Trained as an actress, Barbara Nadel used to work in mental health services. Born in the East End of London, she now writes full time and has been a regular visitor to Turkey for over twenty years. She received the Crime Writers' Association Silver Dagger for her novel *Deadly Web* in 2005. She is also the author of the highly acclaimed Francis Hancock series set during Wo

Praise for Barbara Nadel:

'The delight of Nadel's books is the sense of being the surface of an ancient city which most visitors see for a few days at most. We look into the alleyways and curious dark quarters of Istanbul, full of complex characters and louche atmosphere'

Independent

'A colourful and persuasive portrait of contemporary Istanbul'

Literary Review

'Nadel's novels take in all of Istanbul – the mysterious, the beautiful, the hidden and the banal. Her characters are vivid. A fascinating view of contemporary Turkey'   *Scotland on Sunday*

'Nadel's evocation of the shady underbelly of modern Turkey is one of the perennial joys of crime fiction'   *Mail on Sunday*

'Nadel makes full use of the rich variety of possibilities offered by modern Istanbul and its inhabitants. Crime fiction can do many things, and here it offers both a well crafted mystery and a form of armchair tourism, with Nadel as an expert guide'   *Spectator*

'The strands of Barbara Nadel's novel are woven as deftly as the carpet at the centre of the tale . . . a wonderful setting . . . a dizzying ride'   *Guardian*

By Barbara Nadel and available from Headline

The Inspector İkmen series:
Belshazzar's Daughter
A Chemical Prison
Arabesk
Deep Waters
Harem
Petrified
Deadly Web
Dance with Death
A Passion for Killing
Pretty Dead Things
River of the Dead

The Hancock series:
Last Rights
After the Mourning
Ashes to Ashes

River of the Dead

BARBARA NADEL

headline

First published in 2009 by
HEADLINE PUBLISHING GROUP

First published in paperback in 2009 by
HEADLINE PUBLISHING GROUP

1

Cataloguing in Publication Data is available from the British Library

ISBN 978 0 7553 3566 4 (B format)
ISBN 978 0 7553 4897 8 (A format)

Typeset in Times New Roman by Palimpsest Book Production Limited,
Grangemouth, Stirlingshire

Printed and bound in Great Britain by Clays Ltd, St Ives plc

Headline's policy is to use papers that are natural, renewable and recyclable
products and made from wood grown in sustainable forests. The logging and
manufacturing processes are expected to conform to the environmental
regulations of the country of origin.

HEADLINE PUBLISHING GROUP
An Hachette UK Company
338 Euston Road
London NW1 3BH

www.headline.co.uk
www.hachette.co.uk

To Alex, Pat and Lisa - fellow travellers
on the road to the east.

Cast of Characters

İstanbul

Çetin İkmen – İstanbul police inspector

Mehmet Süleyman – İstanbul police inspector – İkmen's protégé

Commissioner Ardıç – İkmen's and Suleyman's boss

Sergeant Ayşe Farsakoğlu – İkmen's deputy

Sergeant İzzet Melik – Süleyman's deputy

Dr Arto Sarkissian – İstanbul police pathologist

Fatma İkmen – Çetin İkmen's wife

Zelfa Süleyman – Mehmet Süleyman's wife

Çiçek İkmen – Çetin İkmen's daughter

Bekir İkmen – Çetin İkmen's son

Kemal İkmen – Çetin İkmen's son

Bülent İkmen – Çetin İkmen's son

Yusuf Kaya – escaped prisoner

Ramazan Eren – prison guard

Cengiz Bayar – prison guard

Ara Berköz – prisoner

Mr Aktar – hospital administrator

Dr Eldem – neurologist

İsak Mardin – nurse

Murat Lole – nurse

Faruk Öz – nurse

Sophia – Bulgarian girl, a beggar

In the east

Inspector Edibe Taner – Mardin police inspector
Captain Hilmi Erdur – of the Birecik Jandarma
Seçkin Taner – Edibe Taner's father
Seraphim Yunun – a Syrian monk
Gabriel Saatçi – a Syrian monk
Musa Saatçi – Gabriel Saatçi's father
Zeynep Kaya – Yusuf Kaya's wife
Bulbul Kaplan – Yusuf Kaya's aunt
Anastasia Akyuz – a prostitute
Elizabeth Smith – an American
İbrahim Keser – works for Elizabeth Smith
Lütfü Güneş – a Kurd
Lucine Rezian – elderly Armenian woman

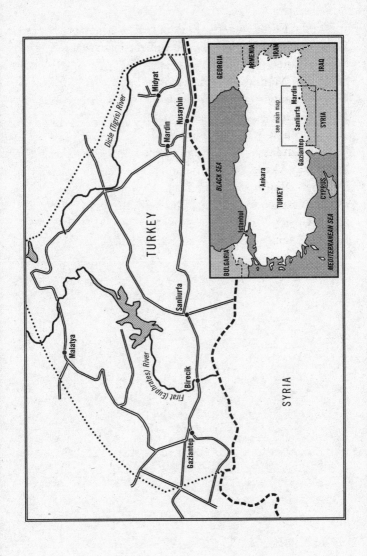

Prelude

'I'm going to be sick!'

The figure in the wheelchair slumped forward as if to emphasise the point. Prison guard Ramazan Eren, who was pushing the chair, said, 'Hang on, Yusuf, we're nearly there.'

'You should have cuffed him,' police constable Mete said angrily.

'He's having a heart attack!' Eren responded sharply.

There were four men with the individual in the wheelchair – two police constables and two prison guards. The man in the chair, their charge, was Yusuf Kaya: drug dealer, murderer and one of İstanbul's most notorious criminals. Late the previous evening, back in his cell at Kartal High Security Prison, he had started experiencing chest pains. The prison doctor had been called and had found little to concern him. But then in the early hours of the morning Kaya's condition had seemed to deteriorate. The prison governor ordered Ramazan Eren, the guard who had first reported Kaya's illness, and a colleague, Cengiz Bayar, to take the prisoner to the Cerrahpaşa Hospital for further tests and possibly treatment. There they had been joined by two police officers. Yusuf Kaya was known to be a very violent offender and, sick or not, no chances were being taken.

The officers had just rounded the corner on their way to the cardiology clinic when Yusuf Kaya began to complain of feelings of nausea. Up ahead was a group of young men, a couple of whom appeared, to Cengiz Bayar, to be in uniform.

'Look, Yusuf, there are some nurses,' he said. 'We'll get them to find you a bowl or something.'

He called out to the men, four in all, who began walking towards the officers and their wheelchair-bound charge.

'We're taking this man to cardiology,' Cengiz Bayar said as the group drew level with them. 'Could you—'

But the pain from the knife or whatever it was that one of the men thrust into his chest was so awful it took his power of speech clean away. One of the police officers began to shout, but Yusuf Kaya soon put a stop to him. Miraculously well again, he leapt up from the wheelchair, took something sharp from the hand of one of the unknown men and killed the policeman stone dead.

The last two things prison officer Cengiz Bayar saw in this world were his colleagues collapsing around him in fountains of blood and a very fit Yusuf Kaya running off to freedom down the hospital corridor.

'Who are you?' Kemal İkmen asked.

'Who are *you*?' the man with the thick gold chains round his neck replied. There was something aggressive in the man's approach that Kemal, for all his teenage bravado, didn't like. There was also, more strangely, something about him that was vaguely familiar too.

'Listen, son, does Inspector Çetin İkmen live here or not?' the man continued gruffly. 'If he does, I'd like to see him, and if he doesn't—'

'Yeah, but who wants to know?' Kemal interrupted. The boy's father, Çetin İkmen, was a high-ranking and successful officer in the İstanbul police force. He therefore had a lot of enemies as well as some very odd and unnerving relatives who, like Çetin İkmen's late mother, came originally from Albania. It was well known that some Albanian gang members could be very 'flash', just like this gold-covered creature at the apartment door.

'You're beginning to get on my nerves, boy!' the man said.

Kemal, for all his bluster, felt his face go cold with fear.

'Does Inspector İkmen live here or not?'

If this man was a relative he was, if Kemal were honest with himself, really out of character. The Albanian relatives were weird – one of them even dressed up as a woman – but they weren't exactly frightening, not like this man. Cold sweat invaded the underside of Kemal's shirt collar. Almost unconsciously he said, 'Dad?'

But his father didn't appear. Instead it was his mother's voice that came from inside the apartment.

'Kemal, who is it?' Fatma İkmen said.

The man in front of him blinked as if reacting to something irritating around his eyes, and nervously licked his lips.

'It's a . . .' Kemal began, but then his words simply faded in his throat. 'It's . . .'

'Oh, for the love of . . .' The sound of a woman grunting somewhat painfully to her feet was followed by the shuffling of slippers across carpet. Fatma İkmen, her head covered with a floral scarf, burst out of the living room into the hallway behind her youngest and, she often thought, silliest child Kemal. How difficult was it to answer a door? She pushed Kemal roughly out of the way, and then she stopped.

Kemal, who could only see the strange man's face from where he was standing, frowned when he saw this person give his mother what he felt was a very familiar smile. His mother in response said only, 'No!'

'Oh, yes!' the man said as he opened his arms in front of her. 'Oh yes it is!'

'I can't . . .'

'Mum, it's me, Bekir!' the man said.

'It is? It *is*!' Fatma İkmen threw her short, plump body into the arms of someone Kemal had always thought of as almost a myth. Bekir, his bad boy rebellious brother, had run away from home when he was fifteen. Kemal hadn't even been born then. And until this moment not a word had been heard nor hair been sighted of him since. His father, Çetin İkmen, who had followed the boy's mother out of the living room and was now standing beside Kemal with a smouldering cigarette between his lips, had privately believed that his third son had died some years before. While Fatma cried copiously into the arms of her long-lost child, Çetin didn't move from his position at all. He just looked. And when the man Kemal now knew was his brother smiled at their father, the youngster noticed that Çetin İkmen did not smile back. In fact, if anything, Inspector İkmen looked appalled about the appearance of this ghost from the past.

Chapter 1

Every police officer in the city of İstanbul spent almost every waking moment looking for the escaped convict Yusuf Kaya. For three days and nights the entire city, or so it seemed to its residents, was turned upside down. Every bar, every night-club, every bathhouse – anywhere Kaya might have had a market for his cocaine and his heroin – was raided. Every one of his old neighbours in his home district of Tarlabaşı was questioned. Those not drifting into or out of a heroin-induced haze claimed to know nothing about him. Those drugged up to the eyes didn't know what year it was. But the investigating officer, Inspector Mehmet Süleyman, knew Tarlabaşı of old. Yusuf Kaya had in fact been arrested by the handsome and urbane Süleyman the previous summer. On what had probably been the hottest day in that July, Süleyman and his men had raided Kaya's crumbling fifth-floor apartment and found a considerable quantity of heroin and two dead bodies. One was Kaya's mistress, a Syrian prostitute called Hana; the other was a rival drug dealer, a Russian called Tommi Kerensky.

When Süleyman and his men raided the apartment, Hana had been dead for some days. But as the inspector's informant had intimated, Tommi had been tortured for many hours and had only just died when the police arrived. Kaya, calmly as was his wont, was sawing one of the Russian's legs off when he was arrested. That someone so dangerous – 'psychopathic', the psychiatrist who had assessed him after his arrest had said – was free once again was a frightening thought. And while his colleague Çetin İkmen worked on trying to determine from the Cerrahpaşa Hospital just who those nurses and cleaners who freed Kaya might have been, it was up to Süleyman to find out whether the prisoner had been or was back home.

Less than a week after the arrest, Kaya's landlord had rented his apartment out to another man. Adem Ceylan was a known heroin user who was a familiar sight in rougher parts of the city like Tarlabaşı. For years he'd been living, on and off, with a German woman called Regina who was also a junkie, known to the police as a very persistent beggar in the main Beyoğlu shopping area of İstiklal Street. Filthy and screaming with hatred for just about everyone and everything, Regina could terrify even quite large groups of tourists into giving her money.

Adem let the tall inspector and his shorter, fatter sergeant İzzet Melik into what passed for his sitting room and then, breathlessly, sat down.

'Those stairs don't get any easier!' he said as he coughed on a soggy hand-rolled cigarette.

Süleyman looked around, unsurprised that the place looked almost identical to what he'd seen of it the previous year. Even the chairs and tables were Kaya's. But then junkies were not the best housekeepers going and he was simply relieved that his officers had cleaned up Tommi's blood before they left. Both Süleyman and Melik declined the foul seats that Adem offered them.

'You know of course about Yusuf Kaya,' Süleyman said without preamble.

Adem nodded. 'Yes,' he said. 'I was a bit frightened that he might come back here. Went to see my landlord as it happens, I was so worried. Not for myself, you understand, but with Regina . . .'

It was hard to reconcile the image of the spitting, cursing Regina with someone who needed to be protected, but both Süleyman and Melik nodded anyway.

'What did your landlord tell you?' Süleyman asked.

He had already spoken to Kaya's old landlord himself. That too hadn't been a comfortable experience. The landlord, though not a drug user or even a drinker, was a man unaccustomed to personal hygiene. As his many, many grime-stained children ran around their father, Süleyman watched in horror as the landlord's hair moved to the rhythm of a million or so blood-sucking nits. It wasn't a sight that an experienced police officer in his forties, like Süleyman, hadn't seen before. But it was one that even now turned the stomach of a man who came from a gracious, if impoverished, Ottoman family. As it happened, the landlord had, as he always did, claimed to know nothing about anything. But maybe speaking to someone not in authority, like Adem, was different.

'My landlord reckons the Christians know something,' Adem said darkly.

'The Christians?'

Adem tipped his head in the direction of the window behind his chair. 'Over at the church,' he said. 'That Hana, the one he . . . Well . . . She was a Christian. Suriani. Every Sunday over at the Virgin Mary church she was. Atoning for her sins, I imagine. But Kaya, so my landlord says, was a Christian too.'

İzzet Melik rolled his eyes at yet another stupid myth. 'Kaya isn't a Christian,' he said. 'I think some people round here would like to think he's different from them. But he's a Muslim.'

'Yes, but my landlord says that the Christians at the church—'

'Kaya comes originally from Mardin, which is a city with a considerable Christian population,' Süleyman said. 'But he himself is not one of them. As you say, his unfortunate victim was, and you may remember that many people, including myself, attended Hana Karim's funeral service at the Virgin Mary church. The clergy over there know little of Kaya.'

Adem shrugged. 'I'm just going on what my landlord said.'

İzzet Melik turned his heavily mustachioed face towards his boss and shook his head. There was no point in continuing the conversation with Adem. He obviously had some sort of fixation, whether in reality taken from his landlord or not, that Yusuf Kaya was a Christian. Anything more about the escapee he claimed not to know.

Once outside the rotten and peeling apartment building, both İzzet Melik and Mehmet Süleyman lit up cigarettes.

'What do you think, Inspector?' İzzet said as he looked down the litter-strewn street, through the tall line of dilapidated nineteenth-century apartment buildings. The church, to the left of where the men were standing, was the only building in the whole quarter that looked cared for.

Süleyman sighed. 'I don't think Kaya came back here,' he said. 'Why would he? His old henchmen are either long gone or dead. I think he's probably abroad by now.'

'The people who sprang him were certainly professional,' İzzet Melik said.

'Absolutely. To kill three officers and effectively disable, probably permanently, a fourth takes some doing.' He looked around at the hot, filthy street with distaste, and then added, 'You don't find people like that in Tarlabaşşı. Or rather' – he smiled – 'I don't think you do.'

'It's only the priests at the church who aren't stoned out of their minds round here,' İzzet said.

'Yes, and Kaya himself when he lived here,' his superior agreed. 'Until the unfortunate Tommi tried to move in on the quarter, Mr Kaya had this very big market for his products all to himself.'

'Kaya never used himself?'

Süleyman smiled again. 'Oh, no, İzzet,' he said. 'Yusuf Kaya was a very good drug dealer. He never, ever touched his own products. It was because he was always straight, basically, that he killed Hana Karim.'

İzzet frowned. 'What do you mean?'

'It is said that Yusuf noticed that Hana's behaviour changed some time towards the end of 2004. He watched her and discovered that she was having an affair with another man. If he'd been off the planet on heroin he would never even have noticed. Doesn't mean he's not a raving lunatic, however, as we well know. One does not cross Yusuf Kaya.'

Tucked away behind a small suite of lecture rooms, the office of the administrator of the Cerrahpaşa Hospital was both clean and quiet. Mercifully distant from the chaotic medical business of the hospital, it was a place where, he hoped, Çetin İkmen could interview the facility's senior managerial official in peace.

'What you have to understand, Inspector, is that hospital cleaning staff come and go all the time,' the administrator, a small, tired-looking man behind a large dark-wood desk told him. 'Some, of course, mainly the middle-aged women with families, have been with us for years. But two young men like the ones on the security footage . . .' He shrugged.

İkmen had just viewed the somewhat fuzzy security tape

which showed the murder of Yusuf Kaya's guards and his subsequent escape. The cleaners and the nurses – all male – who had liberated the gangster had been both young and quick. Together with Yusuf Kaya, three of them had taken a guard or a police officer and, seemingly without any hesitation or remorse, stabbed him. In all but one instance the wound had proved fatal. İkmen looked across at the clearly shaken hospital administrator and said, 'The surviving guard . . .'

'As you know, Inspector, he is still unconscious. Dr Eldem cannot be sure when or even if the unfortunate man will awaken. Neurology is not an exact discipline, as I'm sure you know.'

'Indeed.' This wasn't the first time İkmen had had to wait for a potential witness to come out of a coma. Some years previously he had actually had to wait for one of his own colleagues to surface before he could question him about an incident. But in this instance, he knew he had to accept that the prison guard, Ramazan Eren, might never recover. Mr Eren's heart had been grazed by his assailant's weapon and he had lost a vast amount of blood. Whether he would ever regain consciousness, and, if he did, whether he would still have normal mental capacity, were moot points.

'As you saw for yourself, the security footage wasn't clear,' İkmen said as he pulled one of the administrator's ashtrays towards him and lit up a cigarette. 'We can't identify any of the people caught by it, even those, like Kaya, whom we know. We may have more to go on once the images have been enhanced but that is by no means a certainty. Do you have any possible names for the cleaners or the nurses?'

The administrator switched on his computer terminal. Hospitals were such *public* places! In one sense that worked against criminal activity, because of the large numbers of people

10

around. But in another, provided the timing was right, hospitals were wide open in that regard. Yusuf Kaya had been rescued very early in the morning, when the hospital was probably at its quietest. The only problems the rescuers had experienced had to have revolved around the timing of the attempt. It had been the prison governor who had made the decision to have Kaya sent to the Cerrahpaşa in the early hours of the morning. True, he had been encouraged to make some sort of decision by members of his staff, including Ramazan Eren, who had apparently been alarmed by Kaya's condition. But unless the governor himself was involved, the placing of the cleaners and nurses at the scene had to have been a speculative act. The hospital administrator had admitted that tracking down a couple of casual cleaners was probably well-nigh impossible, but the nurses could have been, indeed in İkmen's mind had to have been, 'embedded' within the hospital for some time. Even so, on the morning in question, they had to have been activated by someone, told that Kaya was coming. And that someone had almost certainly been a person or persons inside the prison. If that person or persons was either Ramazan Eren or Cengiz Bayar or both, they had paid a very high price for their treachery. But then Yusuf Kaya, as İkmen knew from his friend Mehmet Süleyman, was a ruthless, unfeeling psychopath. The death of two 'bent' prison guards, if that was indeed what they had been, would simply serve to save him anxiety and money, because if cash hadn't been involved somewhere along the line İkmen would be very surprised. In addition, there were the two dead police officers . . .

'There are three male nurses who have not reported for duty since that morning,' the administrator said as he peered at his screen. 'İsak Mardin from Zeyrek, Murat Lole from Karaköy, and Faruk Öz, who lives in Gaziosmanpaşa.'

İkmen frowned. Yusuf Kaya, it was well known, came originally from Mardin. What were the chances of one of these nurses having that name?

'I'll need their contact details,' he said. 'All of them.'

The administrator frowned. 'You'll contact these men?' He looked over at his computer screen once again. 'Lole and Öz work in the same department, orthopaedics. I believe their supervisor has already tried or maybe even succeeded in speaking to them. Would you like to speak to someone in the department?'

'Yes.'

İkmen, or rather some of his officers, would almost certainly be paying all the missing nurses a visit in the very near future, but it certainly wouldn't hurt to speak to their colleagues and superiors too.

Several hours later, when he emerged from the Cerrahpaşa, İkmen had a slightly clearer picture about İsak Mardin, Murat Lole and Faruk Öz. Both Öz and Lole worked on the orthopaedics ward, as the administrator had said. Mardin's speciality was cardiac care, which made sense in relation to his possible appearance on a corridor leading to the cardiology clinic. Lole had been contacted by his superiors since the Kaya incident and was apparently at home with a bad cold. İkmen himself had spoken to the man on the telephone and Lole had readily agreed to be interviewed by the police. Mardin and Öz were seemingly uncontactable. After lighting up a cigarette in the lee of the ambulance station, İkmen called his sergeant, Ayşe Farsakoğlu, and told her to assemble a squad of officers to meet him at İsak Mardin's address in Zeyrek.

When he'd finished the call, İkmen dropped his mobile telephone into his pocket with a sigh. In spite of the seriousness of having a murderer like Yusuf Kaya on the run in the city that was both his home and his passion, İkmen was finding it hard to concentrate. All he could think about was the son who had come home after nineteen long and, for his wife Fatma particularly, painful years. A difficult and at times violent child, Bekir İkmen had begun to take drugs – just cannabis to start off with – from the age of thirteen. No threats about endangering his own liberty or putting his father's career at risk had had any effect, and Bekir had quickly tired of cannabis and gone on to cocaine, acid, amphetamines – anything he could get his hands on. By the time he ran away from home two years later, his brothers and sisters, as well as Çetin İkmen himself, were almost relieved. Living around Bekir and his drug-fuelled rages had been difficult and it was only Fatma İkmen who actually cried when it became clear that her third-born son was not coming home.

Çetin İkmen looked out over the top of the traffic jam on the coastal road, Kennedy Street, at the shining waters of the Sea of Marmara beyond. From the front entrance of the hospital, one could see the many vast tankers that had recently passed through the Bosphorus straits. One could also see much of the city of İstanbul itself. To his left, İkmen could just make out the minarets of the Sultan Ahmet or Blue Mosque. Almost encapsulating the spirit of the city in itself, the mosque had been built in a district that for ever afterwards took on its name. Sultanahmet, the very centre of the old city of imperial mosques, Ottoman palaces and the teeming Grand Bazaar, was where the İkmen family lived. Until Bekir had somehow made his way back, it had been home to Çetin, Fatma and their four youngest children. For the past nineteen years they had been, in totality, a family of ten – eight children and two parents. Now they were eleven, as it was meant to be, as was *right*. Except that, for Çetin İkmen at least, it wasn't. His son Bekir was, to all intents and purposes, a very personable man of thirty-four. By his own admission he'd spent many years battling various addictions. He had, he said, spent the time he'd been addicted to heroin in the crime-ridden district of Edirnekapı, up around the old Byzantine city walls. Walking distance, provided one was fit, from the İkmens' apartment in Sultanahmet. *Walking* distance! One could feel, and his wife Fatma did feel, very guilty about being so near and yet so far from a beloved child for such a long time. Çetin İkmen, however, did not. Now clean and bright and shiny and, he said, gainfully employed in the tourist industry, Bekir was still *wrong*. How, İkmen didn't know. But that he, Bekir, was now on his own in the İkmen apartment with only Fatma for company made Çetin feel uneasy. The superstitious and suspicious blood that ran in his veins, inherited from a mother known for her witchcraft, would not allow the inspector to delight in his son's return.

The landlord of the house where İsak Mardin had lived until a few days before was very certain that the young man had been 'weird' and 'wrong' – after he'd run off without paying his rent.

'He was forever body-building, the woman who lives in the apartment below told me,' Mr Lale told Ayşe Farsakoğlu. İkmen hadn't yet arrived, so Sergeant Farsakoğlu, together with constables Yıldız and Orğa, had found the landlord of the house on Zeyrek Mehmet Paşa Alley and gained admittance to a now empty apartment.

'Bang, bang, bang, all night long, so Miss . . . whatever her name is downstairs said,' Mr Lale continued. He was a thin, lugubrious man of about fifty who, winter and summer, wore a thick knitted hat, as a lot of people who came originally from the countryside did. 'Lifting weights, see,' he said, moving his arms up and down to demonstrate, 'and banging them down on the floor afterwards.'

'Yes, Mr Lale,' Ayşe said with a polite smile. 'I do know what weightlifting is about.'

In spite of the fact that more women were joining the Turkish police all the time, Ayşe still found some male members of the public very patronising. This man wouldn't have dreamed of doing his awful demonstration for either of the young male constables who were looking round the apartment with her. But for her, their superior, Mr Lale obviously felt he had to make himself plain. After all, Ayşe was an attractive woman in her early thirties, so it was almost unthinkable that she wasn't stupid.

'What someone in his profession was doing lifting weights, I don't know,' Mr Lale said as he lit up a cheap, rank Birinci cigarette. 'I mean a nurse, I ask you! What kind of job is that for a grown man?'

Suspecting that this overtly macho attitude towards nursing was allied to a few other prejudicial feelings, Ayşe said, 'So would you want to be handled by a woman if you were in hospital, Mr Lale?'

'I've never been in a hospital in my life!' He relayed this fact as if it were some sort of badge of honour.

'Yes, but if you did have to go in . . .' Ayşe, seeing the look of hostility on the landlord's face, decided to give up. After all, his attitude towards this İsak Mardin was irrelevant. Where Mardin was now, what he was doing and what he had done were the only subjects she should be concentrating on now. After all, this man could have just murdered a prison guard, or one of the unfortunate police officers who had accompanied Yusuf Kaya to the Cerrahpaşa. One of their own . . .

'Mr Lale,' she began.

'Sergeant!'

A call from what had apparently been İsak Mardin's bedroom caused Ayşe to excuse herself to go and see what Constable Yıldız wanted.

The room, which contained little beyond an ancient-looking metal bedstead and the built-in cupboard Yıldız was looking into now, overlooked the Golden Horn. The nineteenth-century wooden house had five storeys and this apartment was on the fifth. So even though there were buildings behind the house, because they were smaller than Mr Lale's place İsak Mardin had had a wonderful view. Even with the thunderous traffic on the Atatürk Bridge pounding across to hip and happening Beyoğlu over the water, the sight of the great inlet with the European city beyond was still absolutely breathtaking. And on a wonderful spring day like this one it would, under normal circumstances, have made Ayşe want to sing and shout from the sheer joy of simply being alive in such fabulous weather. But the circumstances were far from normal.

'I found this in this cupboard,' Constable Yıldız was holding a thin red and gold scarf very gingerly by one corner.

'That's a Galatasaray scarf,' Mr Lale said from the doorway, once again anticipating complete ignorance on Ayşe's part. 'He supported that lot.'

Mr Lale, by referring to what is probably İstanbul's most famous football club as 'that lot', signalled that it was not a particular passion of his own. Ayşe, whose brother was a fanatical Galatasaray fan, smiled.

'Bag it up for forensic, please, Constable,' she said to Yıldız. 'Thank you for that, Mr Lale.'

Any examples of DNA found on the scarf or indeed on the

16

bedding or the other, very few, items in the apartment could be useful; although, as her boss Inspector İkmen had told her earlier, İsak Mardin was probably a pseudonym. Yıldız had just put the scarf into a bag when İkmen, his thin face red and flustered, arrived.

'I apologise for being late, Sergeant,' he said to Ayşe Farsakoğlu as he tipped his head in greeting to Mr Lale. 'But I've just had a telephone call from Commissioner Ardıç. We need to get back to the station – now.'

Chapter 2

Try as he might, İkmen couldn't get away from the fact that the man on the screen had to be Yusuf Kaya. 'Where did this film come from?' he asked as he watched again the short movie footage of Yusuf Kaya eating a plate of pastries.

'A patisserie called the Nightingale is where it was taken,' the large, heavily sweating man puffing on a cigar across the desk replied. 'When was yesterday lunchtime, twelve thirty.'

'I didn't know that patisseries had security cameras,' Mehmet Süleyman said as he sat down next to İkmen and ran the small snippet of film yet again.

'Where does not have at least one camera these days?' the large man responded gloomily. 'I don't know how many speed cameras there are between the centre of the city and Atatürk Airport, but if it goes on like this all traffic officers will lose the use of their legs. Sitting in rooms looking at screens all day long!'

Commissioner Ardıç, who like İkmen was in his late fifties, was not a man with whom new technology sat easily. He had gained enough knowledge to be able to operate his own computer and his mobile telephone and that, to Ardıç, was enough. Wall-to-wall security and speed cameras were, he felt, neither right nor necessary. Except in this one instance.

'Fortunately for us the proprietor of the Nightingale thought he'd seen this particular customer before – on TRT News –

and so he took this down to his local station yesterday evening.'

Yusuf Kaya's image had been all over the media since he'd absconded.

'So where is the Nightingale?' Mehmet Süleyman asked. 'It's not a name that is familiar to me.'

Ardıç lowered his considerable behind into his groaning leather chair. 'Gaziantep,' he said.

'Gaziantep!'

İkmen, still fixated upon the images on his superior's computer screen, said, 'Look at him! An intelligent operator like Kaya must have seen the cameras in that place. You know, I think he's actually enjoying being observed. Arrogant bastard!'

'Yes,' Ardıç said to Süleyman, 'our friend does seem to have got very far east in a very short space of time.'

'If he's eating, as he must be, baklava from Antep, then I envy him,' İkmen said as he leaned back in his chair and lit a cigarette. 'The centre of the pistachio nut universe, Gaziantep. They make the most sublime, nut-crammed baklava.'

'I didn't think that food was very high on your list of priorities, İkmen,' Ardıç said, one bushy eyebrow raised.

İkmen looked up, took a long drag from his cigarette and smiled. 'I make an exception for baklava and chocolate, sir,' he said. 'They are so very bad for one.'

Ardıç, who had to be at least twice İkmen's weight, said, 'Quite.' He turned back to Süleyman. 'On the basis that Kaya originates from Mardin and that much of the profit from his crime empire here in the city went back to his home town, we think that's possibly where he's headed. However, it is also known that he has friends in Antep, and so an Inspector Taner from Mardin has been despatched to investigate that connection. You, Süleyman, will rendezvous with Taner at Gaziantep airport tomorrow night.'

'Sir?'

This seemed, to Süleyman, to be somewhat of an over-reaction. Surely if Mardin were on to it, this Taner person could deal with Kaya without help from İstanbul.

Ardıç looked narrowly at Süleyman. 'It was you who originally apprehended Kaya and he was serving his sentence in this city when he absconded.' He paused to relight his cigar, which had gone out during the course of their conversation. Then he lowered his head a little and added, 'And besides, this time Kaya and his people killed our own.'

Süleyman exchanged glances with İkmen, who drew a long, thin breath into his lungs.

'I don't think that either of you knew Constable Mete or Constable Kanlı.'

He was right. Neither İkmen nor Süleyman had known either of the men who had been killed by Yusuf Kaya's people.

'Didn't know them myself,' Ardıç continued. 'But what I do know is that the only thing those officers were doing that night was their duty. They were called upon to provide escort to a prisoner, which they did, and they died for their pains.' He pulled himself up very straight in his chair then and said, 'Know them or not, Mete and Kanlı were İstanbul police officers. If Kaya is out east, I want him brought back here. I don't want some eastern types getting hold of him.'

'Sir, Kaya was, as you say, imprisoned in İstanbul,' İkmen said. 'Surely, if he is caught, we—'

'Mardin have issues with Kaya,' Ardıç said contemptuously. 'His crime empire here in the city apparently helped to fund still more illegal activities amongst his relatives in the east. They want him and so do we.' He looked across at Süleyman and frowned. 'Make sure you get hold of Kaya, not this Inspector Taner. We want him serving time in İstanbul. He *will* serve time in İstanbul.'

Süleyman sighed. 'So it's a competition, then, between myself and Taner. İstanbul versus Mardin.'

'If you wish.' Ardıç cleared his throat. 'It is one that we will win.'

'Sir, Mardin is a very small city with limited resources and a lot of problems,' İkmen began. 'I don't think—'

'You, İkmen, will continue the investigation here,' Ardıç said. 'Your own sergeant as well as Süleyman's deputy Sergeant Melik will assist you. Now, I understand some male nurses have gone missing from the Cerrahpaşa.'

İkmen told Ardıç about the three men he was currently pursuing, while Süleyman descended into silence. In spite of being a professional woman herself, his wife Zelfa wouldn't like the idea of his going away for an uncertain length of time. For a woman who was half western, and had indeed been brought up in her mother's country of Ireland, she was intensely possessive. But then Mehmet, much as he adored his intelligent and considerably older wife, hadn't always been faithful to her. That said, going to Gaziantep and then maybe on to Mardin was not like going to Paris. Antep was famously dull and ugly and, at only fifty-eight kilometres from the Syrian border, Mardin was the back of beyond. As far as Süleyman was concerned it was not a city famed for its alluring women. In summer Mardin was infested with snakes that, without even visualising a serpent, made Süleyman shudder. Not that the snakes were what really bothered him. Mardin had other associations too – with terrorism and with the internal war Turkish troops had been fighting against the separatist Kurdish organisation, the PKK, for decades. The conflict was bitter and vicious and loss of life on both sides was heavy. In addition, now there were other dimensions too. Hezbollah were known to be operating in the area and there were rumours of al-Qaeda cells also. Anyone, even out of uniform, who represented the Turkish state was at risk. Snakes were nothing compared to that.

Murat Lole lived in a small second-floor apartment on Büyük Hendek Street in Karaköy. It was a location that was sadly familiar to İkmen because it was close to the Neve Şalom synagogue which had been attacked by al-Qaeda-inspired suicide bombers back in 2003. His son-in-law, Berekiah Cohen, who had lived opposite the synagogue had been badly injured in the explosion. The union of İkmen's daughter Hulya, a Muslim, and his old friend Balthazar's son, a Jew, had seemed like an example of tolerance and hope for the future when the two youngsters first got married. But now that Berekiah could no longer work and Hulya by contrast had to work all the time, cracks were beginning to show. The apartment where the Cohens had once lived was now repaired and repainted, which pleased İkmen, even if it did only serve to underline how easily buildings could be fixed compared to people.

When he and Ayşe Farsakoğlu arrived they found the orthopaedic nurse indeed in thrall to a very bad cold. About thirty, slight, with a pleasant face and ready smile, Murat Lole showed the two officers into a poorly furnished but tidy living room, which smelt strongly of coffee. It put İkmen in mind of the coffee houses of his youth, back in the fifties when even enlightened men like his father went to all-male cafés to play backgammon, talk about football and drink the thickest, darkest Turkish coffee imaginable.

'You don't expect to get a really bad cold at this time of

year,' Murat Lole said as he ushered them towards a rather battered sofa under the window. 'But then I don't work with well people, do I?'

'Orthopaedics,' İkmen said. 'Bones not infections.'

'They often come in with infections,' Murat Lole said as he sat down on a small hard chair and blew his nose loudly. 'After all, if you have a cold and then break your leg, it can't just be left until the cold has gone, can it?'

'Mr Lole,' Ayşe said, 'we've come to talk to you about the escape of a prisoner, sent for treatment to the Cerrahpaşa.'

'That was the last day I was at work,' Lole said. 'I wasn't really well then, but . . . That prisoner was being taken to cardiology. I didn't see him, but I heard about it, of course.'

'You have a colleague,' İkmen said. 'Faruk Öz.'

'Faruk and I were on shift together that night,' Lole said.

'All night?'

'We came on at eight the previous evening and I at least finished at eight the following morning. I don't remember seeing Faruk. But then we're not that close and I was feeling very bad by then and wasn't noticing much, to be truthful.'

'During the course of an average shift, do members of staff come and go from the ward very much?' Ayşe Farsakoğlu asked.

'Yes,' Lole said, 'a lot. We go to get drugs, check new patients in, take existing patients to the lavatory . . .'

'Do you know if you were on the ward at four a.m.? Was Faruk with you?'

Murat Lole shrugged. 'I remember I was on the ward when all the commotion reached us,' he said. 'I was actually in the toilet trying to clean up my nose and splash some water on my face to wake myself up. I heard someone scream about people being stabbed. I don't know where Faruk was. Obviously, I was alone at the time.'

'Can you remember seeing Faruk Öz in the hour or so before the incident?' İkmen asked.

For a few seconds Lole was silent, and then he said, 'No. No, I can't. He may very well have been on the ward, but I was not personally with him. As I said, this cold wiped me out. I shouldn't even have been at work.'

'Mr Lole,' Ayşe said, 'do you have any idea where Faruk Öz might be now?'

'If he's not either at his apartment or at work, then no.'

'You don't know where his family live, where he's from?'

'No.' Lole shrugged again. 'Faruk and I are only work colleagues. Although . . .' He paused, thinking, and then said, 'I think his parents might live in Ankara. I don't know where-abouts.'

Faruk Öz's apartment in Gaziosmanpaşa had been searched by constables Yıldız and Orğa while İkmen was with Commissioner Ardıç. He hadn't been there, even though, unlike İsak Mardin's, many of his possessions appeared to be still in situ. Significantly, however, no one in Öz's block had seen him since the night of Yusuf Kaya's escape. He too had disappeared.

Ayşe asked Murat Lole whether he knew anyone by the name of İsak Mardin. He said that he didn't.

'İsak Mardin is also a nurse at the Cerrahpaşa,' İkmen said.

'It's a big place, Inspector.'

'Mr Mardin worked on the cardiac care ward,' İkmen continued. 'He too has been missing since the incident with Yusuf Kaya. Mr Lole, do you know whether Faruk Öz knew İsak Mardin?'

'No. Inspector, I've never heard of İsak Mardin before. As I said, the hospital is a very big place.'

The interview continued until finally, taking pity upon Lole and his obviously fragile state, İkmen thanked him for his time and prepared to leave. As he rose from his seat, he said, 'Mr Lole, I'm sorry, but I must ask. The smell of coffee . . .'

'Oh.' The nurse frowned, then smiled again almost immediately. 'Sorry, I can't smell anything at the moment. But I know what you mean. That isn't me, Inspector. Next door there's a couple from the east. You know how strong they like their coffee out there.'

Although İkmen himself had barely been east of Ankara in the whole of his life, he knew what Murat Lole meant. Once, years before, he'd had to pick up a prisoner from Nusaybin on the Syrian border. In many ways Nusaybin is far more an Arab than a Turkish town, and the coffee there had been so thick that İkmen had almost been able to stand a spoon in it. As he recalled, Nusaybin was quite close to Mardin, from whose airport he remembered having travelled. He had never seen the city itself, however. As he and Ayşe walked out into the street and back to his car, İkmen identified some feelings of envy for Süleyman. Mardin had always been one of those semi-legendary places, almost an Anatolian Shangri-la. In Mardin, it was said, Christians, Muslims and Jews all lived in harmony in big, beautiful, honey-coloured mansions. The place was infested with snakes but there was some sort of snake goddess who the locals swore protected them from potentially fatal bites. Süleyman, if he did indeed get there, would tell İkmen all about it upon his return. If he returned. Like most İstanbullus, İkmen automatically feared for those going out east. Out east, fabled cities notwithstanding, terrorists and armed clan chiefs were most certainly amongst one's neighbours.

Of course, Ardıç had chosen Süleyman to go after Kaya because he had made the original arrest. That was the reason, because Ardıç had said so. But that İkmen was seventeen years older than Süleyman did cross the older man's mind. Dodging bullets required a certain turn of speed. Unless they already lived out east, it wasn't somewhere the 'old' went. But then, with Bekir back in his life once again, would İkmen really have wanted to be anywhere else? There were things he had to say to his son: details about his past that needed clarification, for instance. And as he looked around at the very ordinary little street in Karaköy where his car was parked, the one with the Neve Şalom synagogue, he was reminded that there was his sad daughter Hulya to support too. With little time for friends and not wishing to bother the already over-burdened Fatma, İkmen's daughter was turning more and more to her father for advice and comfort these days.

As he got into his car beside Ayşe, İkmen looked up and saw Murat Lole looking at him fixedly through the window. He was drinking from a very tiny coffee cup.

Mehmet Süleyman made a point of reading his little boy, Yusuf, his bedtime story that night. Of course, he'd see him in the morning, before the child left to go to the brand new nursery that had just started up in Ortaköy. Zelfa Süleyman had been delighted that somewhere so apparently professional and child-centred had opened up virtually on their doorstep. But then Ortaköy, once a quaint Bosphorus village, had become in recent years a very chic İstanbul suburb. So chic, in fact, that the couple often had difficulty parking their own cars for all the Ferraris, Lamborghinis and Aston Martins that, in the summer months particularly, lined their once very countrified street of wooden cottages. That otherwise very modern young people wanted to be associated with somewhere as quaint and historical as Ortaköy was something that Zelfa, a psychiatrist, had various theories about. Not least amongst these theories was one concerning the fact that very few of the nouveaux riches youngsters who hung around the clubs and bars of Ortaköy came from native İstanbul families. Most of them came originally from dirt-poor villages in the east. By inhabiting a place like Ortaköy, so Zelfa claimed, they were in effect buying a piece of history, or rather buying into a past that was completely alien to them. They thought, she said, it gave them a cachet, legitimised maybe their excessive cars, houses and clothes. Zelfa's husband, like her father, was a genuine İstanbullu as well as being from an Ottoman dynasty related to the now deposed imperial family. There were still people in the city who insisted upon calling Mehmet's father Prince Muhammed Süleyman, even though the old man had been born well after the Ottoman Empire had crumbled to dust. But that was İstanbul.

'You know Gaziantep has got a fantastic museum,' Zelfa said to her husband as he came into the living room and sat down.

'Yusuf isn't very pleased about this trip of mine,' Mehmet said as he lit up a cigarette and then let the smoke out of his nose on a frown. 'He wanted to know when I was going to come home and I just couldn't tell him. When I find, if I find, Yusuf Kaya.'

Zelfa moved away from the television set she'd been watching and sat down next to her husband. Snuggling in close to his side, she changed to English, the language with which she was really more comfortable than Turkish. Her voice, which was husky, was also imbued with a strong southern Irish accent. 'I'm not mad about your going off myself,' she said. 'I suppose Ardıç wouldn't send İkmen out there because of his age.'

'I don't think it's anything to do with that,' Mehmet said. 'And anyway, Çetin is hardly an old man, is he?' he added

28

loyally. İkmen, as well as being a legend in policing circles, was also his friend, and as such İkmen could never truly be old. 'No, I have to go because it was me that arrested Kaya originally.'

'You have an insight into the way his mind works.'

Mehmet frowned. 'I don't know about that,' he said. 'But I am going to Gaziantep and maybe Mardin too and I cannot do anything about it.'

Zelfa sat up and looked at him. 'Well, if you must go to Gaziantep, you can at least try to stimulate your mind by going to the museum. They've got the Zeugma mosaics there – you know, from that ancient site they flooded to build a dam? They're supposed to be the most marvellous examples of mosaic art in the world.'

She was insatiable when it came to cultural things like art. She was also, he knew, trying very hard not to mention or even perhaps think about all the dangers that being out east could involve. 'You'd like a brochure of some sort, Zelfa?' he said.

'I'd like a big book full of beautiful colour pictures of the mosaics,' she replied forcefully. 'God Almighty, Mehmet, if I can't go myself *and* I'm forced to be without you, I have a right to expect something.'

'So Gaziantep baklava . . .'

'Oh, I'll have some of that too,' she cut in playfully. 'And you can get some for your son as well.'

They both laughed. But then there was a serious silence, a moment during which he saw the fear of what could happen 'out there' reflected in her eyes. He was about to lean over and kiss her when his mobile phone rang. He took it out of his pocket and answered it.

Zelfa, cuddling into his side, said, 'If that is Ardıç . . .'

Mehmet said, 'It's Çetin.'

'Ah.'

'Mehmet, I'm so sorry I didn't get very much time with you today,' İkmen said. 'You're off to Antep tomorrow and so I won't see you.'

'No.'

Zelfa, suddenly agitated as she was wont to become at anxious times, got up and walked back towards the television.

'I just wanted to say that I will continue to find out what I can here and I'll contact you every day,' İkmen said.

'I will also pass anything that I find on to you,' his friend replied. 'How did you get on with that nurse in Karaköy this afternoon?'

İkmen told him about his meeting with Murat Lole. He added that although the man's story about what he had been doing at the hospital when Kaya escaped checked out in every available way, he still didn't trust him. Mehmet asked him why.

'It's a stupid thing really,' İkmen said. 'Basically, all the time Ayşe and I were with him, I could smell very strong coffee, like the real hard Turks in the old days used to drink. I asked him about it, because you don't find many people these days who drink that stuff, and he told me that the couple next door, people from the east, were making it. Then after we left I looked up at his apartment and saw him at the window drinking from a tiny coffee cup. Of course he could have been given the coffee by his neighbours, but I don't really think so. I think that he lied to me. A senseless, silly lie that makes me distrust him. Why would he do such a thing?'

'I don't know,' Mehmet said. 'But if you have a bad feeling about this man, Çetin, then we should watch him. I never

30

knew your mother but I trust absolutely the intuition of the Witch of Üsküdar's son.'

'Yes.' Mehmet heard his friend sigh. When he spoke again, the younger man noticed that İkmen's voice was lowered. 'I just wish I didn't have similar – as in bad – feelings about my own son.'

'Bekir?'

'Yes.'

Mehmet Süleyman had never met Bekir İkmen and would probably not do so until he returned from the east. But İkmen had told him a few things over the years: how Bekir had stolen from his brothers from the age of twelve, how he had lied about his drug-taking, and the terrifying stand-up fight he'd had with his father just before he ran away from home.

'We still don't know anything approaching the truth about where he's been, what he's done and what he's now doing,' İkmen said. 'I don't know what it means, but . . .' He raised his voice once again and seemed to cheer up. 'But I just wanted to wish you a good journey, Mehmet.'

'Thank you, Çetin. I'll do my best to acquit myself with honour and dignity in the face of eastern hostility – as well as eastern food, of course.'.

They both laughed. The previous year, Süleyman's deputy İzzet Melik had been sent to the shores of Lake Van, also in the east, in the course of an investigation and had lost several kilos in weight. He had enjoyed the spicy eastern food very much, but sadly it had not suited his constitution.

'Be safe, my friend. Go soon, come back quickly,' İkmen said, and cut the connection. Süleyman put his phone back in his pocket. Suddenly tearful, he turned away quickly lest his wife see his weakness. Çetin was like a very loving older brother, always there, always watching his back. He too knew what the realities of working out east could be. İkmen, like everyone else, read the papers, watched the news from what some called the front. Süleyman was going to miss him very much.

'Oh,' he heard his wife say as she watched the television, seemingly oblivious. 'Gaziantep twenty-eight degrees tomorrow. You'll get a suntan.'

She was trying to make light of it. Süleyman knew that he himself couldn't think about it too much. Couldn't think about his wife, his child, or his friends back in İstanbul either. He thought instead about what Inspector Taner might be like, how far Yusuf Kaya might have got and how strange and foreign 'out east' was going to be. Try as he might to concentrate on how interesting it might all prove, he couldn't help but feel afraid.

Chapter 3

Although it wasn't dark when he arrived, to Süleyman, because he was tired, it felt like the middle of the night. Oğuzlı Airport at Gaziantep was hardly a glamorous or even seemingly businesslike terminal. Surrounded by far more covered women than he was accustomed to, as well as several distinctly rural-looking men who smelt, he suspected, of goat, he had to wait an eternity for his luggage to be unloaded from the flight from Istanbul. When his small suitcase did arrive it looked as if it had been kicked around a dusty floor for the duration of the journey. He took hold of it with a look of misery on his face, wiping his now sweating brow with his other hand as he did so. It was considerably warmer here than it had been in İstanbul. But then spring in the far south-east could be quite hot. In Mardin, which was even further east and to the north of Antep, it could be either as hot as hell or freezing cold. Places like Mardin were unpredictable.

What was not, he felt, unpredictable, however, was what this Inspector Taner was going to be like. He'd be deferential to a man from İstanbul, which was no problem at all, unlike the small-mindedness he would almost certainly exhibit, which would be. Physically he would either be short and thin or short and stocky. People from the far east, in his experience, rarely grew to any great height. He would definitely have a large and luxuriant moustache. And as Süleyman passed through Customs and entered the arrivals hall there, indeed, was a small, thin, middle-aged man holding up a sign with his name on it. His moustache was of heroic proportions. Süleyman, moving forward, forced a smile. When he got near to the small man, he put out his hand. After all, averse as they sometimes could be to hand-shaking in the east, it was his custom and he was the guest, as it were.

But to his surprise and, for a fraction of a second, his irritation, the man with the sign did not take the offered hand. Süleyman was just about to let his arm drop when another hand, a long, slim thing with painted nails, took and shook his fingers firmly. He looked up and found himself staring into the face of a tall, very handsome middle-aged woman.

'Inspector Süleyman?' Her voice was deep and smoke-scarred. 'Edibe Taner.' She shook his hand enthusiastically. Then, looking down at the small man holding the sign, she said, 'This is my cousin, Rafik. He lives here and will drive us into the city. Welcome to Gaziantep, Inspector Süleyman.'

It was late and the hospital administrator was obviously tired. But İkmen needed to get to the truth.

'Listen, sir,' he said, 'I need to know who exactly İsak Mardin and Faruk Öz are. They are both missing, and either one could be implicated in what amounts to multiple homicide.'

The administrator rested his chin in his hands and sighed.

'Now, am I right in my belief that Lole and Öz's qualifications are in order but Mardin's are not?'

'Mr Mardin came to work here only a few months ago,' the administrator said. 'It was at a time when we were experiencing some staff shortages.'

'So Mardin isn't—'

'Yusuf Mardin was engaged by my predecessor, Mr Oner. I was not in on the interview and so I don't know what might or might not have been discussed. All I know is that although there is a note about Mr Mardin's qualifications in his file there are no photocopies of his certificates.'

'As a rule, you photocopy certificates?'

'Yes. As I said, the hospital was under a lot of pressure with regard to staff at that time. Mr Oner might very well have not taken photocopies due to an oversight. Such a thing is not unknown.'

'Well,' İkmen said, 'I suppose we'd better talk to Mr Oner, hadn't we?'

The administrator pulled a strained expression. 'I'm afraid that won't be possible,' he said.

'Why not?'

'Mr Oner died last month. That's why I'm sitting here now.' Then, seeing İkmen's instantly suspicious look, he said, 'Mr Oner had been under a lot of pressure for a very long time. Sadly, he took his own life.'

His suspicions raised even further, İkmen said, 'How did he do it? How did he kill himself?'

The administrator, apparently aware that it was important for his future liberty that he tell the policeman everything he knew, nevertheless lowered his voice. 'He ingested disinfectant,' he said. 'A hideous, hideous way to die.'

In view of his 'hideous' demise, Mr Oner's oversight with regard to Mardin's qualifications could possibly be understood. Although why a man working in a hospital, around so many drugs that could have eased him comparatively gently into the next world, should choose to kill himself with disinfectant was mysterious. It was a very painful way to die, especially in a place where an overdose of everyday painkillers could be obtained with little difficulty. But then if he were truly out of his mind at the time . . .

İkmen had learned quite a few things of interest since he'd come back to the Cerrahpaşa. He'd learned that the cleaners involved in the rescue of Yusuf Kaya could not, so far, be either named or identified by any member of the hospital staff. He'd learned that İsak Mardin was a very new employee while, by contrast, Faruk Öz and Murat Lole had been working at the hospital for eighteen months. Öz and Lole were fully qualified nurses, while Mardin's status was, due to lack of copied certification, more open to question.

'Can you tell me where Mr Mardin worked before he came here?' İkmen asked after a pause.

The administrator looked down at the three files in front of him and picked one up.

Could it have really been some sort of conspiracy, İkmen wondered? Had the late Mr Oner given İsak Mardin a job at the Cerrahpaşa with a view to using the nurse to assist in Yusuf Kaya's escape? Or had Mardin come to Oner and blackmailed him, by some means, into giving him a job? Had Oner known that he planned to enable a very dangerous criminal to escape justice? Had the former administrator killed himself because he couldn't live with that knowledge? And where, if anywhere, did Öz and Lole fit into this picture?

Or was İkmen racing ahead of himself, creating scenarios that did not really have any basis in fact or true validity?

'Mr Mardin worked at the Urfa Hospital in Şanlıurfa,' the administrator said. 'He came recommended by them,' he added.

'Did he?' İkmen cleared his throat. 'Do you have a name I can contact at the Urfa Hospital? I'll need to verify this.'

The administrator copied something down on to a piece of paper and handed it over to İkmen.

'Lead cardiac consultant at the Urfa,' he said. 'Would have been İsak Mardin's overall superior. He will be able to comment on his work. You've not been on to his ward here, have you, Inspector?'

'No. That is one of my tasks for tomorrow,' İkmen said. 'I am going to see the cardiologist who had been due to examine our escaped prisoner.'

'He gave your officers a statement at the time.'

'I am aware of that.'

The administrator didn't reply. It wasn't that he was either evasive or hostile. He just, İkmen felt, had nothing more to add. For himself, the policeman had done everything he believed he could for the present. It was early evening and he had a full diary of interviews and meetings for the following day – not least of which was with his team, which temporarily included Süleyman's sergeant, İzzet Melik.

If, as he was coming to believe was just possible, the plot to spring Yusuf Kaya went back a considerable way, there was a possibility that people still present in the Cerrahpaşa knew about it. And then there was Mr Oner, the now deceased previous administrator. Why had he died in such an unnecessarily painful fashion? Had he in fact been killed rather than taken his own life? Yusuf Kaya was well known for his brutality. Had he ordered a hit on the man İsak Mardin? Had Faruk Öz or maybe even Murat Lole been somehow persuaded to either support or turn a blind eye to his venture? Were any of the three nurses truly involved anyway? The security footage was very unclear and there was not, as yet, any evidence that connected any one of them in any way to Yusuf Kaya.

His brain humming with numerous possibilities, İkmen left the hospital soon afterwards. As he made his way back to his car he found himself thinking about İsak Mardin's previous job in Şanlıurfa. Far down in the deep south-east, 'Urfa', as it was known locally, was not far from Gaziantep where Süleyman had to be by that time. Rather than think about how strange it was that he was so reluctant to go home since Bekir had returned, instead he thought about his friend and wondered how he might be coping, having to work with some peasant from the back of beyond.

The drive from the airport into the city was not exactly a picturesque trip. Gaziantep was heavily populated and industrialised. Factories, car repair garages and line upon line of almost Soviet-style tower blocks marched relentlessly across the dusty landscape like ranks of silent, depressed soldiers. The man at the wheel, Inspector Taner's cousin Rafik, reminded Süleyman a little of Çetin İkmen. Thin and sporting a thick, black moustache, he drove a battered old Mercedes similar to the one that İkmen had kept alive for so many years. Unlike İkmen, however, he did not talk continuously, even if the amount of smoking that went on was very familiar. Inspector Taner herself was quite another matter.

The last thing Süleyman had been expecting, especially way out in the wild, wild east, was a female officer. He had thought about the possibility of Taner's being a young man, but a middle-aged macho character had been what he anticipated. An image of a tall and attractive woman had not even entered his mind. Inspector Edibe Taner was, Süleyman reckoned, somewhere in her forties. Slim without being thin, she had thick shoulder-length hair that was coloured a dull but affecting shade of dark purple. Like her long, red fingernails, her face was heavily painted and she had thick black lines round her eyes that made her look more Egyptian than

Turkish. Everything about her seemed to speak of strength: her long straight nose, her firm jaw, her large and muscular bustline.

'I've booked you into a hotel called the Princess,' she said as they sped past a large and very brash Jeep dealership. 'As I expect you are well aware, Inspector, hotels in general in this part of the world are not up to İstanbul standards. But the Princess, Rafik tells me, is clean if basic.'

'You won't get bedbugs,' the man at the wheel muttered.

Süleyman smiled. They were a direct pair, which he liked, and there was a little private fun to be had for someone whose family had been princes staying in a hotel called the Princess. 'I'm sure it will be fine,' he said.

'Once you've checked in I've taken the liberty of organising dinner,' Taner said. 'It's the best restaurant in town, believe me.'

'Thank you.' Süleyman saw Rafik smile and wondered what it meant. Was Taner joking with him, perhaps?

'We need to talk about what you know of our friend Yusuf Kaya and what developments have occurred with regard to him since I've been here,' the woman continued. She offered Süleyman a long black Sobranie cigarette, which he gratefully accepted, and then lit one up for herself. 'Do you drink, Inspector Süleyman?' she said after a pause.

'Sometimes,' he said. 'I don't have a problem or—'

'I do,' Taner said with a smile and what Süleyman felt was astonishing candidness. 'Rakı.'

'Ah.' There wasn't really very much that he could say to that. Before he could think of any way in which he might move their conversation forward, the car turned into a dark and rutted side street. On one side was a tiny coffee house with several men sitting outside at low tables, playing backgammon. On the other was a six-storey sixties-style block sporting a scruffy sign which said *Princess Oteli*.

'We're here,' Taner said as she swung her long, slim legs out of the car door. The men at the coffee house opposite watched, almost mesmerised, as she stood up and then smoothed her mini skirt a very short distance down her thighs.

'If you get into a fight with a gypsy you have to know what you're doing.'

'Oh, well, I imagine you do!'

İkmen, sitting with his wife in the living room, could hear his son Bekir and his daughter Çiçek talking in the kitchen. Bekir's stories regarding his 'lost' years were becoming a feature of everyone's evenings now that he was back home once again. Relayed in an almost casual tone that could be regarded as modest, they often drew a response of breathless excitement from Bekir's siblings. He was engaged at that particular moment in telling his younger sister about the time he'd apparently spent living on the streets of Sulukule up by the old city walls. A gypsy quarter, it was a place that had a reputation, mainly for the high cost of its dancing girls and the toughness of its men.

'Dad engaged a gypsy fortune-teller for Hulya's wedding,' İkmen heard his daughter say. 'She was very good.'

What a pity the gypsy in question hadn't been able to predict that Hulya and Berekiah's marriage would come under so much strain. But then the fortune-teller wasn't just a seer, she was an artist and one of İkmen's informants too. And although she lived in the district of Balat, she like most gypsies knew Sulukule well. If Bekir had, as he was now telling his sister, a reputation as a fighter up in the gypsy quarter, the fortune-teller would know about it.

'I called myself the Black Storm,' he heard Bekir say. 'And I won every fight I ever had in Sulukule.'

İkmen looked across the room at his wife, who was darning one of Kemal's socks. It was a really old-fashioned thing to do in what had become an era of cheap, throwaway clothes. But Fatma İkmen was not a woman given to behaviour she perceived to be wasteful.

'What do you think about all these stories Bekir tells?' İkmen asked his wife when he finally managed to catch her eye.

'I'm just glad to have him back, wherever he's been,' she replied. 'Aren't you?'

'Well, of course!' He *said* that, but was it true? Çetin İkmen alone had, finally, had to deal with Bekir when he reached the height of his bad behaviour at age fifteen. Fatma and the other children had known about the stealing, of course; he'd stolen from every one of them. They'd also known about the cannabis and the drink. But Çetin had kept quiet about the harder drugs he knew his son was taking. The cocaine and the amphetamines had been between Çetin and Bekir, as had the former's knowledge of the latter's drug-dealing exploits. Bekir at fifteen had been a nightmare. Taking drugs, dealing, getting drunk, fighting . . . There had been women too, İkmen recalled, ladies of his wife's age who, if indirectly, had helped to fund Bekir's various drug addictions. The boy had not, his father could not easily forget, always treated those women with even the most basic kindness. Allah, but the black eyes and cracked ribs that some middle-aged women were prepared to tolerate in exchange for a firm, young body!

Fatma, her concentration on her needlework now broken, said, 'Çetin, are you sure about that? Are you sure you're really happy about Bekir being home again?'

She was no fool. After thirty-seven years of marriage there was little she didn't know or couldn't deduce about her husband.

İkmen took in a deep breath and then leaned forward. 'Oh, Fatma,' he said, 'I don't know. The circumstances of his leaving were so . . .'

'But that was years ago, Çetin!' Fatma said. 'He's changed now. Even you can see he's not on drugs any more.'

Bekir didn't appear to be, it was true. In fact apart from cigarettes he didn't seem to 'do' anything, and that included alcohol. That, in particular, pleased Fatma, who was a sincere and observant Muslim. But all of that notwithstanding, İkmen himself was not happy. A doubt, something he often objectified by envisaging it as the voice of his dead mother whispering in his ear, was nagging. Ayşe, his Albanian mother, the local witch of the Asian district of Üsküdar, was not happy with Bekir. He made her skin tingle. İkmen made a mental note to drop by the fortune-teller's colourful studio in Balat before he returned home the following evening.

During Ottoman times, before the Republican era, Gaziantep was known just as Aintab. Then in 1921, when what is now the Turkish Republic was fighting for its existence against the forces of France, Great Britain and Greece as well as the Sultan's royalist soldiers, Aintab was Turkicised to Antep and given an honorific title. In recognition of the heroic resistance put up by Antep's citizens to the French army in 1921, Atatürk, the Republic's founder and first president, said that from then on the city was to be known as Gazi or 'warrior hero' Antep. Since that time Gaziantep had been a largely Turkish city, but remnants from its more cosmopolitan past remained, as Mehmet Süleyman was discovering. The house that Inspector Taner and her cousin took him to for his meal that night was a case in point. It was located in the old Sahinbey quarter of the city, an area which had a distinctly Arabian feel to it, underlining in effect the comparative closeness of Gaziantep to Syria. Once through the low doorway that led directly from the dark, narrow street into the courtyard of what looked like a great mansion, one could very easily not be in Turkey at all. In fact, Süleyman thought as he watched a pretty marble fountain bubble away gently in the middle of the chequered courtyard, places just like this existed in Damascus, Jerusalem, Amman or any other Arab city one would care to name. The pungent smell of spices that permeated the building added to the general sense of exoticism.

'I hope you don't mind,' Taner said as she directed Süleyman towards a dining table, already set with cutlery and napkins, in one corner of the courtyard. Above it and slightly overhanging into the space below was the upper storey of the house, which was accessed by a broad marble staircase from the ground level. Up there Süleyman could see ornate doorways and delicate fanlight windows of tremendous beauty.

'What a wonderful place,' he said, genuinely impressed.

'Please sit down,' his hostess replied. She did not respond to his delight in his surroundings, nor did she tell him what the place was.

Her cousin left them and walked towards a doorway just underneath the staircase, saying something in a language Süleyman didn't understand.

As they sat down, Inspector Taner spoke. 'As you know, Yusuf Kaya was picked up on security cameras in a patisserie called the Nightingale,' she said. 'Not that that is important now. What is, however, is that Kaya has friends, of sorts, in Gaziantep.'

'Do you know who they are?'

She took a piece of paper out of her handbag and pushed it across the table. It was a map of the centre of Gaziantep.

'There is a house, here, just off Güzelce Lane.' She pointed to what was, to Süleyman, a fathomless spot on the map. 'It is a brothel.'

'You think that Kaya might be hiding out in a brothel?'

'A friend of his runs the place,' she said. 'A woman called Anastasia. Kaya put her on her back when she was little more than a child.'

'That was in Mardin?'

'Yes.' Ardıç had said that Mardin wanted Kaya as much as or perhaps even more than the police in İstanbul. And if he had been turning the city's girls to prostitution . . . 'Do you like lahmacun?' Taner beckoned an old black-clad woman carrying two steaming plates over to the table.

'Er, yes . . .'

Lahmacun is a type of thin bread topped, usually, with rather spicy meat and vegetables. Because it generally involves cheese too it is often referred to as Turkish pizza. In the east, as a rather wary Süleyman knew all too well, lahmacun could be very heavily spiced indeed. As the elderly lady put the plate down in front of him he viewed the pile of slices with some caution.

'Together with the local police I'm going to be raiding the brothel tomorrow morning,' Taner said as without so much as a flicker she folded a great wedge of lahmacun into her mouth. 'We've been watching the place since yesterday, but we don't know whether Kaya is in there or not. However, one thing is for sure: to raid at night when the place is full of customers will only give him any cover he might need to escape. We'll get in there while they're all asleep.' She smiled grimly. 'It will be very strange for me to meet Anastasia again. I haven't seen her for over twenty years.'

'No?' He would have liked to quiz Taner more closely on the matter, but as soon as he'd put the lahmacun into his mouth the whole of his alimentary canal had caught fire. The chillies were lethal!

'Anastasia and myself are of an age,' the inspector replied. 'I am a Muslim, she a Suriani Christian, but we went to school together. She was very pretty, but a nice girl too, you know.' She smiled more openly this time. 'Not many girls are both pretty and nice, Inspector. As a man you may not be aware of that.' Her face dropped and became altogether more grim. 'Yusuf Kaya, who as you know is fifty this year, is a few years older than Anastasia and myself. When she was fifteen he raped her. He wanted her badly, but she didn't like him and so he took her by force. Of course her family didn't want her back.'

The old woman returned, this time carrying a bottle of something clear. She hovered, seemingly nervously, until Taner turned to look at her with a very casual eye.

'Rakı?' Taner asked Süleyman.

He'd finally managed to get through the first slice of lahmacun and was starting on his second. He was, he felt, getting used to it now, maybe because his mouth had been numbed by the pepper.

'Yes. Thank you,' he said.

The old woman didn't even look at him as she poured some of the clear, viscous liquid into his glass. Then she filled Taner's glass and left. There was no sign, or didn't appear to be any sign, of Rafik.

'Yusuf Kaya set up a brothel on the edge of a small village down on what we call the Ocean,' Taner said as she topped

45

up both their rakı glasses with water. Then, seeing his confusion, she added, 'It's what outsiders call the Mesopotamian plain.'

'Ah.'

'Even at seventeen he was enterprising. He had Anastasia because he wanted her and then he let other men have her for money. The Kayas are a very bad clan, Inspector Süleyman. But they have power, you know?'

He'd heard. The clans of Mardin, like the clans associated with some other cities in the east, were notorious for the power they wielded over their members and often over non-relatives around them too. Between the clans and the various terrorists it was difficult to know who was the most dangerous.

'But, Inspector,' Süleyman said, 'you describe this woman, now, as Kaya's friend. Surely if he ruined her life . . .'

Edibe Taner shrugged. 'What can one say?' she said. 'Some women are like that. Some women adore their abusers. Psychologically it can be a way for an abused woman to come to terms with what has happened to her. If she loves her abuser then what has happened cannot be abuse. Yusuf Kaya is a married man but Anastasia Akyuz is still, it is said, in love with him. What is also said is that her daughter, also living in the brothel, is his daughter too.'

'So Kaya is very likely to be with them.'

'He was seen just yesterday here in Gaziantep. It's possible.' She took a swig from her rakı glass and then looked up at the darkening sky above and sighed. 'Inspector, I have spent most of my professional life fighting these clans. They're clever. I can't guarantee what, if anything, will happen tomorrow. But if you want to come along with me, provided you are content to let the Gaziantep police take the lead, you may do so.'

Was that stuff about letting the Gaziantep police take the

lead some sort of code for 'we know how arrogant you İstanbullus are, we know you always want to take over'? If so, then it was probably best to let it just go over his head. After all, what did a country bumpkin like Taner know about him? She might be wearing a smart suit and expensive make-up, but that didn't stop her being merely a big fish in a very small pool. He said he'd like to observe the raid just as the next course, ribs of lamb that appeared to be stuffed with rice, appeared. It was then that Taner's mobile telephone rang.

She looked down at the instrument and said, 'I have to take this.' Then, without another word, she got up and left the table.

'You'll want to wait for her, I suppose,' the old woman, who was still standing by the table waiting to serve them, said. 'To eat?'

'Oh, er, yes,' he said. 'Yes, I will, thank you.'

'As you wish.' There was a slight foreign tinge to her voice. But then a lot of people in this part of the country did not speak Turkish as their first language. Maybe the old black-clad woman was an Arab? Perhaps that was the language he had heard Rafik speaking earlier?

She was just about to leave when Süleyman, his curiosity piqued by this place he knew absolutely nothing about, said, 'What is this building? Can you tell me?'

The woman, who was small and he could see now was very angular, almost like one of those pictures of witches one some-times saw in books of European fairy stories, stopped. 'You want to see the Zeytounian house?' she said.

Süleyman instantly recognised the name as one of Armenian origin. The old woman, who did not give him her own name at any point, led him up the stairs to the first floor of the building. Just to the left of the stairs was a large doorway surmounted by a very ornate stained glass fanlight. The door

47

was ajar and Süleyman could just make out that the interior was lit by a flickering flame, possibly candlelight.

'The house was built by Dzeron Zeytounian in the nineteenth century,' the old woman said. 'The Zeytounians were rich, educated people.'

She pushed the door open and he found himself looking into another world. The old woman quite clearly knew this, because what she said next indicated that she had, perhaps, read Süleyman's mind.

'These rooms belong to the Cobweb World,' she said. 'They exist in a time not even I can remember.'

He could see three rooms, all with worn but still beautiful parquet floors. Curtains faded almost to white hung at the few windows, and the rooms were indeed lit by four large collections of flickering candles. Although the furniture was sparse, Süleyman could see that it was both old and very good. Two sagging but still regal armchairs graced one room, their once bright brocade covers nibbled by vermin. In another room, on top of a small bamboo and teak table was a radio almost as big as a modern TV set, the international stations on its dial given in French: Londres, Maroc, Allemagne.

But it was not the furniture or even the fabulous floors that really held his attention. The walls and the ceilings, which were panelled in ornate cream-painted wood, were also covered with paintings. Great fluffy clouds above his head barely concealed cherubs casually leaning upon golden harps. At picture rail level, large arched hunting scenes predominated: illustrations that looked as if they would be more appropriate for the country house of an English gentleman than the mansion of a wealthy Armenian. Finally, between panels painted with a Grecian urn motif and cupboards fronted with delicate wooden filigree, there were portraits. The women, unveiled

48

and wearing clothing typical of nineteenth-century Europe, stared out solemnly from hooded oriental eyes. The men wore fezzes, their faces also solemn but this time in some cases recognisable.

'That is Dzeron Zeytounian,' the old woman said as she pointed to a particularly severe-looking portrait. 'This one here is Midhat Paşa.'

Midhat Paşa Süleyman knew. It had been Midhat who had tried to persuade the autocratic and paranoid Sultan Abdul Hamid to grant his people a modern constitution back in the 1870s. He had paid for his social concern with his life. Strangely, next to Midhat's portrait was one of the sultan concerned, his dark skin and hooded eyes making him look as if he could almost be related to the Zeytounian ladies.

Instinctively – for this long dead sultan, for all his faults, was one of Süleyman's forebears – the policeman put his hand up towards the portrait.

The old woman said, 'You have a connection to the Cobweb World. I know it and I can see it too.' He turned to look at her and saw that she was smiling. 'The Cobweb World is Ottoman, it is Armenian, Syrian, Jewish. Ancient, even beyond the Byzantine times. It has always been,' she said. 'You will find the Cobweb World everywhere if you go to Mardin.'

He wanted to know how she apparently knew about his possible trip to Mardin; how she knew or claimed to know that he was from an Ottoman family, for that matter. But he just went on staring at the portrait of Sultan Abdul Hamid. During the latter half of his reign some of his opponents had 'accused' him of having Armenian blood. 'This Cobweb World of which you speak . . .'

'Is what remains of things gone by. Meaningful things,' she said gently. 'In other places things die, but here . . . Belief means that some corpses retain some life. Then again, some things never die in the first place. Some faiths are alive and—'

She was cut off by a furious female voice coming from the ornate doorway. Turning slowly and reluctantly from the portrait in front of him, Süleyman saw the angry figure of Inspector Taner berating the old woman roundly. What language she was speaking he didn't know, but the effect it had on the old woman was instant and she moved away quickly without another word. Taner, breathing heavily, looked across at Süleyman and smiled. 'I apologise for that,' she said. 'She speaks out of turn. Madly.'

'She was actually quite interesting,' Süleyman said. 'And this building—'

'It's very late,' the policewoman cut in, rudely, he thought. 'The stupid old woman has let our food get cold. Rafik will take you back to your hotel now. We have to start early in the morning.' She held her arm out towards him in a gesture that he felt would brook no argument. 'Come. Let's go.'

'This is a marvellous place. It—'

Taner moved forward and took Süleyman physically by the arm. 'It's an old, dead house,' she said matter-of-factly; 'it has no interest or meaning for someone like you. Dinner is over. Come.'

She pulled him roughly out into the cool, southern night.

Chapter 4

Secretly, İkmen had expected more. Scientific procedures were so sophisticated now that near miracles were, or seemed to be, almost daily occurrences. He passed the photographs in his hands over to the pathologist and sighed.

'Useless,' he said. 'They tell us nothing.'

Dr Arto Sarkissian adjusted his spectacles on the bridge of his nose and squinted. 'Çetin, to be fair,' he said, 'these men are wearing stockings over their faces. The enhancement shows that very clearly. We couldn't see that before. All we had was some security film of men dressed as cleaners and nurses.'

'Now we have men dressed as cleaners and nurses with stockings over their faces,' İkmen responded caustically. 'Hardly useful.'

'Hardly possible, in the real world, for photographic enhancement to peer through the distorting effect of ladies' hosiery,' Arto said, himself peering sternly over the top of his glasses at the policeman. 'I think that the laboratory has done extremely well.'

İkmen grunted. Arto Sarkissian and Çetin İkmen had been friends since childhood. Their fathers had been friends also and the two boys, together with İkmen's brother Halil and Arto's brother Krikor, had spent almost every waking moment together when not at their respective schools. Although financially far and away above İkmen with his huge, riotous band of children, the pathologist retained a closeness to his old friend that was entirely free of competition or artifice of any sort.

'I suppose now I've got to start looking for ladies' stockings in dustbins and on landfill sites,' İkmen said gloomily.

'At least you know now that you have to look for stockings,' Arto replied. 'The men who freed Yusuf Kaya may even have discarded their masks amongst the clinical waste at the Cerrahpaşa. There are many avenues you can go down in pursuit of DNA samples, Çetin.'

'Mmm.' İkmen lit a cigarette and sighed. The doctor had come to the policeman's office in order to discuss the post-mortems he had performed on the police officers and the prison guard who had died during Yusuf Kaya's escape. That he'd walked into an examination of stills from the Cerrahpaşa security camera film footage was purely accidental.

'I thought that stockings were a thing of the past these days,' İkmen said, still miserably. 'I thought those wishing to hide their faces these days wore scarves or novelty George W. Bush masks.'

Arto laughed. 'Maybe Yusuf Kaya's team are just old-fashioned boys,' he said. Then, pointing at the photograph in his hand, he added, 'But maybe not. You know that the weapons used to kill the men I examined were not knives.'

'Not knives?' İkmen frowned.

Arto waddled heavily over towards his friend and put the photograph on his desk. He was a short, very stout man just on the brink of actual obesity.

'What the enhancement shows very nicely here is an absence of knives,' he said, pointing at the photograph. 'See here. Something glints, but as to what that thing is . . .'

Çetin peered downwards and then said, 'Yes, but the glinting is . . . Admittedly I can't actually see anything . . .'

'That's because the weapons they used were glass,' Arto said.

'Glass?'

'Admittedly large and very sharp shards of toughened glass, but glass nevertheless,' Arto said.

His friend looked up and asked what even he knew was a pointless question. 'Are you sure?'

Arto Sarkissian was always sure; that was why he was so good at his job. 'Wounds to all three bodies contain glass particles. Also, the shapes of the incisions are so irregular they can't have been produced by a conventional blade. These stills, which show an apparent absence of actual weaponry, only serve to confirm my findings.'

'Yes, but . . . Glass?'

Arto stumbled back to his chair and sat down again. 'Why not?' he said. 'Glass is very effective as a weapon, and if a piece of glass is found on a cleaner or a nurse it is unlikely to be confiscated even by a police officer.'

'Well . . .'

'They could be in the process of disposing of a dangerous shard found on a ward or in a corridor. Glass can turn up anywhere. In the right context, like that of a cleaner, being found in possession of glass can be viewed as a good thing.'

He was right. It could be looked upon as entirely innocent. But far from giving the policeman a sense of progress in the Kaya case, the new information only served to unsettle him still further. Frowning again, he said, 'The more I learn about Kaya's escape the more I am convinced it was planned down to the last second. Glass! They might have considered different weapons for weeks . . . months!'

'And yet planning at such an exact level implies, to me at least, complicity from the only person who could possibly engineer Kaya's escape from the beginning: the prison governor. Or am I being simple-minded?'

Çetin İkmen nodded his head. 'I can see your point,' he said. 'And yet so far I can find no evidence for that. The governor made a decision based upon what the prison doctor and then the guards told him about Kaya at the time. It took him some hours to come to the conclusion he reached and Kaya's condition had deteriorated before he did anything. You don't send a dangerous psychopath out of incarceration unless you're very certain that something is really wrong.'

'What about the prison doctor?'

'He was interviewed only hours after Kaya's escape,' İkmen said. 'The officer who interviewed him reported that he smelt of alcohol, although whether or not he had examined Kaya whilst drunk isn't known. He says he didn't recommend immediate transfer to the hospital. Kaya had raised blood pressure but in the doctor's opinion he was more likely to be having a panic attack than anything else.'

'So how did Kaya come to get a transfer to the Cerrahpaşa?' Arto asked.

'The governor says that his guards recommended it,' İkmen replied. 'They claimed, he says, that Kaya was breathing with difficulty and had turned an alarming shade of grey. The governor duly went to see Kaya and found him as he had been described. He then called the Cerrahpaşa to request an ECG and asked the guards to prepare the prisoner for transfer.'

'That's his version of the story,' Arto said.

'Without Yusuf Kaya himself and with the only surviving prison guard still in a coma, there can only be one version at this time,' İkmen said. 'I've looked at telephone calls into and out of the prison, both landline and mobile – I've found nothing in the least bit suspicious.'

'And so you question absent nurses and speculate about chimerical cleaners,' Arto said. 'By the way, DNA samples gathered from the scarf said to belong to one İsak Mardin came up with no matches to anyone known to us.'

İkmen sighed. 'Oh, joy,' he said gloomily.

The doctor cleared his throat. 'So Mehmet Süleyman is out east in pursuit of Yusuf Kaya.'

'He's in Gaziantep at the moment,' İkmen replied. 'Kaya was picked up on a security camera at a patisserie down there.'

'What happens if Yusuf Kaya isn't in Gaziantep?'

İkmen shook his head wearily. 'Then my friend will have to go to his home city of Mardin.'

'Oh, yes, of course, I remember now,' Arto said. 'A real eastern boy, Yusuf Kaya.' They sat in silence for a moment and then he said, 'You know, I've an old friend in Mardin, a Syrian. Seraphim Yunun he's called. He's a monk at the monastery of St Sobo, which is just outside the city.'

İkmen, who had never heard of Seraphim Yunun, said, 'How did you get to know him?'

'Oh, Christian circles, you know,' the Armenian said breezily. Not that he was religious in any way, as far as İkmen was aware. But unlike the policeman, who was nominally a Muslim, Arto was nominally a Christian, and in a country that was over ninety per cent Muslim, like Turkey, the minorities did tend to know one another.

'Nice man, Seraphim,' the Armenian continued. 'I wonder, if Mehmet Süleyman does go to Mardin, whether I should put him in touch? I mean, I don't want to labour the point, but one cannot encounter too many friendly faces in such an outlandish place.'

'Call him on his mobile.'

'Mm.' Arto frowned. 'I might just do that,' he said. 'My

recollection of accommodation in Mardin, admittedly some years ago now, is not a pleasant one. I imagine that much has changed in twenty-odd years, but if Inspector Süleyman does find himself in need of a clean bed and intelligent company, he could do worse than stay at the monastery of St Sobo.'

'Police!'

Less than a second later, and without further warning, a constable smashed in the front door of the brothel with a pickaxe. Inside, women screamed while the deeper voices of their erstwhile customers howled in fury. Armed police, both plainclothed and in uniform, pushed their way into the building shouting, 'Stay where you are!' Taner and Süleyman, bringing up the rear, arrived inside when the raid was all but over.

Some of the brothels in İstanbul, in Süleyman's experience, were rough but this filthy little house in Gaziantep was just pathetic. The madame, the Anastasia Akyuz of whom Taner had spoken the previous evening, had obviously once been attractive. Now in her late forties, she was overweight, unkempt and disappointed. Badly dressed in a thin, dirty-looking house-coat, she stood smoking beside the shattered front door of her premises as officers from the Gaziantep police constabulary made her various 'girls' and their clients step outside. Several 'respectable' people from nearby flats and houses hurled random insults at the women as, in dribs and drabs, they appeared.

'I haven't seen Yusuf for years,' Anastasia said to a clearly sceptical Taner, when she and Süleyman emerged from the sad little house of ill repute.

'Anastasia,' Taner replied with a smile, 'don't protect him. He married a Muslim girl and gave her a lot of children. Money but no active support, you know how he is. He was convicted in İstanbul for, amongst other things, the murder of his mistress. Who knows how many more women he has, how many children? Yusuf Kaya is totally faithless and not worth a thought!'

Anastasia Akyuz put her hands on her ample hips and said, 'Edibe, I don't know where he is.'

'He's a shit!' the officer from Mardin said.

Two women, neither of whom Süleyman felt could be under sixty years of age, came out of the brothel clutching ugly nylon nightdresses around their skinny varicose bodies. Someone in a house nearby shouted out, 'Filthy whores!' Inside the brothel the sound of crockery being smashed against floors and walls underlined the fact that the local police were being far from low-key about this raid.

One of the sixty-year-old hookers looked at Süleyman, cleared her throat and then said, 'What are you looking at?'

He didn't respond.

Inspector Taner, who didn't turn a hair at all the violence and shouting emanating from the brothel, said, 'Anastasia, where is Gülizar? Is she with her father?'

'Gülizar is at college in Damascus. She's a good girl,' the woman said.

'You brought her up in this brothel!'

'Yes, and I protected her!' Anastasia pointed to her own chest, a large mound of flesh surmounted by a thick, gold crucifix. 'I sent her to university! I pay!'

'Not Yusuf Kaya?'

'No! I don't see Yusuf, as I told you.'

'Yusuf Kaya who, until he was arrested in İstanbul last year, was in charge of a drugs empire worth tens of thousands of dollars,' Taner said. 'Not a kuruş for his daughter, though, no?'

Süleyman remembered that squalid flat in Tarlabaşı where Yusuf Kaya had lived. Thousands and thousands of lire in sports bags in his filthy bedroom as well as in bank accounts all over the city.

'Give him to me, Anastasia.' Taner bore down relentlessly on her victim. 'He's been seen here in Gaziantep. Where would he stay if it wasn't with you, eh?'

Before the woman could answer, one of the Gaziantep officers put his head out of an upstairs window and shouted, 'Inspector Taner!'

She looked up at him, shielding her eyes from the early morning sun with one long, thin hand.

'Something you might like to see, Inspector,' the officer said.

'I'll come up,' Taner said. She turned back to Anastasia and pointed rudely into her face. 'If you have been concealing things from us, Anastasia . . .'

She walked back into the house and up the stairs. The raid itself had been a pretty standard hit on a brothel in that it had involved a degree of wanton destruction, women well past their prime crying and screaming and unattractive men attempting to escape across neighbouring rooftops. Neighbours and passers-by gawped, and some of the younger police constables looked decidedly sheepish. Süleyman had seen it all before and, if he were honest, he hadn't had enormously high hopes of finding Yusuf Kaya in this brothel. Psychopathic he might be, but Kaya was far too devious to make the mistake of staying with someone as obvious as Anastasia.

In truth, Süleyman was still puzzling over what the old woman at the Zeytounian house had meant by the 'Cobweb World'. If it was that such places are stuck in the past by virtue of neglect, he could understand it. But whether intended or not there had been, he felt, something more esoteric behind what she had said. Unlike Çetin İkmen, who had a natural sympathy with and understanding of things unseen, Süleyman was far from comfortable with the metaphysical, in spite of the old woman's words. And yet he'd felt something in that room beyond natural curiosity, and the old woman had said that going to Mardin was going to expose him to more of the Cobweb World. The thought of it made him shudder. Now that Kaya was not, it seemed, in Gaziantep, it was very probable that he'd gone back home to his dreadful clan in Mardin, apparently the epicentre of the Cobweb World. In his mind he conjured pictures of his befezzed Ottoman ancestors. Would he feel them at his side when he went to Mardin? Was the Cobweb World a kind of permanent and possibly tangible haunted state of being? He was linking that thought to why, possibly, Inspector Taner had been so keen to get him out of the Zeytounian house when he felt a tap on his shoulder.

'She's not right, you know.' Anastasia Akyuz blew a lungful of cigarette smoke into his face.

'I'm sorry?' It was like waking violently from a very peculiar dream.

'Edibe Taner,' the woman continued. 'I knew her at school. She wasn't right there either.'

Süleyman frowned. 'What?'

'Well, why would she want to go and join the police? Why would any woman?' Anastasia moved in closer to Süleyman and looked him critically up and down. 'I heard her say you are from İstanbul.'

'Yes, I am.'

'You know Yusuf.'

'Yusuf Kaya is known to me,' he said. He didn't tell her he'd arrested him.

'Edibe thinks that I still keep in touch with him, but I don't,' she said. 'Why does she think that I send my daughter to university in Syria? I am Suriani, yes, but Turkey is my country. I send Gülizar to study in Damascus because I don't want her father to find her. I know what Yusuf is, even—'

'Anastasia!'

She looked up. The voice came from the top of the tatty stone and mud brick house. Inspector Taner was waving what looked like a small piece of paper at her.

'You need to see this.' She disappeared from the window.

Anastasia shook her head and closed her eyes. 'God!' she murmured.

Outside with Süleyman and the brothel keeper again, Taner pushed the paper underneath Anastasia's nose.

'Why is there a photograph of Yusuf Kaya underneath your bed, Anastasia? I think it was taken recently, and it was taken here in this house.'

Briefly, the brothel keeper put her head in her hands. Then she looked up and said, 'Look, Yusuf came here last year, I admit it. Maybe two months before he was arrested. I . . . Look, Edibe, I admit I still had a thing for him then, we went to bed . . . but I don't let him see Gülizar and I don't know where he is now. I haven't seen him since that time, I swear to God.'

'Why should I believe you?' the Mardin policewoman said. 'You told me you hadn't seen Yusuf for years. That was a lie.'

Anastasia groaned. Edibe Taner put the photograph into a small plastic bag and slotted it into her handbag.

'Miss Akyuz,' Süleyman said urgently, 'if you know anything at all about where Yusuf Kaya might be you must tell us – now. Aiding and abetting an escaped prisoner is, as I am sure you know, a very serious offence.'

The woman's dark, make-up-smudged eyes darted round nervously for a moment until she said, 'I haven't seen Yusuf this year, I swear. I swear! But I know that one of his aunts lives at Birecik. She broke from the Kaya clan in Mardin and married this farmer from there. They don't speak to her, but I know Yusuf has used her place in the past. He'll use anyone.' She cast her eyes downwards. 'Her name is Bulbul, that's all I know. She lives on a farm outside Birecik with her husband. He's a lot older than her, I think.'

'Where is Birecik?'

'South of here,' Edibe Taner said. 'It's on the Euphrates.' She smiled at the woman and said, 'Thank you, Anastasia. You did the right thing.'

Furious now, Anastasia Akyuz turned away with tears in her eyes.

Inspector Taner flicked her head at Süleyman, indicating that they should go. But before she left she put one of her hands on Anastasia's shoulder and said, 'And next time, if there is a next time, Yusuf seeks the warmth of your bed for the night, be kind to yourself, Anastasia, and say no.' She let go of the woman and took Süleyman by the arm.

'Where are we going?' Süleyman said, looking down at Taner's strong hand on his bicep.

'To headquarters here and then on to Birecik,' she answered casually. 'No point being here if Kaya is elsewhere.'

'Ssh! Ssh! Ssh!' Fatma İkmen put her fingers to her lips and waved her other hand as if in warning. 'Bekir is still asleep!'

'Mum, it's eleven o'clock,' her son Bülent replied. 'Even I'm up!'

When he had returned from performing his military service the previous year, Bülent, who was now in his early twenties, had gone to live with his sister Çiçek in an apartment near Atatürk Airport. Like his sister, Bülent worked as cabin crew for Turkish Airlines and, again like Çiçek, he flew all over the world on a regular basis. Unlike his sister, Bülent didn't really remember his brother Bekir. He did not therefore share her apparent joy at seeing him again. In fact, Bülent found the older man not a little patronising and his mother's attitude towards him irritating in the extreme. Fatma was behaving as if Bekir was a baby.

'So what tasty little treat have you been cooking up for him today?' Bülent said as he entered the kitchen, which smelt strongly of cooked sugar and butter.

'Bekir was always a great one for baklava,' Fatma said as she turned the heat up on the samovar in the corner of the kitchen. 'Tea?'

'Yes, thank you. You're making baklava?' Bülent said, astounded. 'Mum, you can buy that stuff from the patisserie down the road. Did you make the pastry and—'

'Yes, yes, yes! What is wrong with that?' his mother interrupted angrily. 'Do I have to ask you what I may or may not do in my own kitchen?'

'No, of course not,' her son said. 'But Mum, I know that if you make baklava from scratch, as in you make the pastry too, it's really hard and time-consuming, and—'

'My mother did it without complaint,' Fatma said, pouring tea from the samovar pot into a small tulip glass for Bülent.

Baklava, which consists of nuts, a lot of sugar and layer upon layer of very thin buttery filo pastry, is not an easy dessert to make. All but the most enthusiastic cooks did as Bülent had suggested and bought the stuff ready made from a pastry shop. Fatma İkmen did indeed like to cook, but even she had, to Bülent's knowledge at least, always drawn the line at baklava.

'So where have you been this week, my son?' Fatma said as she ushered Bülent, a tall and still very thin young man, into a chair by the kitchen table.

'Holland,' he said, slipping a hand into his denim jacket and taking out a packet of cigarettes. 'We were meant to be just shuttling there and back but on Tuesday the plane developed some sort of engine trouble and we had to lay over for the night.'

'Oh?' Fatma sat down across the table from her son and watched him light up a cigarette. Just like his father. She didn't approve, but she accepted that smoking was something that most of her children did. 'In Amsterdam?'

'Yes.' There was another smell underneath the sugar and the butter that was really quite unpleasant. What it was, Bülent couldn't imagine, beyond knowing that it was organic in some way. Something of rot or mould . . .

'That you are having the opportunity to visit so many places is very nice for you,' Fatma said. 'But also you must be careful too, Bülent. In some of these places . . .'

He knew full well what this was about. 'Mum, in Amsterdam I did not, I promise you, use either drugs or women of easy virtue,' he said. To use even the word 'prostitute' would have outraged her. That said, he wasn't lying. He'd got very drunk in Amsterdam but he hadn't done anything else beyond look at what others got up to. 'I'm not stupid, you know. Not now.'

When he was a teenager, Bülent had had the odd brush with drugs, but nothing, Fatma knew, on the scale of Bekir's involvement. What had happened to her third son and what he had done as a result of it was unique within the İkmen family. Only the day before she had learned that there had been a period in Bekir's life when he had begged for money for drugs. Then, apparently, he had been literally on the street.

Cold in spite of the fierce summer heat, he had pulled at the clothes of rich European and American tourists to get their attention. Then he'd asked for money for some mythical child's life-saving operation, money he would later use to buy heroin.

'I think I'd feel better if at least some of my children paid attention to religion,' Fatma said. 'I know your father doesn't care for Islam but you know, Bülent, at times, for me, my religion has been the only thing that has sustained me. I—'

'Oh, Mum, not religion.' The voice was tired, smoke-scarred and lazy. Bülent looked up into the tanned and rather amused face of his errant brother.

Fatma, instantly on her feet and alive with what could have been anxiety, said, 'Bekir, my son, do you want a glass of tea? I'm cooking baklava for you, and—'

'Mum, calm down!' Bekir said as he watched Bülent light up another cigarette. 'Can I have one of those, brother?'

With a shrug Bülent tossed a Marlboro across the table. Fatma almost ran towards the samovar.

'Mum, it's OK,' Bekir said. 'There's no hurry. You don't need to fuss.'

But she did and Bülent at least knew why. His mother was afraid that if she didn't do exactly what Bekir wanted, he'd leave again. The first time he left, apparently, it had been because he wasn't getting his own way all the time. But he'd been a teenager back then.

'So, Mum, are you ready for the dentist?' Bülent said once his mother had given his brother some tea.

'Dentist?'

Bülent rolled his eyes. 'Mum, that's why I'm here,' he said. 'You've an appointment at midday over in Beyoğlu, remember?'

Fatma put a hand up to her mouth and said, 'Oh, my . . .'

She had forgotten. 'You're always frightened and one or other of us always takes you,' Bülent said.

'Oh, Bülent, I . . .'

'Oh, well, no harm done,' he said. 'Get your coat and we'll go. There's time.'

At first she didn't answer. She was thinking about something that very soon, and to Bülent's intense irritation, became apparent.

'Bülent, I'm sorry,' she said, 'but I can't go to the dentist today.'

'Mum, you have toothache, or you had it last week,' Bülent replied. 'You've got to go.'

'Oh, but . . .'

'Mum, if you have toothache you must go to the dentist,' Bekir said.

She put a hand on his arm. 'Bekir, darling, I have so much washing to do. And then there's baklava baking . . .'

'Do the washing another time,' Bekir said. 'And if you tell me what time to take the baklava out of the oven, I can do that for you. I'm not going anywhere today.'

But Fatma was adamant. 'No, no,' she said. 'I can't have you doing that, Bekir.' She looked across at Bülent. 'I'll go and telephone the dentist. Cancel.'

Without another word, she left the room. This, Bülent knew, was not healthy. His mother wasn't leaving the apartment in case her prodigal son suddenly upped and disappeared again. Bekir knew it too, Bülent felt. In spite of his soothing words Bekir was sitting across the table from him looking very smug. Bülent knew he'd have to speak to his father about it soon, and also about that quite irritating musty smell that seemed to be all over the apartment these days.

Chapter 5

About an hour's drive to the east of Gaziantep (or forty minutes with Inspector Taner behind the wheel) is the town of Birecik. Sitting astride the Euphrates river, Birecik is famous for two things: the dam of the same name that lies to the north of the town and the fact that the shores of the Euphrates at this point are home to a particularly ugly, if rare, bird called the bald ibis. So unusual is this creature that every year people come from all over the world to see it. Not so the dam, the building of which necessitated the flooding of numerous local villages including the site where the fabulous mosaics of Zeugma, now in the Gaziantep museum, had been discovered. As they drove at lightning speed towards the town, Süleyman thought gloomily that he'd never managed to get to the museum on Zelfa's behalf. Even though he knew that his wife had only mentioned Zeugma as a distraction from the fear she felt at his going away, he was sorry he hadn't been able to see the mosaics. Now he didn't know whether it was ever going to be possible. He and Taner had brought all their luggage with them on this trip. Chances were they were either going to stay in Birecik or move on eastwards.

It was midday by the time they reached what was a rather scruffy town, albeit one with a fabulous Roman fortress that Taner told him had been captured by Christian crusaders in the tenth century. Not that such a span of time was considered to be that vast in the east. As the Mardin policewoman was very quick to point out, her father had older things in his yard back home.

The Euphrates river is to the west of the town and is spanned by a bridge that was constructed back in the 1950s. It was in a teahouse on a cliff overlooking the bridge and the river below that Taner and Süleyman met the captain of the local Jandarma. Clad in the familiar green uniform of the paramilitary force that polices many rural areas in Turkey, Captain Hilmi Erdur, whom Taner had contacted by telephone earlier, was young and very tired-looking.

'Sir, madam,' he said, bowing to both Süleyman and Taner as they approached him, 'I do apologise for my appearance. I'm afraid we had an incident last night and as a consequence I have not slept for almost two days. Please . . .'

He pulled out chairs for them and then called for tea and a clean ashtray.

As usual, Inspector Taner got straight to the point. 'Captain, we're looking for a woman called Bulbul. She comes originally from my city of Mardin and she is the aunt of the escaped convict Yusuf Kaya. I don't know her exact age but I made a call back to the station in Mardin just before we left Gaziantep and a colleague there reckons she must be somewhere in her sixties. He, my colleague, thinks that Bulbul is probably the sister of Yusuf Kaya's father. Apparently, or so it is said, she met a Birecik man in the bazaar in Mardin back in the late fifties and love blossomed. She left with him, and there was quite a scandal at the time. I don't know the man's name; apparently it is not spoken of in Mardin. All that is known is that he is a farmer and he is a lot older than his wife.'

Captain Erdur looked grave. 'Like everyone else, I have

heard of Yusuf Kaya, and I know that his family are powerful and dangerous. I didn't know that his aunt lived in Birecik.'

'You know a lady fitting this description?'

'A Mrs Bulbul Kaplan lives with her elderly husband Gazi on his farm just to the east of here,' the captain said. 'The Kaplans are involved in olive-growing. They have money and a lot of power round here. I am surprised to learn that Bulbul was once a Kaya – if indeed that is the case.'

'Are the Kaplans known to be violent?' Taner asked.

The captain shrugged. 'What can I say? I don't know of any actual criminal connection. But they have money and their men have been known to defend the family honour against outsiders. The Kaplans always have the best of any clan-based fight here in Birecik.'

A young boy brought three glasses of tea and an ashtray, set them all down in front of the officers and left.

'At the time, back in the fifties, apparently people wondered why the Kayas didn't go after Bulbul when she left Mardin with her lover,' Taner said. 'But if her lover was a member of a very powerful clan maybe it was deemed unwise to challenge them. After all, Bulbul was only a girl, wasn't she? Hardly worth spilling male blood for, was she?'

The overt bitterness in her voice made both of the men, for a moment, look away. Süleyman at least wondered just how hard life for a woman on the force in Mardin could be. He suspected it wasn't at all easy.

'But anyway,' Taner said, recovering her composure, 'we think that Yusuf Kaya may have been or indeed may be even now staying with his aunt here in Birecik.'

The captain frowned. 'You think Kaya would stay with someone who had dishonoured his family? Who told you such a thing?'

'We learned that Kaya might be staying with his aunt from a woman who has been involved with him for many years,' Süleyman said. 'And, Captain, as for Kaya's having any qualms about staying with someone like this aunt, he is a person entirely free of such concerns. He's a psychopath, and as such he will use anyone or anything to achieve his objectives or preserve his own life.'

'You arrested him in İstanbul?'

'I did.'

The young jandarme rubbed the sides of his face with his hands and then stared out into the distance, across the Euphrates, apparently deep in thought. Taner and Süleyman let him do so for a while, but when the silence went on the Mardin officer said, 'Captain, what are you—'

'Oh, no, not again,' he murmured in reply. 'Not again!'

'Not again? Captain . . .'

He rose quickly to his feet and pointed to the river in front of them. 'There,' he said, 'there in the Euphrates, another present from bloody Iraq! Another creature forsaken by Allah!'

Süleyman looked in the direction in which the jandarme was pointing, but all he could see was a small patch of what looked like sand in the middle of the Euphrates river.

'So Yusuf Kaya was in here when he first became unwell,' İkmen said.

'Yes.' The governor of Kartal Prison looked across the small room at the policeman and blinked owlishly through his thick, round spectacles. In spite of the day's being warm it was cold in that dark little cell and the governor shuddered. 'Kaya fought with another prisoner earlier in the day. He went berserk. He was put into solitary both to protect the other inmates and as a punishment. I'm sure you know how it is, Inspector.'

Çetin İkmen did. Unlike, or so he had heard, most western European prisoners, Turkish inmates loathed being in solitary for even the shortest period of time. Most of them, also unlike their western counterparts, hated two- and three-man cells as well, favouring the large dormitory style of incarceration that was now being phased out across the whole of Turkey.

'Do you know what the fight was about?' İkmen asked.

'No.' The governor was quite blunt and also seemingly unconcerned. But then that was no surprise. Prison was a harsh place; sorting out differences between individuals was not something the authorities did a lot of. As if to underline his position the governor said, 'We keep order, Inspector İkmen, as you know. Keeping order when those in your care are murderers, rapists, terrorists and drug dealers takes up all of your time.'

'I understand that, sir,' İkmen said. 'But I will need to speak to the prisoner with whom Kaya fought.'

The governor looked at him steadily through his spectacles and said, 'Do you think that Kaya might have had help to escape from within this institution?'

İkmen took a deep breath of the fetid, damp air around him. 'I don't know, sir, but—'

'Because, Inspector,' the governor added quickly, 'if you think that any of my officers were involved you are very much mistaken. Apart from anything else, officer Bayar died during the course of the escape, while officer Eren is still fighting for his life. Other prisoners are one thing, but my officers . . .'

'Sir, you said yourself that no other officers apart from Eren and Bayar were involved with Kaya that night,' İkmen said. 'We can't speak to Eren yet, but we have spoken to the other significant person, your doctor, who gave it as his opinion that Kaya was only experiencing a panic attack that night.'

'Yes, I know that. I—'

'You, sir, as far as I can tell, on the advice of Officer Bayar made the decision to send Kaya to the Cerrahpaşa because you and or Bayar were afraid that he might be having a cardiac arrest.'

The governor sighed. 'Our doctor, between you and me, Inspector, is sometimes . . .' He frowned. 'Well . . .'

'Sir, we know that the doctor drinks,' İkmen said. 'I can understand why you sent Kaya to the hospital, believe me I can. But what interests me is how he got there.'

'How?'

İkmen looked down at the small hard bed built into the cold cell wall and decided that he didn't need to sit down *that* much, however hard his back was aching.

'Sir, it occurs to me that if Kaya had not been in solitary that night the chances of your detecting his supposed cardiac problems would have been slim. On the dormitory his cries for help may well have been drowned out by the moans and cries of other men, as well you know,' İkmen said. 'As you also know, when Kaya escaped from the Cerrahpaşa he ran out of there like a teenager, and so I think that we can safely say that he was faking his cardiac arrest. The doctor's assessment was therefore accurate – any prisoner just about to put an escape plan into action would be panicking and his blood pressure be raised. So now I need to speak to the prisoner he had been fighting with earlier in the day. Because it is that prisoner who put Kaya into solitary. That prisoner, sir, whether by accident or design, allowed Yusuf Kaya to escape from this prison.'

Three of Captain Erdur's men were on the shoreline when Erdur, Süleyman and Taner arrived. Two of them made sure that people stayed as far back as possible while the third waded out into the river to retrieve the dead body.

'This is what had me up all night last night,' the captain said wearily to the two visiting officers.

'Another body in the Euphrates?' Süleyman asked, genuinely surprised.

'When I said they came up from Iraq, I wasn't lying,' Captain Erdur said.

'You mean from the conflict with the Americans?'

'Oh, yes,' Erdur said. 'Insurgents, terrorists – whatever they're called – maybe. Often I think just poor ordinary people caught up in that nightmare over there. We're rarely able to identify them. The one we found last night was a woman, a young one.' He looked down for a moment and then muttered, 'It's tragic.'

Inspector Taner, whose stiletto heels were sinking a bit in the thick river mud, said, 'What do you do with them? Do you repatriate, or—'

'Captain Erdur!' The man in the middle of the river with the apparently yellow-clad body was waving.

'Yes?' Erdur said. 'What is it?'

'This is an American soldier,' the young jandarme said.

'*What!*' Without another word Captain Erdur plunged into the waters of the Euphrates and waded towards his man and the waterlogged body.

Süleyman, alone now with a decidedly unsteady Inspector Taner, said, 'Can it really be an American soldier, do you think?'

'I've heard stories about Iraqi bodies being found in the Euphrates,' she said. 'It's been happening for a while. But I've never heard anything about any Americans. Maybe it isn't. Let's see.'

She stumbled a little as the mud sank beneath her, but Süleyman resisted the temptation to assist her. She would not, he felt certain, appreciate it. As a woman in what was very much a man's world, Taner felt she had a lot to prove. Female officers were somewhat like this in İstanbul, although there the distinctions between men and women were much less marked than he imagined they would be in Mardin. His thoughts were interrupted by the sound of retching coming from the middle of the Euphrates. The young jandarme who had originally gone to retrieve the body was being sick.

'Yüksel! Güzer!' Captain Erdur yelled over at his remaining men on the banks of the river. 'Come and help!'

The two young men left the few curious locals they had been talking to and ran into the water. As they went in so the other officer came out, looking decidedly white around the face. Süleyman went up to him and said, 'Are you all right?'

The young man shuddered and then said, 'Not really, sir.'

'Had you never seen a body before?'

'Oh, I've seen bodies before, sir. Several, actually, but never like that. Not ever like that!'

His eyes had a glint of horror in them. It was something, this shocked and appalled look, that Süleyman had seen many, many times before amongst victims of crime.

'Was it an American soldier?' Taner asked.

'Oh, yes,' the young man said. 'I recognised the uniform. But . . . but – madam, sir – the body, it . . . it had, it has, no face! Someone has . . .' He leaned forward, retching again. When he stopped he said, 'Someone, some . . . some *animal* has scraped it all away!' He vomited, missing Süleyman's shoes by at most a centimetre.

Süleyman looked up at Taner and then at the figure of Captain Erdur emerging slowly from the river. His face, though not white and shocked, was grey with both strain and fatigue. When he got close to the little group he said, 'Nightmare! An American soldier without dog-tags. Where do I even start?'

'You'll have to pass it up to your commander,' Süleyman said. 'The American military will have to be informed.' It was self-evident, but he said it anyway. 'Captain, the face of the body . . .'

'Gone,' he said, confirming what his still heaving officer had just told them. 'Looks like it's been hacked off with a knife. Anything goes over in that poor wretched country these days! People are turning into beasts.' He looked down for a moment and then scanned the cliff behind them, where a few local people had gathered. Then he frowned. Touching Süleyman on the arm, he said, 'Inspector, turn round and look behind you.'

'What?' But he did as the captain had asked and turned round to look up at the cliff, the track that led up to the top and the tea garden they had just left.

'Up there, on top of the cliff,' the captain said. 'The lady with the green headscarf, that is Bulbul Kaplan.'

Süleyman squinted up into the sunlight and saw a short, dumpy woman whose head was indeed covered with shiny green silk. Unlike the rest of the onlookers, she was, he felt, looking not so much at what was happening in the river as directly at him.

İkmen didn't as a rule have a lot of time for prison guards. In his experience they were often people who were really frustrated police officers. Having failed to make the grade for the police, many prison guards slotted resentfully into the incarceration service and spent much of their time taking out their ire on the prisoners. But they had their uses and at this moment

İkmen was very glad that he had a couple of big brutish examples with him. The governor had agreed that, provided he didn't take Ayşe Farsakoğlu with him, he could interview the inmate who had fought with Yusuf Kaya on the day of his escape. Apparently the man in question, Ara Berköz, was a violent rapist on whom just the sight of an attractive woman acted as a provocation. İkmen entered the room the governor had set aside for the interview and found himself looking at a huge, black-bearded man with small but intensely bright blue eyes. On his shoulders were the firmly planted hands of the two guards always allocated to Ara Berköz every time he had a visitor. The rapist, the governor had told him, had a tendency to bite when agitated and so letting him sit without restraint of some sort was not really an option. İkmen told the huge man who he was and why he was asking for help.

'You fought with Yusuf Kaya, just before he escaped, out in the yard, didn't you, Ara,' he said.

Ara Berköz didn't speak for a very long time. Irritating though this was, it did give İkmen a chance to take the man in. On first glance one saw only the bulk and those extraordinary eyes, but now that İkmen really looked he could see the scarring too. Not just on his barely clad torso but on what could be seen of his face also, tens if not hundreds of sealed-up cuts. İkmen wondered where he'd got them, who had inflicted them. Less mysterious was the way in which Ara Berköz's black, tangled hair moved in rhythm to a plague of hungry headlice.

'Anyone,' the deep, low voice said menacingly, 'who criticises Yıldız the Body is going to have it coming.'

İkmen blinked. Yıldız the Body was a young supermodel. Born in the very run-down and troubled district of Edirnekapı, Yıldız Efe had been dubbed 'the Body' by the modelling agency that had hired her, aged sixteen, in 2003. Three years later she was a multimillion-lire industry and owned one house in İstanbul and another one somewhere on the south coast. Girls all over Turkey idolised the Body mainly because she was so very, very thin.

Just to clarify, İkmen asked, 'You fought with Yusuf Kaya because he was critical of the supermodel Yıldız?'

Ara Berköz's face distorted briefly into something that might have been pain. 'He said nasty things,' he said. He moved, seemingly to put one of his hands into his trouser pocket. The guards took his arms and held them hard. Ara's eyes filled with tears. 'I just want to get my picture!' he said. 'Let me get my picture!'

Beyond knowing that the psychiatrist who had assessed Ara Berköz after his arrest had given him a mental age of twelve, İkmen knew little about the man before him. He looked up and said to the guards, 'Let him have his picture.'

The guards looked at each other and then the one on the left said, 'Ara, you can have your picture if you let me get it for you.'

Ara Berköz made a thin whining noise in his throat. Both guards pushed his arms up and then the one on the left put a hand at the top of his hip.

'Ara,' he said, 'do you have a blade in with your picture? If I hurt myself getting the photo out there will be repercussions.'

The rapist, his arms raised up in the air, hands hanging into his filthy, tangled hair, looked like a trapped animal. The guard on the right leaned towards İkmen and told him what the policeman felt he knew already. 'Ara here hurts himself when he gets upset,' he said. 'He likes to cut. Got a body like a war zone.'

'I haven't got a blade,' Ara Berköz said. 'I wouldn't put a blade in with any of my pictures, especially not my special pictures.'

Carefully, the guard on the left put his hand into Ara Berköz's trouser pocket and pulled out a piece of paper. He threw it gingerly on to the table in front of the prisoner, whose eyes lit up when he saw it. Once his hands were free again, Ara Berköz very gently opened out the folded sheet and with a contented sigh smoothed it out and stared at it. It was a topless shot of Yıldız the Body lying flat out on a beach somewhere. Although thin to the point of danger, her breasts were enormous, artificially enhanced and to İkmen really quite painful-looking. Once the rapist had settled himself and seemed content, İkmen spoke to him again. 'Ara,' he said, 'when you fought with Yusuf Kaya about Yıldız, who started the fight?'

'Don't know.' Fixated on the picture, he wasn't really listening. Or didn't want to listen.

'Did Yusuf insult Yıldız first or was there a conversation before you started to fight?' İkmen asked.

'Don't know.' This time his voice was, if anything, even softer and more somnolent than before. Maybe letting Ara have his picture hadn't been such a good idea. Far from helping him to relax and open up, the photograph appeared to be mesmerising him. İkmen looked up at the guards holding Ara Berköz and, seeing no interest in either of their faces, came to a unilateral decision to help things along in his own way. After all, the guards were meant to be there to protect him.

He leaned forward and snatched the photograph out of Ara Berköz's fingers. A howl of agony from the prisoner was followed by a terrifying break for freedom which had İkmen, until the guards managed to get their charge fully under control, cowering against the wall.

'What in the name of . . . Why did you do that?' the guard on the left said as he wrestled a spitting Ara Berköz back into his seat.

'You're lucky he didn't bite you!' the other guard observed. 'Allah!'

'Ara,' İkmen said breathlessly, completely ignoring the prison officers, 'Ara, did Yusuf Kaya or anyone around him want you to fight him the day he escaped? Did he—'

'Give me back Yıldız! Give her back to me!' He gnashed his teeth and cried at the same time. 'Give her to me!'

'We'll have to take him back to his cell!' the guard on the left said. 'Can't have him like this!'

'No!' İkmen said. 'No, don't do that!' Then, looking straight into Ara Berköz's tiny furious eyes again, he addressed him directly. 'Ara, if you tell me exactly what happened before you fought with Yusuf Kaya you can have Yıldız back. I swear it!'

'Give her back! Give her back! Give her back!'

'Tell me the truth and you can—'

'We're out of here,' the guard on the right said as he and his colleague pulled Ara Berköz out of his chair.

'No!' İkmen wailed.

Allah, but what was this? He was supposed to be interviewing this man! But it had all gone wrong and now it looked as if his chances of getting at something, anything, were slipping away.

'Ara,' İkmen said as he walked towards the prisoner, 'tell me what happened and you can have your picture – now!'

He held the rumpled photograph out towards the wild and furious man, who stopped and looked at it. It was just out of reach. Then Ara raised his head and said, 'Yusuf said he'd give me that lovely photograph if I had a row with him. I could even beat him, too.'

'Is that the truth, Ara?' İkmen said. 'Are you sure?'

'Yes.'

The guards were pulling him out of the room now. 'That's enough, inspector,' one of them said. 'You're tiring the poor brute.'

İkmen, following nervously, handed the photograph back to the prisoner and said, 'Thank you, Ara. Now look, did anyone else know . . .'

The guard on the left pulled Ara Berköz out of the room just as he was saying something İkmen could neither hear nor understand. The guard on the right stayed behind and said to İkmen, 'He's far too agitated now. He needs to cool right down.'

There was a look that could have been alarm on the man's face. Had it been the suggestion of some other person's being involved in Yusuf Kaya's escape that had got this man and the other guard so very agitated? That Kaya's escape had been facilitated by both inmates and guards at the Kartal Prison was not a new or revolutionary notion. Now Ara Berköz had admitted that the contention was, at least in part, true. He had, in exchange for a photograph of Yıldız the Body, argued and then fought with Yusuf Kaya on the day of the latter's escape. The fight had ensured that Kaya was put into solitary confinement, after which he had gone into his cardiac arrest routine. But if Berköz had helped him then maybe others had too. Maybe others amongst his jailers . . .

'I'll be back to see Mr Berköz again soon,' İkmen said as he stared very steadily at the guard in front of him. 'Make sure that he stays well, won't you?'

In spite of Bulbul Kaplan's far from fashionable appearance, she and her husband were obviously wealthy. Their house, a new villa-style building with multiple balconies – just like those holiday homes of the rich down on the south coast – was full of things like plasma screen televisions, American fridges and tiny, intricate CD players. Outside, surprisingly, there was no car, but the reason for that soon became apparent.

'My husband, Gazi, is resting,' Bulbul Kaplan said as she ushered Süleyman and Taner into her considerable living room. 'He's elderly.' She looked down briefly, and then added, 'And blind.'

Hence the lack of car, Süleyman thought. Bulbul Kaplan, once she had, like her neighbours, tutted and shaken her head at the appearance of the dead American soldier in the Euphrates for a little while, had agreed to talk to Süleyman and Taner very readily. She didn't know what it was about, of course, but she did know that it had to concern her old home town in some way. She had indeed had the surname of Kaya before her marriage. On the way over in Inspector Taner's car she had commented upon the policewoman's own surname.

'I knew a Taner back in Mardin,' she had said. 'Şeymus Taner was a coppersmith in the bazaar.'

'My grandfather,' Taner had responded immediately.

'Your grandfather!' Bulbul Kaplan had opened her big blue eyes very wide. 'Allah! But he was a Master of Sharmeran too, was he not?'

'He was,' Taner said. 'Now my father Seçkin has that honour.'

'Seçkin? You are Seçkin's daughter? Allah! But now I can see it in you! Yes, the good bones . . .'

She had wittered on about how attractive, kind and intelligent Taner's father was, although quite what the designation Master of Sharmeran might mean Süleyman didn't know. As far as he was aware the Sharmeran was a mythical eastern

Turkish snake goddess. An ugly thing, he had always felt, the Sharmeran had the head and torso of a woman and the tail and belly of a snake. To be candid, this image, which one saw occasionally on pictures and plates in antique shops in İstanbul but apparently just about everywhere east of Kayseri, gave him the creeps. What on earth did a Master of Sharmeran do, and did the fact that such a bizarre title even existed mean that the people of Mardin and places like it actually believed in the existence of that deity? Surely someone like Edibe Taner was far too pragmatic and modern to take any notice of such nonsense?

But the Sharmeran wasn't spoken of for long and later, at the farmhouse, talk turned to other things. While Bulbul Kaplan prepared tea, she and Taner spoke of other Mardin characters, the bazaar, the new and apparently very smart hotels, and the Ocean, the great luminous Mesopotamian plain below the city. Maybe, Süleyman thought, if they did have to go to Mardin he could stay in a hotel after all. They sounded, from the way Taner described them, really quite good. That said, the monastery Dr Sarkissian had recommended just outside Mardin, St Sobo's, would certainly be more peaceful, and the doctor's old friend, the Syrian monk Seraphim Yunun, had sounded charming. The doctor had called to let him have Seraphim's details just that morning. Apparently the Syrian, like Süleyman himself, was very appreciative of old buildings.

'Mrs Kaplan,' Taner said as she took a glass of tea out of the older woman's hands and sat down, 'we have to talk to you about your nephew, Yusuf Kaya.'

Bulbul Kaplan looked upwards, presumably to where her husband was sleeping, and then sat down beside Taner. She looked, Süleyman felt, strained now. Up on the cliff with a dead body below her she had been fine, but . . .

'I . . . I don't see my family, Inspector Taner,' Bulbul said slowly. 'There was a . . . a falling-out, as I am sure someone back home would have told you.'

'I know that you left Mardin in order to marry your husband, yes,' Taner said. 'But, Mrs Kaplan, any enmity that might have resulted from that did not I think impact directly upon your nephew Yusuf.'

Bulbul Kaplan looked at Taner, genuinely struck. 'Not impact? Inspector, I left my clan! You are from Mardin – you know! I married a man they did not want me to marry! How could that not impact upon the son of my brother? I know that Yusuf is a criminal but he is still a Kaya; he still protects the family honour!'

'And yet, Mrs Kaplan, we have reason to believe that you have seen Yusuf in recent times.'

'Who?' Bulbul Kaplan was indignant. Again she looked upwards. She lowered her voice before she spoke, but she was obviously upset. 'Who says that I see Yusuf? Yusuf is in prison in İstanbul!'

'Mrs Kaplan, it doesn't matter who says what,' Taner said. 'Have you seen your nephew Yusuf in the last few days?'

'Last few days? He's in prison! Yusuf Kaya is—'

'He escaped, Mrs Kaplan,' Taner said. Both she and Süleyman looked at the two working, if silent, plasma television screens in the room. Bulbul Kaplan, unlike her husband, could see, and if she could see she, like the rest of the country, had to know that Yusuf Kaya had escaped from Kartal Prison the previous weekend. She was lying and Inspector Taner as well as Süleyman and Bulbul Kaplan herself knew it. Not that Taner even began to allude to such a notion.

'Have you seen or spoken to Yusuf Kaya in the last few days, Mrs Kaplan?' Taner asked.

'No!' She was trying to keep her voice down but her tone was still hurt, though quite forceful too.

'So did you see him before he went to prison?' Taner asked.

'No!' Bulbul Kaplan leaned towards the other woman and said, 'I don't have anything to do with my family. That all finished when I married Gazi. They don't see me, I don't see them.'

'And yet how did our informant know about even your existence if you have no contact?' Taner asked. She would not reveal Anastasia's name or where she lived, but she was going to use what she had said to get the truth from Bulbul Kaplan. 'The information we received is not from a person you could possibly know. Yusuf does know this person and through him, so this person says, he or she is aware of you and of your relationship with Yusuf Kaya. Mrs Kaplan, if Yusuf Kaya came here—'

'All right!' She flung her arms up into the air and then let them rest in her lap. 'All right, Yusuf came here.' It was not much more than a whisper now.

'When?'

'Last year.'

'When last year?'

'I don't know! Last year!'

'Why? Why did he come here, Mrs Kaplan?'

The older woman sighed. 'Yusuf was just a baby when I left Mardin,' she said. 'Last year he came and found me.'

Taner frowned. 'What for? Weren't you worried about that?'

'In case he took revenge on behalf of our clan? No,' Bulbul Kaplan said. 'He came offering the hand of friendship and I saw no reason not to take it from him. To me he was kind and polite.'

'And your husband?' Süleyman asked. 'What did your husband make of that?'

Clan rivalries, especially in the east, were notoriously intractable. He could no more imagine Yusuf Kaya and Bulbul Kaplan cosying up after such an incident than he could see the convict figuratively in bed with her husband.

Bulbul Kaplan looked down at the floor. 'Gazi was in hospital at the time. His eyes . . . He has operations from time to time . . .'

'So Yusuf Kaya came to visit you when your husband was in hospital,' Taner said. 'Did it not occur to you, Mrs Kaplan, that perhaps that was planned? For Yusuf to see you alone? To accept your hospitality . . .'

'Yusuf appeared and I have no doubt that it was planned, but . . .' She smiled a little. Her face was round and pleasant, only her amazing blue eyes giving a clue as to the beautiful girl she must once have been. 'My husband's family have been good to me, but they are not my blood. Yusuf,' she looked up and said simply, 'is. He's a nice man, at least he was to me. What he has done—'

'Yusuf has killed people,' Süleyman said. 'Until we arrested him he was one of the most powerful drug dealers in İstanbul.'

Bulbul Kaplan shrugged. 'He is my nephew. When I spoke to Yusuf it was like talking to my father once again.'

'Did he ask you for money?'

'I gave him food and drink, he stayed one night,' she said. 'He came because he was curious to meet me, that was all.' She sat up straight and added, 'I appreciated it too. But I haven't seen him since. I couldn't allow it anyway, not with Gazi . . .'

'No.'

She seemed to be genuinely sad about not being able to

see her nephew again. They must have got on well but, as Süleyman at least knew only too well, whatever their relationship might be it was purely on Yusuf Kaya's terms. Bulbul Kaplan might think that Yusuf Kaya loved her, but that was unlikely. Yusuf Kaya loved only himself. He'd come to her in all probability because he needed somewhere in the Gaziantep area, apart from Anastasia's brothel, to hide out at the time.

After they left, Inspector Taner confirmed his suspicion. 'Kaya was seen back in Mardin in March of last year,' she said. 'We received a report that he and his brother Metin, another delightful character I do not think, were doing drug deals with some of the gypsies out on the Ocean. But when we arrived the two men had gone and we were left with one young boy with powder round his nose and a woman out of her mind on ketamine. I assume Yusuf headed up here after that.'

'He wasn't seen again in Mardin?' Süleyman asked.

'No, but Metin was,' she said. 'I found him myself with his head down the toilet of a local restaurant. Dead.'

'Dead?'

'Coke overdose. That or his brother made him snort enough to kill him. That would not be outside Yusuf's range of behaviours, as you know. Not of course that his family would ever believe that.'

Süleyman looked up above the olive trees outside the Kaplan house towards the now darkening sky. It had been a long and ultimately frustrating day. 'What now?' he said to Taner as she fired up the engine of her gutsy Volkswagen Golf.

Taner lit a cigarette and said, 'If Kaya isn't in Gaziantep any more and he isn't here . . .'

'You don't think he's here in Birecik?'

She shrugged. 'Bulbul Kaplan could be lying. She did lie, as we know, when we first spoke about Yusuf. Her relationship with him, if it indeed exists, is odd for those involved in clan business. I will ask Captain Erdur to keep watch on Bulbul Kaplan and her farm.'

'And so . . .'

'And so on to Mardin,' Taner said with a smile. 'As far as we know Kaya has not left the country and if he hasn't done that then he'll be with the people who love him most. His family.'

Chapter 6

There was no way anyone could have got any sort of idea what the Mesopotamian plain looked like under cover of darkness. All Süleyman knew as he sat beside Taner as she wrestled her car over uncomfortably rutted road surfaces was that he was exhausted. After a night of very little sleep, he'd been up since the crack of dawn and now here he was powering on into the back of beyond where the only lights that could be seen came from tanks on their way out east to fight the Kurdish separatists, the PKK. Someone – an informer, the local Jandarma had reckoned, Taner told him – had been beheaded by one or other group of terrorists in a village near to Mardin. It was not, after all, just the PKK who operated in this area. There was also Hezbollah and possibly al-Qaeda too, Taner expounded breezily, as well as some other little splinter groups – Marxists, religious fundamentalists, ultranationalists. That she seemed to be happy going back to what to Süleyman appeared to be a hotbed of violence was odd. But then Edibe Taner was not your run of the mill policewoman.

Through half-closed, bloodshot eyes he looked at her. She was a very attractive woman and yet, strangely for him, he felt nothing for her. Mehmet Süleyman was and always had been in love with his wife. But that he had a weakness for other women he was the first to admit. It was partly because he himself was attractive and women came on to him. But he could also make the running himself, as he knew only too well. Inspector Taner had the look of a woman who would make any feelings she might have for a person well and truly apparent. But maybe that was just an illusion. Maybe the fact was that, however professional and liberated she appeared, she was still an eastern woman with all the modesty and restraint that went with such a background. But then again, perhaps in view of the fact that she had shown absolutely no romantic interest in him he was just choosing to think that that was so. It was possible she was indeed a very liberated woman who simply did not fancy him.

'You'd still like to stay at St Sobo's?' she said suddenly, in that harsh staccato way of hers.

The monastery where Dr Sarkissian's friend lived was, so Taner had told him, about ten minutes by car from the centre of Mardin. In the scheme of the geography of the city it was no further away from police headquarters than the hotel Taner had had in mind for him. That Taner herself obviously wanted him to stay at one of the new hotels in town was evident – she was nothing if not a woman imbued with civic pride – but that was not really his problem. Brother Seraphim and a degree of peace and quiet had the feel of something far more attractive to Süleyman.

'Yes, I would,' he replied into the darkness of the road ahead.

'I don't blame you,' Taner said with a sigh. 'The monks are interesting and, like you, educated. In the hotel you'd be bombarded with Syrians who've come over the border for the Easter services at our churches and monasteries.'

He turned to look at her. 'Easter? Is it Easter?'

'Next weekend, yes,' she said. And then she yawned. 'We'll all be on duty then – cops, Jandarma, military.'

'In the churches.'

'Protecting the Christians, yes,' she said. 'We wish them happy Easter as they go in to worship while we wait outside with tanks and guns just in case any lunatic or band of lunatics might have ideas about killing them. But then I believe you protect the churches in İstanbul, don't you?'

There was a measure of security in all places of worship in the city, but rarely were tanks employed as part of the process.

'Yes . . .'

Far, far away in the distance, unless he was very much mistaken, a glimmer of light was just beginning to be discernible. He didn't have any idea about how long they had been on the road, whether he had in fact slept for a short time or not, but he felt that dawn had to be happening some time soon. That could be the beginning of it.

'We're about an hour away now,' Taner said as she lit yet another cigarette. She'd chain-smoked ever since they'd left Birecik. 'When we reach Mardin we'll get some breakfast first and then I'll take you out to the monastery. I expect you'll want to sleep for a while.'

He looked across at her. 'Won't you?'

She laughed. 'Maybe. Paperwork, you know?'

He did. From İstanbul to Mardin and beyond, they all had paperwork. Süleyman's head slumped forward and he went to sleep, to Taner's amusement, yet again. When he woke up he was looking down upon what appeared to be a vast, green sea.

İkmen had just finished e-mailing the main points about his visit to the Kartal Prison the previous day to Süleyman when

İzzet Melik entered his office. Such a marvellous thing, e-mail! And everyone had it! Even monasteries! Arto Sarkissian said it would be absolutely no problem for Süleyman to pick up his messages at St Sobo's.

Melik shut the door behind him and sat down.

'Yes,' İkmen said, still staring fixedly at the screen with an expression of wonder on his face.

'That nurse, at the Cerrahpaşa, sir,' İzzet Melik said, 'Murat Lole . . .'

'What about him?' İkmen said as he closed down his system with a contented sigh. It had only been in the last month that he'd been able to do this.

'He's gone back to work at the hospital, sir,' Melik said.

'No reason why he shouldn't,' İkmen said. 'We have no evidence that he was involved in Kaya's escape.'

'Sir, we're coming up negative with searching the hospital rubbish.'

'You've found nothing that could be a nurse's uniform? Stockings?'

'No.'

İkmen frowned. 'Glass?'

'Oh, there's a lot of that,' İzzet said wearily. 'Tonnes. But it's going to take forensic some time to first sift through it and second match any blood found on the glass to that of Kaya and his accomplices or victims. The glass has to be matched to the fragments Dr Sarkissian found inside the bodies.'

'No shards have been found that could conceivably have been used as weapons?'

'The killers either smashed them up or took them away,' İzzet replied. 'Wouldn't you?'

İkmen looked gloomily down at the top of his desk. 'No

news about the surviving prison guard, I suppose, İzzet?'

'No, sir. Still in a coma, I'm afraid.' He rose to his feet and made ready to go. 'I tell you who I do have news about however, sir, Hüseyin Altun.'

İkmen looked up sharply. 'The king of the Edirnekapı beggars?'

'The same.'

'What of him?'

'He's dead,' İzzet said with an unconcerned shrug. 'Been so for some time, apparently. Stabbed.'

İkmen was shocked. Not that he'd actually known Hüseyin Altun personally. For all his faults the talented beggar, who came from and lived in the run-down district of Edirnekapı, had never killed anyone. Even when his need for heroin had been at its most acute, Altun had always preferred street-based extortion – often via his ragged gang of street kids – to murder. Altun, İkmen knew, was known to have bought his drug of choice from dealers in or around his begging beat in Beyoğlu. Whether he had ever bought from Yusuf Kaya, İkmen didn't know. But Altun had been a junkie and so anything had to be possible. İkmen made a mental note to try to find out about the circumstances of Hüseyin Altun's death and what the dead beggar had actually been stabbed with.

'Do you know, İzzet, whether a post-mortem was performed on Altun's body?' he asked.

'Yes,' İzzet replied. 'Dr Sarkissian's assistant did it.'

'Thank you, Sergeant,' İkmen said as İzzet Melik left his office. A very brief visit from his friend's junior but one that had provided some illumination. As he watched İzzet figuratively dance round Ayşe Farsakoğlu in the corridor, İkmen pondered yet again on how well Yusuf Kaya's escape had been planned. So far there was no evidence at all, either material or human.

'Now you see why we call it the Ocean,' Edibe Taner said as she swept her arms outwards to encompass the vast plain below them. Although she had planned to take Süleyman actually into the city of Mardin for breakfast that morning, a telephone call to Brother Seraphim at the monastery of St Sobo had changed her mind. The Brothers would be delighted to offer Inspectors Süleyman and Taner breakfast in their refectory. Now, parked on an outcrop of rock just outside the ancient honey-coloured monastic building, Taner and Süleyman were standing beside her car looking down upon just a fraction of the Mesopotamian plain.

'Perhaps because this area, whether you are religious or an atheist, is acknowledged as the cradle of civilisation it has many names,' Taner continued. 'The plain in its entirety from Diyarbakir to Baghdad is called Al Jazeera. That is an Arabic term meaning "the island".'

'The island? I thought it was an ocean,' a horribly weary Süleyman replied. There was a slightly chill wind coming off the vast patchwork of bright green, pale green and yellow fields and settlements below. Contained only by the mountains and hills that seemed to provide almost a frame for the vast shimmering plain, the 'island' was an almost overwhelming onslaught of colour, shape and competing smells – flowers, animals, the earth itself. Süleyman felt dizzy.

'To the Arabs it was an island, but to the Suriani this area is called the Tur Abdin,' Taner continued. Remarkably she seemed to be not only awake but really quite fresh-looking too. 'Tur Abdin, which is Aramaic, means the "Slaves of God" which refers to the fact that this place was, and to some extent still is, a place of monasteries. It is a sacred place, special.' She looked at him pointedly. 'I believe this, even though I know that it is tainted.'

'Tainted?'

She breathed in the cool air deeply, all cigarettes well and truly out now. 'By gangsters like Yusuf Kaya,' she said. 'People like that make trouble for the ordinary people of Mardin. I don't like that. There are others too, but . . .' She stopped there, as if she'd said too much, and then she smiled. 'People here in Mardin do not always speak what you would recognise as Turkish,' she continued. 'We are close to Syria here and so many people speak Arabic. The Suriani speak Aramaic amongst themselves. Then there are the Kurds who have their own dialects. I speak both Arabic and Aramaic and so you don't have to worry about those. The Kurdish dialects . . .' She looked down at the ground briefly. 'We can manage.'

They, as in the Mardin police, would have to manage the Kurdish dialects somehow, Süleyman thought. Although relatively quiet in recent months, the whole area had been by turns closed to outsiders and under curfew for many years, in part, at least, because of the Kurdish separatists. Even through his half-sleeping state, Süleyman had noticed how much military traffic – tanks, armoured cars, troop carriers – there had been on the road east of Birecik. He looked around at the wonderful and yet frightening absence around him and, although not exactly cold, he shuddered.

'I have just the thing for cold bones,' a deep male voice cut in.

Süleyman turned round and saw a very upright man of about sixty standing behind him. Heavily bearded, he was dressed in a long black robe, while on his head he wore a dark cap embroidered with stars. Inspector Taner, on seeing him, first smiled and then stepped forward to take one of his hands, which she kissed.

'Brother Seraphim.'

'And this, I take it, Inspector Taner, is Inspector Süleyman from İstanbul.'

'Yes, Brother.'

He held his hand out to Süleyman which, for a moment, gave the İstanbul man pause. Was he supposed to shake the monk's hand or kiss it? Things were obviously done very differently out here, but then Brother Seraphim as a friend of Dr Sarkissian had to know that. Süleyman smiled and shook the monk firmly by the hand.

'Come inside,' the monk said as he led the two officers towards the huge stone monastery building. Its walls were studded with numerous arched and latticed windows and covered with intricate, if to Süleyman incomprehensible, carvings.

'I do hope that you will like the room we have prepared for you, Inspector,' Brother Seraphim said as he mounted the stairs towards the main door of the monastery. 'It is simple, I am afraid, but clean.' And then he turned round and looked upon both of them with troubled eyes. 'We live, sadly, in difficult times.'

He put the strange dream he was to have later down to the unaccustomed location, his utter exhaustion and that damn coffee too!

Once inside the monastery, Brother Seraphim had ushered him and Taner into a very light and clean dining room. There, seated at a plain wooden table, they had been plied with a variety of food and drink, including bread, cheese, preserves and meat, fruit juice and coffee. Literally sick with tiredness by that time, Süleyman had opted just for coffee. He had not paid attention, however, to the kind of coffee he was being given.

Mirra coffee is a traditional beverage in south-eastern Turkey. Bitter and thick in a way that ordinary Turkish coffee does not even approach, it is boiled and reboiled so many times over a twenty-four-hour period that, eventually, it achieves the consistency of dark syrup. Beloved by the people of the south-east, especially Mardin, it has a kick like a bull and can stain a china cup on contact. It is also deemed exceedingly rude to refuse one of the tiny cups of mirra one is routinely offered by almost everyone on the Ocean. Süleyman eventually drank three of these thimble-sized cups which led to the kind of head-spinning experience one would normally associate with alcohol poisoning. Luckily Brother Seraphim was well aware of the rapid change of state in his guest and, while Taner carried the İstanbul officer's luggage, the monk very gently raised Süleyman from his chair and took him to his room. As they all walked into what was a small but bright and clean-smelling chamber, the monk said, or rather Süleyman thought he heard the monk say, 'We've looked and looked and still we can't find him. I think he must have gone to *her* . . .'

Then he lost consciousness. He was adrift on a sea of green fields being tossed and turned by what looked like vast snakes or eels. Strangely these creatures did not provoke any sort of fear, rather a curiosity that extended to the fact that although he was under water he could, somehow, breathe.

'Inspector Süleyman. Inspector Süleyman.' It wasn't said along with physical movement, as in someone shaking him awake. It wasn't even said with much urgency. But he was nevertheless brought out of his serpent-filled world by a voice that was firm in its intention.

Süleyman blinked. 'Brother Seraphim?'

Whether the monk was smiling underneath that huge beard of his was impossible to tell. But his voice was soothing and apologetic. 'I am so sorry to wake you, but Inspector Taner has arrived and apparently you need to go somewhere with her,' he said. 'Were it up to me I would have let you sleep, but . . .'

Süleyman, with some difficulty, sat up. Still fully clothed, he must, he now saw, have just collapsed on to that small but comfortable bed and then not moved a muscle. He looked out of the narrow arched window at his side and saw a huge, green 'sea' sweeping down into a misty nothingness, just as in his dream. He shook his head and said, 'What time is it?'

'It is midday,' the monk replied. 'I have telephoned my friend Arto Sarkissian to tell him you have arrived. He sends his greetings and was relieved to know that you were safe.'

Safe? Süleyman rubbed his face with his hands and tried to make his brain think straight. Now that he was in the east, of course people would routinely enquire about his safety.

'I need to have a wash,' Süleyman said at length. 'Can you please tell Inspector Taner I'll be with her as soon as I can?'

'Of course.' The monk rose to his feet and began to walk back towards the door.

'Oh, Brother Seraphim?'

He turned. 'Yes?'

'Do you know if Inspector Taner has managed to get some sleep too?'

Brother Seraphim shook his head. 'Oh, no,' he said as if this were the most natural thing in the world. 'She doesn't need to.'

'Doesn't . . .'

'Her father, Seçkin Taner, is a Master of Sharmeran,' the monk said gravely. 'Those people are not like the rest of us, Inspector, as I am sure you will very soon learn.'

Chapter 7

It was difficult to see what the prison guard Ramazan Eren really looked like. Lost underneath a spider's web of tubes, canulas and tapes he could have been any age; almost, İkmen felt, any sex. Dr Eldem, Eren's physician, standing on the other side of the bed from İkmen and Ayşe Farsakoğlu, said, 'He sustained one stab wound to the chest which grazed his heart. We've stopped the bleeding, but as to the damage caused . . .' He shrugged. 'To be honest with you, Inspector, this man is lucky to be alive on any sort of level.'

'I know it is impossible to say when he may regain consciousness,' İkmen began. 'However—'

'However nothing,' the doctor responded shortly. 'It is not *when* he regains consciousness, it is *if*.'

'His brain is exhibiting electrical activity,' Ayşe Farsakoğlu said as she looked up at the monitor above Eren's head.

The doctor, offended as some physicians can become when confronted with a non-medic with some knowledge, blustered, 'Just because his brain is showing activity doesn't mean that he will ever recover. If he wakes he may be perfectly normal in every way but then again he may emerge a blithering idiot. One must be patient, madam. He who owns patience, owns Egypt, as is said!'

It was not a saying with which either İkmen or Ayşe was familiar, but they got the gist of it anyway. İkmen, who thought the whole conversation had become far more hysterical than it needed to be, said, 'I'm going to continue to post a guard at the door of the ward just in case one of Kaya's people should try to come back and finish Mr Eren off.'

'You do as you wish,' the doctor said as he made his way over to the door leading out of the room. 'Whether this man recovers or not is in the hands of Allah!' And then he left.

Ayşe Farsakoğlu breathed a sigh of relief. 'Not very helpful,' she said, watching Ramazan Eren breathe with the aid of a respirator.

'What else can he say?' İkmen shrugged. 'None of us can know when or if this man will wake. Until he does, of course, we can't know exactly what happened when Yusuf Kaya was rescued. All we do know is that Eren was supposed to die and so we have to guard him for the foreseeable future. By the way, Ayşe, did Sergeant Melik tell you about Hüseyin Altun?' He knew that she'd arrested the beggar a few times in the past when she was still a constable working the beat.

'Yes,' she said without emotion. 'No loss.'

'Stabbed, wasn't he?'

'Apparently,' she said, still without any great interest.

İkmen took his eyes off the waxen figure beneath the pipes and the tubes and looked into Ayşe's face. 'I spoke to Dr Sarkissian's assistant. It was she who performed the autopsy on Altun earlier this morning,' he said. 'Apparently he was stabbed with a serrated metal blade of some sort. Not glass.'

Ayşe frowned. 'Glass? You think that Altun may have been killed by the same people who killed the police officers and the prison guard?'

İkmen shrugged. 'Altun died just after Kaya escaped. He hung out around Beyoğlu, he was a junkie, the chances are he knew Yusuf Kaya. It's . . . well, it's . . . Kaya has seemingly

102

cleaned up so much in the wake of his escape, I find myself wondering whether Altun could have been a part of it.'

Still frowning, Ayşe said, 'You have one of your . . . intuitions, sir?'

'Maybe, maybe not, Ayşe,' İkmen said. The further away in time he got from his late mother, the witch of Üsküdar, the more unlikely her powers and his own seemed to be. Or at least that was how he had come to feel about it recently. This was after all the twenty-first century, and no one sane believed in such things, did they?

Yet although Hüseyin Altun did not have any observed connection to Yusuf Kaya, his feeling that one did indeed exist was strong.

'Ayşe,' he said as they prepared to leave the hospital room, 'you arrested Hüseyin Altun several times. Did you ever get involved with the kids in his street gang?'

'When I or some other officer could catch them, yes,' she said. As they left the room she added, 'There were several boys I think I might know by sight. A girl too. Blond hair and I think she might have been foreign, Bulgarian maybe. This was years ago; they must all be grown up now. Oh, and there was a boy called Aslan too. I think that was his name, Aslan . . .'

Just before she closed the door behind her, Ayşe heard a very faint groan from the man on the bed. She and İkmen went and got Dr Eldem immediately, but he said the groan was only a physical response to the pain the patient was probably still experiencing even in coma. It meant nothing. It did not signal the end of Ramazan Eren's sojourn in darkness. He gave him more diamorphine for the pain and all three left.

The twenty-first-century city of Mardin is actually two very different places. Both exist in the shadow of the fortress of

Mardin which sits atop the peak that dominates the whole area, Mazi mountain. To the west of this huge, craggy pile is New Mardin. It consists of high-rise apartment blocks, supermarkets, bus stations and most things modern people need to lead a reasonably comfortable modern life. In the lee of the fortress itself is Old Mardin, which is quite another place. Basically, Mardin city is clustered around one street which is actually called Avenue One. Above and below this street exist the many winding lanes, alleys and literally thousands of stone steps that make up the old city. The buildings, which are made of yellow limestone, seen from the vantage point of the Mesopotamian plain below the city, seem to almost hang from the side of the mountain in waves of washing-draped confusion. Between Avenue One and the much newer road far below it that delineates the southern boundary of the city, Avenue Two, are very few places accessible to anything bigger than a motorbike. So it was that Edibe Taner and Mehmet Süleyman were forced to walk down to their destination from the place where she parked her car on Republic Square, which is about a third of the way along Avenue One.

For Süleyman, who had travelled in Taner's car along Avenue Two in order to get into the city and had therefore stared open-mouthed at yet more immense views over the Mesopotamian plain, the main focus of the city, Republic Square, proved to be a disappointment. As well as being an important stop for the many minibuses running to and from the new city and the surrounding villages, the square also acted as a somewhat makeshift car park. Taner parked her vehicle in front of the entrance to a branch of Akbank, outside which two of her uniformed colleagues stood leaning their elbows on the stocks of their sub-machine guns. Süleyman stepped out into a thin layer of mud and litter and looked up at a range of buildings that looked as if they had originated in the 1960s. An ugly kebab restaurant with plastic flowers on a tatty upstairs veranda was only bested by a truly hideous building that announced itself as the Hotel Bayraktar. Almost Soviet in its blockishness, the Hotel Bayraktar had noticeably more bullet holes in its masonry than unshattered windows. Süleyman imagined that this had to be a legacy of the violent struggle between the Turkish army and the PKK that had caused Mardin to be closed to outsiders from time to time. He was in fact going to ask Taner about it when suddenly he noticed that he was surrounded by a group of tiny boys.

'You like guide?' one asked him in English.

It was a surreal moment. He hadn't long been awake, he was in a place that so far looked like a cross between some sort of mythical mountain land and Leningrad, and he was being spoken to by a child with a wildly divergent accent in a foreign language. For a moment, he just stood silent, like a mute.

'He's with me. Go away!' was what he thought he heard Inspector Taner say, although he couldn't be sure. What she spoke was Turkish, but only just. The little boys melted back into the almost invisible alleyway whence they had come.

'I'm sorry about that,' Taner said as she wandered towards him, a cigarette hanging idly from her lips. 'Kids here can smell an outsider. And as you see, this is not a wealthy city, so if you do feel like slipping them the odd kuruş to go away, that's up to you.'

As he looked at her, Süleyman became aware of the truly wonderful building behind her. Constructed of yellow sandstone, it was reached via a sweeping staircase made from the same material. It was a three-storey, flat-roofed building fronted by a series of graceful arches on each level. In effect the building was terraced to allow upper storeys to have semi-private spaces where one could walk, seek the shade or shelter from the rain. Unlike the Zeytounian house in Gaziantep, this mansion, as he imagined it had to be, was not surrounded by a thick, high wall.

'That is the Mardin museum,' Taner said when she saw him looking up at it. 'One of the newer buildings in the old city.'

'Newer?'

'It's nineteenth-century,' she said. 'It was built as the Syrian Catholic Patriarchate. Now it's our museum. Come.'

She led him across the square, past the 1960s kebab restaurant and into an alleyway that, in terms of architectural style, owed more to Damascus than to İstanbul. It was bounded by high stone walls, and as they walked towards Yusuf Kaya's family home they passed many donkeys and mules laden with all sorts of bundles and baggage.

'In Mardin we use donkeys to carry our rubbish away,' Taner explained as they approached a tiny doorway in a very high, yellow wall. 'You have trucks in İstanbul, we have donkeys here.' She smiled. 'In terms of global warming, I think we are better.' And then she stopped. 'Now, Inspector, when we go through this doorway we will be in the family home of Yusuf Kaya. Unlike most of the mansions of Mardin, which are divided into flats, this house is just one dwelling for one family. So everyone you will see from now on will be connected to Yusuf Kaya in some way. As I told you in the car, I interviewed his wife, his mother and a whole host of relations when he first escaped from prison and our officers have been watching this property ever since. But now I want you to meet them too. Or rather I want them to see that you, the officer who arrested him in İstanbul, is not easily going to let Yusuf go. They will be very nice and polite to you, even though they hate you almost as much as they hate me. They'll make you drink mirra. I'm sorry.'

'Hate you? Why do they hate you?' Süleyman asked.

Edibe Taner, who still hadn't slept since Birecik, said, 'Because I'm a woman and a police officer and therefore very unnatural. I belong to a different clan, my father is a Master of Sharmeran . . .'

'Which means? Master of Sharmeran?'

'Come on, we must go inside now,' Taner said, bending her head to get through the tiny door in the thick high wall. 'We are expected.'

Süleyman, still none the wiser about the exact nature of a Master of Sharmeran, followed. As he went through he pushed past a man whose head and face were almost totally obscured by a thick woollen shawl. The man looked at him briefly though glittering black eyes and then ran off down the alleyway in the direction of Avenue Two.

Çiçek İkmen found only her youngest brother Kemal at home when she turned up at her parents' apartment in Sultanahmet. In between their various flight shifts, Çiçek had learned enough from her brother Bülent about their mother's behaviour to make her feel alarmed. As one of the older İkmen children, Çiçek remembered all the trouble Bekir had caused before he ran away and all the heartache his departure had left behind it. But her mother and Bekir were out, so she had to try to get some sort of view on her mother's behaviour from her sullen teenage brother Kemal. Bülent had also mentioned some sort of smell that seemed to be suddenly present in their parents' home.

'Kemal,' she said as she sat down behind her mother's large kitchen table, 'how are things? With our brother Bekir?'

The boy, who was fiddling rather ineffectually with the samovar, looked sheepishly across at this sister who was old enough to be his mother. 'OK,' he said, pushing a hank of greasy black hair away from his spot-encrusted forehead.

'Do you think that Mum spends a lot of time with Bekir?'

'Maybe.' He had poured some tea into a glass for his sister and was now trying to top it up with water from the samovar, but he was trying to turn the handle the wrong way. Like almost all of her brothers, Kemal had been indulged by their mother to such an extent that he was domestically useless. Only Bülent seemed to have emerged from this child-like dependence upon women and that was because Çiçek, who lived with him, flatly refused to indulge him.

But she had to make an exception and help this boy because otherwise he was going to break the samovar. 'Out of the way.' As she pushed him aside she felt the heat from his blushing face. She also smelt something very unpleasant and, as Bülent had put it, 'musty' too. It was coming, she felt, from Kemal. Knowing, because she knew her mother so well, that it couldn't possibly be the smell of dirty or unaired clothes, she had to assume that it came from something else Kemal was doing.

'What's that smell, Kemal?' she asked as she finished making up her glass of tea.

'Smell?' He blushed again.

'Yes, smell,' his sister said. 'Like a sort of yeasty or musty smell.'

He didn't respond. She took, she knew, an evil delight in his embarrassment. But then he was a moody, awkward and tedious boy. Her mother had been over forty when she'd had him and he'd aged her. 'You must be able to smell it, Kemal.'

'Cream for my spots,' he mumbled. 'It's a new one. Smells a bit.' His entire head was red now and she noticed he was actually sweating. Finally she felt ashamed of herself. Poor Kemal. He was the only one of her siblings to have suffered horribly with acne and now he was having to apply vile-smelling creams in an attempt to alleviate his misery. But at least there wasn't some sort of damp or rot in the apartment that she needed to tell her father about. Not that Çetin İkmen would exactly go into overdrive in order to fix such a problem. He was nothing if not totally careless about his home. But it had bothered Bülent enough, together with their mother's behaviour, to warrant a visit from Çiçek, and now that the smell was dealt with she went on to other matters.

'Kemal,' she said as she drank her tea and then lit up a cigarette. 'Mum and Bekir—'

'I'm not going to say anything against him if that's what you think! You're just like Bülent, just totally jealous and stuff!' her still brick red brother flared. 'Bekir's cool! I like him!'

And without another word he stomped out of the kitchen and went to his room. Çiçek, alone in the kitchen now, was frankly rather shocked. Kemal had never been easy even as a small child, but one thing he had never been before was in any way partisan with regard to his siblings. He had, in the past, either hated or disregarded them all with equal force. Now suddenly he had a favourite. Çiçek wondered why. But then, recalling how manipulative her brother Bekir had been when they were children, she thought that perhaps Kemal's behaviour wasn't that difficult to understand. Bekir, as she recalled, had always delighted in playing people off against each other. He'd done it with her and her older brothers who had actually fought, basically over Bekir. What, she wondered, was he doing with Kemal now? Who was he pitching the boy up against, or was it everyone?

Later, bored with Kemal's seething silence and fed up with waiting for her mother, Çiçek left. As she walked down the hall to retrieve her shoes from the rack by the front door, the musty smell if anything got even stronger.

The house the Kaya family and their attendants now lived in had once been the home of a wealthy Syrian Christian family. The two-storey house was arranged in the traditional way in that the family lived on the upper storey and used the court-yard and the rooms down below for cooking, storage and servant and animal accommodation. Not that they had servants, as such. Those wild-eyed men who served Süleyman and Taner with mirra coffee at the request of the women of the house were not like the ancient retainers the man from İstanbul could remember his grandfather employing. These were no soft-spoken remnants from a previous age, not with guns in their belts and resentment on their faces.

Süleyman had seen Yusuf Kaya's wife, Zeynep, before. She, together with one of her sons and some other women, had attended her husband's trial in İstanbul. Compared to many gangsters' women he had come across in the past, Zeynep Kaya was very low-key indeed. Whereas some would scream, curse and even fight those around them when their men were sentenced to long prison terms, Zeynep Kaya had remained silent behind the chiffon scarf that had covered her head and mouth for the whole of the proceedings. One of her sons, a boy in his early teens Süleyman reckoned, had done enough of the other sort of thing for both of them. But this time no young boy, nor indeed any children, were in evidence. There was just Zeynep and an old veiled woman who Taner told him was Yusuf Kaya's mother, Bilqis.

As they sat down on the floor beside the table upon which the mirra was being served, Taner said to Süleyman, 'Bilqis Kaya speaks only Arabic. I will translate.'

As they sat, Zeynep Kaya followed them solemnly with her dark, wrinkle-encrusted eyes. She looked to be about the same age as her husband, but now that her face was uncovered Süleyman could see that much of what she must have felt at Yusuf's trial had settled bitterly around a mouth that was small, tight and mean. There was something else too: a tattoo which she wore on her left cheek. Süleyman could see that it was a scorpion.

The older woman growled something which Taner told Süleyman was a greeting. In his turn he thanked her for her hospitality, which she seemed to understand. She then told him to drink his mirra, something which Edibe Taner translated with some hesitation. Her guest so obviously did not like the stuff. But Süleyman gamely raised the small cup he had been given to his lips and took a sip without so much as a murmur.

'I haven't seen my husband and neither has any of our family,' Zeynep Kaya said without looking at either Taner or Süleyman.

'To hide Yusuf, who is a convicted criminal under prison sentence, would be counted as an offence,' Taner responded in, Süleyman noticed, the same rather harsh accent as the gangster's wife. 'Whatever your feelings might be, Zeynep, you have children to consider.'

'And my husband is the father of those children,' the woman snapped with now raw and open hatred. 'They are my world, all of them.'

111

'Zeynep, you're not a fool,' Taner said. She calmly sipped her coffee and then lit a cigarette. 'Yusuf has other women from here to İstanbul, and probably beyond. He—'

'Yusuf is my husband—'

'Yusuf killed the prostitute he was living with in İstanbul,' Taner butted in forcefully. 'He murdered her, as you know from the trial. When Inspector Süleyman here arrested your husband, Yusuf was in the process of sawing the legs off a business rival he had just tortured to death!'

The old Arab woman said something that, to Süleyman, sounded vicious and spiteful. Edibe Taner responded, he noticed, in kind. When she had finished speaking the Mardin officer said to Süleyman, 'Bilqis Kaya has just reminded me that as a native of Mardin I should not be helping outsiders against my own kind.'

Süleyman raised an eyebrow.

'I have told her,' Taner continued, 'that her son Yusuf is in no way "my own kind", that she herself should want her very dangerous and disturbed son to be caught for his own sake if nothing else, and that anyway you as well as all your colleagues in İstanbul will not rest until Yusuf is apprehended.'

'Anyway, how could my husband even get into the city without *you* seeing him?' Zeynep said, leaning across the table towards Taner. 'No one does anything without *you* having your eyes and ears everywhere, knowing—'

'And now I have an officer from İstanbul with me,' Taner responded with a smile on her face. 'Someone you won't be able to even think about influencing. Zeynep, if you or any member of your family knows where Yusuf is and I find out, I will make sure that as many of you as possible are punished for it.'

'Oh, you are so spiteful, Edibe Taner!' Zeynep Kaya said. 'Spiteful and alone!'

There was a moment of silence while Taner looked at Zeynep Kaya with a studiedly casual expression on her face. They were of an age, Taner and Yusuf Kaya's wife, the latter maybe a few years older. But one was married and one was not and in places like Mardin that would always give a woman like Zeynep the higher status whatever job her rival, as it were, might choose to do.

'You only persecute those no longer in your circle,' the gangster's wife pushed on. 'At least we don't harbour guns for terrorists. Not like your Christian friends—'

So quickly did Taner jump to her feet that for a moment Süleyman wondered whether she had accidentally dropped her coffee in her lap. She certainly looked as if she might have been scalded.

'What others may or may not be doing is nothing to do with you!' Bent at her slim waist, she hissed down at the gangster's wife still seated by the table on the ground.

'You believed him, your "saint",' the woman continued. 'Can't believe your own blood, no! But some monk whose own family are terrorists—'

'Shut your mouth, Zeynep, or I will shut it for you!' Taner looked as if she might be about to spit at the woman before her. 'And don't you talk to me about blood, don't ever talk to me about blood!'

The police officers left, Süleyman in Taner's furious wake. She explained nothing about whatever had just happened in the Kaya house beyond saying to Süleyman, 'Well, now the bitches know who you are!'

In silence they passed up the litter-strewn alleyway that led back to Republic Square. Distracted by the overwhelming smell of mirra that seemed to be coming from almost every-where, Süleyman didn't notice the old man come up behind them until he was actually level with Taner. When she saw the old man, a small flat-capped peasant in a sheep's-fleece jerkin, suddenly and spectacularly Taner smiled. Then, after a short and tender embrace, they spoke. What they spoke in, Süleyman couldn't even begin to fathom. All he knew was that it was neither Turkish nor Kurdish nor even Arabic.

They talked, Taner and the man, for minutes rather than seconds, the policewoman saying not a word by way of expla-nation to the clueless Süleyman. During the course of their conversation her face was by turns grave and joyful and, when the old man finally left her to disappear down some tiny, dark passageway, she bade him farewell with a smile and a kiss. Then, her face set straight once again, she was going to walk on without another word when Süleyman challenged her. 'Who was that?' he asked.

'No one,' she replied, with harsh lack of grace that was so rough it was almost as if she had slapped him in the face.

Chapter 8

The e-mail from İkmen to Süleyman was very typically the product of one who had grown up without either Internet access or text messaging. It began with Dear Mehmet, and it ended with his own full name, Çetin İkmen. But what it contained was informative and that was the main thing.

Apparently Yusuf Kaya had been helped to get into solitary confinement at the Kartal Prison by another inmate. 'Glamour' pictures had, so İkmen said, changed hands in return for this favour. However, İkmen was still not convinced that this prisoner, Ara Berköz, had been the only person in the prison involved in Kaya's escape. The wounded guard was still in a coma and so he couldn't enlighten anyone, but İkmen was still sure neither about him nor about any of his colleagues. In addition, the two nurses, Faruk Öz and İsak Mardin, were still nowhere to be found. Apparently İkmen had tried to call the doctor in Şanlıurfa for whom Mardin was supposed to have worked before coming to İstanbul, but no such person existed. The previous administrator of the Cerrahpaşa, a Mr Oner, had according to Mardin's file spoken to this non-existent man. But Oner had apparently committed suicide and so wasn't available for comment. Lole, the third nurse who had gone 'missing' after Kaya's escape, had returned to work. Lole, or rather his coffee, had disquieted İkmen as Süleyman recalled. Finally there was a message, sent via İkmen, from

Ardıç. It basically reiterated his desire for Süleyman to 'beat the locals to Kaya'.

'Inspector?'

He turned round to see Brother Seraphim standing behind him.

'I know it's late, but there is a man at the monastery gate, a Kurd, who is insisting upon seeing you,' the monk continued. 'I know him. His name is Lütfü Güneş. He is not a troublesome man in my experience and I think that he is genuine in his desire to see you.'

'You don't know why he wants to see me?' Süleyman asked.

'No, he won't say. I've let him into the monastery compound but I can ask him to leave just as easily.'

Süleyman shut down his e-mail and stood up. 'I'll see him,' he said wearily.

It hadn't been İkmen's idea to hang around Beyoğlu looking for beggars. Ayşe had been quite happy to try to find any remnants of Hüseyin Altun's child gang by herself. It was after all a pleasant evening and plenty of people were about, visiting the clubs, bars and restaurants of İstiklal Street and its environs. But then İkmen wasn't just with Ayşe for professional reasons. He couldn't bear the way that his wife was obsessing over Bekir. It was excessive and it made him fear for her. Because Bekir would hurt her again; İkmen knew that to the very bottom of his soul. The boy might be back, ostensibly clean, tidy and ready to put his life back together, but that didn't mean that his father had to trust him. Somehow Bekir was going to mess things up again, and just at the moment İkmen couldn't bear to even be in the room with him. So he was out on the streets with Ayşe watching gangs of probably foreign children sit outside the Tünel railway station, staring at tourists' handbags.

'I haven't heard one of that lot speak Turkish,' he said, tipping his head towards a large sprawl of kids leaning against the ATM machine just inside the station entrance.

'Eastern European Roma, I think,' Ayşe replied. 'Not that Altun didn't have some of those on his payroll. No one could ever have called Hüseyin a racist. He'd allow anyone, regardless of their race or religion, to share in his criminal lifestyle.'

The sun was setting now and although the day had been warm it was still early in the year and the evenings could be cold. As they came out of the station, quite a few of the tourists stopped to put on jackets and cardigans. Sometimes as they did so they put down bags and rucksacks which the lolling kids, as well as the adult men who were always lurking around children like this, would view hungrily. Hüseyin Altun had been one of the first and probably the most notorious adult leader of a child criminal gang, but he had, in recent years, faced some very stiff competition. İkmen watched carefully as the latest group of tourists readied themselves for a night out on the town, scanning the scene for signs of small hands diving with amazing speed into unattended bags. But although the children seemed largely unaware of anyone looking in their direction, the smart men in sports wear with them did not. One, a very muscular character probably in his early thirties, stared directly at İkmen for some time before saying something to a boy of about twelve in a language İkmen couldn't understand.

But in spite of the obvious suspicion that the men and their kids were harbouring, none of them moved. One of the antique red and gold trams that run up and down İstiklal Street disgorged people at the station and then took on more passengers just off the strange little funicular railway that carries people up the steep hill that rises from Karaköy at the bottom

117

to the southern end of İstiklal Street at the top. A well-trodden tourist route, Tünel had been targeted by genuine beggars as well as by thieves for some years.

İkmen looked away. Staring at these men and their kids wasn't achieving anything, and besides, he and Ayşe were not there to catch street urchins stealing wallets, they were there to look for remnants of Hüseyin Altun's gang. Although ostensibly prompted by one of his 'feelings', the notion that the escape of Yusuf Kaya from prison and Altun's death were connected in some way was not really mystical in origin at all. Kaya was a drug dealer who had been in the city on and off for many years, Altun a native İstanbullu had been a junkie. Both of them had wandered up and down İstiklal Street for years and had to have at least known of each other. An increasing number of people seemed to have been either killed, injured and maybe bribed too around Kaya's escape. Why not a pathetic junkie who might or might not have harboured the escaping convict? After all, Kaya must have needed to hole up somewhere before he took off for Gaziantep. İkmen's eyes strayed on to a dark art nouveau building known as the Botter House. It was one of his favourite city buildings and it saddened him that it was now so unkempt. With so much of Beyoğlu under repair or repaired already this building stood out as a rare sad case. The word was that apparently there was some problem over the ownership of the place. A pull at his elbow ended his musings.

'Sir, over there,' Ayşe whispered, 'by the simit seller's cart.'

He looked across the square in front of the station towards the glass-cabinet-topped cart from which an old man was selling the bread rings called simit. He was taking money from a girl with long blond hair. She in turn clung on to the simit he had given her as if her life depended on it. But then she was probably hungry. Thin though she was, the girl was also in the advanced stages of pregnancy.

'That's Hüseyin Altun's Bulgarian girl,' Ayşe said to İkmen. 'I wonder who the father of her child can be?'

İkmen said, 'Let's ask her, shall we?'

They both walked over to the simit cart.

It was the man with glittering black eyes who had pushed past him outside the Kayas' house in Mardin.

'Yusuf Kaya has a second wife,' the Kurd said without even a pretence of preamble.

He wouldn't actually enter the monastery buildings, so they had to talk in the freezing cold courtyard at the middle of the monastery complex. Süleyman was wearing his overcoat but even so it was still far from warm and he remained exhausted. But the Kurd, who was himself wearing a thick woollen shawl, had insisted. He didn't want the monks 'involved' as he put it. They were good people.

'She is a foreigner,' Lütfü Güneş continued.

Süleyman, surprised to say the least by this revelation, was also straining to understand the man's eccentric accent. 'What kind of foreigner?' he asked.

'American.'

'American?' That out in a place like Mardin was very, very foreign. 'Are you sure?'

'He keeps her in a house out by Dara,' the Kurd said.

Süleyman didn't know either what Dara was or where it was.

'Dara is a village out on the Ocean,' Lütfü Güneş explained. 'She is an American, she is his wife and she lives there surrounded by wormwood.'

Thinking that perhaps he had misheard, Süleyman said, 'Wormwood? As in wormwood the—'

'Wormwood,' the Kurd interrupted. 'As I say.' He held up one silencing hand. 'But I'll say no more. No one else will tell you that this woman exists and you need to know.'

'Do Kaya's mother and his wife Zeynep—'

'Of course they know!' the Kurd said contemptuously. 'But they won't speak and you need to know.'

'Why?' Süleyman asked. 'Is Kaya with this American wife? Is he hiding with her now?'

Lütfü Güneş shrugged. 'I don't know and I don't care,' he said.

'If you don't care, why are you telling me?'

The Kurd looked down at the ground. 'I don't want a war with the Kayas,' he said. 'I don't personally bear them any ill will. But Yusuf wrongs everyone and my name should not be spoken to his clan.' He looked up, his eyes wet with either the cold or emotion or both. 'I rejoiced when Yusuf Kaya went to prison. Someone must put him back there and it must be someone from outside.'

'Inspector Taner—'

'No one will tell Taner anything,' the Kurd said with bitterness in his voice. 'She betrays her own kind! The only reason she is still alive is out of respect for her father.'

Seçkin Taner, the famous and mysterious Master of Sharmeran, as Süleyman recalled. 'Master' – whatever that might mean – of a mythical snake goddess, what nonsense! And yet it meant something powerful to these people seemingly irrespective of their ethnicities or religions. It also apparently helped to keep the local inspector breathing.

The Kurd took a cigarette out from underneath the folds of his shawl and lit up. 'Go to the American wife,' he said, 'and find Kaya. Only a person without a clan can arrest him without starting a war in the city and out in the Ocean.'

He turned to leave, but Süleyman put a restraining hand on his shoulder. 'Have you seen Kaya since he escaped from prison? Have you seen him here in the Tur Abdin?'

The Kurd looked at him with obvious distaste. 'No, I have not,' he said. 'Why would I?'

'And wormwood? What—'

'Ask your unnatural woman about that,' he said, echoing the sentiments, Süleyman recalled, of the Kaya women. Taner was unnatural because she was a policewoman and maybe for other reasons too. Maybe her being the daughter of a Master of Sharmeran put her in an ambiguous place. Maybe people around her were both jealous and fearful, admiring and awestruck in equal measure.

The Kurd left and then, in spite of the lateness of the hour, Süleyman called Edibe Taner.

The Bulgarian girl told İkmen and Ayşe Farsakoğlu that her name was Sophia. Whether that was in fact her real name was not ascertained at that point. She did not however, whatever her name was, want to talk about Hüseyin Altun. Nevertheless, mainly due to Ayşe Farsakoğlu's easy and tactful manner, she was persuaded that accompanying the officers to one of the cafés in the lovely Belle Époque-style passage known as Tünel Geçidi was going to be far more pleasant than going with them to police headquarters. As she plonked herself down grumpily in one of the wrought-iron chairs amid the luxuriant plants that almost overwhelmed the passage she said to Ayşe, 'I want latte and a piece of tiramisu.'

Ayşe looked at her boss for confirmation. 'Get the lady

what she wants, Ayşe,' he said. 'I'll have tea if places like this do tea.'

She went into the indoor section of the café they had chosen to sit outside – mainly because no one else was sitting there – and ordered. İkmen, although anxious to discover what, if anything, Sophia might know about Hüseyin Altun's associates, kept quiet until his deputy returned. He did not, after all, know this heavily pregnant, and heavily accented, girl at all.

'So, Sophia,' Ayşe said when she re-joined them at the table, 'it's been quite a while. I see that you're pregnant. Congratulations.'

The girl looked up at Ayşe with a sneer on her lips. 'What you want, Sergeant Farsakoğlu?' she said. 'I don't do nothing now, you know.'

'Sophia, I didn't see you begging,' Ayşe said. 'I just want to talk.' She fixed the girl with her eyes. 'About Hüseyin.'

Sophia shrugged. 'Is dead, I hear.'

'Yes, he is dead,' Ayşe said. 'Someone killed him.'

'Hüseyin, he was a bad man, he use heroin,' Sophia said without either surprise or emotion. 'I am away from him.'

'Sophia.' İkmen smiled at her. 'I am Sergeant Farsakoğlu's superior. I know you've done nothing wrong. But we need to find out if Hüseyin knew a man called Yusuf Kaya. He was a drug dealer, lived over in Tarlabaşı.'

Sophia did not respond in any obvious way to this. 'A lot of drug dealers in Tarlabaşı,' she said.

'Yusuf Kaya is a middle-aged man. Tall, dark, apparently attractive to women,' İkmen said. And then he added, 'Last year he was convicted of the murder of a Suriani prostitute and a Russian drug dealer known as Tommi Kerensky.'

At this last name, Sophia looked up. This time there was

fear on her face. 'Tommi? The man who kill Tommi? Is in prison—'

'Is out of prison now,' İkmen said. 'Escaped.'

Whether consciously or otherwise, Sophia's hands grasped her enormous belly and she said, 'That is very bad, I think.'

'Sophia, do you, or rather did Hüseyin know this man, this Yusuf Kaya?'

The waiter appeared then and so at least a minute was spent organising drinks while İkmen took in the enormous size of the cake Sophia had made Ayşe order for her. As the girl spooned the first great cream-laden glob into her mouth she briefly closed her eyes. Only when İkmen repeated his question did she open them again. Then she frowned.

'Some years ago and once only I go to the apartment of the man who kill Tommi,' Sophia said. 'I recognise the place from the television last year. They show this as the place Tommi died.'

İkmen looked briefly across at Ayşe and then said to Sophia, 'How did you come to go to that apartment, Sophia? Why?'

The Bulgarian girl put her spoon down beside her gooey tiramisu, as if she had suddenly gone off her food, which indeed she had. But she said nothing for some time and so Ayşe, after a pause, answered for her.

'Sir, Sophia was a heroin user.'

'Well, I—'

'I don't do the junk no more!' the girl said vehemently. 'But I . . . Then I . . .'

'Just tell us about your visit to Yusuf Kaya's apartment,' İkmen said. 'You're not in any trouble and whatever you did while you were there is a long time ago and of no concern to us now.'

Ayşe put a hand on Sophia's shoulder. 'Just tell us,' she said. 'It's OK, honestly.'

Sophia swallowed hard and then said, 'I go there to buy junk.'

'From Yusuf Kaya?'

She nodded. 'Hüseyin know him.'

'Hüseyin took you there?'

'No.'

İkmen frowned.

'Hüseyin tell Aslan to take me,' she said. 'Aslan tell me this man he is Hüseyin's friend.'

İkmen had heard the name Aslan before, from Ayşe. He looked at her now for an explanation.

'Aslan is one of Hüseyin Altun's lieutenants, sir,' Ayşe said. 'Used to be one of the street urchins. He's been with Hüseyin for years.'

'Maybe we should go and talk to this Aslan,' İkmen said as he lit up a cigarette. The name Aslan had also, he now recalled, possibly caused a reaction from the comatose prison guard, Ramazan Eren. When Ayşe had uttered the name, he had stirred. It might have been, as the guard's doctor had said, just a coincidence, but nevertheless İkmen did feel a need to see this Aslan person, whoever he was. 'Where does this Aslan live?'

'He is gone,' Sophia said. Still not touching her food, she looked incredibly sad. 'Before Hüseyin body is discovered he is gone.'

'Sophia,' Ayşe said, 'you just told us you haven't been seeing Hüseyin Altun. You've given up heroin, so you say, and—'

'I do give up junk!' Sophia said, tears now in the corners of her eyes. 'But . . . but I don't give up Aslan.' She looked

124

down at her swollen belly and began to sob. 'Aslan is father of my baby! He live with me, but now he have gone.' She rose quickly from her seat and looked down into İkmen's face. 'I am afraid he is dead, like Hüseyin.'

'Why do you think that, Sophia?' İkmen said. 'Why do you think that Aslan might be dead?'

'Why else he leave me?' she said tearfully. 'Why else he leave his baby?'

And then with a turn of speed amazing in a pregnant woman, even a young one, she ran headlong back along the passage towards İstiklal Street. Ayşe ran after her but after a few minutes' desperate searching out on the main thoroughfare she had to admit defeat and returned to the café and Çetin İkmen. Sophia had been and probably still was a beggar. She knew the streets and all the hiding places they concealed.

Chapter 9

Below Mardin and the monastery of St Sobo, the Mesopotamian plain stretched into a misty and unknowable place. As flat as a salt-pan, the plain was nevertheless a very interesting and intricate jigsaw of multicoloured fields, dusty roads and the occasional rough, mudbrick building. On the roads, which on this unexpectedly bright spring morning were clear save for the occasional errant goat, the only other humans on the move were a group of gypsies. No more than twenty in number, the gypsies looked at Edibe Taner's car as it passed with blank, closed-off eyes. The women, whose faces and heads were completely uncovered, wore bright dresses, many of them covered with sequins that reflected the pale yellow light of early morning, making their wearers look like carriers of stars.

'The turn off to Dara is just here,' Taner said, pointing to a track which led off to the left. The signpost actually said Oghuz, which was the name, apparently, of the modern village that had grown up around the ancient site of Dara.

When Süleyman had telephoned Taner late the previous evening, after Lütfü Güneş had come to see him at the monastery, she would have liked to set out for Dara straight away. Partly because she believed that Süleyman was exhausted, but mainly because she knew that looking for anyone out on the Ocean in the dark was going to be diffi-cult, she had agreed to leave the journey until the morning.

But she had started early. That Yusuf Kaya apparently had an American wife was something completely unknown to her and she was intrigued. She and a constable called Selahattin had called at St Sobo's at five a.m. Luckily Brother Seraphim and the other monks were accustomed to early rising on account of their devotions, so it hadn't taken Taner long to have Süleyman roused and then pushed inside her car with a tiny glass of tea in one hand and a cigarette in the other. As they came out of the city, she explained what she felt Süleyman's guest had meant when he had said that Yusuf Kaya's American wife was surrounded by 'wormwood'.

'Kaya's clan, like all of us who belong to families from the plains, tattoo themselves,' she said.

Süleyman remembered seeing a tattoo on Zeynep Kaya's left cheek. It had been, as he recalled, a scorpion.

'This kind of tattoo we call Dakk,' Taner said. 'Well, the Dakk for Kaya's clan includes a wormwood flower in the design. They are known locally as the "wormwoods" for this reason. When your informant said that the American woman was surrounded by "wormwood" what he meant was that this woman is guarded by members of the Kaya clan. To leave the wife of such a prominent man, even a foreign wife, alone is unthinkable.'

'So not—'

'Oh, don't get me wrong, actual wormwood does grow on the plains. The Dakk that we wear reflect our environment and the Kaya family do grow and sell herbs including wormwood. But we are, trust me, looking for a house that is guarded by Kaya family members or retainers. Although how such a unique event as an American can have been kept secret . . .' She tipped her head back and called to the constable behind her. 'Selahattin, have you ever heard of such a thing?'

'No, Inspector,' the young man said. 'But then each clan is a closed book, isn't it? That much I have learned since I came to work in this city.'

'Selahattin is from Trabzon,' Taner said. Then she smiled. 'Black Sea people too busy trading to be bothered with clans and such nonsense, eh?'

The young man smiled. People from the Black Sea coast, probably because of their proximity to sea and land routes to other cultures, have a reputation for cunning business practice.

Once they had turned off the main route from Mardin down to the D400 and thence to the Syrian border, they soon came upon what looked to Süleyman like a series of vast overturned monoliths. Massive grey sharp-cut rocks stuck out of the ground at alarming angles. Seeing where his gaze was fixed, Taner said, 'Those were the quarries that provided the stone needed to build Dara. Just before we get into the village is the ancient necropolis. Dara's first inhabitants were Byzantine and so the graveyard is Christian. Inspector Süleyman, did you get any sort of idea from your informant about where this house might be?'

'No.' And then a thought struck him. 'Inspector,' he said, 'about Dakk. Kaya's wife Zeynep was tattooed, I noticed. But not with a wormwood flower – with a scorpion, on her left cheek.'

'Zeynep Kaya was not born a member of his clan,' Taner said. 'There is some level of marriage between relations within the clans, but clan members do marry out, particularly if the match is advantageous.'

'So the scorpion . . .'

'Is the Dakk of the Taner clan,' she said. She turned her head away from the road for a moment and rolled up the sleeve of her jacket. 'Like this.'

The tattoo was on her forearm. Long and black, its stinger held threateningly above its head, this scorpion was much more expertly drawn than Zeynep Kaya's had been.

'Zeynep is my cousin,' Taner said. 'She is the daughter of my father's younger brother. Because of what my forebears were and what my father is, many clans want a connection with us.'

This was obviously the Master of Sharmeran business again. But Taner related to Zeynep Kaya . . . Süleyman was shocked. He knew that he shouldn't be, because that was just how things were, or could be, out in the east. Everyone was related in the end to everyone else. That notwithstanding, his İstanbul-raised sensibilities were rather rattled.

'Inspector . . .'

'Of course no one in Dara will tell us whether or not a foreign woman connected to Kaya lives hereabouts,' Taner said. 'Yusuf Kaya has always been feared and, by some, admired on the plains.'

Deciding that now was probably not the time to ask Taner about her father – if such a time indeed would ever come – Süleyman turned his mind back to the job in hand.

'So we look for a house, houses . . .'

'No.'

He looked across at her face, which was smiling in profile.

'Selahattin,' she said, 'will take you sightseeing. Dara is a very interesting site and one that you should see while you are here. In fact, I'd go so far as to say that local people will expect you to see it.'

The woman who lived on the fourth floor of Mr Lale's boarding house in Zeyrek had been going on for months about the garden at the back of the building. Mr Lale had told her that if it bothered her that much maybe she should plant some flowers or something in it herself. That had shut the old bitch up!

But ever since that nurse, that İsak Mardin, had just upped and left without paying his rent, the top flat had been empty, and Mr Lale needed the money. A couple of people had come to have a look since the nurse disappeared, but none of them had wanted the flat. To be honest, it wasn't very big, and besides, word had got out that the police had searched the place and that had put people off. Mardin was after all missing and the last thing any putative tenants wanted to face was the possibility of suddenly coming across the nurse dead underneath their floorboards. So when elderly Miss whatever on the fourth floor suggested that tidying up the garden might help to encourage prospective tenants, Mr Lale had decided that that was what he would do.

No gardener, he nevertheless made an early start. Dragging a shovel and a bag of flowers behind him, Mr Lale strolled miserably round to the back of his property and surveyed the bald lumpen patch of earth that was his garden. It wasn't a very promising vista. But then, as Miss whatever had told him, some people made really fabulous flower displays out of very much less. As he began to dig, at random really, Mr Lale mused on the fact that none of the existing tenants used the garden. Occasionally the young man in the basement parked his bike against the back fence but more often than not he kept it inside. However, as Miss whatever had said, summer was only round the corner and a pretty garden would make people stop and look and not in a bad way.

It had rained a few times in the past few weeks, as it often did in İstanbul in the spring. So the ground was variable, dry in some places, muddy in others. Because of this, Mr Lale gained no impression that the earth had been turned over by anyone else. But that must have been the case because after about an hour, in a corner of the garden nearest to the passage at the side of the house, his shovel hit something hard. Closer inspection of the object revealed it to be one of those very thick plastic bags sometimes used to cover electrical goods. There was something in it, too. But what it was was not electrical. It was a human arm, just beginning to break down and rot. Horrified, Mr Lale could see that the arm had once been very large and well developed.

Süleyman didn't see the logic of what happened next. He asked Constable Selahattin what he thought.

'They do some very strange things around here, sir,' the constable said as he too followed the troupe of teenage tour guides into the heart of Dara. Edibe Taner had simply handed the two men over to the boys while she went off to make enquiries on her own. 'I imagine the inspector has gone to see something or someone she feels might be of use. There are some people here, sir, well a lot really, who won't speak to outsiders. They won't even speak to one of their own while an outsider is present.'

'My understanding, however, is,' Süleyman said, 'that this American wife is a person unknown to anyone outside the Kaya family.'

'And yet your informant knew, sir. Amazing to me he should care to talk to you, but . . . And you say he wasn't a Kaya. So if he knows maybe others do too. I imagine this is what the inspector is assuming.'

Lütfü Güneş, so Brother Seraphim had told Süleyman, wasn't even distantly related to the Kayas. So, Süleyman reasoned, if he knew so indeed could others. But how did

Taner know who, if anyone, she could talk to about words spoken by a man Süleyman had refused to name? Constable Selahattin in part answered this question.

'There are all sorts of alliances and pacts and things between the various clans that no one from outside can possibly understand,' he said. 'They won't talk to the likes of us unless there's really no choice, or it would actively endanger them to talk to their own.'

Following the group of boys down a rutted, bramble-strewn track, they came to the ruins of a massive cistern cut into the rock.

'You can't even draw lines along ethnic divisions around here,' Selahattin continued as the boys, guides educated and paid by the local municipality, waited for the men to catch up with them. 'Half of these kids here are Arabs and in Mardin itself you find Turkish families who only two generations back were Arabs or Christians or Jews or all three! So the alliances there, even now, can be confusing.' He smiled. 'But I leave all that to the locals. I just catch the odd pickpocket from time to time.'

Süleyman was certain that wasn't entirely true. After all, why employ someone as apparently neutral as Selahattin if there wasn't some higher purpose in mind? The young man was intelligent and obviously very fit. Perfect for hiking out into the mountains in pursuit of terrorists of all kinds.

The boy guides, who were indeed largely of Syrian Arab ancestry, began their spiel about Dara. As the smallest of the lads talked about how the city had started life as a Byzantine garrison town known as Anastasiopolis, Süleyman was struck by two things. First how durable some ancient names were. Yusuf Kaya's Christian lover in the brothel in Gaziantep had been called Anastasia. And second, he wondered whether that

133

really was Edibe Taner's car driving out of Dara back towards the Mardin road?

'Dad!'

İkmen was just outside police headquarters when he was stopped by the sound of Çiçek's voice. He turned and smiled. Breathless from running to catch him up, Çiçek tottered into her father's arms and kissed him on the cheek.

'I came home to see you all yesterday, but only Kemal was in,' she said as she put a hand up to her heaving chest.

'He didn't say anything about your visit,' İkmen said as he returned her kiss and took one of her arms in his.

Çiçek raised her eyes to the sky in exasperation. 'Kemal!'

'So, my soul, what was your visit about?' İkmen asked. 'Was it just a social call or did you want to talk about something in particular?' He suspected from the rather serious look on her face that it was the latter.

Çiçek had never been a person to mince her words. 'Dad, I'm worried about Mum,' she said. 'More specifically, I'm worried about Mum and Bekir.'

'Ah.' İkmen put his free hand in his pocket and retrieved his cigarettes.

'I know that she is going to be more protective about Bekir than she would be normally for a while,' Çiçek continued. 'But when Bülent was at home the other day he saw Mum cancel a dental appointment she made ages ago in order to stay in with Bekir. What's more, Bülent said that although Bekir did make various noises to Mum about how she should go to the dentist, once she'd cancelled he looked smug and pleased with himself.' She drew still closer to her father and took one of the cigarettes that he offered her. 'Dad, Bülent can barely remember Bekir but I do and, glad as I am to see him again, he was trouble.'

İkmen lit up their cigarettes and sighed. 'He says he's changed, that he's off drugs . . .'

'And Kemal is coming under his spell. Thinks that Bekir is "cool"!' Çiçek drew shakily on her cigarette and then said, 'Dad, I know it's suspicious and cynical but I can't and don't trust Bekir. What he put us all through, years ago, but with such obvious delight . . .'

'Çiçek.' İkmen put a hand on her shoulder. 'My darling, I must be honest and say that I don't trust him either. I can't tell you why; I have no evidence that he is or has been doing anything wrong. He says that he will leave us soon. Apparently he has a job down on the south coast for the summer.'

'Do you know what it is?'

'No.' He rubbed his face wearily with his hands. 'I want him to go. I don't know why, he's not being unpleasant and he is my son, but . . . He says he's leaving soon and I want your mother to have some good times with him first. She doesn't know about this yet and you're not to tell her. I mean, yes she is behaving in a silly fashion right now, but how can I tell her that? Her son has returned after one and a half decades doing who knows what—'

'He says he fought gypsies, travelled and all sorts,' Çiçek cut in.

'Yes, and I must try to find the time to go to Balat and talk to my gypsy connection,' İkmen said. 'I'm not saying that I don't believe any of Bekir's stories, but . . . You know, Çiçek, I think that your mother does know on some level what is going on with regard to Bekir and her behaviour towards him. She's not a fool.'

'No, I know.'

İkmen puffed hard on his cigarette and said, 'I will go and see my gypsy. She knows everyone.'

'Sir!'

It was, İkmen recognised immediately, Ayşe Farsakoğlu's voice. Turning towards his place of work he saw her standing in the doorway holding a mobile telephone to her ear.

'Ayşe?'

'Sir, we have to go out to Zeyrek now! İsak Mardin's landlord has found something that could be significant in his garden!'

İkmen smiled at his daughter, kissed her again and took his leave of her. Çiçek, used to such oblique and unexpected partings, began to go about her business. As she left she said, 'Oh, and Dad, there's a smell in the apartment. Don't know what it is. Kemal says it's his spot cream, but . . .'

'Yes, it is, apparently,' İkmen said as he ran off towards the station. 'Ghastly, I know, but . . .'

'OK, Dad,' Çiçek said. 'I'll leave it with you.'

But her father had gone.

Interesting though the history of the ancient city of Dara was, Süleyman felt that there had to be more constructive things he could be doing with regard to the recapture of Yusuf Kaya. All this detail about Byzantine garrisons and wars with the Persians was making him feel as if he were on the edge of the world. And when one of their young guides pointed towards some tiny white cube-like buildings in the distance and said, 'Syria,' it only served to increase his sense of dislocation. But there was nothing he could do. Inspector Taner was running this investigation and she'd taken off in her car to who knew where over an hour ago.

The young guides told the officers that they had been employed to take tourists round the site mainly because visitors had complained that they were being hassled for money by gangs of greedy kids.

'They are mainly gypsies, of course,' one of the lads said when they all sat down at the end of the tour at a tea garden on the edge of the town. The children in question probably weren't exclusively gypsies, but Süleyman let it go.

The tea, which was served to them by an elderly man, was hot and strong and was very welcome in spite of the now rapidly increasing heat. Constable Selahattin said, 'When the sun does come out at this time of year, it can be very hot.' He smiled. 'It can also still rain and even snow on occasion too. This place is unpredictable.'

They sat and talked of this and that with their young hosts for almost an hour and then, as quickly as she had gone, Edibe Taner reappeared. Once back inside the car, she didn't speak to either of the men about where she had been until they had well and truly cleared Dara village. Even when she did speak she didn't say from where or from whom she had gained her information.

'There is an old house at the back of the necropolis,' she said, 'that belongs, I am told, to the Kaya family. Occasionally, generally after dark, a tall veiled woman is seen taking exercise outside in company with armed men.' She pointed out of the car window, beyond the tumbling tombs of Dara's former masters, towards a large sandy hillock at the back of the graveyard. 'Behind all that. I think we should return tonight and—'

'Inspector, forgive me,' Süleyman said, 'but now that we have this information, wouldn't it be better to investigate now? Yesterday you felt that night-time was not the best time to be out here. I mean, I don't know who your informant was, but surely that person could tell the woman and her guards that you have been told about this.'

She looked away from the road for a moment, her face

proud and stern. 'They won't talk,' she said with absolute certainty. 'They wouldn't dare.'

It was not a statement that invited any sort of response, and Süleyman kept his counsel. Had Taner been perhaps to see Lütfü Güneş, the Kurd who had come to see him? It wasn't likely. In line with the man's request, he hadn't told Taner his name, and anyway, if Lütfü had wanted to talk to Taner he would have done so a long time before. No, she had seen some other person or persons and quizzed and probably threatened them with something or other too. She was, he was coming to see, a very powerful woman – daughter of a Master of Sharmeran or not.

'I will arrange for a squad to surround the house tonight and then you and I will go in and talk to the inhabitants,' Taner said to Süleyman after a pause. 'It's safer that way. That's my decision.'

She clearly knew her territory and her people, so there was very little in that to argue with. Not that it didn't leave Süleyman feeling uneasy. To surround the house at night seemed to him an unnecessarily aggressive act. Surely, to stop at the house and maybe for him to ask for directions in order to get the lie of the land would be a better plan? But then he didn't know the area or the people. What he did know *of* it was, he had to admit, more tense, violent and generally unstable than anything he had ever come across in İstanbul. Apart from all the different ethnic groups and terrorist organisations active in the area, there was drug growing and trafficking and last, but certainly not least, the powerful clans that controlled life both up in the city and down on the plain.

'Now we will go to Mardin Prison,' Taner said as she accelerated the car past a herd of startled goats and made for the crossroads. 'There is someone there I would like you to meet, Inspector Süleyman.'

'Oh?'

From the back of the vehicle, Selahattin said, 'Musa Saatçi.'

Taner said, 'Indeed.'

Süleyman, frowning, said, 'Is Musa Saatçi something to do with Kaya?'

'Oh, no,' Taner said breezily. 'Not at all. Musa Saatçi is the father of a man who is a living saint.'

A living saint? Süleyman squashed down his suspicions and said, 'So why is he in prison, this father of a saint? What is his crime?'

'He is on remand and so has not yet been convicted of any crime,' Taner said. 'But just under eight weeks ago, an old friend of Musa Saatçi when visiting him discovered that the old man's house was full of weapons: guns, grenades and rocket launchers. That old friend is one of our officers.'

'So this Musa Saatçi is a terrorist?'

Edibe Taner sighed and shook her head sadly. 'No,' she said. 'He is a very pious Christian man whose son has performed miracles in this area. The guns are not Musa's. But he won't tell us who they do belong to.'

'And now Gabriel has gone missing,' Selahattin said from the back of the car.

'Gabriel?'

'Gabriel Saatçi, Musa's son,' Taner said. 'He is a monk at St Sobo's. But shortly after his father was arrested, he disappeared. Everyone is looking for him. When we were at the Kaya house yesterday I spoke to a neighbour about him. We are all very worried. Even if one is a Muslim, Gabriel Saatçi is very special.'

'Why is that?' Süleyman asked.

Without a hint of scepticism in her voice, Edibe Taner said, 'God via the Sharmeran gave Gabriel the power to withstand snake bite when he was a young child. Gabriel Saatçi was bitten by vipers and yet he lived unharmed. He is an immortal saint.'

Chapter 10

Mr Lale was not a man to take a tongue-lashing from anyone. Not even a senior police officer.

'I had to know whether it was him or not,' he said to İkmen as he looked across, without emotion, at the plastic-bag-framed face of the dead body that was currently being examined by the police pathologist, Arto Sarkissian.

'By "him" I take it you mean İsak Mardin your ex-tenant?' İkmen said tightly. The bloody stupid man had tampered with a crime scene!

'Who else would I mean?' Mr Lale replied. 'Of course İsak Mardin!' He sighed. 'It was a relief to find that it wasn't him. I mean, I know he owes me rent, but—'

'So having tampered with the body in order to satisfy your curiosity—'

'My peace of mind!' Mr Lale interrupted. 'To put my mind at rest that the body in that bag wasn't one of my tenants. With that great big arm sticking out at me, it could easily have been him. He built his body; it was his obsession. And if it had been him maybe one of my other tenants might have killed him. Imagine that! Imagine living with the knowledge that someone in your house had been killed by someone else in your house. Imagine—'

'Mr Lale, hysterics will get us nowhere!' İkmen snapped. 'I'm quite rightly angry because you have contaminated a crime scene. You pulled that bag apart to reveal the face and in the process you have almost certainly destroyed at least some of the evidence this man's assailant may have left behind. This man is clearly not İsak Mardin. I have to find out who he is and why he was buried in your garden.'

It was at this point that the pathologist rose to his feet and beckoned to Çetin İkmen. 'Ah, Inspector . . .'

İkmen looked over at his friend and then, without another word to the landlord, he made his way over to him. 'Arto.'

The Armenian looked on as the policeman lit up a cigarette and then said, 'Cause of death, as far as I can deduce right now, is a deep stab wound to the neck.'

Thinking back to the other recent stabbings connected with the absconding of Yusuf Kaya, which by virtue of happening in İsak Mardin's garden this one could also be, he said, 'Glass?'

'No, short-handled knife. Probably a flick knife. He's about thirty. In good health as far as I can see.'

'ID?'

'He's naked.'

İkmen groaned.

'Forensic are on their way,' Arto said. 'They'll have to turn over the property.'

'Won't please the landlord too much,' İkmen said, nodding his head in the direction of Mr Lale.

The Armenian looked at the small, woollen-capped man with some disdain and said, 'He contaminated the scene?'

'Yes.'

Arto sighed.

'Thought it might be his missing tenant, our missing nurse, İsak Mardin,' İkmen said. 'I must admit that I thought it might be him too. But it isn't.' He sighed. 'I wonder who it is and whether he has or had anything to do with Mr Yusuf Kaya or not?'

'I do not know,' Arto said as he bent over the body once again.

İkmen, puffing heavily on his cigarette now, hunched his shoulders in misery.

But just before he hunkered down to go about his work again, Arto Sarkissian turned and said, 'Oh, and he has a tattoo.'

'A tattoo? Where?'

'On his left bicep. It's a flower, wound around with what look like tree branches. Quite well done. I have seen worse.'

'Oh, well, that's something,' İkmen said. Tattoos were, he knew, often a good way of tracing an unknown person. And if no other evidence pointing to the identity of this man was found, that tattoo could prove very useful.

It was strange to see anyone, unrelated to that person, kiss a prisoner's hand. But Edibe Taner did just that when Musa Saatçi was brought into the interview room. It was, Süleyman decided, a foul place. Not that any prison could be described as pleasant, but this place, maybe because of its remoteness, felt worse than any other jail he had visited before.

The prisoner himself, however, was probably cleaner and tidier than the usual run of such individuals. Short and stooped, Musa Saatçi was probably somewhere in his late seventies. He had a long white beard, not unlike those Süleyman had seen on the monks at St Sobo's, and, behind small wire-rimmed spectacles, a pair of very lively bright green eyes. Taner, noticing the look of slight confusion on Süleyman's face, said, 'The guards look after him. He isn't a criminal.'

She looked and sounded absolutely sure about it. She was

143

also adopting a deferential manner with this old man that Süleyman had not seen or associated with her before. It was almost as if all her toughness and ambition had suddenly dropped away from her.

The old man sat down in the chair Taner brought over for him and made himself comfortable. A conversation in what Süleyman imagined was probably Aramaic ensued, after which Taner said, 'My dear uncle here speaks Turkish. I have told him you are a completely neutral and fair officer from İstanbul. He will listen to you.'

She obviously had a great deal of affection for the old man, but then so did the guard who brought him in a large glass of tea. He too addressed the prisoner affectionately as 'uncle'.*

'Yes, I will listen,' the old man said in a deep, heavily accented voice. 'For Edibe's sake, I will listen.' He then turned to Taner and added, 'But it will change nothing.'

'Just listen, uncle dear,' Taner said. And then she looked across expectantly at Süleyman. He cleared his throat. According to Taner, Musa Saatçi had admitted neither guilt nor innocence with regard to the arms the police had found at his home. All he would say was that whatever was wrong would be all right once his son, the missing 'miracle' monk Gabriel, returned. The problem was that no one, Musa apparently included, seemed to know when that would be.

'Mr Saatçi,' Süleyman began, 'Inspector Taner has described your situation to me in some detail. I understand you believe that all will be well when your son returns. But . . .'

'When Gabriel comes back everything will be clear,' Musa Saatçi said with a smile on his broad, brown face. 'My son is a saint, young man. Everything will be well upon his return.'

---

* 'Uncle' is used by Turkish people as a term of respect for their male elders.

'Sir, I am . . .' Süleyman, a man who once believed in God and now didn't any more, felt embarrassed in the face of such, to him, blind faith. 'Mr Saatçi, unless your son is coming home now, we don't have the time. If you are innocent, as Inspector Taner believes, then you must tell us so, and you must also tell us who is actually the guilty party in this matter.'

Musa Saatçi looked down at the floor and frowned. 'I have nothing to say to you, young man.'

Süleyman looked across at Taner, who just shrugged her shoulders helplessly. He leaned forward and whispered so that only the old man could hear him. 'Mr Saatçi, I am from İstanbul. I belong to no clan or group, I have no religion and I have never been bought by anyone. I hate to see an obviously revered man like yourself in a place like this. Tell me the truth and I assure you that . . .'

He stopped because the old man was laughing. Not loudly or with a cackle in his voice, but sadly, with much shaking of his shaggy white head.

'Young man,' he said when he had finished, 'I know that you mean well. I know that Edibe here has only my interests at heart. But if I speak before my boy returns and it gets out . . .'

'It won't get out!' Taner said, leaning forward to squeeze one of the old man's hands in hers. 'Tell Inspector Süleyman only, if you like!'

'And he will tell you, and . . .'

'I won't tell anyone, I swear it!' she said. 'I will simply find who has really committed this crime and arrest them.'

'Which is exactly what I do not want!' Musa Saatçi thundered. 'Not until Gabriel—'

'Mr Saatçi, you are charged with a terrorist offence,' Süleyman said. 'If your telling us the truth is dependent upon your son's returning to St Sobo's then he needs to do that very quickly. Mr Saatçi, do you know where your son is?'

Musa Saatçi turned away and said softly, 'No.'

Süleyman looked again at Taner, who spoke to the old man. 'Uncle Musa, if you know where Gabriel is—'

'I do not!'

'Uncle Musa, is it that you fear that the people who really own those weapons will hurt Gabriel in some way?'

There was a long and very still silence. It told both Taner and Süleyman almost everything they needed to know.

The man from İstanbul leaned forward once again. 'Mr Saatçi,' he said, 'if we knew where your son was we would, and I would personally oversee this, protect him.'

The old man's eyes were full of tears when he looked up once again. 'You couldn't protect Gabriel,' he said. 'My son is immortal, a living saint.'

'So why do you fear for him so very much?' Taner asked.

The old man shook his head. 'There are more ways to kill a man than just by destroying his body.'

'You fear for his soul? These people have dominion over Gabriel's soul? How can that be?' Taner said. 'Uncle, Gabriel is a saint, he is a perfect soul! No one can change that! No one!'

But the old man didn't answer. Süleyman, lost or so he felt in some sort of medieval world of saints and souls and miracles, leaned back in his chair again and sighed. He'd come out to Mardin to find Yusuf Kaya, not to get involved in something that to him felt like an episode from one of his son's Harry Potter books.

The old man rose slowly from his chair and then leaned down to cup Edibe Taner's chin in his hands. 'All I ask is that you speak to your father for me,' he said. 'Ask him to ask the Sharmeran to protect my son.'

'Uncle.' Taner got to her feet and embraced the old man. 'Gabriel is the Sharmeran's own dear son, you know that. She will never, ever desert him.'

If Süleyman hadn't known for sure that Taner was a Muslim he would have sworn that she was Suriani. Talking in reverent tones about a Christian holy man! But then of course there was the Sharmeran, too. What a thick brew people were in the east! Taner and the old man spoke in Aramaic again, until the guard returned to take Musa Saatçi back to his cell. Taner, her eyes wet with tears, followed. Süleyman, bringing up the rear, was flummoxed, confused and completely determined to find out just what this Sharmeran thing was really all about.

Like Zeyrek, where İkmen had just come from, Balat is one of those İstanbul districts that line the Golden Horn. Traditionally Balat had always been a Jewish quarter and some Jews did indeed still inhabit its ancient winding streets. But in recent years new people had come into the area – migrants from Anatolia who had come to the city in search of work, and also a small number of artists. This latter group included İkmen's informant, whom he was visiting now. A tall and very beautiful middle-aged woman, she had lived and worked in Balat for some years.

'I imagine you've heard that Hüseyin Altun, the beggar king of Edirnekapı, has died,' İkmen said after one of the gypsy's many daughters had given him tea.

The gypsy offered İkmen a fierce Birinci cigarette, which he took with gratitude, and then lit one up for herself.

'Many of our people used to live in Edirnekapı,' she said after a pause. 'Long ago now. But I still keep an eye on what happens over there. Hüseyin was not one of our own, but I knew him. He was a beggar, a thief, a drug addict, some said an abuser of children . . .'

'Do you know a lieutenant of Hüseyin's, one of his ex-street kids, Aslan?'

'Yes, I know Aslan,' she said. And then she leaned forward in order to look intently into İkmen's eyes. 'He's nowhere to be found now Hüseyin has gone.'

'I don't suppose you—'

'Know where he is?' she said, and then she sighed. 'No. What I do know, however, İkmen, is that you move in pursuit of Yusuf Kaya, the escaped convict.'

'A man from the east,' İkmen replied. 'Not one of your kind.'

'A dangerous and cruel man,' the gypsy said. 'Did Hüseyin Altun have any connection to him?'

'We think that Kaya may have dealt drugs to Altun. But there is no established connection between the two except via Aslan who, it is said, once went to Kaya's apartment in Tarlabaşı.'

The gypsy smoked hard, nodding her head as she did so.

'Since Yusuf Kaya escaped from Kartal Prison,' İkmen said, 'this city has experienced a lot of death. Two police officers and one prison guard were killed at the Cerrahpaşa, Hüseyin Altun was stabbed to death, Aslan has disappeared and just this morning I was called to a crime scene that may or may not have a connection to Yusuf Kaya. I believe it is possible that Hüseyin, Aslan or both of them may have aided Kaya's flight from the city. It is further my opinion that our man from the east is systematically eliminating witnesses to his escape as he goes along. That is certainly how it is looking here in the city.'

Out beyond Gaziantep, according to Süleyman, things were rather different. But then not only were the people out there

Yusuf Kaya's own but none of them, so far, had even hinted at catching sight of the escaped convict.

'I have never heard anything about Aslan being involved with Yusuf Kaya,' the gypsy said. 'He traded with drug dealers all over the city, Beyoğlu and beyond. That was just part of the job that Hüseyin had given him.' She sighed. 'What I do know is that Aslan left, went missing or whatever you call it, on the day that Yusuf Kaya escaped from prison.'

'And . . .'

'And the rumour is,' she held up one finger in order to silence him, 'that Aslan made a bid for power and that it was he who killed Hüseyin. That he did it at that time would seem to be coincidental.'

İkmen eyed the gypsy narrowly. 'But you and I, we don't hold unquestioningly with coincidence? Do we?'

'If Aslan did indeed make a bid for power,' she said, 'then it failed. Hüseyin's kids have scattered. His other lieutenant, Rahmi, runs a few of them, but he is weak . . . İkmen, the truth as I hear it is that Aslan is still alive but no one knows where he is. It is said he and Hüseyin were alone together the night Kaya escaped, the night when Aslan disappeared. With Hüseyin dead, who can say what truly occurred?'

'Look, can you describe this Aslan to me?' İkmen asked. 'My Sergeant Farsakoğlu who over the years has had, on occasion, some dealings with Hüseyin Altun's kids cannot reliably do that because she's seen him very infrequently. We did speak to his Bulgarian girlfriend yesterday but we didn't manage to get to what her lover looked like because the bloody kid gave us the slip!'

The gypsy smiled. 'Poor İkmen, the street people have been giving you a hard time! Aslan is, from my recollection, a man who must now be about thirty. I wish I could say that he had some sort of distinguishing mark or feature, but I can't. He has straight black hair, is of average height, weight . . . I've seen him maybe twice as an adult.'

'You can't say where or who . . .'

'No.' She smiled again.

'No.'

He asked her whether she knew anything about the meaning of the flower tattoo he'd seen on the body of the young man at Mr Lale's house in Zeyrek. She said that she didn't. What he described didn't have any meaning for her.

And so, the business of their conversation apparently over, they chatted of this and that until İkmen finally left about half an hour later. Before he went, however, he did have one last question to ask.

As he stood on the doorstep of her ramshackle studio, he said, 'Have you ever heard of a Turk called Black Storm? A fighter by all accounts. Had some memorable bouts amongst your own men up in Sulukule.'

'One of you fighting one of us in Sulukule and winning?'

'Apparently so.' His son Bekir had always been full of stories even as a child. He feared and hoped in equal measure that his incarnation as Black Storm was one of them.

Various small and dirty children, some of them the gypsy's own, watched as she burst into laughter.

'Oh, İkmen, that is priceless!' she said. 'That one of your men would beat one of our men in Sulukule? God help us, but that is just impossible! Impossible!'

'Yes, but Black—'

'Black Storm?' She laughed again. 'Black Storm? İkmen, I've never heard of such a person. If such a person did exist and did beat one of our men in a fight in our own quarter then you can rest assured that Black Storm is no longer in the land of the living now!'

And then she closed the door on him. İkmen walked back towards Zeyrek, closing his mind to at least one of Bekir's stories as he did so.

Edibe Taner still hadn't answered Süleyman's question about just exactly who a Master of Sharmeran was or what such a person did. But when they got back into the city of Mardin, rather than drop him off at the police station along with Selahattin, she took Süleyman to one of Mardin's two markets, the Revaklı Bazaar. Various tradespeople work at their chosen crafts in this area, including coppersmiths. It was to one of their workshops that Edibe Taner took Mehmet Süleyman now.

'We have a saying here on the Ocean,' she said as she led him towards a truly old, dingy and blackened portico, 'that he who owns patience will own Egypt.' She smiled. 'I think that you have earned your place in the land of the pyramids.'

There was no sign up on the wall to tell the world who the hectic little coppersmith's workshop belonged to. But two things were immediately apparent. First, there was a large brazier in front of the shop on top of which was a pot Süleyman recognised as a very large mirra coffee pot. Second, almost every copper artefact on view was characterised by the image of the Sharmeran. Hanging from the columns at the entrance to the shop, the wares provided a bright and shiny frame to the almost impenetrable darkness within. It was in fact only when Süleyman really looked hard that he noticed that there was another brazier or fire right at the back of the premises. He only saw that a living being was in the shop when Taner called into the blackness.

'Papa? Papa, it is Edibe. Are you there, Papa?'

A few seconds later a small, soot-stained man appeared. Of indeterminate age, he wore a thick canvas apron over what looked like one of the oldest brown suits in the world. When he saw Edibe Taner, his large mouth split open into a smile revealing teeth the colour of black treacle.

'Edibe!' He walked forward with his arms outstretched. The normally upright and stately Edibe Taner crouched down into her father's embrace and then bent down even lower to kiss both his hands. Just as she had done with Musa Saatçi, Edibe Taner was apparently putting aside her detached, professional persona once again

'Edibe.' The coppersmith went on to speak to his daughter in one of those languages that were completely unknown to Süleyman. Whether it was Arabic or Aramaic he couldn't even begin to know. When they had finished, the Mardin police-woman introduced Süleyman to her father.

'Inspector Süleyman, this is my father, Seçkin Taner,' she said. 'Papa, this gentleman is the policeman from İstanbul I have been working with.'

No handshakes were exchanged. Just the polite bow of one eastern gentleman to another. Süleyman was not entirely comfortable with this, but he smiled anyway and said, 'Sir, it is a pleasure. It is an honour to work with your daughter.'

Seçkin Taner took these compliments with a straight but contented face and then invited his daughter and Süleyman to join him in his shop. To Süleyman's relief, he appeared to speak fluent Turkish, even if what he said next filled the İstanbullu with horror.

'You must take mirra, Inspector,' he said.

'Papa's mirra is the finest on the Ocean!' his daughter enthused. 'You will like *this*, Inspector. I know you will.'

'Oh. That's nice. Thank you,' he replied without enthusiasm.

The coppersmith pushed several plates along the bench at the back of his shop to make space for them to sit. Now that he was closer, Süleyman could see that the fire was enclosed by a low, dark wall whose top was cluttered with what looked like branding irons of various sorts.

'The smith's forge,' Seçkin Taner said by way of explanation. Then, smiling to reveal those heavily stained teeth yet again, he added, 'Copper like any metal must always be coaxed into position by fire. Please sit down, Inspector.'

With one eye on Edibe Taner, who appeared to be doing something worrying with the mirra pot and a handful of not such small cups, Süleyman sat. Seçkin Taner sat down next to him and said, 'Now, my daughter tells me you want to know about the Sharmeran.'

'Yes, although to be truthful, sir, it is your role as what your daughter describes as a Master of Sharmeran that really interests me,' Süleyman replied. 'Unless I am mistaken, this would seem to be some sort of social duty?'

Seçkin Taner put a restraining hand on Süleyman's thigh. 'I will come to that. First things first.' He picked up a large plate with the serpent image on it and said, 'This here is the Sharmeran, my mistress. Queen of snakes and protectress of Mardin. Back in the dark times before the Prophet Muhammed, blessings and peace be upon him, before even the Prophet Isa of the Christians, there was a young boy who was tricked by his friends into getting lost in the caves that cover the mountains around here. In trying to find his way out the boy only succeeded in getting himself deeper and deeper inside the mountains until eventually . . .'

'He found himself in a cave full of poisonous snakes,' Edibe Taner said as she passed a slightly reddening Süleyman a cup of steaming mirra. 'He called upon his god to help him but still the snakes writhed at his feet and snapped at his ankles. Just as the boy had given up all hope a strange figure came into view . . .'

'The Sharmeran!' Seçkin Taner clapped his small hands in delight. 'Queen of the snakes! She ordered her children to leave the boy alone and then, because she is a good and tender-hearted goddess, she told the boy she would show him how to get out of the caves and find his way home.'

His daughter took a large gulp of mirra from her cup before continuing the story. 'Of course the Sharmeran in her great wisdom made this conditional on the boy's promising not to reveal her location to anyone. A goddess can have only certain human visitors, you understand.'

Süleyman smiled in what he hoped was not a hugely embarrassed fashion.

'The boy promised. But he was faithless!' Seçkin Taner said with regret in his voice. 'The sultan of the city as it was then was dying. On the advice of his vizier he had offered the hand of his daughter as well as half the kingdom to anyone who could tell him where the Sharmeran lived.' He leaned towards Süleyman suddenly, and whispered, 'The meat of the Sharmeran can give eternal life! The sultan wanted to catch her and eat her!'

'Which of course, with the boy's help, he did,' Edibe said. 'Or rather he ate some of her flesh. The sultan's men only managed to cut a small amount of flesh from her because she fought them off. The Sharmeran was wounded, but she recovered. She escaped and lives still, unlike the sultan.'

Süleyman frowned. 'Yes, but you . . .'

'Young man.' Seçkin Taner smiled and patted the policeman's knee once again. 'Do you not think that if the Sharmeran can bestow life, she can also take it away? The Sharmeran may offer a man her flesh to give him life. But if he takes it for himself, he will be doomed. The sultan died as did the faithless boy, as do all who abuse our Sharmeran. She, however, lives still both in the mountains and in our hearts.'

'My father makes representations of the Sharmeran,' Edibe Taner said, smiling at her father. 'She allows certain people to do this. My father is a Master of Sharmeran because my grandfather also had that honour and his father before him. Father knows and loves his Sharmeran with all his heart.'

There were some parts of this story that could be interpreted as pure examples of faith, of love in the heart of something divine and yet unseen. But Süleyman had the distinct impression that nice smart Inspector Taner and her father were talking about a being that actually existed in the flesh. That, clearly, had to be a misunderstanding on his part.

Seçkin Taner leaned towards Süleyman once again and said, 'I also, alone but for one other, know where my mistress lives. That is why I am the Master of Sharmeran. That is why people respect a mere coppersmith whose father could not either read or write.'

So there was no misunderstanding after all. Süleyman felt quite cold. Edibe Taner, seeing the slightly chilled pallor on his features, fetched him a fresh, hot cup of mirra to help revive his colour.

'Only Gabriel Saatçi knows the secret too, but he is the Sharmeran's own true child,' Seçkin Taner continued. 'The Sharmeran's children are bound to protect her from faithless humanity. Thirty-five years ago, by accident he says, Gabriel walked into the Sharmeran's cave and was bitten on every part of his body. But he didn't die because the Sharmeran and the Prophet Isa together ordained that Gabriel should be a beacon for mankind. A living saint.'

'Ah, Gabriel, whose father—'

'Papa, I took Inspector Süleyman to meet Uncle Musa. I thought, because he is an outsider, he might encourage Musa to talk. But nothing happened.'

'Nothing would,' Seçkin Taner said. 'Musa has no control over Gabriel. The boy will return when God and the Sharmeran will it and not before.'

Süleyman frowned. It was a mild expression of what he was feeling within. This conversation was, he thought, rather like several he had had over the years with various wilder members of Çetin İkmen's family. In the realm of the unseen he was, he knew, out of his depth. The only way forward was to attach as much of this fantasy as possible to something that might be provable and observable.

'Was Gabriel Saatçi treated by a doctor?'

'Of course,' Seçkin Taner said. 'The doctor said that he should have died.'

'So if Gabriel is missing, could it not be that he is with the . . . in the cave where you believe the Sharmeran—'

'You think I haven't looked?' the coppersmith interrupted. 'I am the only other human who knows the location of that cave, and I can tell you that unless my mistress is hiding Gabriel for some reason, he is not there.'

'So where do you think he might be?'

'I don't know.'

Süleyman turned to the coppersmith's daughter. If any progress was to be made these people needed some reality imposed upon them. 'Musa Saatçi is of the opinion that everything will be all right when his son returns.'

'Yes,' she said. 'When Gabriel comes back there will be a resolution.'

'But what if Gabriel doesn't return?' Süleyman said.

'What if Musa or Gabriel or both of them *are* terrorists? What—'

'Gabriel cannot be a terrorist. He is a living saint,' Seçkin Taner said. He was beginning, Süleyman could tell, to grow agitated with the man from İstanbul's seeming lack of understanding about his world. 'That just isn't possible!'

'But what if it were possible?'

'It isn't!'

There was a pause. While Seçkin Taner inwardly railed, Süleyman looked into the face of his daughter Edibe and thought that he saw just a very little seed of confusion on her features. Not that she said anything apart from simply reiterating, softly, her father's beliefs and position.

'Edibe, you should take your friend away now,' Seçkin Taner said, getting up and turning back to face his forge once again.

Edibe Taner, obviously embarrassed now, first shrugged at Süleyman and then said to her father, 'Papa, Inspector Süleyman has not come here to help us find Gabriel. He is here to find Yusuf Kaya. I took him to meet Uncle Musa only because I am fearful for him. To be accused of terrorist offences is such a serious thing. I thought that talking to an outsider might help him.'

Seçkin Taner turned to face his daughter with fury on his features. 'You of all people should know that when Gabriel returns is beyond our control! No outsider or anyone else can change that!' He turned back to his forge and murmured again, 'You should know that.'

'Yes, Papa.' She lowered her eyes just for a second and then, moving out of the shop, she flicked her head towards Süleyman, indicating that he should follow her. 'We must go now. We must work.'

As he left, Süleyman saw Seçkin Taner's shoulders shrug. He saw hurt on Edibe Taner's face as well as that slight suggestion of confusion he had seen earlier. Maybe, he thought, staying in the mythical past was easy for a Master of Sharmeran, maybe that was what being a Master of Sharmeran really meant. But being the daughter of one as well as a serving police officer was, he could see, far more complex. What he could only now appreciate too was why Edibe Taner had resisted his questions about the 'Master of Sharmeran' appellation for so long. He imagined she felt that men from İstanbul could not be expected to understand such things. In the case of this particular man, she was right.

Chapter 11

The nurse had of course been quite right to call the patient's doctor to his bedside. Ramazan Eren, the prison guard, the only survivor from Yusuf Kaya's bloody break from the hospital, looked as if he might be starting to regain consciousness. Dr Eldem, his physician, came immediately. The nurse stayed for a moment while the doctor looked at the various monitors that surrounded the supine body of the guard. He was as she had found him, gently murmuring, his eyelids fluttering open to reveal bruised, jaundiced eyes and then closing again just before she left. Dr Eldem was, after all, quite capable of dealing with whatever might happen next and, if he needed help, he could always ring to summon other doctors and nurses on the unit. In the meantime, as Dr Eldem himself had told her, there was another coma patient who needed turning. She didn't need telling twice. She'd seen enough pressure sores on coma patients in her time to make her terrified at the thought of such abominations on *her* ward. The doctor also told her not to tell the police guard at the entrance to the ward about what might be going on. Ramazan Eren may or may not be waking up. There was no need to tell the world about it yet.

Once she had left the room, Dr Eldem eyed the patient Ramazan Eren and his seeming struggles to regain consciousness with some distaste. After a few seconds had passed, and totally at odds with received hospital guidance, Dr Eldem took his mobile phone out of his pocket and switched it on. He searched through the phone's directory until he came to the number that he wanted and then selected it. Just under a minute passed before the automatic answerphone clicked in. Dr Eldem snorted impatiently.

'Where are you? It's Eldem,' he said flatly. 'He's awake. What the hell do you want me to do about him?'

The afternoon had been spent preparing for the activities of the night to come. Edibe Taner had had to obtain permission from her superiors to search the as yet unknown Kaya house down on the plains. If the woman, Kaya's second wife, was indeed an American citizen, she wanted to avoid any sort of diplomatic gaffe. Once permission had been given she was obliged to construct a team to carry out the operation. This she created entirely from officers not native to the area, including Mehmet Süleyman. Together in her car on their way to Dara, Süleyman finally plucked up enough courage to tackle his colleague on the subject of her father.

'Inspector, I did not mean to cause offence to your father,' he said, looking at her strong profile silhouetted against the fading sun as it dipped behind the mountains. As usual she was driving, fast.

Edibe Taner smiled. 'It's all right,' she replied. 'I understand. You probably find us here in Mardin very strange. I don't imagine that personal relationships with snake goddesses are common occurrences in İstanbul.'

'No.'

'What you have to understand is that Mardin is one of those places where the differences between states of existence are small.'

Mehmet Süleyman didn't comment. This could, he felt, very quickly turn into one of those conversations that he sometimes had with Çetin İkmen: worrying conversations about the nature of reality, if indeed such a thing even existed.

'My father has a relationship with the Sharmeran. One day I too will do so. I must be introduced to her soon, as my father is old now. When he dies I will take his place,' Inspector Taner said. 'That said, Inspector, with my "modern" head on I can think that utterly impossible. Maybe my father experiences some sort of delusion or hallucination when he goes into that cave, I can think. Maybe what he calls his relationship with the Sharmeran is in fact just a series of internal musings in his head. But to him and to the many other people round here who claim to have seen or heard the Sharmeran moving across the Ocean in the night, it is very real and it does bring comfort, joy and reassurance of the continuance of our lives here. I'll be honest, I believe in the Sharmeran with my whole soul. I am a police officer working for my country, which I love. But I am also convinced that when I am a Master of Sharmeran, my mistress will come to me. The Sharmeran is *our* deity; that we alone can see her is only right. As for Gabriel Saatçi . . .' She shrugged. 'I am sorry that I got you into all that. It was desperation on my part. I know that those weapons in Musa Saatçi's house are nothing to do with him. But his insistence upon not saying a word until Gabriel comes back is driving me insane!'

'Why do you think that Gabriel has gone missing?'

'I don't know. I wish I did. Gabriel is a . . . well, he is a friend, and . . . None of the monks at St Sobo's have a clue. He just left.' Very briefly she took her eyes off the road ahead and looked at him. 'But know this, Gabriel Saatçi is no fake. I saw him, all those years ago, his body covered in bites, his mind half mad from snake venom. His survival was a miracle.'

She looked back at the road again then and briefly flashed the truck behind which contained the five other officers who had been assigned to the operation.

'This is where we turn off,' she said.

'Right.' Although Süleyman was thinking about the upcoming mission and feeling nervous about what they might find beyond Dara – after all, in this part of the country seemingly straight-forward scenarios had in the past turned out to be terrorist traps – he was also still concerned with issues supernatural. 'So, Inspector, would you say that Mardin and its legends are by way of being a sort of halfway house between what I under-stand as reality – the present, the concrete – and some sort of other consciousness, echoing back to the past, maybe?'

'My city, Inspector Süleyman, is certainly a place that at the moment owes much to the past,' Taner said. 'Albeit a rather fragile past at times.'

Süleyman, recalling what the old woman in the Zeytounian house had said to him, murmured the phrase she had used. 'The Cobweb World.'

'The Cobweb World? Where did you hear that?' Taner said.

'That old woman who served us dinner back in Gaziantep used it to describe the just barely living world of the past in which she exists,' Süleyman said. 'I think she either knew or deduced that I am descended from an Ottoman family – one doesn't get a lot more redundant than that – and applied it to me. She said that Mardin was part of the Cobweb World too and that if I went there I would understand it.' He smiled. 'If only that were true!'

There was a silence that went on just a little bit too long to be natural. Süleyman turned to Taner, whose eyes were fixed firmly and now grimly upon the road ahead.

'Forget the woman in Gaziantep,' she said. 'People say she is mad. Maddened by such thoughts.'

'She related her world of the past directly to me,' Süleyman said.

'But your Ottoman past is just that,' Taner replied. 'You cannot disappear back into it. You can only feel its sorrow. You are not like us, Inspector. You do not live half in and half out of different worlds. Your lack of understanding is quite normal.'

'That is not what the old woman said,' Süleyman countered.

But Taner didn't answer him.

Ayşe Farsakoğlu was accustomed to the fact that her boss, Çetin İkmen, often worked long into the night. Mehmet Süleyman was less inclined to operate in this fashion and so İzzet Melik found that he was rather more reluctant than his other two colleagues when he finally joined them at just before eight p.m. Not that İkmen was making any of them work within the grim surroundings of the police station. Because the evening, though cool, was very pleasant, he had chosen to meet in one of the tea gardens on Sultanahmet Square. Opposite the incongruously Gothic fountain that had been donated to the city by Kaiser Wilhelm II just before the First World War, the tea garden in question was famed for the fact that it offered its customers water pipes. By the time İzzet joined them, both İkmen and Ayşe were very happily smoking on the mouthpieces of cloth-covered tubes connected to large, ornate water containers.

'My late father used to smoke the straight tobacco, tömbeki, whenever he had a narghile,' İkmen said as he let a large lungful of smoke out on a sigh. 'He would consider my only being able to stand the apple-flavoured tobacco indicative of a lack of a sense of adventure. Poor Father.' He looked up and saw İzzet Melik standing in front of him. 'Ah, İzzet!' He patted the carpet-covered cushions on the bench beside him and said, 'Sit down and tell us what you have been doing. Would you like a narghile?'

İzzet Melik said that he would, with molasses-flavoured tobacco, and then he sat down. Ayşe Farsakoğlu, with whom İzzet had been enamoured for a number of years now, gave the slightly rough-round-the-edges officer a small, tight smile. She was fond of İzzet but, in spite of her single status, she was not fond of him in *that* way. İkmen called for another narghile as well as three glasses of tea and then began to quiz Süleyman's sergeant who, earlier in the day, he had given a very important job.

'How did it go at the mortuary?' he asked once the waiter had left to fulfil their order.

'I took the consultant orthopaedic surgeon from the Cerrahpaşa with me and he identified the body as that of Faruk Öz,' İzzet Melik said. 'According to the consultant, Öz was a very good worker.'

İkmen sighed. 'So now we know for certain that at least one of the nurses who went missing directly after Yusuf Kaya's escape is dead.'

'Dr Sarkissian confirmed that cause of death was loss of blood due to severance of the carotid artery. Stabbed in the neck with what the doctor reckons was a straight-bladed knife,' İzzet said.

Ayşe Farsakoğlu puffed on her narghile and then said, 'Time of death?'

İzzet shrugged. 'Doctor can't be certain. The body's been in plastic and under the ground for some time. Some days, he reckons.'

'Which could mean,' İkmen said, 'that he was killed at or around the time of Yusuf Kaya's escape.'

'If we take it as read that Kaya or his agents are killing those who have assisted him in order to confound our investigation,' Ayşe said.

'Indeed.' İkmen frowned. 'Well, whatever may be the truth we will have to get Murat Lole in and ask him some questions.'

'Of course, the person we really need to speak to is İsak Mardin,' Ayşe said. 'But . . .'

'Mardin is still missing,' İkmen said. 'But, of course, that Öz's body should turn up in Mardin's garden in Zeyrek cannot be, I think, coincidental. Zeyrek is a long way from Öz's home in Gaziosmanpaşa. Not that they were friends or even knew each other, according to Murat Lole.'

'Lole denies that he was friendly with Mardin too, doesn't he?' İzzet asked as the waiter turned up with his narghile and tea for all three of them.

'He does,' İkmen said as he took the narghile from the young waiter and indicated that he would set it up for İzzet himself. He wanted to get on with their discussion without further interruption. 'But Mardin, we think, is originally from the east and may very well have some sort of connection to Yusuf Kaya. He gave a hospital in Şanlıurfa as reference for his job at the Cerrahpaşa. But that was a lie that the then director of the hospital, the one who killed himself, apparently colluded in. With the help of the current administration I have discovered that there is no record of İsak Mardin working at any hospital in Şanlıurfa.'

'So Mardin could have been a plant?' Ayşe said. 'Someone sent in to be part of Kaya's escape plan?'

'Yes.' İkmen puffed on his narghile and then said, 'Lole

and Öz were at the Cerrahpaşa some time before Kaya was sent to prison. So the likelihood of their being plants is slim. Kaya wasn't even in prison when they started nursing there. But Mardin, who has not been at the hospital for long, could have recruited them when he took up his post. Nurses don't earn much; the offer of big money could have swayed any dedication to their profession. Maybe Mardin and Öz took Kaya back to Zeyrek after the incident at the hospital and then one or other of them killed Öz in order to silence him.'

'What about Lole?' Ayşe asked.

İkmen shrugged. 'I don't know. Maybe he's part of it, maybe he isn't. There were only, we think, two nurses involved in the actual escape, remember.'

'Yes, but could he be in danger if Mardin is still out there?'

'*If* Mardin is out there,' İkmen said. 'Maybe he's lying dead somewhere too.' And then, turning to İzzet, he asked, 'What about forensics on Öz's body?'

'They're working on it, sir,' İzzet replied. 'But nothing obvious yet. However, I did find out what that tattoo he had on his arm was.'

'Oh?'

'It's the flower of the wormwood plant,' İzzet said.

İkmen frowned.

'It's the stuff that gives absinthe its potentially lethal effect.'

'I know what wormwood is, İzzet,' İkmen said. 'I'm just trying to imagine what, if anything, it might mean. I went to see my gypsy earlier today and asked her about tattoos. The gypsies are rather fond of them, as you know. But a wormwood flower?' He frowned again. 'I've never heard of anyone in the city, not even the gypsies, being involved in the production of absinthe. La Fée Verte has never, to my knowledge, been one of their particular passions.'

'La Fée Verte?'

'It means "the Green Fairy",' İkmen said. 'It's what absinthe was called during its heyday in nineteenth-century Paris. The Green Fairy was a beautiful and addictive mistress and is implicated in the deaths of numerous French artists.'

'My grandmother used to put wormwood leaves in with the winter blankets when she put them away for the summer,' Ayşe said. 'Wormwood has a strong smell which helps to keep the moths away. There was some sort of stomach remedy which used to contain wormwood too, but I don't know what that was called. I know they used to grow wormwood near her village.'

'Where was that?' İkmen asked.

Ayşe shrugged. 'I don't really know,' she said. 'Out east. There was some sort of trouble – when isn't there out there? Anyway, my grandparents moved first to Afyon where my father was born and then here in about 1930. But I can still remember my grandmother using wormwood in her remedies and laying the leaves amongst the blankets. The horrible smell tends to stay with you.'

'Mm.' İkmen puffed thoughtfully. 'Murat Lole.'

The other two looked at him for several moments before, at last, İzzet Melik spoke.

'Sir,' he said as he put the mouthpiece of his narghile down and then drained his tea, 'shouldn't we pick him up? For his own safety if for no other reason?'

Çetin İkmen smoked without comment.

'Sir,' Ayşe said, 'I think that Sergeant Melik has a point. Whether Lole is innocent or guilty we do need to get to him, and soon.'

After yet another pause, İkmen nodded sagely. 'I agree,' he said. 'With one little difference.'

167

Ayşe and İzzet looked at him questioningly.

'If', İkmen said, 'Murat Lole is in league in some way with Yusuf Kaya, maybe if we make him think he is in no danger from us he might lead us to some very valuable information. I say we have him watched, followed day and night. That way we can learn something about what he is doing as well as providing some level of protection too. What do you think about that?'

Neither Edibe Taner nor Mehmet Süleyman nor indeed any of the officers with them knew exactly what was behind the front door of the house outside Dara. They were all well aware that they could very easily be walking into a trap. The PKK had been quiet for some time in and around Mardin, but Süleyman's informant about this house had been a Kurd. Then there was Hezbollah . . . How difficult would it be for one of their people to mislead a police investigation team into a trap?

Taner knocked with her fist on the ancient wooden door, which was covered in carved Armenian script. Civilisations had always met in this place of confluence. They also fought, died and sometimes, like the ancient Persians, disappeared completely.

'Police!' she called out, confident that she had carefully positioned three of her officers at the back and sides of the property. 'Open up!'

But not a sound came from either outside or inside the building. Instinctively, Süleyman looked down at the ground for any evidence of wiring. Soon Taner's officers would have to force the door and the man from İstanbul did not want any of them to fall foul of such a basic thing as a booby-trapped entrance.

As if reading his mind, Taner said, 'Don't worry, we won't force it unless we're sure it's OK.'

'Right.'

She took her gun out of her jacket pocket and smiled. 'But I guess we'd better get ready in case someone comes out—'

'What do you want?'

The door snapped open simultaneously with the sound of a man's voice. The man in question, a tall young individual carrying an AK-47 assault rifle, regarded the police team with what looked like fury.

'Police,' Taner reiterated as she moved her gun from her right hand to her left and took out her ID card.

'What do you want?'

Taner, frowning at the man now, said, 'Aren't you—'

'Oh, stop playing silly games like a little boy pretending to be a soldier!'

The voice was female, it was annoyed, it came from somewhere behind the man at the door and it spoke in English. Taner stepped into the house and the 'little boy' in front of her stood to one side, suddenly looking, in spite of his weapon, really rather sheepish. Süleyman followed.

The woman in front of them was not exactly beautiful. But she was tall, slim and angular and had the most startling cascade of thick red hair hanging down her back. She was, Süleyman reckoned, probably somewhere in her mid-thirties. When he, Taner and the two officers behind them had all crossed the threshold, they'd seen that the woman was surrounded by a group of heavily armed local men. Seemingly they had been waiting for them. The woman, when she spoke again, did so once more in English. She had an American accent. For a while Taner, Süleyman and the others assumed it was the only language available to her.

'We always have at least one man a kilometre in front of the house,' she said in what Süleyman could now tell was probably an east coast, New England type of accent. 'The house is not accessible by road from any other direction. We knew you were coming. What do you want?'

Edibe Taner cleared her throat. She knew, by sight at least, all of the men who surrounded the woman. They'd passed her on the streets of Mardin before. There was one man in particular with whom she knew she had shared polite greeting in the past. But not now. Now all of them stared down the officers with snarls on their faces. 'I have papers to search this house,' she said in English, holding up her authority to search for all to see.

'Search this house?' the woman said as she just very slightly smiled. 'Whatever for?'

'We think this house is property of a prisoner who escaped,' Taner said.

'Oh, you mean my husband? Yusuf?' The woman laughed. Then, turning very pointedly towards Süleyman, she said, 'I assume you are in charge—'

'No,' he interrupted. 'Inspector Taner is lead officer here. My name is Inspector Süleyman. I come from İstanbul.'

The woman raised her eyebrows. 'Of course. It was you who arrested my husband.'

'I put Yusuf Kaya in prison for what should have been his whole life,' Süleyman said. 'I saw first hand, madam, what your husband was capable of.' Her face quickly clouded.

'What is your name?' Inspector Taner asked.

The woman looked her straight in the eye and said, 'Hürrem.'

The men around her, though armed, shifted nervously. Süleyman hoped that none of them lost their nerve and accidentally let off the odd automatic magazine. No one in the house would survive.

'Your American name,' Taner persisted.

'My—'

'You are a foreign person,' Taner said. 'I must see your passport.'

'I don't know that I have it to hand. I—'

'Just tell us your name for the moment,' Süleyman cut in. He was getting tired of this woman's game-playing and wanted to get on with the search. While all this was going on, Kaya could be trying to slip out of the building. 'What is it?'

The woman sighed. 'My passport is in the name of Elizabeth Smith, the name I was given at birth.'

'Thank you,' Süleyman said. 'So, Miss Smith, I assume that all of these guns you have here are registered?'

'But of course.' She smiled.

'Excellent.' Süleyman bowed his head slightly and then turned to Taner and said in Turkish, 'Let's go through this place.'

The armed men in front of them moved forward as if to try to mount a challenge, but Elizabeth Smith told them, in Turkish, to put their weapons down. Continuing now in Turkish, she told the officers, 'We don't, after all, want to have any sort of accident, do we? Yusuf my husband isn't here. Search anywhere and everywhere you like.'

'You can speak Turkish,' Edibe Taner said.

'Well, of course I can,' Elizabeth Smith responded acidly. 'Your country is my country now. I have adopted it. I said before, do your search. Get on with it.'

And so they did. For the secret love nest of a wealthy gangster, Yusuf Kaya's house was very sparse. It was traditional too. There were no beds here, just rolled-up mattresses. No apparent concessions to someone who at least sounded like an educated American lady. Outside, empty outhouses gave forth nothing, as did the large cellar beneath the building.

'When did you last see Yusuf Kaya?' Taner asked the American as their search was coming to a close just over two hours after it had begun.

'I saw my husband at his trial in İstanbul,' Elizabeth Smith replied. She then added sneeringly, 'Only the once. I went with your cousin, Zeynep. Yusuf's other wife.'

But Edibe Taner betrayed no obvious emotion. She had deduced some time before that her cousin and Kaya's mother and probably all of his family had to know about this Elizabeth Smith. On some level at least they obviously told her things about themselves, like who they were related to. One of the men guarding the American rolled up one of his sleeves, revealing the wormwood flower tattoo on his arm. The scorpion within Edibe Taner wanted to hiss with disdain. But she was not in this house to pursue old clan rivalries. Besides, in her position both as a police officer and as the daughter of a Master of Sharmeran she had to be above all that. After all, her own family, if reluctantly, had allowed her cousin Zeynep's marriage to a hated wormwood.

'Your husband was handed down a life sentence by the court in İstanbul,' Süleyman said to the woman as he looked around the hall in case there was any piece of evidence present that he might have missed. 'I personally requested that he serve a minimum of thirty years. Why do you stay? Your husband is never going to be able to live with you.'

Elizabeth Smith smiled again. 'But Yusuf is out of prison now.'

'Oh, yes,' Süleyman said. 'And I do hope, Miss Smith—'

'Mrs Kaya, please.'

'Mrs Kaya,' he said with some irony in his voice, 'that you did not assist his escape. Because if you did . . .'

'I would spend a very long time in a Turkish jail. Inspector Süleyman,' she said, 'I stay because I have made this place my home. I have nowhere to go back in the States. My husband has left me well provided for here. I have money, a home, I am guarded, I have friends . . . Also I can visit Yusuf. My home town, Boston, is a very long way from Kartal Prison, İstanbul.'

'Mrs Kaya,' Edibe Taner joined in, 'this house is very empty. With your guards you are six people. But there is very little here. Are you going somewhere?'

'No.' Elizabeth Smith shrugged. 'I live simply. What can I say? Besides, it's Lent. Christians don't adorn their homes until after Easter. It's not the custom, is it?'

'You are a Christian, Mrs Kaya?'

'No, but a few of the men are. And I was raised a Christian. Now I attend the Suriani services when I can. Because that's what we do in the Tur Abdin, isn't it? We all join in with and respect each other's beliefs. Or we should. My husband is of course a Muslim and has Muslim children by Zeynep. But he respects other religions and beliefs.'

'My recollection of your husband, Mrs Kaya,' Süleyman said, 'is of a man not overly given to religion. And as for this area being free from factional strife . . . Why do you think that the army is here, Miss Smith? Why do you think the Turkish Republic guards places of worship out here?'

The room went silent as the rough men who guarded this woman looked at the guns at their feet with relish. They then looked at Süleyman with equal homicidal fervour. But under the gaze of the small troop of police officers, none of them moved.

'Mrs Kaya,' Edibe Taner said after a moment, 'please do not leave the environs of Dara.'

'Ah, but the Easter service in Mar—'

'You may attend church in Mardin on Easter Sunday,' Taner said. 'In fact I will be there to make sure that you can go. But otherwise stay where you are, where we can easily see you. Oh, and I will need your mobile phone number too. I assume you have one of those.'

Elizabeth Smith said nothing then until Taner and Süleyman were nearly at her front door. Suddenly and angrily she burst out, 'I've done nothing wrong!'

'Haven't you?' Süleyman turned to look her straight in the eye. 'Madam, how much do you know about this country?'

The American woman frowned. 'Why?'

'Did you meet your husband shortly before you married or were you together for some time prior to that?'

'I lived in Turkey five years before I met Yusuf,' Elizabeth Smith replied. 'I was teaching English in İstanbul. I met Yusuf in İstanbul. I was with him for a while, you know.'

Süleyman resisted the temptation to ask her how she, an apparently decent American teacher, met a local drug dealer. There had been no drugs found in the house and so, on the face of it, this woman probably wasn't a junkie. There was something else, however. 'Do you understand where Turkish law stands on the subject of polygamy?'

'I know it is illegal, but—'

'Absolutely,' Süleyman said. 'It is illegal and yet you—'

'Oh, for heaven's sake!' she said, slipping into English. 'People out here don't worry about that. They—'

'Well then people out here should worry!' Süleyman replied, also in English. 'Polygamy is against Turkish law. You, madam, will not leave this area until this matter, if not the return of your "husband", is resolved.'

He then turned back to follow Edibe Taner and the other

officers out of the door. Once out in the cold night air, he breathed deeply in order to settle his nerves. The officers who had been patrolling the outside of the house came over to join them.

'Nothing here tonight,' Taner said with a look of disappointment on her face. She then turned to Selahattin, who had been searching through the outhouses, and said, 'We'll keep the house under surveillance.'

'Yes, Inspector.'

She told the men to get in the truck and head back towards the city. Just before she got in her car to follow on behind, Süleyman took hold of her arm, sniffed hard and then said, 'What's that smell? Sort of sharp and musty?'

Edibe Taner shook her head and assumed a lugubrious air. 'That's the smell of you being right,' she said.

Mehmet Süleyman frowned.

'You conjectured that Kaya's American woman was actually surrounded by wormwood.'

'She was, as you had predicted, surrounded by men of the wormwood clan.'

Edibe Taner smiled. 'She's also surrounded by actual wormwood too. It seems that the family grows it just behind the house. And the Kayas are traditionally growers of herbs. That smell you're getting is the reek of the plant itself. Horrible, isn't it?'

Chapter 12

Çetin İkmen didn't get round to making a call to Mehmet Süleyman until nearly midnight.

'I had to check first of all that Murat Lole was still alive before I assigned someone to watch him,' the older man said. 'Couldn't, after all, give over precious human resources to a dead man. Think of the waste!'

Süleyman, although now very sleepy, nevertheless smiled. Everything in the city was budget-related these days. It was almost as if the police department had been hijacked by a party of particularly sour and puritanical accountants.

'But anyway, Lole is under surveillance,' İkmen continued. 'All we have to do now is find nurse number three, İsak Mardin.'

'You say that the dead nurse, er . . .'

'Faruk Öz.'

'Faruk Öz had this wormwood tattoo on his bicep?'

'Yes. Which, if what you told me earlier, Mehmet, is so, could denote membership of Yusuf Kaya's clan.'

They'd talked about the 'wormwoods' as well as the 'scorpions' earlier on in their conversation. The possible tattoo connection between Faruk Öz and the city and people of Mardin, as well as actually to Yusuf Kaya, had been a revelation. Öz, it had been thought, had originated in the west; now this was open to doubt. That Öz had started working at the Cerrahpaşa well before Kaya's arrest meant that he could in no way have been a plant. But he had in all probability been a fortuitous resource with regard to Yusuf Kaya's escape.

'Öz may or may not have been his real name,' Süleyman said. 'But I'll speak to Inspector Taner. Maybe if you can e-mail us a photograph . . .'

'I'll certainly get Ayşe to e-mail you a photograph,' İkmen replied. Süleyman smiled. The older man, famously, didn't 'do' technology, and although he could use e-mail now he was still way off sending attachments and preferred that his sergeant did that. 'So you have discovered a second wife then, Mehmet. A woman, you say, surrounded by men with worm-wood tattoos.'

Lying on his narrow but comfortable monastic bed, Mehmet Süleyman wearily shook his head. 'Yes. Wormwood grows in the fields around the house where she lives, too. Stinks. She's an American, the woman. Educated, a teacher by profession, quite attractive. What can she possibly get out of a relationship with a man who is not only in prison but already married to someone else?'

'Exoticism? Adventure? That odd thing some women have for murderers? But then, Kaya has money . . .'

'True, but there's more to life than that. Kaya's a cretin,' Süleyman said. 'I'm sure this woman could do better.'

'Maybe she really does love him,' İkmen said gloomily. 'Maybe she is besotted by his bad boy image, or perhaps the strange myths that surround Mardin keep her inside what to me sounds like a harem-style fantasy.'

Süleyman shook his head and sighed. 'I know my own wife is half Irish, but she has always known this country. What is it with these western women? What brings them here, makes them cover themselves in some instances?'

'The irresistibility of the Turkish male,' İkmen said, and laughed. 'But seriously, maybe there is something here that they find chimes with them, a meaning they have not found back in the west.'

'They're running away.'

'Or running to something.' İkmen sighed. 'You know, when I was a boy, I often used to dream about working in a foreign country. I think it is a common fantasy amongst women and men.'

'Possibly.' Süleyman paused to light a cigarette and then said, 'Çetin, you know this snake goddess they have out here?'

'The Sharmeran. Yes, I know of it.'

'You know it's real to the point that people actually believe that they see the thing?'

'Some members of my family, as you know, Mehmet, come originally from Cappadocia,' İkmen replied. 'Land of strange volcanic shapes and eerie cave houses. Seemingly quite rational Cappadocians claim to see, from time to time, the famous local fairies.'

'Do they claim to be able to communicate directly with them?'

'Sometimes,' İkmen said. 'Your Inspector Taner – rather esoteric, is she?'

'Underneath the toughness, yes,' Süleyman said. 'Not that far underneath, as it happens. I respect her enormously, Çetin. She has a difficult time as both a woman and a police officer in this city. I think she's only really tolerated by the population because her father is a member of this scorpion clan and is a Master of Sharmeran. It's some sort of companion to the being, or . . . That said, I'm not always comfortable with her judgement when it comes to things of an unseen or spiritual nature.'

İkmen asked him what he meant and Süleyman told him about the Christian family known as Saatçi, about Musa the father and Gabriel the miracle son.

'Mm, that all sounds very eastern indeed,' İkmen said when he had heard his friend out. 'Have you spoken to any of the monks about this Gabriel?'

'I did speak briefly to Dr Sarkissian's friend, Brother Seraphim,' Süleyman said. 'All he told me was that Gabriel Saatçi was perfectly fine up until the arrest of his father. Apparently Gabriel went to see Musa at Mardin police station just after the arrest was made and the cops there, Taner included, let the two of them speak in private for a few minutes. Immediately afterwards Gabriel walked out of the city and seemingly disappeared.'

'My logical police sense would cause me to think that perhaps Gabriel is implicated in this crime,' İkmen said. 'After all, there are many and various terrorist groups operating in that area, aren't there? But if he is a real Suriani . . . Living saints rarely wage war, do they?'

'Musa the father believes that once Gabriel returns from his sojourn with God, the Sharmeran or whatever, he will make everything right.'

'On the basis that a man who can withstand the bite of a hundred vipers is probably pretty special . . .'

'But my point, Çetin, in all this is that there is a possibility that Musa Saatçi is guilty, that he *was* hiding arms in his house for one or other terrorist group,' Süleyman said. 'Inspector Taner however will not have it, not in any way. Musa is innocent, and although I know that Taner's mind is rather more open than that of most people around here, she is still basically a person who is totally comfortable with magical solutions.'

'Well, that's me too, Mehmet, as you . . .' İkmen's voice tailed off into silence.

Frowning, Süleyman said, 'Çetin?'

When the older man spoke again it was in a low whisper.

'I think that Bekir has just come back in,' he said. 'I need to speak to him.'

'Why?'

İkmen lowered his voice still further. 'Certain behaviours of his I am not happy with. Certain stories he has been telling that do not wholly accord with reality. In other words a replay, in part at least, of the behaviour that years ago resulted in his leaving his parents' home and taking to the streets.'

'Çetin, I'm sorry. I—'

'Must go! I'll call you tomorrow!' İkmen hissed and then, suddenly, he was gone.

It was well past midnight by the time Edibe Taner got back to her small apartment in the city quarter known as New Mardin. Situated on the flat plain below the old city, New Mardin is where the greatest civic expansion has taken place in recent years in the form of new apartment blocks, municipal buildings and modern hotels. Taner was just digging into her handbag for her keys in front of her own, almost completely darkened block when she became aware that she was not alone. Instead of continuing to look for her keys she put her hand in her jacket pocket and drew out her pistol. For several seconds she just stood, waiting to see what happened. But then the feeling of threat passed. Nothing so much as moved or even drew breath in or around the entrance to her apartment block, and so after a few more seconds Taner put her pistol away, took her keys out of her handbag and let herself in. Although rattled by the activation of an instinct that, over the years, she had grown to trust, Edibe Taner was convinced that whoever or whatever had been with her outside had meant her no harm. In fact, whatever it had been had, she felt, probably been a friend. Before she headed for the lift up to her fifth-floor apartment, she put her head outside the main door again and called, very softly, 'Gabriel? Is that you, Gabriel?'

As it often did, Gabriel Saatçi's gentle face had come suddenly and unbidden into her mind. He could do that, her friend Gabriel, *her* saint Gabriel. Or was it because after she had dropped Inspector Süleyman off, she had remembered where she had seen and spoken to one particular guard at the American woman's house before? The man was a neighbour of Gabriel's father. A village man originally, and a nice enough person by all accounts. Or not. 'Gabriel, my . . . my friend.' Was he close by, perhaps? Was he looking at her and smiling as she wrestled with conflicting feelings of need for him and dread? Gabriel had always been a prankster.

But even after almost half a minute there was no reply and so she closed the door again and went and got into the lift. Why she thought it had been Gabriel she didn't know. Maybe because she had grown up with him she had developed a sort of a sense as to where he might be. Or maybe it was to do with the deeper feelings she knew she possessed. But if that were the case, why couldn't she find him? It was something that her father might be able to enlighten her about at some time. If of course Seçkin Taner was still speaking to his daughter. The meeting between her father and Inspector Süleyman had not gone well. But then how the Ottoman from İstanbul could be expected to understand Mardin beliefs and customs Edibe Taner didn't know. At times it was a struggle for her. She hadn't seen the Sharmeran; she'd heard her a few times, but . . . Then there was the 'Cobweb World' of which, apparently, Cousin Rafik's mother had spoken to poor Süleyman. That kind of phenomenon was best kept dark but then maybe Rafik's mother just had to blurt it out sometimes. After all, she, if anyone, was part of the Cobweb World. Just as the name of one of the suspect nurses in İstanbul was part of the Cobweb World. Lole. She would have to tell Süleyman about that name at some point and why the young man who owned it couldn't possibly be from Mardin. The Loles had disappeared into the Cobweb World for good. Difficult if not impossible sometimes to talk about that.

Taner opened the door to her apartment and put on the light in the hall. She slipped her shoes off at the door and then walked into her bedroom.

Captain Hilmi Erdur had not expected a visit from the American military, especially not in the middle of the night. The body of the faceless American corpse was still in the mortuary in Birecik and therefore under his jurisdiction. But tissue samples and fingerprints had gone off to the Americans and Erdur was, as far as he was concerned, simply waiting for confirmation from that quarter as to the man's identity.

According to the information on the body's dog-tags, which had eventually been found in one of the pockets of his trousers (odd in itself), he was a Private Jose E. Ramone. His uniform, which was characterised by a blue spade insignia, belonged to the 26th infantry regiment who were, so Erdur now knew, currently stationed in Ramadi in central Iraq. Once his identity was confirmed, Erdur could release the body to the US authorities and, when a Captain Chalabian of the US 26th arrived at the Jandarma station to see him, he thought that the American had come to arrange just that.

'Private Jose Eduardo Ramone was killed two weeks ago

183

in Baghdad,' Captain Chalabian said without preamble and in perfect Turkish. 'What's left of his body, which is in Baghdad, is waiting repatriation to the US.'

'So what—' Erder began.

'What you've got here, Captain, I don't know,' Chalabian interrupted. He was tall and fair and seemed to give the lie to his obviously Armenian surname. Armenians were not, Hilmi Erdur thought, like this. 'But that Private Ramone's dog-tags should turn up on an unknown body is of concern to me. There's a lot of insurgent activity in the Iraqi territories to the south of your country.'

Captain Erdur wondered whether to mention the somewhat vexed issue of active Kurdish PKK terror cells in that area, but the American got in first.

'Whatever may or may not be said officially, the Kurds go in and out of Iraq,' he said baldly. 'You've Hezbollah also to contend with here, as do we.'

'This is not the first time we've found body parts in the Euphrates,' Erdur said.

'Yes, I know. But, Captain, this is the first time you've found a US serviceman. Or not. You should know that the US military have not been able to identify the corpse.' He shrugged. 'We've run those DNA sequences and we've looked hard at those fingerprints but whatever we do we can't make any of them fit any of our personnel. He could be an Iraqi, civilian or military, dressed in US uniform to disguise his identity.'

'He has no face,' Erdur said.

'Exactly. Someone doesn't want us to know who he is, do they? Look, I can run his prints and DNA past our Iraqi military colleagues, but I think we could have the body of an insurgent here.'

184

Erdur sighed. What he'd do with the body of an unknown Iraqi civilian he didn't know.

'In the meantime I'd like to take a look at him, if I may,' Chalabian said. 'If he was someone active around our base, I could maybe recognise something that remains about him. I knew Ramone, of course, and I know it isn't him. Ramone had his head shot to shit by a sniper.'

Erdur took his American colleague to the mortuary. On the way he complimented him on his Turkish. It was very good. However, as soon as the words were out of his mouth, Erdur knew he'd done the wrong thing. This tall blond man, he had forgotten, had an Armenian surname.

'My father's people came originally from Diyarbakir,' Chalabian responded tightly. 'My grandparents only knew Turkish. Oh, and Armenian too, of course. But no one speaks that now. Turkish was useful. My dad encouraged me to learn it. We forgot Armenian. You know?'

There was no tone of challenge in Chalabian's voice, just a little bit of anger. Erdur thought that the American would probably want him to ignore it, which he did.

'Here,' he said as he pulled one of the refrigeration drawers out of the mortuary cabinet. He pulled the sheet covering the corpse aside to allow the American to see what lay beneath.

As soon as Chalabian saw the body, he frowned. 'How long was he in the water before you picked him up?' he said.

'We are not yet sure,' Erdur replied. 'Only one of our local doctors came to him when we found him. No one else was available. The pathologist from Urfa is due tomorrow.'

'I don't know because I'm not an expert,' Chalabian said, 'but to me he doesn't look as if he's been in the water all that long.'

They walked out into the chilly night air and Chalabian offered Erdur a cigarette, which he took.

'Captain, you and I both know that your borders here in the east are porous,' Chalabian began.

'We do our best,' Erdur replied with some heat in his voice. Confounded Americans! What did they know about dealing with multiple terrorist threats over decades? 9/11 had been dreadful but compared to the terrorist experiences of people in Europe and the Middle East over the past forty years, it had been a drop in the ocean. 'We have Hezbollah to contend with,' he continued. 'There are al-Qaeda cells operating, we know that. And then there is the PKK.'

He didn't elaborate upon that final group. It was well known that the US government was somewhat lukewarm in its condemnation of that particular organisation. Chalabian, as if a little embarrassed, lowered his head slightly.

'Yes, well . . .' He cleared his throat. 'Captain, what exercises me is the fact that Ramone's dog-tags have ended up inside Turkey. We've either got insurgents slipping over the border from northern Iraq or you've got people coming over to our side. Backwards and forwards, there's movement anyhow.'

Erdur puffed hard on his cigarette and then looked up at the stars. 'There is the drug trade too,' he said after a pause. 'Opium grows very well in these border valleys. We try to control this trade as best we can. But during the time of Saddam Hussein things on the Iraqi side of the border were often quite unrestrained. Now, of course . . .' He looked up at Chalabian and saw what he thought was a face that could be open to the truth. He gave it a shot. 'Little has changed in that respect. If anything, in fact, the trade is more violent, the drugs more hotly contested.'

'I know,' Chalabian said with a sigh. He then, quite unexpectedly, put a hand on his Turkish colleague's shoulder and said, 'We've made a fucking mess of the whole thing, I know that. But, Captain, I knew Private Ramone and I liked him. I need to find out who stole his dog-tags and why. If people are throwing bodies carrying US ID into rivers then they have an agenda we don't yet understand. We need to understand it, and soon.'

Captain Erdur nodded his head in agreement. 'When the doctor comes from Urfa he will take more DNA samples. Then, maybe, we will find out who this man is.'

Çetin İkmen hadn't been able to close his eyes. He'd tried, because he didn't want to feel tired at work the following day. But he'd failed. Even before he'd been denied his own bed, the argument he'd had with Bekir, or rather the memory of it, had put paid to sleep. Not only had his son stuck to his grandiose lies about being a famous fighter of gypsies, he had been vicious in his resentment of his father.

'How dare you check up on me!' he'd roared when Çetin İkmen had told him about his conversation with the gypsy. 'I know you resent me coming back, but—'

'Bekir, you were a nightmare when you lived at home before,' İkmen had countered. 'You lied, you took drugs, you—'

'I'm a different person now and you don't like it!' Bekir had screamed. Fatma, by this time crying in the kitchen, had begged her husband to stop.

'Look what you're doing to Mum!' Bekir had said when he heard her cries and her tears.

'It's because of your mother that I need to be sure of you,' İkmen had said. 'Because if you break your mother's heart again, Bekir, I will break every bone in your body!'

Bekir had gone to what had once been Bülent's room then, slamming the door in his young brother Kemal's face as he did so. This had put Çetin İkmen in trouble with both his wife and his youngest son, who accused his father of being a 'fascist'. Fatma just very icily told her husband to sleep on the sofa. And so Çetin sat, wakefully, smoking heavily until at just before six o'clock his mobile phone began to ring.

'İkmen,' he said gloomily into what he persisted in thinking of as its tiny, tiny mouthpiece.

'Sir, it's İzzet,' he heard Süleyman's sergeant say. 'We've just received a call from Dr Eldem at the Cerrahpaşa. The prison guard Ramazan Eren died half an hour ago.'

İkmen sighed and then groaned. With Eren dead, any chance of questioning a witness to Yusuf Kaya's escape had gone. 'How?'

'Multiple organ failure,' İzzet Melik said. 'The doctor said it's not uncommon in patients in coma.'

İkmen knew that was so. He'd seen a few people both die in and recover from coma over the years. But Ramazan Eren wasn't just anybody. He was possibly one of the last links in the chain that led back to Yusuf Kaya's escape. He was certainly the last witness to the actual event whose whereabouts were known. His death was therefore, for Kaya, really rather convenient. İkmen took his jacket off the cushion beside him and put it on.

'And because Eren was under medical care when he died there will be no post-mortem,' İkmen said as a statement of fact.

'No, sir.'

'Unless of course we order one,' İkmen continued as he checked his pockets for car keys and money.

'Sir?'

188

Suddenly energised, İkmen rose to his feet. Far too many people were dying around Yusuf Kaya for his liking. 'The police,' he said decisively. 'I'm going to go over to the Cerrahpaşa now and I'm going to find out who was with or around Ramazan Eren before and during his death. I'm also going to order a post-mortem which I will want a police pathologist to perform.'

'But sir, I understood from Dr Eldem that Eren's body was going to be released to his family.'

'Then it will have to be un-released,' İkmen replied. 'I want Dr Sarkissian to take a look at Ramazan Eren before he meets his maker.'

'But sir, what will that—'

'Look like? I don't care,' İkmen said. 'If necessary I will say that I suspect foul play because maybe I do.'

Even in a secular state like Turkey, Muslims are usually buried within twenty-four hours of death unless something about the demise is reasoned to be unnatural.

'A lot of deaths have occurred around Yusuf Kaya's route out of this city. Let's see if we can at the very least find some sort of connection here,' İkmen said. 'Meet me at the Cerrahpaşa in fifteen minutes, İzzet.'

'Yes, sir.'

İkmen cut the connection and then walked determinedly out into the hall of his apartment. Kemal, who had just finished in the bathroom, scuttled nervously past him and back to his bedroom. The musty smell of his acne cream made İkmen wince.

Chapter 13

'Tomorrow is Easter Sunday,' Edibe Taner said to Süleyman as they walked towards the high yellow wall that surrounded the Kaya family home in Mardin. 'So all leave is cancelled and I for one will be in church.'

'Protecting the Christians?'

'In part, yes,' she replied. 'There will always be people who wish to harm others on the basis of their beliefs. The innocent have to be protected. But I will also be there to see whether Kaya's American woman does indeed turn up.'

'Which church?'

'Mar Behnam Suriani church is where everyone goes,' she said. 'Musa Saatçi's relatives will be there.'

'Minus Gabriel.'

She shrugged. 'Who knows? It's Easter. Gabriel is a very observant man. Maybe he will just turn up for the service. Who knows?'

The gate that led into the Kaya family compound was closed. Taner rapped on it hard and then stood silently next to Süleyman while they waited for someone inside to respond. Almost a minute passed before soft footsteps were heard approaching from inside. When the door opened they found themselves looking into the heavily kohl-rimmed eyes of Yusuf Kaya's first wife, Zeynep.

'What do you want?' she said, addressing Edibe Taner. 'I've nothing to say to you.'

'Not even about Yusuf's foreign woman down by Dara?'
Taner said as she pushed roughly past the woman and entered
the courtyard. 'I think that you do, Zeynep.'

Zeynep Kaya looked her cousin straight in the eye and said,
'Foreign woman? I don't know what you're talking about!'

'Don't you?' Taner glanced around the seemingly deserted
courtyard and then pulled Zeynep Kaya into the open door to
a stable. Süleyman, looking round to see who may or may
not be coming to Zeynep's assistance, followed them. Beyond
themselves, not a thing appeared to stir.

'Well, the second wife in Dara, an American woman, knows
you!' Taner said as she held Zeynep Kaya up to the wall in
front of her. 'And, Zeynep, let me tell you, some of your
husband's thugs were guarding her.'

'I don't know anything about any woman!' Zeynep persisted.
'It's all lies!'

'It isn't, and you know it,' Süleyman put in. He wasn't
happy to witness what was in effect one woman bullying
another, but Zeynep Kaya needed to know that her continued
lying was futile. She must surely be aware that her husband
had a second wife. There was far too much evidence to support
that contention.

'Your husband was imprisoned in İstanbul for killing the
prostitute he was living with,' Taner said. 'He has a daughter
by Anastasia Akyuz. I don't know how many other women
he's slept with over the years since he married you but I would
imagine that it runs into double figures. Yusuf is a shit! He
always was!'

'He is my husband!' Zeynep Kaya made as if to spit into
Edibe Taner's face, but then, with sudden terror in her eyes,
she stopped.

'Don't you dare!' the policewoman roared. 'Don't even

think about it!' Suddenly, and with a force that surprised even Süleyman, she slapped Zeynep Kaya across the face. The woman's cheek reddened immediately. 'Like it or not, Zeynep, you remain a scorpion and as a scorpion you will accept my authority!'

'Inspector Taner, I . . .'

She turned and gave Süleyman such a cold look it was almost like gazing into the face of a snake. Then she turned back to her cousin.

'Zeynep Kaya, if you lie to me, I will make sure that the Sharmeran never favours you with good fortune ever again!' The woman beneath her hands looked terrified. 'You know that I can do this! You know that my father can and will curse your rotten adopted family who, by the way, are nowhere around to protect you now, are they?'

'Bilqis Hanim* is out,' Zeynep said. 'The men have taken her to see her sister in Nusaybin. She – the sister – is dying; she . . . Oh, Edibe, please, please do not curse us! I love Allah but I truly love my Sharmeran too . . .'

'Then tell me the truth, Zeynep! Tell me now!'

There was a pause. One of Taner's hands was at Zeynep Kaya's throat, but it wasn't the physical consequences that were frightening the woman, it was the spiritual ones. Being cut off from or cursed by the Sharmeran was a very big deal indeed.

'She, the woman, she is much better with Yusuf in terms of business,' Zeynep said.

'You mean she helps him run drugs and murder his rivals?'

'I don't know what she does!' Zeynep said. 'She fell in love with my husband in İstanbul. I – I think it was partly because

---

* Hanim. Polite form of address for a woman.

of this place. She knew of the Tur Abdin. She was fascinated by it. She wanted to hear about the Sharmeran. And . . . Look, Yusuf told me he never loved her but she was good at business. It's what he said! She is American and good at business. What do I know? I don't understand Yusuf's business!'

'Oh, so you don't know how or why he gives you expensive jewellery, buys up property and dresses like an Italian politician? What—'

'No! No, I don't know!' Zeynep said, almost in tears now. 'I don't get involved in business! I have children, Yusuf's children!' And then suddenly her face turned into something less frightened and much more bitter. 'That foreigner can't give my husband children! My children, Muslim children, will have everything when my Yusuf dies! That's all I care about! That's all that anything in this world might mean to me!'

'So the fact that Yusuf has been fucking—'

'I don't care about that,' Zeynep said. 'I just—'

'Where is he, Zeynep?' Taner asked. 'Where is Yusuf now? Tell me and no one need ever know that you were concealing information from us. Don't tell me and I can't be responsible for what happens – here in the city with the law, or beyond . . .' she leaned forward and whispered into Zeynep's ear, 'out amongst the caves where the snakes gather and bask, the children of—'

'I don't know! I don't know!' As Zeynep spoke she shook in every part of her body. Süleyman had seen terror in his time but rarely had he seen it engendered by reference to things that to him were clearly only mythical. But then these people were not from his part of the world. These people were, he was coming to understand, almost wholly alien.

'If I knew where Yusuf was I would tell you,' Zeynep Kaya sobbed. 'Do you, Edibe, think that I would risk the displeasure of my Sharmeran? I have children! I would never ever put them in the way of danger, not even for my husband!'

Slowly Edibe Taner released her grip upon Zeynep Kaya's throat and Süleyman began to breathe more easily again. In spite of the fact that the house was empty apart from Zeynep, he had been worried. What would the Kayas have done if they had come back and found Edibe Taner with her hands at Zeynep's throat?

'If they knew she'd spoken to us, they'd kill her,' Taner said when, later, they walked back towards Republic Square.

'Then why did she answer the door?' Süleyman said. 'She must have known, or had an idea at least, that it could be the police?'

Edibe Taner sighed. 'As a member of my clan, she cannot deny me,' she said. 'She knows who and what I am and what I can threaten her with. Around Kaya's family she does whatever they dictate. But alone with another scorpion she must tell the truth. She opened that door because she wanted me to know what was real.'

For Taner to be talking about anything 'real' seemed more than a little odd. This daughter of the Master of Sharmeran had more than a hint of the snake about her. Not that such things were in any way real to Mehmet Süleyman.

'When are we going to start combing the surrounding countryside?' he asked as they reached Avenue One and began making their way back towards the police station. 'In İstanbul, we—'

'In İstanbul you go tearing into all sorts of situations, I am sure,' she responded breezily.

'Inspector Taner, if you are implying that we somehow have it easy in İstanbul, then you are very much mistaken,' Süleyman said. Her tone had irritated him. 'Our problems are just as

195

intense as your own. But when someone escapes from prison we do search for them. Here, beyond terrorising the rest of the Kaya family and only very slightly upsetting, as far as I could see, that American woman, we have investigated nothing.'

'Oh, so I went to Gaziantep for *nothing*?'

'No, I—'

'Look.' She took one of his arms in hers and then looked up, smiling now, into his face. 'I did not mean to cause offence, Inspector, but . . . We work very largely with informants here. Many are gypsies who don't of course belong to native clans. They are sometimes of use and sometimes not. But this region is a land of fortified cities and villages with allegiances even I do not always understand. On top of that we have to contend with many different armed groups. We are close to the border with Syria, not much further from the border with Iraq. Inspector, my officers and I cannot go bursting into places without compunction. We could die. You yourself were nervous when we were outside the house in Dara. Organisations like Hezbollah have bombs, they stockpile the things! And how do I really know that Yusuf Kaya is not associated with such people? I don't.'

They had stopped in front of a little tobacconist's shop above and behind which were three huge and magnificent arches. It was as if one of Mardin's great mansions were hiding behind a humble and disproportionately small shop, which was indeed the case. Süleyman looked up at the structure and Taner looked at Süleyman. She sighed. It was now or never.

'This is what is known as the Cerme family mansion,' Taner said. 'It was built at the beginning of the twentieth century by one of Mardin's most famous sons.'

But he changed the subject back. 'Inspector, I am sorry if I failed to understand your problems—'

'The architect Serkis Lole,' she said. The look on Süleyman's face changed. 'We should have had this conversation before, but—'

'Lole? But I told you about Murat Lole when we were back in Gazi—'

'I know. Serkis Lole was an ethnic Armenian,' Taner said. 'He built many beautiful palaces here in Mardin.'

'So Murat Lole—'

'Cannot be connected to Mardin,' Taner said. 'The Lole family, they . . . er, they emigrated in the First World War.'

Süleyman and Taner looked silently at each other. Both Turks, neither of them even wanted to breathe about the alleged massacre of Armenians by Ottoman forces in Turkey in 1915. That the Lole family had emigrated from the city at around that time was difficult for the two officers. The Turkish Republic doesn't recognise the Armenians' allegations. The Armenian Republic, for its part, continues with this claim. And in the east it was an issue that was more sensitive and current than in the large western cities.

'No person with the name Lole has been in this city for nearly a century,' Taner said. 'It is no longer a name associated with Mardin, except as something from the past. That man can have no connection to this place.'

'You could have told me all this before,' Süleyman said bitterly.

But she didn't answer him. She just looked long and hard into his eyes and then she walked away.

Çetin İkmen was very sorry for Mrs Eren, who only wanted to take her husband's body away from the hospital and have him buried. But he wasn't prepared to let sentimentality cloud his judgement in this case.

'I have to be certain this man died of natural causes,' he said to an obviously furious Dr Eldem.

'If, İkmen, you are impugning my honour or my professionalism—'

'I am impugning neither,' İkmen said. 'But, Dr Eldem, Mr Eren here,' he pointed to the sheet-covered body on the bed behind him, 'was the last known witness to the flight of Yusuf Kaya. He might very well have been able to tell us some more facts about that incident.'

'But he won't be able to do that now, will he?' the doctor cut in shortly. 'He's dead.'

İkmen looked back at the body once again and said, 'Clearly.'

Mrs Eren, a small headscarfed lady in her thirties, wept silently and alone in a corner.

'This poor lady—'

'Is going to have to wait for her husband's body,' İkmen said. 'Doctor, I have to be sure that Mr Eren died of natural causes.'

'As I told you, multiple organ failure—'

'Yes, quite common in those in coma. But it can also occur when certain substances are introduced to the body with the intention of killing the subject,' İkmen said in as low a voice as he could, given the presence of the weeping widow. 'Now, Doctor, do you have a list of nurses, doctors and other members of staff who attended Mr Eren, please?'

After glaring at İkmen for a second or two, Dr Eldem went off in search, apparently, of information. Almost immediately İzzet Melik arrived.

'Sorry I'm late, sir,' he said in a low voice as he sidled up to İkmen. 'Got a call from Inspector Süleyman. He tried to call you but of course your phone was off.'

'Mmm? And?' İkmen was not comfortable with the widow

Eren still in the room and hoped that Arto Sarkissian would arrive soon to take charge of the body.

'Inspector Taner in Mardin had never heard of Faruk Öz, but if we could send over that photograph she might be able to identify him as someone else,' İzzet said. 'However, she does know the name Lole.'

'As in Murat Lole,' İkmen said.

'Not exactly,' İzzet said. 'Years ago a very famous architect called Serkis Lole lived in Mardin. He was Armenian. Taner told the inspector that there are now only two Armenian families in Mardin. Neither of them is called Lole.'

'So our Lole could be a descendant of a famous architect.'

'Apparently Inspector Taner thinks not, sir,' İzzet said, and lowered his voice. 'The, er, the Loles left Mardin in the First World War. Emigrated, so Inspector Taner told Inspector Süleyman.'

'I see.' İkmen understood. 'So where does he come from, this Murat Lole?'

'Originally? Don't know,' İzzet replied. 'I don't think we asked him.'

'Then we must ask him,' İkmen said. 'If he is involved in some sort of conspiracy he'll lie. Maybe if Inspector Taner says there are no Loles left in Mardin that name is an alias anyway. Go and see him, İzzet. Tell him that his colleague Faruk Öz has died.'

'Don't you think he knows?'

'Maybe.' İkmen shrugged. 'Gauge his reaction.'

'Yes, sir.' The younger man began to walk away.

'Oh, and İzzet . . .'

İzzet Melik turned. 'Sir?'

'Can you e-mail Öz's photograph over to Mardin? And one of Murat Lole?'

'Already done, sir.'

'Good.'

İzzet turned to go again but once more İkmen stopped him. 'İzzet!'

'Sir?' There was a tired if not downright obstreperous look on his face now. İzzet Melik was not a man easily pushed around even by his superiors. İkmen went over to him and took him to one side.

'Also phone the Kartal Prison for me, if you will,' he said. 'Speak to the governor. I want his personal assurance that the prisoner who was instrumental in getting Yusuf Kaya into solitary, Ara Berköz, is being protected. If deaths around the escape of Yusuf Kaya are going to accelerate, I don't want even Berköz to become yet another statistic. Kaya's reach is, as I am only now beginning to fully appreciate, long. If you have any trouble with the governor, get him to contact me.'

'Yes, sir.'

'Oh and İzzet,' İkmen concluded, 'not a word about this background to the family Lole. Not to anyone. Not relevant anyway, not as yet. Keep it in mind, though. I will.'

İkmen waved İzzet Melik on his way and then went back to contemplating the sheet-covered corpse on the bed and the woman weeping in the corner. He wished fervently for the swift arrival of Arto Sarkissian.

Inspector Taner tapped the image of the man on the computer screen and said, 'His name is Hasan Karabulut.'

'This is the dead nurse? Faruk Öz?' Süleyman said as he peered across at the screen, frowning.

'It is what your colleagues from İstanbul have sent us,' she said. 'Hasan Karabulut is a distant cousin of Yusuf Kaya. He has a clan Dakk to prove it, although Hasan in my experience was a decent lad, not at all in favour of drugs or violence or anything else that Yusuf Kaya does.'

'Hasan Karabulut trained as a nurse in Van,' Constable Selahattin said, referring to a cardboard-covered file as he spoke.

'Hasan Karabulut was an orphan,' Taner continued. 'But he was taken in by his mother's sister, a spinster lady. She looked after him and kept him away as much as she could from his father's family, the Karabuluts, who are related to the Kayas.'

'Yes, but if he had a Dakk . . .'

'Hasan was tattooed as a child. A lot of people are,' Taner said. She sighed. 'I knew that he had left the city to seek his fortune somewhere else. But I had no idea that he had taken on an assumed name.'

Süleyman hoped that she was telling him the truth. Their altercation outside the Cerme mansion had left him unsure. Between her impenetrable beliefs and her civic loyalty and her apparent inability to discuss such difficult issues as Murat Lole and his possible antecedents, Taner was making him nervous.

'Do you think he took on another name in order to be able to assist Yusuf Kaya?' he asked.

'I don't think so.' She shook her head. 'Apart from the fact that the timing doesn't work – Hasan/Faruk was working at the hospital in İstanbul before Kaya even went to prison – he would never have done that.'

'Why?'

'Because Hasan's beloved aunt, the one who took him in and cared for him when his parents died, hated Kaya. She hated what he did and the power that his family exerted on almost everyone around them.'

'So maybe if we speak to her . . .'

'She lives in a hospital out beyond Midyat,' Taner said sadly. 'She doesn't even know what her own name is these days. Hasan must have gone to İstanbul to make a new life. There was nothing but heartache or a life of crime for him here. Maybe, somehow, Yusuf Kaya or those around him got to know where he was.'

'What about the other picture?' Süleyman said. 'The so-called Murat Lole?'

Edibe Taner sat down on her ancient office chair and lit a cigarette. 'I don't recognise that face at all,' she said. 'It doesn't look anything like the pictures of the Lole family members they have in the museum. At least I don't think so.'

'Do you have any idea where those Loles might be now?' Süleyman asked.

'No. As I told you,' she said, 'they left Mardin.'

'But that said, this Murat Lole could be a member of the —'

'Whoever that is,' Taner said as she continued to stare at the picture, 'he doesn't come from Mardin. If this man was part of the plot to spring Yusuf Kaya from prison he did not do so because of any local connection. But Hasan?' She became animated again. 'Hasan, of all people. Maybe Yusuf offered him money?' Then she shook her head. 'No. No, there has to be some other explanation.'

'The third nurse, called İsak Mardin,' Süleyman smiled grimly at the name, 'was employed at the Cerrahpaşa under false pretences, with the knowledge of the then director.'

'The one who killed himself?' Taner said.

'Yes.' Süleyman sighed. 'İsak Mardin's qualifications from a hospital in Şanlıurfa didn't check out. Theoretically he's still out there somewhere.'

Taner looked up. 'And the cleaners? What of the people

dressed as cleaners who were supposed to have been at the scene too?'

'Of those we have no knowledge,' Süleyman said. 'The hospital's records with regard to cleaning staff is sketchy to say the least. Inspector, I know that you said that Hasan Karabulut's aunt was ill . . .'

'Demented.'

'But maybe we should go and see her? Maybe even through dementia the old lady might know something?'

Edibe Taner didn't say that she agreed but she did promise to call the hospital where the aunt was living in Midyat. Then she took him back to St Sobo's. Easter Sunday was, she said, going to be a busy time for all of them and Süleyman, at least, should now try to get some rest.

'The American woman will be coming up from Dara with her guards,' Taner said as she leaned out of her car to speak to him at the gates of the monastery. 'One of them I know quite well. He lives in an apartment across the courtyard from the Saatçis. He's a new resident in as much as he came to the city as an infant. Comes originally from the plains. I think he's a Suriani. I want to speak to him if I can. I think he's one of only a few Christians who work for the Kayas. His loyalty may well be a little looser than the other guards'.'

Süleyman smiled. In his experience it was money rather than religion that generally bound people together.

'I'll come and get you at seven thirty,' Taner continued. 'And don't eat anything; there's a huge meal laid on in the church after the service. Everyone is invited.' She fired up the engine of her car but then thought of something else and said, 'Oh, and my father will be attending the service too. Men and women sit separately in Suriani churches, so he will look after you.'

And then she left. The smile on Süleyman's face faded as he thought once again about how Edibe Taner had concealed information from him. Unpalatable information, but information none the less.

Chapter 14

As soon as he got home from school that afternoon Kemal İkmen, as had become his custom of late, went straight to his brother Bekir's room. But Bekir wasn't there, so he went first to the family living room and then to the kitchen. His mother was standing at the sink washing up tea glasses. The only other occupant of the apartment, seemingly, was his brother Bülent.

'Looking a bit worried, Kemal,' Bülent said as the youngster put his head round the door and frowned into the room. 'What's up?'

'Do you know where Bekir is?' Kemal mumbled.

'In his room,' Fatma İkmen said. 'He was tired after last night.' She shook her head at the memory of the argument Bekir had had with his father the previous evening. Just like the bad old days! 'He went for a lie-down.'

'He isn't there,' Kemal said.

'Oh, well, then maybe he's watching TV.'

'He isn't in the living room. I've looked.'

Fatma's face turned white. Bülent saw it, stood up and immediately took charge. In all probability Bekir had just let himself out to go and buy cigarettes and not bothered to tell anyone. Such thoughtlessness was typical of him. Such terrified over-reaction in his mother was, these days, typical of her.

'Let's have another look,' he said to his brother. The two of them set off from the kitchen and went round the apartment until inevitably they came to what had become Bekir's room. Bülent, whose room it had been, looked at the unmade bed and the dirty glasses on the floor with some distaste. He hadn't been the tidiest person in the world when he'd had this room, but he'd only been a kid then. Bekir was years older than Bülent was. What a slob!

Kemal began searching on the floor and looking in the cupboards for some reason. Bülent, frowning, said, 'You won't find him in there.'

'No, I . . .'

The boy looked hot, red-faced and flustered. Only when he finally lighted upon a small rucksack underneath the bed did he finally stop and sit down breathlessly on the floor. 'Oh, he's left his rucksack, so . . .' He held the thing on his lap like a trophy. 'He must be about.'

'He's gone out, that's all,' Bülent said. He then lowered his voice and continued, 'You know, Kemal, you really mustn't over-react like this. Mum's already anxious enough about Bekir. I know you really like him too and that's great. But you have to try to be a bit calm for Mum's sake.'

Before the boy could answer, Bülent heard his mother's voice from the kitchen. 'Boys, have you found your brother yet?'

Bülent turned towards the bedroom door and said, 'I think he's just out, Mum. There's nothing to worry about.'

But by the time he turned back Kemal had opened the rucksack and seemed to be searching frantically inside it for something. There was an expression on the boy's face that Bülent didn't like. His panic also, seemingly, was making that bloody spot cream he insisted upon using smell even worse than usual.

'Kemal! What are you looking for?'

The boy looked up, his reddened face slathered in sweat.

'Er . . .'

There was guilt there too. Bülent had been a teenager himself not long before; he knew that kind of look. He made a dive for the rucksack, which made his brother scream.

'What are you doing?' Kemal squeaked. 'It's—'

'It's Bekir's, not yours, so give it here!' Bülent said as he tussled with the boy on the floor. 'Give!'

'No!'

'Kemal, what is in this bag? If you don't show me I'll . . .'

'Ow!' Kemal cringed as his older and stronger brother prised his pudgy fingers away from the bag. 'No, it's private! Mum, Bülent is bullying me!'

'Bülent?' Fatma İkmen couldn't believe it. Bülent was such a kind and considerate boy. She began to move towards the bedroom.

But now Bülent had the rucksack in his possession and was looking inside. Kemal, crying on the floor, was making threats apparently on behalf of Bekir about what would happen to people who 'messed with his stuff'. But Bülent wasn't listening. The first thing he took out of the bag was a small sprig of greenery that smelt alarmingly like Kemal's face. The second thing he pulled out, and luckily just avoided hurting himself with, was a used and bloodied syringe. As his mother entered the room, he was in the process of dabbing one of his fingers in the small amount of white powder that had gathered in one of the bag's side seams. Not that Bülent, who had been to a few night clubs in his time and was also a policeman's son, didn't know what that was.

'Allah, what have you got there!' Fatma said as she looked at the syringe in her son's hand.

Bülent just touched his tongue with the powder and said, 'Coke.'

'Coke?' Fatma frowned and then looked down at Kemal, still crying on the floor. 'Coke?'

'Cocaine,' Bülent said bluntly. And then, holding the bloodied syringe up to the light, he added, 'Not this, I don't suppose, however.'

'What . . .'

'He couldn't even be bothered to dispose of his syringe!' Bülent said angrily. 'I could have stabbed myself on it! Allah alone knows what he's got floating around in his blood!' Seeing that his mother either wouldn't or couldn't understand, he said, 'Mum, Bekir has been shooting up heroin.'

'But you said coke . . .'

'I don't know why he's got cocaine too,' Bülent replied. 'Maybe he just deals that, or takes it as well as heroin. Who knows?' He picked up the sprig of greenery he had taken out of the bag first and said, 'And as to what this is . . .'

'You mean he's on drugs? He said he'd done with all that,' Fatma said. 'He said he was clean!' Her attention was caught by her weeping youngest son on the floor and she frowned. 'Kemal?'

'Kemal here was rather more worried about getting hold of this bag than he was about finding Bekir,' Bülent said. He leaned down towards his brother. 'Kemal, have you been taking drugs with Bekir?' he said in what to the teenager was a very menacing fashion. 'Has he been giving them to you? Tell me the truth, boy!'

Seraphim Yunun had never had a moment's doubt about his vocation. Even when in the past it had seemed sometimes as if St Sobo's could not possibly survive another year, he had always known that it would. As he had lived, so, he knew, he would die under holy orders. If only Brother Gabriel would return, then all would be well whatever might or might not be going on outside the monstery walls. Although he hadn't seen the miracle for himself, Brother Seraphim knew many who had been there when Gabriel Saatçi had walked back into Mardin covered in snake bites. He'd seen the report the doctor had written on Gabriel's injuries at the time. No one could survive such an onslaught! Only a saint with God at his right hand. Easter Sunday would arrive in the morning and Seraphim would pray even more fervently for Gabriel's return. Maybe the saint would, like the Christ himself, rise again triumphant on the third day.

'Brother Seraphim!'

It was the policeman from İstanbul, Arto Sarkissian's friend. Brother Seraphim smiled. 'Inspector?'

Mehmet Süleyman had spotted the monk as he was about to go back to his room. Now he jogged across the central courtyard of the monstery to speak to him.

'Brother, if I may have a moment of your time . . .'

'Of course.' Brother Seraphim opened his hands in a gesture of acceptance. 'Would you like to come and sit up on the roof? It's a lovely afternoon and the view from up there is definitely something you should see before you leave St Sobo's.'

'Thank you.'

The monk led Süleyman up a steep flight of outdoor steps cut into the side of the building, which led from the courtyard up to a large flat roof. At one corner was the ornate, fluted bell tower while at another, beside a smooth white dome, was a stone bench that Brother Seraphim took Süleyman over to now. As they sat down the policeman looked around at the rolling vineyards in front of the monastery and the jagged and forbidding-looking mountains behind. Near the tops of the peaks were what looked like very rudimentary buildings. Although how anyone would or could get up to such a place and then build, Süleyman could not imagine.

As if reading his mind, Brother Seraphim pointed to the structures and said, 'Those are very ancient. I don't know when they were built or by whom, except that brothers most certainly made them.'

'Monks?' Süleyman sat down on the bench, still looking at the mountains beyond.

'They are hermitages,' Brother Seraphim said. 'Constructed by brothers whose road to God was to be of a solitary nature. It is an ancient and honourable Christian tradition, although few choose the life of the hermit these days. The last of that kind here in these mountains died back in the 1960s.' He smiled. 'But when Brother Gabriel went missing we, or rather some of the younger brothers, did risk venturing up into the old dwellings to look for him. It has been feared for some time that terrorists might haunt some of the old hermitages. But our brothers didn't find them, thank God, or sadly Brother Gabriel either.'

'Some people think he's with the Sharmeran,' Süleyman said. It came out, he thought, with a tinge of irony. The reply however was totally and utterly straight.

'Maybe he is.'

And then they both just looked. Down in front of the building men in wide salvar trousers were raking the ground between the neat rows of grapevines. Above, in a sky that, though cold, was a deep and almost sea-like blue, an eagle hovered silently on invisible thermals. Without noise or great movement the world of the Tur Abdin outside the cities and settlements was one of timeless and eerie beauty.

'What you have to understand, Inspector,' Brother Seraphim said in a low, slow voice, breaking the silence, 'is that many people of religion here accept a certain blurring of the edges of doctrine.'

Süleyman frowned.

'Tomorrow, I understand, you will attend the Easter service in Mar Behnam church. There you will see a lot of things that at first sight might appear contradictory. For instance, as well as cloth pictures depicting the lives of our saints, Mar Behnam has a representation of the Sharmeran on its walls. In addition to Christians, both Suriani and Armenian, there will be Muslims also – Turks and Kurds. They will take the service as seriously as their Christian brothers and sisters, and many people whatever their religion will pay homage to the Sharmeran.'

'Inspector Taner said that her father would be attending,' Süleyman said.

The monk shrugged. 'Seçkin Taner, like you a Muslim, is a man of enormous faith. Seçkin Taner is a prime example of the blurring of the lines of belief.'

'But, Brother,' Süleyman began, 'you must see how this is a struggle for someone like me to take in.'

'Of course.'

Again a moment of silence passed while the eagle swooped down upon something beyond the vineyards.

'I don't know and often don't understand where allegiances lie here,' Süleyman continued. 'I am obliged, because of my ignorance, to take much on trust. Part of the time I don't even know what people are saying because I don't speak any languages apart from my own, English and French. I've come here to apprehend Yusuf Kaya and yet . . .'

'And yet you feel no closer to him now than you did back

in İstanbul?' Brother Seraphim smiled. 'If Yusuf Kaya is in the Tur Abdin then he will be so well hidden that only a lapse of concentration on the part of his guards or the man himself will give him away. It will come about by accident. Edibe Taner knows this.'

'And yet,' Süleyman said, 'people were sometimes willing to tell Inspector Taner things. Where certain people might be, and—'

'Gypsies,' the monk said simply. 'They're poorer than most folk. Sometimes they sell information to the police, sometimes they work to help the clans with their guns and their drugs. There are other informants too, I believe.'

'Lütfü Güneş, who came here to see me just after I arrived,' Süleyman said. 'He told us some—'

'You went off to Dara the following day,' Brother Seraphim cut in. 'I, of course, do not know what it was you did there.'

Exasperated, Süleyman said, 'Yes, but by saying that, by implying you do, you—'

'Inspector, the Tur Abdin is a very beautiful and very dangerous place. A man, or a woman, must wear many faces in order to survive.'

'And so *anyone* may or may not know *anything* . . .' He paused, started to rake his fingers frustratedly through his hair but then lit up a cigarette instead. 'Brother Seraphim, what do you know about Lütfü Güneş? I haven't seen him since he came to see me. Do you think that he might have led us in the direction he did for reasons associated with an agenda of his own?'

The monk sniffed the cigarette smoke with obvious pleasure. He had only given the habit up six months earlier. 'What I know of Lütfü Güneş is that he is a Kurd who loves only others of his own kind,' he said. 'His family is not a great

212

clan even though I know his people have ambitions. It is one of those groups who have been known to assist those more important than themselves in the past. My understanding is that some of Lütfü's people have had some involvement with drugs. A couple of the clans, as you know, involve themselves in peddling that misery; the Kayas are only one of them. I don't know whether the Güneş family have ever helped the mainly Turkish Kayas, but they have been involved with some of the other, Kurdish clans. Therein may lie his motive for informing. I'm not saying that is so, but . . .'

'But I may have to return to İstanbul without Yusuf Kaya,' Süleyman said.

'If God wills.'

Süleyman took in a deep breath and let it out again slowly. 'Brother Seraphim, have you ever heard of something called the Cobweb World?'

There was a pause during which Süleyman turned to look at the monk, who was frowning.

'Where did you hear that expression, Inspector?'

'An old woman used it to me in Gaziantep. She said that I was part of the Cobweb World on account of my coming from an Ottoman family.'

'An Ottoman family? You are from an Ottoman family?'

'Yes.'

Brother Seraphim shook his head and said, 'And the woman, she was . . .'

'I don't know,' Süleyman replied. 'I was met in Gaziantep by Inspector Taner and her cousin and they took me to this house, an old Armenian place, where the woman was a sort of cook.'

'Mm.' Brother Seraphim put a hand up to his heavily bearded chin. 'The cousin, was it a man called Rafik?'

213

'Yes.'

'Ah.' He nodded gravely now. 'Yes, well, that would explain it.'

'Explain what?'

'The woman you met was Lucine Rezian. She is Rafik's mother and although once married to Seçkin Taner's brother, she is an Armenian.'

'But I thought . . .'

'Armenians remain here. A few,' Brother Seraphim said. 'Like the Suriani, the Yezidi Kurds and Ottomans like you, they are part of the Cobweb World. What do I mean by that? Inspector, the Cobweb World is what just about remains from the past. The modern world of the Tur Abdin is about the PKK, Hezbollah, the military and the divisions that some want to drive between religions and clans. Things that in the old days would have been ignored. Our reality, the Cobweb World, is delicate and fragile and it clings precariously to the old buildings here just as surely as it clings to old men like me.' He smiled. 'You are young. But if you are an Ottoman then you must know that world too. For you, I think, it must be one of diminished status, of the sadness you must sometimes feel when your fine manners are ignored. And I expect that you probably speak French with a very fine Parisian accent.'

Süleyman too began to smile. What the monk was saying was very familiar, as was his assessment of Süleyman's own place in this abode of the past, the dead and the dying out. His father, the prince, he knew would be the last of his family to be referred to by that title.

'But the Taner family are good people,' Brother Seraphim said. 'Inspector Taner's grandfather, Şeymus Taner, was not entirely happy for his second son to marry an Armenian Christian, but he allowed the match. He was genuinely sad

214

when his son, Lucine and young Rafik moved to Gaziantep for work. Lucine is a slightly guilty secret in that family. Even now, even in private, how does one speak about Armenians and what might or might not have happened long ago? I lay no blame anywhere but . . . Edibe Taner, you know, speaks Armenian, but she would never use the language in your earshot. She has difficulty with Lucine, with her place in the past. But she loves her. Edibe recognises things of herself in the old woman. The Kayas, on the other hand . . . They were furious when Yusuf's aunt Bulbul decided to go off with a man from the town of Birecik.'

Süleyman told him he knew something about this story and had indeed met Bulbul Kaplan in person.

'The husband was upstairs when we visited,' Süleyman said. 'We were told he is blind . . .'

'Gazi Kaplan is blind,' Brother Seraphim said. 'It is said that Yusuf Kaya's father put his eyes out with his own hands. His punishment, apparently, for marrying his sister in secret.'

When a child is at risk, all thoughts of other things fly from the mind of a parent. For once Çetin İkmen's mobile telephone was off.

'What did you take?' he said to the cowering figure of Kemal as the boy stood in front of his father's chair in the İkmen living room. Over by the door out to the balcony, Fatma İkmen was being hugged and comforted by her son Bülent. 'Kemal!'

The teenager tried to stop himself from shaking but without success.

'What has that no-good brother of yours been giving you, Kemal?' İkmen said in a way that everyone else in the room knew was terrifyingly controlled.

'Çetin, we don't know that Bekir—' Fatma began.

'He was a lying, drugged-up thug at fifteen, why should he be any different now?' İkmen said.

'Çetin!'

İkmen threw his arms in the air, finally giving way to the fury inside. 'I only let him stay to please you, Fatma! I would have thrown him on to the street without a thought!' And then he leaned forward and glared up at Kemal yet again. 'What did he give you, Kemal? What did you take from that snake of a brother of yours?'

But Kemal could only cry. Hot, fat tears sliding down his hot, red face.

'Kemal!'

'Dad, as I told you, there was coke loose in the bag,' Bülent said. 'The syringe . . .'

'The syringe I will send off to the forensic institute for analysis,' İkmen said. He looked up pointedly at Bülent and continued, 'In the meantime, I want Kemal to tell me what—'

'C-coke,' the teenager stuttered out between sobs. 'I – he – he let me sniff it. It was—'

'Got you as high as a Boeing 747 no doubt!' İkmen yelled. He stubbed the cigarette in his hand right out and instantly lit up another. 'Did you like it? Coke?'

The youngster hung his head and whispered, 'Yes.'

'Did he give you anything else? Anything in a syringe?'

'What, heroin? No,' Kemal said. 'No, he kept that for himself.'

The room became very quiet then. It went on for some time. The silence was finally broken by Çetin İkmen rising sharply to his feet. He looked at his watch.

'It's six o'clock now,' he said. 'When was Bekir last seen?'

'I saw him go into his room just after two,' Bülent replied.

And then, holding on tightly to his mother, he said, 'What are you going to do, Dad?'

There was another, this time very short silence. Çetin İkmen swallowed hard and said, 'I'm going to report the fact that a thirty-four-year-old man was giving my child drugs. I'm going to circulate Bekir's details and description and have him arrested.'

No one either moved or spoke again until Fatma said softly, 'I took a photograph of Bekir the other day, Çetin. Çiçek put it on the computer for me. You can have that if you think it will do any good.'

And then she went over to her youngest son, took him in her arms and kissed him. 'Allah forgive me,' she said softly.

'I don't understand,' Edibe Taner said to the veiled woman who stood in front of her. The light over the plains was fading now and soon Dara would be in darkness.

Underneath her veil, Elizabeth Smith smiled. 'What don't you understand? Why I dress like this outside the house? My marriage? Yusuf? What?'

'Any of it,' the policewoman said.

She had intended to go home after she left Mehmet Süleyman at St Sobo's. But then, as she had done periodically ever since Gabriel's disappearance, she had gone out looking for him. She had not, however, ended up in Dara purely by chance. She had an officer watching the place and she wanted to check up on him too. Elizabeth Smith was such an oddity in that setting that when she had seen her strolling in her garden, fully covered, the temptation to go and talk to her had been overwhelming.

'I cover myself when I'm outside the house out of respect,' the American said.

'Women in the Tur Abdin do not generally cover their faces, just their heads,' Taner replied.

The heavily made-up eyes above the veil closed and then opened again. 'You know, Inspector,' Elizabeth Smith said, 'I may have been born and raised in Boston, but my people were Southern Baptists.'

'What does that mean? Is it a religion?'

'Southern Baptists are very strict and austere Christians,' the American said. 'They go the extra kilometre, as you would say. No drinking, no cussing, no sex outside marriage. I lost contact with all that years ago. I wanted to travel and my folks didn't approve of that and so I left. But I still have some of the old values. The respect, at least.'

'So now you go to the Suriani church . . .'

'It's a fine spectacle, yes.'

'Miss Smith, I . . .'

'What's a nice American girl doing marrying a gangster, covering her face and living in a house without running water?'

'Miss Smith, you live in a house surrounded by armed men! You are a prisoner. Willing, but . . .'

The clanking sounds of the bells that some people put round the necks of their goats drifted over from the vastness of the Ocean's fields. The veiled woman looked up into the darkening sky.

'When a person finds herself alone in the world, different priorities can take over,' she said. 'My respect for this place and its people, its purity, is paramount.'

'The people of the Ocean are not perfect,' Edibe Taner said. 'Your husband is a drug dealer and a murderer.'

'Mm.' She didn't deny it. But it didn't seem to bother her too much either. 'I first came here ten years ago,' she said. 'On a tourist trip. The place possessed my soul!' She looked up into the sky once again. 'This is a place where things are brought to life – empires, faiths. Between the great rivers the Tigris and the Euphrates. This is where civilisation began. I envy you growing up here, Inspector.'

'I wouldn't wish to be from anywhere else,' Taner replied. 'But, you know, this place does have its problems.'

'Yeah.' The American's face darkened somewhat. 'New Mardin. The crap apartments down there.'

'I was thinking more about the conflict that exists here,' Taner said. 'The various terrorist organisations who base themselves here, war in Iraq, the dictatorship in Syria.'

There was a moment of silence as these two very different women looked at each other. Then the American said, 'But things can change. They do and will.'

'I wish I had your confidence,' Edibe Taner said.

Whatever expression Elizabeth Smith made in response to this was hidden underneath her veil.

'Miss Smith,' Taner said, 'you must know that the guards the Kayas have employed to protect you are not just for show. People are killed out here.'

'Clan rivalry. I know,' Elizabeth Smith said. 'I know also that your cousin Zeynep, Yusuf's other wife, would probably rather I was dead. But I also know she won't do anything.'

'No.' Zeynep had obviously accepted the situation. However, Edibe Taner did have one question. 'But, Miss Smith, why does Yusuf, or why did he, keep your existence such a close secret? I mean, it isn't as if he cares about the law with regard to polygamy.'

The American laughed. 'No. No, I was a secret, Inspector, because Yusuf feared his rivals might try to kidnap me. Hence all my guys in the house. Hence, in part, the reason I cover up in public. Foreigners fetch a good price here.'

'Yes.' Edibe Taner knew of several such cases of foreigner kidnap and it was undoubtedly very lucrative for the clan or group perpetrating the crime. 'But I still don't understand why you're here, Miss Smith,' Taner said. 'Whatever you may have run away from in the USA cannot, surely, have been bad enough to make you want to become a willing prisoner?'

There was silence, and then the American said, 'I told you, I love this place. It has possibilities. If one has money and loyal protection, as I do, one can build something special here.'

'Something special?'

'A life amongst the ruins,' the American said. 'A new life on the broken stones of the past.'

And then she left to go back into her house. It was only when Edibe Taner returned to her car that she realised that Yusuf Kaya's American bride had only spoken about him in passing. She hadn't once expressed what she might feel for him. She had actually exhibited more affection for her guards.

Chapter 15

Süleyman was not unaccustomed to security outside a church, although the level was rather higher than what he had experienced before. At the bottom of the narrow lane leading up to Mar Behnam there was an armoured car blocking off any vehicular access. Up to the church itself and just inside the precinct there were very many policemen and some women too. Edibe Taner greeted all of them. Looking very smart in a modest black suit, she was accompanied by Süleyman and her father Seçkin.

Constructed from the same honey-coloured stone as all the other ancient Mardin buildings, Mar Behnam was accessed via a small doorway in a tall, very blank-looking wall. Having seen the vast mansions with humble entrances in Gaziantep, Süleyman was unsurprised to find that in common with traditional Arab structures Mar Behnam was actually a church and outbuildings – the priest's house, a school and assembly rooms – in considerable grounds. There was also a large marquee, a temporary structure where, Taner told him, the banquet the Surianis were giving after the service was to be held. He had expected the church itself to be huge, but it wasn't. In fact the approach to the altar down between the rows of wooden benches on both sides was quite narrow. On either side of the benches were rows of arches which gave on to still more benches and small areas of devotion around paintings and cloth pictures on the walls. One of these representations was, as Brother Seraphim had told him, of the Sharmeran. Overhead there was a large and ornate chandelier from which strings of tiny fairy lights were suspended across to the ancient arches. Built originally, so Brother Seraphim had told him, in 569, Mar Behnam was definitely part of the Cobweb World. Just the memory of that term made Süleyman shudder, recalling as it did his recent conversation with the monk about Yusuf Kaya's aunt Bulbul Kaplan. What her brother had done, putting out the eyes of her husband Gazi, must have made her hate her family. Such a thing was inhuman and if, as was obvious, she had found love and acceptance from Gazi and his family, why on earth would she even consider entertaining her nephew Yusuf? It seemed to be counter-intuitive and he wondered whether Edibe Taner might be able to shed some light upon it later.

Some sort of ceremony was taking place when Süleyman and the others entered the church. The red-and-gold-robed priest at the altar was intoning something in a language Süleyman imagined was Aramaic. A young boy in a white robe stood next to him, just to one side of the altar, which was bare with the exception of a simple metal cross and a painted altar cloth representing the Last Supper.

'The service has not started properly yet,' Edibe Taner said to Süleyman as they walked through the door. 'The priest is just preparing for the ceremony now.' She turned to her father and said, 'Will you show Inspector Süleyman Mar Behnam, Papa?'

Seçkin Taner nodded his assent. 'Please follow me, Inspector.'

Süleyman followed him straight up the aisle and to the right of the altar. The priest and the young boy appeared to take no notice of them at all. Various rough niches in the stone held boxes, candlesticks and, in one instance, a very old-looking skull. The Master of Sharmeran pointed to it. 'That is the skull of Mar Behnam,' he said. 'He was the son of a Syrian king, a pagan.'

'This church is named for him?'

'And for his sister Mort Saro,' Seçkin Taner said. 'The father king killed Mar Behnam and Mort Saro because he didn't like them being Christians. Then from beyond the grave the brother and the sister began to work miracles and the wicked father repented. If you are sick, Mar Behnam can make you well, so the Suriani believe.'

Süleyman smiled. Miracles were not really his area. He felt Çetin İkmen would have been far better placed to talk to this man about them than he was. Just then, however, there was a noise behind him and he looked round. A large group of people, the women with their heads covered by small lace scarves, the men very obviously in their best suits, were pouring through the door into the church.

'Now the service begins,' Seçkin Taner said. 'Come, we must sit.'

The Master of Sharmeran and Süleyman sat on the right hand side of the church with the rest of the men. Edibe Taner, seated with the woman on the left, smiled over at both of them.

'Now that we know from Inspector Süleyman that the nurse we thought was called Faruk Öz came originally from Mardin, and that there is at least a theoretical connection between Mardin and the name Lole, we must consider carefully what we do next,' Ayşe Farsakoğlu said to İzzet Melik. 'We always had a suspicion that Murat Lole was part of Yusuf Kaya's escape plot. He possibly lied to us, too. Öz's people are not, clearly, from Ankara. Although he may have told Lole that they were from the capital for some reason.'

'The also significantly named Yusuf Mardin is still nowhere to be seen,' İzzet replied gloomily. 'As for the cleaners . . .'

'I don't know whether we'll ever be able to trace them,' Ayşe said as she looked down at the bulging ashtray on her desk. She sighed. 'It's possible, given the number of deaths that seem to be mounting up around this escape, that they may very well have been disposed of. We mustn't forget either that there were only two nurses at the scene when Kaya escaped from the Cerrahpaşa.'

'I contacted the Kartal Prison as İkmen asked to try to get them to protect the prisoner Ara Berköz,' İzzet said. 'But if the corruption there is as widespread as it could be at the Cerrahpaşa, I wouldn't like to make a bet on his chances.' He looked up at his colleague and frowned. 'You know, Ayşe, I always knew that Yusuf Kaya was a rich and powerful drug dealer, but don't you think that all this buying of people, all this killing, is excessive even by his standards?'

Ayşe sat back in her chair and crossed her arms over her chest. She at least was not supposed to be working on this particular Sunday but she'd been unable to settle to anything not work-related at home. The hunt for Yusuf Kaya and the various twists and turns in that investigation was obsessing all of them. Crass though he could be, İzzet was a good person with whom to discuss theories and ideas.

'He does seem to have a lot of power now,' she said.

'Tommi Kerensky, the Russian he killed, was at the top of the tree amongst the eastern European dealers,' İzzet said. 'There are quite a few Russians in the Kartal Prison that I would have at least imagined might have had a go at ending

224

Kaya's life inside. It's all about revenge in their world, after all. And then there was the beggar king Hüseyin Altun, found stabbed . . .'

'We know that Kaya and Altun knew of each other at least. Kaya supplied Hüseyin or his people with drugs. But the connection only really exists through Hüseyin's lieutenant Aslan and his girlfriend Sophia. Altun's death may or may not be connected.'

İzzet didn't answer. Like Ayşe he just sat and looked ahead at nothing much really. The station was quite quiet, a lot of the uniformed officers having been assigned to the various Orthodox Christian churches in the city which were celebrating Easter. The official protection of most places of worship now was a sad fact of modern life. Some people, or so it seemed, would not even consider leaving others alone to do what they wanted to do in peace. But then peace wasn't something İzzet and Ayşe were to experience for very much longer themselves. İkmen, looking even more tired and worn out than usual, burst into his office in a vast ball of grey cigarette smoke. For a moment he just looked at his sergeant sitting frowning at her desk and at İzzet Melik and then he said, 'We've got to find this man.'

He held up the photograph of Bekir that his daughter Çiçek had put on to the computer for Fatma. Bülent had printed this copy out on to a large piece of photographic paper. İzzet looked up at the picture and said, 'Who is he? What's he done?'

'He's a shit who gives cocaine to children!' İkmen said with real poison and yet at the same time real misery in his voice too. 'He's—'

'That's Aslan!' Ayşe Farsakoğlu said as she peered at the picture, nodding her head as she did so. 'Hüseyin Altun's old lieutenant. That's a really good picture. Sure he sells cocaine to kids, I don't know about giving . . . Sir?'

İkmen had almost fallen down on to the top of his desk. 'Are you sure? You've seen him so infrequently,' he said in what for him was a very small voice. '*This* is Aslan?'

'We're looking for him anyway, aren't we?' İzzet said. 'Handy to get a photograph though, sir. Where did you get it from?'

There was a pause during which both Ayşe Farsakoğlu and İzzet Melik became rather concerned about the extraordinarily pale colour İkmen's face had gone.

'I got it from my printer at home,' İkmen managed to say at last. 'This man – Aslan – is also known as Bekir İkmen. He is the third and most troublesome of my sons.'

There had been no signal that Süleyman could discern to suggest that the service had actually started. The church just filled up with men wearing either very cheap and unfashionable suits or ensembles so up to the minute and expensive he was almost jealous. The old man who stood next to him was one of the former, a peasant in a jacket and trousers he had probably been married in. Beside him, all in a shade of cream that had, Süleyman recalled, been quite the thing for a while back in the 1970s, was a 'simple' man of about fifty. In all probability he was the older man's son. Occasionally he made strange hooting noises and rolled his eyes and drooled, but nobody took any notice. Not even the headscarfed, clearly Muslim ladies who sat on the benches at the back of the women's area of the church. In front of them were the far more aquiline and elegantly dressed Suriani ladies. Although much taller than most of the other women, Edibe Taner, right in the middle of the Christian group, looked very different from those around her. Her face was broader, more Asiatic. These Surianis were plainly Arabs. There was not, however, as yet, any sign of the American woman Elizabeth Smith, or of the Kaya men who guarded her.

The priest raised a smoking thurible of incense up until it swung and then proceeded to walk up and down the aisle blessing the congregation with its pungent contents.

Ayşe Farsakoğlu had been to İkmen's apartment several times before. She knew it as a joyfully chaotic place where food and drink were always being pushed on anyone who came over the threshold. This day, however, was different. For a start, either the younger İkmen children were out or they were unnaturally quiet and Mrs Fatma İkmen was nowhere to be seen. Once Ayşe and İzzet had taken their shoes off at the door, İkmen led them to their left and into a small messy room.

'This was Bülent's room,' İkmen explained as he closed the door behind them. 'We let Bekir stay here when he turned up out of the blue. Then my youngest son, Kemal, began spending a lot of time with him. You can smell, even now he's out, that ghastly spot cream or lotion or whatever it is that Kemal has taken to slathering himself with lately.'

Ayşe didn't know what İkmen meant. The smell he was referring to meant something quite different to her. But she put on the plastic gloves they had all brought with them and began looking around.

'My wife and the two younger children are spending the day with family,' İkmen said. Fatma had taken the kids over to the home of the eldest İkmen child, Sınan. A doctor, Sınan was due to go abroad for a job interview the following day. If things went to plan he would soon be working in London.

Just the thought of it made İkmen's chest tighten a little with tension. Of course if Sınan got the job in London he would have to take it; it was what he wanted. But the loss of him on top of Bekir was not going to be easy for Fatma. Her children were almost gone now. Even her youngest was no longer really a child. İkmen tried hard not to think about Kemal snorting coke probably from the back of a battered old tobacco tin or something equally disgusting. His mobile phone began to ring. Ayşe Farsakoğlu picked up what had been Bekir's rucksack and looked inside.

İkmen signalled for her to put the rucksack down and then said, 'İkmen.'

'Çetin, it's Arto,' the familiar voice of the Armenian pathologist said. 'It's about your dead prison officer.'

'Ramazan Eren?'

'Yes,' the doctor said. 'I'm afraid I have some bad news.'

İzzet Melik, who had been looking at the old Galatasaray football posters on the walls, turned round and looked at İkmen, frowning.

'Yes?' İkmen asked the Armenian. 'And so?'

'The toxicology came back with a positive result for diamorphine,' the doctor said. 'Enough to kill an ox. This death was not natural, Çetin. Who was the attending doctor over at the Cerrahpaşa?'

'Eldem,' İkmen said after a pause.

'Well, Dr Eldem has some questions to answer,' Arto said. 'I suggest you get him in right away.'

'I will,' İkmen said. After thanking the doctor for his prompt attention he closed his telephone up.

'Dr Eldem in trouble, is he?' İzzet asked.

'Yes,' İkmen replied. 'It would seem that someone gave Ramazan Eren an overdose of diamorphine.'

'Dr Eldem.'

'He would seem to be the most likely candidate at this time,' İkmen said. 'İzzet, I'd like you to get over to the Cerrahpaşa and pick him up. If he isn't there get the director to give you his details. At the very least, Dr Eldem has some explaining to do.'

'Yes, sir.'

'Once Sergeant Farsakoğlu and myself have finished here, we'll go back to the station and hopefully see you there,' İkmen said as he escorted İzzet Melik back to the front door of the apartment.

'Eldem may already have gone,' İzzet said just before he left. 'He was behaving cagily at the hospital yesterday, wasn't he?'

'If that is the case then I'll have to go to Commissioner Ardıç,' İkmen said. 'As it is I think we'll soon be needing more men and more powers to really get to grips with just where the trail of Kaya's influence is taking us.'

'Yes, sir.'

İkmen returned to Bekir's bedroom where Ayşe Farsakoğlu was still looking down at the rucksack he had asked her to leave.

'Bülent found the syringe in there,' he said. 'And some cocaine powder. I want the whole bag analysed. There are some twigs or something in there too. Not cannabis, but—'

'Wormwood,' Ayşe said with absolute confidence. 'Like the tattoo on Faruk Öz's arm. I recognised the smell as soon as I entered the apartment. The leaves in that bag are wormwood leaves.'

'Ah, but the smell is Kemal's cream.'

'No, sir. If Kemal told you that was the smell of his cream, he was lying. The smell is wormwood,' Ayşe said. 'My

229

grandmother used to put wormwood leaves amongst her clothes to discourage moths. It's awful. I'd know it anywhere. This room reeks of it!'

'We assumed that because Kemal was using some new cream,' İkmen said slowly, 'it had to be him. Since he developed spots he's used some foul things on his skin. He told us he was using some new stuff. He told us it smelt just like this.'

'As I said, he lied to you. The smell is wormwood,' Ayşe persisted. 'And, sir, I would suggest that it was being used to cover the scent of any narcotics Bekir might have been carrying in that bag. Your son was using heroin himself, as well as sniffing coke and giving that to your other boy. He might have been carrying cannabis too at some stage and that really can smell. But with wormwood around he'd know no one would be able to detect anything else he was carrying. He'd even maybe be confident enough to leave the apartment and go down the street with the stuff. Only our own drug dogs would get past wormwood – maybe. And your son wasn't likely to come up against one of those, was he? Have you found any more drugs in this room?'

İkmen, suddenly deflated by being taken for what he felt was a fool, sat down shakily on Bülent's old bed. 'No . . .'

'Have you looked?'

'No, not . . .'

He looked awful. Ayşe went and sat down next to him.

'Sir, I will look round and then we will, as you have suggested, call forensic,' she said gently. 'I suspect if your son had a large amount of heroin, cocaine or whatever here in this room he has now taken it with him. You have no idea where he might have gone?'

'No.'

'Well, sir,' Ayşe said as she looked around the room once again, 'all I can suggest at this stage is that, assuming that your son Bekir and the late Hüseyin Altun's lieutenant Aslan are one and the same, we pick up Sophia the Bulgarian girl again.'

'Sophia?' For a moment İkmen looked confused. But then as light began to dawn in his brain he said, 'Of course, Sophia! The girl who was, er, um . . .'

'The girl who is pregnant, she says, with Aslan's child,' Ayşe said.

There was no accompaniment of any sort. When the beautiful young women in the Suriani choir began to sing their voices soared alone until they were answered by the deeper sounds of the men's choir which now, as if by magic, appeared from behind a large spangled cloth that hung beside the altar. Beyond was a rough-cut stone doorway out of which now processed men and boys of all ages from ten to eighty. Both men and women continued to sing until the areas to both sides of the altar were filled with people and with sound. The service had been going on, so far as Süleyman could tell, for at least an hour and a half. Where on earth was the American woman and why didn't Edibe Taner look at all agitated about the fact that she hadn't shown up? But then, if she had the house outside Dara under surveillance, maybe she knew something that he didn't. He looked across the aisle meaningfully, or so he thought, at the policewoman, but she didn't respond. She was, like the rest of the congregation with the exception of Süleyman, singing. More unintelligible minutes passed. Then the priest, carrying before him a large metal cross wrapped closely in a blood red cloth, began to process round the church, followed by the men's choir.

He'd heard Arab women ululating before – from a distance. Close to, as it was now, it was both eerie and deafening. What it meant in this context he didn't really know, although from the tears in the people's eyes he assumed they were probably mourning the suffering of their Christ. All of them wanted to touch the red-robed cross as it passed, and if they managed to do so they smiled at those around them. It was as he was watching the procession move round the back of the church that he saw a covered woman, surrounded by the guards he'd seen at Elizabeth Smith's house, walk through the door. The group separated, she slipping to the women's side of the church and her guards coming to stand behind Süleyman and Seçkin Taner on the men's side. No one had reacted in a noticeable fashion to their arrival. The women's ululations continued to roll around the inside walls of the church, making every hair on Süleyman's head and body stand up as, in his mind at least, the Cobweb World all but enveloped him.

Chapter 16

Between his apartment on Büyük Hendek Alley and some nameless little street somewhere, probably less than a kilometre away in the district of Cihangir, Murat Lole managed to lose his police 'tail'. One young constable, whose first time on such an assignment this was, plus one slightly older and more experienced officer were the culprits. Apparently the younger one had been distracted by the sight of a group of dancing girls crossing a street on their way to one of the nightclubs of Beyoğlu. His older colleague had clearly been equally entranced. İkmen was incandescent with rage, but not just with the two officers. In fact he didn't spend very much time berating them at all, because when İzzet Melik brought Dr Eldem in he turned his attention to him.

'Our pathologist, backed up by toxicology reports from the forensic institute, has proved that the cause of the prison officer Ramazan Eren's death was not spontaneous multiple organ failure,' İkmen said as he sat down opposite the doctor. 'Cause of death was poisoning via a massive overdose of diamorphine. You were in charge of this patient, Dr Eldem. Explain this, will you.'

The doctor didn't answer. He sat, impassively, in front of İkmen and İzzet Melik, his face expressionless. For a moment İkmen just looked back until he turned to İzzet Melik and said, 'Sergeant, did you say that Dr Eldem has waived his right to legal representation?'

'Yes, sir,' İzzet replied. 'I don't know why; he wouldn't say.'

İkmen leaned across the interview room table towards the doctor and said, 'That wasn't very bright, Dr Eldem. As the responsible physician to a man who has died via an overdose of hospital quality diamorphine you're not in a particularly good place at the moment.'

'Other people had access to that room apart from me,' Dr Eldem said calmly. 'I know I didn't kill the guard. It's up to you to prove it.'

'And I will,' İkmen said. 'Apart from the fact that nurses are not in the habit of walking about unsupervised with lethal doses of diamorphine . . .'

'I think you'll find that sometimes they do,' Dr Eldem said. 'After all, it's nurses you've been questioning up until now with regard to this prison break thing, isn't it? Wasn't it nurses who were supposed to have helped that man, whoever he was, escape?'

'Yes, although, Dr Eldem, we do now think that in order for Yusuf Kaya's plan to fully realise itself he had to have help from some people rather higher up the food chain than a few young nurses,' İkmen said. 'And besides, if I look at the nurses we have been considering and what they were doing when Mr Eren died I find that one has completely disappeared, one spent the day in and around his home in Karaköy and the other one is dead. You, Doctor, so the sergeant here tells me, were packing to leave to go somewhere when he arrived.'

There was a moment of silence as the doctor appeared to take in what had just been said to him. There was also a very faint flicker of what İkmen felt could possibly be fear.

'Er, the nurse in Karaköy, he . . .'

'We have been following him,' İkmen said with a smile he had to really force on to his face. Murat Lole, unless rediscovered soon, was going to be a very sore point. 'The other one we found dead outside the lodging of the third nurse in Zeyrek.'

'Oh, well then, the nurse from Zeyrek, the third one, must have killed him,' Dr Eldem said. 'There is your answer. And just because he, this other nurse, is missing doesn't mean that he isn't around. He could have come into the Cerrahpaşa and killed my patient and—'

'Yes, he could,' İkmen said. 'Theoretically. But, Doctor, I don't think that he did. İsak Mardin, the name by which this nurse goes, worked in cardiac care. Now, he hasn't been on his own ward since the night of Yusuf Kaya's escape. He'd cause a stir if he turned up there now, but on an unknown ward he would stand right out. Especially a ward with a police officer, remember, on the door.'

'But if this Mardin killed this other—'

'Oh, we don't know that Mardin killed the other nurse,' İkmen answered with a smile. 'The body was found outside his lodging house. Anyone, in theory, could have done it. Personally I think that Nurse Mardin is either a very long way away or dead.'

'Why do you think that?'

'Because a lot of people are dying around the fact of Yusuf Kaya's escape,' İkmen said. 'In all probability Yusuf or those who work for him are clearing up the "mess" around the incident as quickly as they can. After all, when you buy a lot of people, you have to be certain that your investments are going to do as they have been told. There's only one way in which you can be absolutely sure of that, however.'

'Say you won't pay up until the job is over and then kill the person before he can collect,' İzzet Melik put in with a smile.

Both İkmen and Melik had imagined that the doctor would be fazed by such a revelation, but he didn't seem to be. His face remained impassive and he did not appear to be unduly uncomfortable in his seat.

'Unless, of course,' İzzet Melik said, 'this, whatever it is, isn't just about Yusuf Kaya's escape.'

İkmen looked at Süleyman's sergeant questioningly. The doctor cleared his throat.

'What if it's about something bigger?' İzzet said. 'Yusuf Kaya is a drug dealer. Significant, but not a huge player. The Russian dealer he took down, on the other hand, was very powerful indeed, and yet not one of Tommi Kerensky's fellow gang members in the Kartal Prison even tried to avenge their old leader's death. Kaya was left alone. Kaya got out of prison with help, possibly from Eren or the other dead guard, possibly from who knows who! Then, at the Cerrahpaşa, help again!' He leaned forward and snarled into the doctor's slightly whitening face. 'We're struggling to keep the dealers in check, keep the addicts we already have under control. But I think that something bigger is in the pipeline and I think that Yusuf Kaya and at least some of his little minions, including I think you, Dr Eldem, know what it is.'

Every so often İzzet Melik made connections like this. It was at such times that his often irritating macho swaggering was worth putting up with. İkmen looked at his colleague with admiration as various elements of his own and Mehmet Süleyman's recent experience began to click into place.

'Dr Eldem,' he said after a pause, 'what does wormwood mean to you?'

The feast the parishioners of Mar Behnam had prepared in the marquee in the church garden was considerable. It was also, Seçkin Taner took pains to point out to Süleyman, entirely pork free.

'As Christians they can eat pork,' he said. 'But they all have Muslim friends and relations sometimes too and so out of kindness to us they don't do that. They serve wine, of course,' he shrugged as if this other Islamic prohibition were nothing, 'but one can take or leave that.' He moved very close to Süleyman's ear and said, 'But take it if you can is my advice. They make truly excellent wine.'

Süleyman smiled and then watched as Seçkin Taner took a plate and helped himself to a very generous portion of the feast. The man's daughter was not long behind.

Edibe Taner looked up at Süleyman and raised a questioning eyebrow.

'I understood nothing beyond the blessing of the Republic, but that said it was very interesting,' he said in answer to her silent query. 'I've been to Orthodox churches before but I've never seen anything like that. Is the congregation usually that large?'

'At Easter people's relatives from Syria come across the border to spend a few days in the city,' Taner said, and then she lowered her voice. 'According to the officers watching the Dara house Elizabeth Smith and her men didn't leave until well after the Easter service had started. She is either not as keen on Suriani spectacle as she would like us to believe or something in her house detained her.'

'I'd forgotten she'd be covered,' Süleyman said, referring to the American's veil.

'To remain a secret, she'd have to be when she left the house,' Edibe Taner replied. 'That's what she told me when I stopped in Dara yesterday.'

'You visited her?'

'She was in her garden, covered. I was intrigued.'

Süleyman wondered what Taner had been doing in Dara without him. But he didn't ask and moved on to present events.

'Are any of her guards still at the house?'

'Two,' she replied. 'But I doubt whether there is very much to see there. I think that she will have anticipated that we might want to take a look while she is away. However, she and her entourage did arrive in a very large truck. I can have that searched. Especially today, especially with it parked out on Avenue One.'

Süleyman looked over and watched as several people kissed Elizabeth Smith's hand. The language she spoke to them in was clearly Aramaic. She was obviously a woman who learned fast.

'Don't you think that someone like her is too clever to carry what she shouldn't in her car?' he asked.

Edibe Taner was about to answer when some sort of commotion began to bubble up amongst the group of people who were standing at the entrance to the church grounds. Quite a few of the people appeared to want to get out.

Süleyman said, 'Any idea what's going on?'

'No, but I'll go and see,' Edibe Taner said. And then with just the lightest of touches on his arm she added, 'You wait here.'

She ran down to the now boiling knot of people, shouting at them to let her through as she did so. Seçkin Taner, who was eating a very fat stuffed vine leaf, came over to Süleyman and said, 'What's going on?'

'I don't know,' Süleyman replied. 'Your daughter has gone to sort out some sort of incident down by the entrance.'

Seçkin Taner shrugged. 'Some idiot wanting to come in and shout and protest about the celebration of Easter, I expect,' he said gloomily. 'Inspector, the older I get the less tolerant I become with intolerance.'

Süleyman smiled.

'If people don't like something I don't know why they can't just keep their prejudices to themselves.'

By this time many of the people who had been inside the marquee eating, drinking and talking had come outside to watch what was going on down by the entrance. Edibe Taner had disappeared. Süleyman could see one police uniform in the midst of the crowd, but its wearer was very isolated and was shouting something in Aramaic that the man from İstanbul couldn't understand.

'What—'

'He's telling them to get out of the way,' Seçkin Taner said. 'Look, now they're clearing to either side of the door.'

They were, if reluctantly, moving out of the policeman's way. Some of the women, particularly, were crying. What on earth could possibly be upsetting them so much? Once the officer had moved the people there was a pause. Then, alone at first, the tall slim figure of Edibe Taner walked across the threshold and into the church complex again. Just inside she turned and paused. It was as if, Süleyman thought, she was talking to someone behind her. He was very soon proved right when the figure of a man, his clothes ripped and muddy, his beard and hair straggly and unkempt, stepped into the church grounds behind her. The whole great crowd

239

of people both down by the entrance and outside the marquee gasped.

'Mar Gabriel!'

Süleyman turned quickly to Seçkin Taner, but he knew what the Master of Sharmeran was going to say before he said it.

'Gabriel Saatçi has returned to us,' Seçkin said. Then, raising his hands to heaven in a gesture of supplication, he added, 'May Allah be praised.'

'According to Mardin police station, Inspector Süleyman is at church,' İkmen said as he lowered himself down into the chair behind his desk. 'That's why his mobile phone is off.'

Ayşe Farsakoğlu sighed. 'Those Orthodox ceremonies last a long time, sir.'

'I know.' İkmen lit a cigarette and leaned back in his chair. Ayşe didn't usually have any trouble talking to her superior but on this occasion she was finding being alone with him hard. That the slimy Aslan of the old Hüseyin Altun gang was his son was both appalling and incredible. Although İkmen himself had had little to do with Altun or his child thieves in the past, the police as a whole were always picking up one or other of the youngsters for various infringements of the law. Not that Aslan had ever been in police custody to Ayşe's knowledge. The little shit had been one of Hüseyin's early recruits and was consequently very cunning and street savvy. Still, the fact that Aslan had not once been arrested in spite of his involvement with drugs was—

'I never helped my son, you know, Ayşe,' İkmen said in one of those eerie moments when he appeared to be reading her mind.

'Sir, I . . .' Flustered, she stammered a rebuttal, but her face was red and sweating and told, to İkmen, a slightly different tale.

'It's all right, Ayşe,' he continued. 'I know that I will have to answer questions about Bekir and quite rightly so.' He cleared his throat. 'I came into contact with Hüseyin Altun only once, when the junkie who lived next door to him was murdered for less than a quarter of a gram by some even more desperate addict. I spoke to Hüseyin but neither he nor the dead-eyed kids in his kitchen knew anything. They were, just coincidentally, telling the truth. But my son wasn't there. I think I would have felt something if my own blood had been in that room.'

There was a pause and then Ayşe said, 'I believe you, sir. You've certainly had no dealings with Hüseyin since I've worked for you. But as for me?' She shrugged. 'I've had little contact with Hüseyin since I've worked for you too. Before, though, I knew him quite well and Aslan I knew by sight. He was cocky and sneaky and I know that he got some of the younger ones hooked on heroin, including Sophia.'

'The mother of my grandchild,' İkmen said softly.

As soon as she'd made the connection between Bekir İkmen and Aslan, Ayşe had been haunted by this notion. 'Yes,' she said and then very quickly changed the subject. 'Sir, I didn't know that he was your son. Only now, looking at that picture and then looking at you, can I see any resemblance. But it isn't strong, sir.'

'No.' He tapped on the top of his desk with his fingers. 'I'll have to tell Dr Sarkissian.'

'He knew your son.'

'Of course.' He smiled and then, sighing, he frowned once again. 'But later. Ayşe, I have called Commissioner Ardıç, on his day off, and he is not, as you can imagine, very pleased about that.'

A mental picture of the commissioner's red and angry face came into Ayşe's mind. That was Ardıç on a reasonably good day. 'Sir?'

'If I want to instigate a full search for my son, I have to go through him,' İkmen said. 'Total honesty is the only way I can move forward with this. I also have to tell him, as I am telling you, that I think the timing of my son's sudden reappearance was no accident.'

'What do you mean?'

'I mean I think it is possible that my son might have been mixed up in Yusuf Kaya's escape,' İkmen said. 'I don't know how. But Sophia told us that Aslan knew Kaya. My son turns up at my home on the same day that Kaya escapes. Hüseyin Altun has been killed.'

'Yes, but—'

'Coincidence or not,' İkmen interrupted, 'Altun, an albeit petty drug peddler, goes to join luminaries like Tommi Kerensky whose "soldiers", as İzzet pointed out earlier, did not take revenge upon him when he was in prison. My son appears with drugs and wormwood. Wormwood grows around one of Yusuf Kaya's houses in Mardin. All the names of the nurses at the Cerrahpaşa lead back to Mardin . . .'

'Sir, it's all circumstantial.'

İkmen lowered his head.

'Until Inspector Süleyman or someone finds Yusuf Kaya or until someone speaks to make these connections real in some way, we won't know,' Ayşe said. 'Sir, believe me, I can see why Sergeant Melik thinks that there's some sort of conspiracy at work here.'

'Yusuf Kaya didn't just escape to escape but to *do* something specific too,' İkmen said. 'Ayşe, I don't have to tell you how competitive the drug trade is now.'

'Since the Taliban were effectively taken out of the picture in Afghanistan, it's gone crazy, yes,' Ayşe said. 'I hate the Taliban; they're so violent towards women it makes me want to weep. But they did control the heroin. Now it's anyone's game and there's so much money to be made it is ridiculous.'

'Kaya behaved with total recklessness when he murdered Tommi Kerensky,' İkmen said. 'Inspector Süleyman told me at the time that at his trial Kaya didn't appear to care about where he was or what was happening to him. What if Kaya was in the process of making the biggest deal of his life?'

'But sir, the drug trade moves very quickly,' Ayşe said. 'When Yusuf Kaya was put in prison someone else would have jumped into his shoes if he had an outstanding deal.'

'This is true,' İkmen sighed. But then he frowned again and said, 'Unless it was bigger than a deal . . .'

'Bigger than a deal?'

İkmen's telephone rang and he leaned across his desk to pick it up. 'İkmen.'

Bigger than a deal? What could possibly, for a drug dealer, be bigger than a deal?

İkmen put the receiver down and then stood up. 'Ardıç is in his office,' he said. 'I must go and see him.'

Just before he left, and although her mind was still puzzling over what he had just said, Ayşe told her boss that she personally would look for Bulgarian Sophia.

'If you find her, then bring her back here,' İkmen said with a smile. 'Sophia should know who Aslan is from me. I'd like to help her if I can, but . . . Oh, and Ayşe, Sergeant Melik has gone back to the Cerrahpaşa. He has some notion that possibly the administrator may have some more to tell us.'

* * *

Underneath all the filth and beyond the obvious lack of nutrition, Gabriel Saatçi was clearly a good-looking man in an ethereal sort of way. It was impossible to even guess at his age, but if he had been to school with Edibe Taner then he was probably in his mid to late forties. As he moved through the silent crowd, Süleyman noticed that he was laying a trail of blood behind him which looked as if it had to be coming from his feet. Filthy hands held a wooden box out in front of him, and his dark, almost fierce eyes concentrated on it intently. No one spoke. Edibe Taner, walking behind the monk, did so with obvious caution. Then suddenly Gabriel Saatçi looked round at the assembled company and spoke in a low, deep voice. What he said Süleyman couldn't tell, and although he knew that Seçkin Taner would in all probability translate for him, he was loath to speak to anyone at such a seemingly delicate moment. All he could make out was the name İbrahim in there somewhere.

Not one member of those assembled moved for a long time. Even Edibe Taner remained absolutely still behind her old friend Gabriel. It must have been a good five minutes before one of Elizabeth Smith's guards stepped down from outside the marquee and approached the living saint. He was a short, tough-looking man of again probably about forty-five or so. Süleyman remembered seeing him at the house outside Dara. As the man approached him, Gabriel Saatçi began to berate him. This time Seçkin Taner leaned over towards Süleyman and provided a translation.

'Brother Gabriel says this man, İbrahim Keser, must no longer torment his father. He says that he must face him himself, like a man.'

'What does that mean?' Süleyman asked. 'Whose father? Gabriel Saatçi's father?'

Seçkin Taner shrugged. 'I imagine so. The man, Keser, is neighbour to Musa Saatçi. That is all I know.'

As he stood, shaking either with rage or under the force of a torrent of Aramaic abuse, İbrahim Keser bowed his head.

'Brother Gabriel says this man is a dog and an unbeliever,' Seçkin Taner said.

'The man is a Christian?'

'Yes. But Brother Gabriel means in general, I think. I think he means that Keser is a man without God, you know?'

A man not unlike himself, Süleyman thought. Years ago he had loved Allah and the Prophet. He'd gone to the mosque regularly with his father, his grandfather and his uncle. When had he banished Allah from his life? It wasn't as if he were even a happy atheist like Çetin İkmen!

A loud click made Süleyman attend to the scene before him again. It was followed by gasps of shock from everyone around him. The monk had opened the wooden box now and was holding it up. Two sinuous snakes' heads appeared at the opening and one of the creatures began to writhe. The monk spoke in a low, trembling voice while the man standing in front of him sweated. Edibe Taner, still behind the monk, spoke softly to him whilst holding back the officer at her side with one hand. The policeman in question had drawn his pistol.

'Brother Gabriel says he will prove to this dog that his miracle is real,' Seçkin Taner said to Süleyman. 'My daughter says he must not do this here with all the ladies and the children around.'

'But . . .'

Edibe Taner spoke again.

'My daughter says that if the snakes get away the police will kill them.'

The monk apparently ignored her then, and Süleyman

watched as Edibe Taner's face went grey. Gabriel Saatçi picked one snake up in each hand and then held the two of them aloft. He said something which Süleyman didn't understand. But this time he didn't get a translation because Seçkin Taner had run down to take charge.

Chapter 17

'Mr Oner, your predecessor, died last month as a result of ingesting disinfectant,' İzzet Melik said to the pale man in front of him. 'It was Mr Oner who gave İsak Mardin a job here in the hospital. Last year Mr Oner also employed the nurses Lole and Öz. Öz, whose real name was actually Hasan Karabulut, a relative of Yusuf Kaya, the escaped convict, is now dead, and Lole deliberately gave our officers the slip earlier today. Now, sir, one of your patients, a man who was a witness to the prisoner Yusuf Kaya's escape from this very hospital, has been declared unlawfully killed by an overdose of diamorphine. We have questioned the doctor entrusted with his care, Dr Eldem, and we are not satisfied with his explanation of that death.'

'Why not?' The hospital administrator shook as he spoke. Once he'd given this thuggish policeman Eldem's address he hadn't expected to see him again. Well, not so soon, anyway. 'Why aren't you satisfied?'

'Because we don't believe that Dr Eldem is telling the truth,' İzzet replied. 'Everything comes back to this hospital and I want to know why. Öz we know knew Kaya, Lole is a name famously associated with Kaya's home town of Mardin and of course Nurse Mardin has a connection that speaks for itself. It also, sir, speaks of an arrogance and a confidence on the part of whoever has been orchestrating these events.'

'These events? What do you mean "these events"?'

'I mean, sir,' İzzet said, 'the ease with which Kaya and whoever was with him got out of this building. I mean the way that the tape in your security cameras is so frankly over-used and fuzzy.'

'The men on the film were wearing stockings or some such over their heads. Of course nothing much could be seen! Your superior told me so!'

'Did he?' İzzet looked round quickly to make sure the door to the administrator's office was closed. It was and, since it was a Sunday, there was no noise coming from the corridor outside. 'Well, I'm telling you that was only part of the problem we had with that film. It was fucked! Old damaged tape! How many times did you use it, eh? How much money did that save you?'

'I—'

İzzet pulled one large arm back and then hit the hospital administrator sharply, if not hard, across the face. His lip split open, just a little bit, immediately.

'You can't—'

İzzet walked round to the back of the administrator's desk and took his head in the crook of his arm. 'I can do whatever I like,' he hissed. 'And I will until you, sir, tell me just what is going on here!'

A thin dribble of blood oozed down on to the administrator's chin. 'I – I can't . . .' He struggled to breathe, let alone talk. There was a long pause before either of them spoke again.

'Sir, I am very sorry that I hit you,' İzzet said. 'I am truly very sorry for that. But you must understand that people are being killed. Sir, to be party to an escape from prison, to even be involved in drugs is one thing. But to be an accessory to murder . . .'

248

'I am not an accessory to murder!'

'Dr Eldem will eventually tell us what we need to know,' İzzet said. 'He was packing his bags for a journey when I got to his house. That makes me very suspicious.'

'About me?' İzzet had loosened his grip slightly upon the administrator's throat now, enabling him to speak much more easily. 'It was I who gave you Eldem's address. Were I in league with him for some reason, why would I do that?'

After a moment, İzzet let him go and walked round to the front of the desk again. He sat down and put his head in his hands. 'I'm sorry,' he murmured through his fingers. 'I am really, really sorry. I . . .'

There was a pause. The administrator took a tissue out of the box on his desk and held it up to his bleeding lip. After a few moments' apparent thought he said, 'Well, you have a hard job to—'

'Oh, that's no excuse,' İzzet said, as he looked up red-eyed into the administrator's face. 'I just had this theory and people were listening to me for once and . . .'

'You got a little carried away,' the administrator said.

İzzet swung his arms out to his sides in a gesture of hope-lessness and then said, 'Sir, if you wish to complain you may do so. I have no defence to offer whatsoever.'

The administrator sat back in his chair and once again dabbed the tissue against his lip.

'I'll even, sir, support you,' İzzet said. 'I have a problem with my temper, or I can do, and—'

'Sergeant, I don't think that there will be any need for that,' the administrator said. 'I . . .' He looked down at his desk and smiled and then he said, 'Accept that I don't know anything about this Kaya business, which is the truth, and we'll say no more about it.'

İzzet sat and considered what had just been said to him for some little time. Or looked as if he was.

'There's no risk to you,' the administrator said. 'I'm telling the truth, after all.'

A little more time passed in silence before İzzet Melik stood up to shake hands with the man beside his desk. 'I'll write up that you simply had nothing to add,' he said. Then, in what could have been interpreted as a gesture of affection, he placed one of his hands on the top of the administrator's arm.

'Sergeant . . .'

And then he pulled the shirt sleeve, hard. The arm that had been concealed inside was thin and covered in a spider's web of angry track marks.

İzzet stared the man straight in his frightened eyes and said, 'I thought I caught a glimpse of something when you rolled up your sleeves to get into Dr Eldem's Personnel file. You just about caught yourself in time, but I saw you. I had to be sure, however. Now I am.' Then he called out to the officer he knew had been outside the door all the time. 'Constable? Get in here!'

The door opened while the administrator just looked down at his own arm with horror. 'You, you . . .'

'Now, sir, in answer to your question about why you would give me Dr Eldem's address if you were in league with him, let me tell you that, as you well know, there isn't much a junkie will not do to save his own skin.' He turned round to face Constable Doğa. 'Let's get this man down to the station.'

'Seçkin Bey is asking for Mar Gabriel to give the snakes to him,' the young Suriani girl said to Süleyman. 'They will not bite Seçkin Bey. He is their master.' The daughter of one of the Master of Sharmeran's friends, she had come over to translate for the man from İstanbul.

Süleyman looked down at the girl in horror. 'What kind of snakes are they?'

'Vipers.'

Seçkin Taner was approaching the monk now, his arms outstretched. As he moved past the terrified figure of İbrahim Keser he spoke softly and gently to Gabriel Saatçi who, though trembling also, Süleyman could see did appear to be listening to him now.

'Seçkin Bey says that this is not the way, that the Sharmeran will be displeased with him if he hurts anyone,' the girl said.

The monk screamed then, a hail of what to Süleyman sounded like pure invective.

'Mar Gabriel says that this man, Mr Keser, must confess his sins. He says that he will perform his miracle now.'

Arms as thin as tree branches raised the snakes high up into the air as the monk began to sing. Seçkin Taner very calmly carried on talking.

'What . . .'

'Mar Gabriel will now let the snakes bite him,' the girl said. 'I wasn't born the first time that he performed his miracle.'

The implication being that this was all very exciting. Edibe Taner, still behind the now swaying monk, looked about as far from excited as one could get. She said something and almost immediately the monk dropped to his knees. For a moment Süleyman thought that he had been shot. Then he remembered about the snakes. They were no longer in the monk's hands.

Someone screamed and Edibe Taner, the armed constable still at her side, shouted something into the air. But whatever she said had little effect upon the people in the courtyard and the garden, who were running as far away as they could from where the monk had fallen. It wasn't until almost a minute had passed that anyone, including Süleyman, realised that Seçkin Taner now had a viper in each hand and was holding them aloft for all to see. He was smiling and, though restrained, the two serpents seemed to be comfortable enough in his company. His daughter, now down on the ground beside the monk, was calling for help. A balding man of about fifty and Süleyman himself ran over. As he passed Seçkin Taner he saw that the Master of Sharmeran was placing the snakes back in the box they had come from.

'Dr Kozlu,' Edibe Taner said to the balding man in Turkish, 'he just collapsed.'

The doctor took the monk's thin wrist between his fingers and then looked at his watch. But Süleyman could see that the monk was, if very shallowly, breathing.

'I thought he'd been shot,' he blurted as Edibe Taner regarded her friend with great concern.

She ignored him. 'Doctor . . .'

'Well, he has a pulse,' the doctor said. 'Just collapsed. But from the state of him I'd reckon he's probably dehydrated.' He took a mobile phone out of the pocket of his jacket and switched it on. 'I'll admit him to the hospital.'

'He'll be all right, won't he, Doctor?' Edibe Taner asked. But Dr Kozlu was too busy on the phone to answer her. She looked down at the monk's face and, with tears in her eyes, said something to him in Aramaic. All around people were gathering to see what had happened to their saint. But now more police officers had come into the grounds and they were holding a lot of the people back.

When she finally did manage to speak to anyone apart from the monk, Edibe Taner said to Süleyman, 'The American woman's guard is İbrahim Keser. İbrahim Keser, Uncle Musa's neighbour. Gabriel was goading him. Accusing him! Inspector, will you make sure that Keser doesn't leave the church, please?'

Süleyman said he would. However, search as he might, he couldn't find Keser, Elizabeth Smith or any of her other guards anywhere. He ran out on to Avenue One to see whether a large truck was still parked by the pavement. But it wasn't.

Sophia the Bulgarian girl was almost certainly not a regular churchgoer. But pregnant and alone in a foreign country she would in all probability, Ayşe felt, make an exception for the Easter service.

The church where the Bulgarian and Macedonian community in İstanbul worship is called St Stephen of the Bulgars. Situated in the old Greek quarter of Fener it stands in a small iron-fenced park beside the southern shore of the Golden Horn. It is a unique building in that it is constructed entirely of prefabricated cast-iron sections. Cast in Vienna, it was floated down the Danube and then erected piece by piece in Fener in 1871. An ornate, heavily ornamented building in the neo-Gothic style, St Stephens is, to those unaccustomed to it, an oddity. As Ayşe Farsakoğlu walked past those members of the congregation leaving the church she looked around the dark and in places rusted interior with some curiosity but not very high hopes. Although Orthodox ceremonies did go on sometimes for many hours it was late and she imagined that Sophia had probably returned to wherever she was living now. But she was proved wrong. At the back of the church, underneath a particularly dark and rusted ornamental niche, sat the girl, seemingly lost in thought.

'Sophia?'

She looked up and Ayşe saw that her eyes were very sore and red-looking. She said nothing, so Ayşe sat down beside her and offered her a tissue from her handbag. Clearly the girl had been crying, but there was no need to state the obvious.

'Sophia, we need to talk,' Ayşe said, after a pause during which the girl blew her nose loudly.

'What about?' Her voice was thick with both phlegm from what sounded like a cold and misery.

'About Aslan.'

'Piece of shit who did . . .' Sophia shook her head and then looked up into the roof of the building and said, 'I am sorry to the God! Sorry! Sorry!'

'Sophia . . .'

The girl got up and walked out of the church. Ayşe, following, stayed silent until Sophia stopped at the top of the steps up to the building and said, 'Sorry. I cannot be in church and say bad words.'

'That's OK, I understand,' Ayşe said. And then, aware that other worshippers were looking at them, she said, 'Sophia, come on, let's sit on one of the benches in the garden.'

It was a lovely day and the girl shrugged her agreement easily enough. Waddling down the steps and into the garden she looked as if she were about to give birth any minute. Once they had found an appropriate bench the two women sat down, Sophia with some difficulty.

'Doctor says baby is big,' she said as she plonked herself down with a grunt. 'Blood pressure is bad, so I will be glad when baby comes.'

'I'm sure you will,' Ayşe said with a smile. It was not ideal to be talking about things that Sophia obviously found difficult in the final stages of her pregnancy, but Ayşe really didn't have any choice. 'Aslan . . .'

'Shit!' Sophia put her hand into the pocket of her dress and took out a packet of cigarettes. Not a good idea, as Ayşe knew, in pregnancy, but she let it go. It was not, after all, strictly her business. 'Last night he come after so long! I say if he think he can have baby he can fuck off!'

Ayşe felt her face colour at this news. So Bekir İkmen had been to see his very pregnant and now rapidly smoking girl-friend.

'Do you know where he had been?'

'Been? No. Has gone now.'

'Gone where?'

Sophia shrugged. 'He say there is a lot of trouble. I say, did you kill Hüseyin? He get very angry, say no, say he just have to go away.'

'Sophia,' Ayşe asked, 'did Aslan stay with you last night?'

'Yes,' the girl said, 'sure. He wants the sex but I say no because I am like elephant. I give him blow job.'

'Ah.' Some of the eastern European girls were very frank, and although no prude by any means, Ayşe was sometimes a little bit shocked if she were honest. Also, although Sophia didn't yet know it, the man she was talking about was actually Ayşe's boss's son.

'He leave this morning,' Sophia said. 'I say him he go this time, he go for good! But he go!' She shrugged her arms wide and sniffed. 'Fuck off. He won't see baby. I will not permit. Fuck off to him!'

In Ayşe's experience Aslan had always been a shit, which made equating him with the close and loving İkmen family so hard. When İkmen had said that he wanted to help Sophia he had meant it. He knew she was a foul-mouthed, former (possibly) junkie. How different the father was from the son! If any revelations were to be made, however, that was for İkmen and him alone to do.

'Sophia,' Ayşe said, 'do you remember Inspector İkmen, the man I introduced to you the other day?'

'Your boss?'

'Yes.'

Sophia shrugged.

'He'd like to speak to you, about Aslan,' Ayşe said. 'It's all right – he won't ask you lots and lots of questions. I think you've told us probably all we need to know. But he would like to talk to you. I've got my car with me if you don't feel up to walking.'

İzzet Melik literally jumped out of his seat when İkmen entered his office.

'Sir, I have the administrator of the Cerrahpaşa downstairs,' he blurted. 'He's a junkie, sir. I suspected before, but—'

'So if he's a junkie, what of it?' İkmen said. 'Did you find heroin in his office?'

'No, but—'

'Then why is he here?' İkmen asked. 'We have Dr Eldem who might or might not have killed the guard Ramazan Eren. Do you have reason to believe that the administrator was in on that with him?'

'Well, no, not directly, but junkies are very vulnerable as we know, sir, and if this plot involving Kaya did indeed go right through the institution . . .'

'We don't *know* that it did.'

İzzet Melik knew of course about İkmen's son Bekir and he was aware that the inspector had also just come from Ardıç's office, so it was understandable that he was subdued. However, he had thought that İkmen was in all probability at least willing to run with his notion of something big involving Kaya and drugs and maybe the deal of a lifetime.

'The administrator has, by the look of him, a very big habit,' İzzet said, his eyes shining with his need to go with this. What of course he couldn't tell İkmen was that the administrator had tried to bribe him. By offering to 'forget' about the slap the policeman had given him in return for backing up his story about knowing nothing about Yusuf Kaya, he had attempted to pervert İzzet's investigation. But İzzet had slapped him, and even though he had done so to force the administrator to do what he did, it was still not something the sergeant wanted to own up to. After all, as a means to an end it had been both clumsy and desperate.

İkmen sighed. The interview with Ardıç hadn't been easy. His superior had been sympathetic to his situation and believed that İkmen had been unaware of his son's alter ego, Aslan. But Ardıç was also urging İkmen to exercise caution. He had accepted that if Kaya had indeed escaped when he did for a criminal, drug-related reason, then people both high and low in the hospital and in the prison could be involved. However, because of İkmen's 'involvement' via Bekir and the possibility that that could soon be public knowledge made Ardıç tell İkmen to tread softly. He then issued instructions instigating a full search for Bekir İkmen plus a warrant for his arrest. At the very least he had given illegal drugs to İkmen's son Kemal, a minor.

'Sir,' İzzet continued, 'I know you think, as I do, that Kaya's escape is about much more than just his freedom. So much money must have been either handed over or promised to make what happened possible. And even if money didn't change hands then promises were made and I think they must have been big promises. Sir, Mr Oner, the current administrator's predecessor who gave jobs to Lole and Öz and underwrote Mardin's questionable work record, killed himself for some reason. He was solvent, married with children, no mistresses or creditors as far as I can see. Why did he do that if he wasn't either guilty about something he'd already done, or scared about what was about to happen on his watch? Or was he indeed killed by someone else because maybe he was weak and unreliable?'

'İzzet!'

Melik was getting carried away now and, although İkmen agreed with a lot of what he was saying, he could not force his investigation onward using only circumstantial evidence. He also, as Ardıç had been quick to point out, had to consider his own rather delicate position now.

'İzzet, I will talk to the administrator,' he said. 'But I don't think that I can yet prove that all these people are actually involved in any sort of conspiracy. Dr Eldem we know was packing to leave when we picked him up, and Constable Roditi is minutely examining the hospital drug records as we speak. But we – well, I – you know that my son could possibly be part of this. I—'

His mobile phone began to ring. With a sigh he took it out of his pocket and said, 'İkmen.'

What İzzet saw then was a change in his superior's already grave expression. His face dropped and then he put one of his hands over the telephone and said to İzzet, 'I'm sorry, a personal call. Would you mind?' He pointed towards the office door. 'I'll be with you when I can, İzzet.'

İzzet Melik left and İkmen took his hand away from the phone. 'Where the hell are you?' he hissed. 'And why did you leave one of your filthy syringes in the bedroom I so generously let you use? Do you hate us all so much?'

On the other end of the line, Bekir sniffed. 'No I don't hate you. I used you, yes. I needed to be somewhere where no one would even think of looking for me. Not even Hüseyin knew where I came from and so being with you was OK. The syringe? Dad, I'll be honest: I'd found a bigger bag underneath the bed that was much more suitable. So I put all my stuff in there and then I needed to get high and so I threw my used works in the old bag. Doesn't matter to me now that you know I'm still on the gear.'

'I never thought you were off "the gear",' İkmen said. 'Your mother, however, was and is another matter. And Kemal . . .'

'Little monster caught me jacking up so I gave him a few lines of coke to shut him up,' Bekir said as if what he was saying was something of absolutely no importance. 'You and Mum have spoilt that boy. He's a vile brat.'

'Where the hell are you?'

Bekir laughed. 'Dad, I am away,' he said. 'Things haven't worked out quite as I had hoped, and—'

'What do you mean, things haven't worked out as you had hoped?'

'You'll see,' Bekir said lightly. 'I imagine that because you're such a good police officer, such a good man, the whole country is looking for me now. You won't find me.'

'Why—'

'Because that's what it's all about, Dad,' Bekir said: 'routes. Routes in, routes out, routes for the movement of whatever you may want.'

'Bekir, what was the drug dealer Yusuf Kaya to you? What—'

'Goodbye, Dad, and thanks for the free food and board.'

There was a sharp click and the connection descended into a low, dead whine. For a few seconds İkmen attempted in vain to try to find the number from which his son had called, but it had been withheld. Strictly, of course, he should have at least tried to record the call, but he hadn't. What, however, Bekir had told him, if indirectly, was that he was leaving the country. Routes in and routes out, routes for anything a person may want . . .

İkmen jumped to his feet, opened his office door and ran back down the corridor towards Ardıç's office.

Chapter 18

Looking at Edibe Taner sitting beside Gabriel Saatçi's hospital bed was like watching a middle-aged married couple try to cope with sudden, catastrophic sickness. The arm not attached to the glucose and saline drip that was now beginning to revive the monk was pressed against the side of Edibe Taner's face. From time to time she would move her head to kiss his brown, parched flesh. The inspector was not, Süleyman knew, married. Maybe Gabriel Saatçi was the reason behind that? If Taner was, as seemed more than possible, in love with him, maybe other men had never stood a chance. But he had chosen God. Whether he had chosen God over Edibe Taner, Süleyman did not know. What was clear to see, however, was that there was a great affection and understanding between these two.

'Oh, Inspector Süleyman,' she said when she saw him. 'Come and sit with us.'

There was a chair already beside hers and he went and sat on that. As he did so she said something to the monk in Aramaic.

'I've just told Gabriel that we must speak in Turkish,' she said. 'You need to know what has been happening, Inspector Süleyman.'

He looked over at the monk, who smiled. For a contemporary of Taner's he had aged badly. But then that was probably in part due to the harshness of his vocation. Brother

Seraphim had told him that no one prayed harder or fasted more rigorously than Brother Gabriel. All the lines and dryness on his face aside, Süleyman could see why his colleague might find so much in this man to be in love with. The huge, upward-slanting green eyes were part of it, as were the plump if rather pale lips. The greater portion of his allure, however, was the facility he seemed to have, without effort, of holding one's attention. As soon as those eyes were on someone's face it was as if that person and only that person existed for Gabriel Saatçi. Süleyman felt genuinely and almost hypnotically drawn to this man.

'Inspector Süleyman,' the monk said in his deep, dark voice. 'The man from İstanbul.'

'Yes.' He smiled. 'Brother Gabriel, I have been looking forward to meeting you.'

'Have you?' The monk frowned. 'Looking forward to seeing how the snakes cannot kill me?'

'No.'

'I was,' he said with yet another of his sudden glittering smiles. 'I was telling Edibe that was what the days and weeks have been about. Preparing myself.'

And then he looked away from Süleyman and smiled up at Edibe Taner. Returning his smile, she said, 'Gabriel prayed and fasted in the caves and the mountains. To God to give him strength and courage and to the Sharmeran to assure her that he would never harm her children.'

'When Christ rose I knew I was ready,' he said. 'I gathered the serpents and I came down the mountain.'

'OK, but why? Why do something, or rather replicate something, that Inspector Taner told me you did many years ago?'

There was a pause then while the monk looked at Süleyman as if he didn't understand what he had been saying.

After a while it was Edibe Taner who explained. 'Inspector Süleyman, Gabriel did what he did to clear his name. İbrahim Keser, the guard of the American woman I told you to go and try to find at the church, lives next door to Gabriel's father. He and his family came from the plains when İbrahim was an infant. İbrahim Keser says that he saw Gabriel's miracle of the snakes out in the desert when he was a child. He says he spied upon the attack, saw everything and then followed Gabriel as he made his way, pouring with blood and venom, back into the city.'

'And is this true?'

'İbrahim Keser was certainly behind Gabriel when he came into Mardin,' Taner said. 'But he said nothing about seeing anything untoward, either as a child or even later on in his life. But then a few months ago he went to Musa Saatçi and told him that he wanted him to do a favour for him.'

'He asked my father to conceal some weapons for him in his house,' Gabriel Saatçi said. 'My father of course refused. İbrahim had never been, as far as my father knew, involved with any terrorist organisation. But there was a connection to the Kaya family and they are not people to become involved with. But then İbrahim threatened my father. He said that if my father didn't do as he said he would tell everyone that what he saw me do with the snakes in the desert was nothing more than a parlour trick. I was, he said, a charlatan.'

'And so your father did as he asked in order to protect you, or rather your reputation.'

'Yes. I know that the miracle I was granted truly happened,' Gabriel said. 'I also know that many of my people take comfort from that proof of God's love. These are nervous times. Our people do not need uncertainties.'

'Uncle Musa didn't tell Gabriel about any of this until after the arms had been discovered and he was at the police station,' Taner said.

'I went to the mountains to pray and to gain strength because I knew that the only way I could defeat İbrahim was to let the serpents have me again,' the monk said. 'My father would not countenance just going to the police and telling them about the blackmail. I had to prove myself and then reveal the story behind my actions afterwards. But . . . but I failed—'

'You didn't fail anything!' Edibe Taner said as she once again gripped hard on to his arm. 'I was trying to stop you and then you collapsed. You were very dehydrated, Gabriel.'

'My father will be furious I didn't manage to do what we had agreed.' He coughed a little and then took a sip of water from a small glass beside his bed.

'But I am glad,' Taner said. 'Not because I think the snakes would have harmed you, I know that they would not. But now I can release Uncle Musa.'

'Father will say there is now a shadow over my vocation . . .'

'No. He won't. He won't!' She reached up and very tenderly touched his eyes and his lips with her fingers. 'He will know as I do that it was the will of Allah that you collapsed and through the good offices of the Sharmeran that my father was there to take good care of her children.'

They looked into each other's eyes as if no one else existed in the world. These two, if a long time ago, had been meant for each other. The monk had given up much to follow his God. Süleyman cleared his throat after a moment and Edibe Taner looked round.

'So, Inspector,' he said, 'the arms.'

'Whose are they? We don't know,' she said. 'İbrahim Keser didn't tell Musa Saatçi anything.'

264

'But because he works for the Kaya family it would seem reasonable to assume that they are—'

'Maybe. But Keser doesn't work for Yusuf Kaya's family in the city, remember. He is employed to look after the American woman.'

'And so?'

'And so Zeynep Kaya or even Yusuf's own mother herself may not know anything about them,' she said. 'The weapons came from İbrahim Keser, remember, based out at Dara. Now I know that Zeynep knows about the American woman, but it is my belief that it is Elizabeth Smith and not Zeynep who knows where Yusuf is.'

'Why do you think that?'

'Because Yusuf is a man of "honour",' she said, rolling her eyes at the irony inherent in the term as she did so. 'I don't believe he would put his wife, his mother and his family in the city in harm's way. The American woman is expendable. The arms came via one of his men in Dara, where she is.'

'Were there many weapons?' Süleyman asked.

Edibe Taner frowned. 'There were ten AK-47 assault rifles, two crates of grenades and a rocket launcher. It would be a good haul from a terror organisation. From a clan it is impressive.'

'Who were they hoping to attack with so much hardware?'

Edibe Taner sighed. 'I don't know,' she said. 'Hopefully we will find out more when we pick up İbrahim Keser. A group of our officers are joining up with the small local force in Dara right now. With luck, by the time the day is over we'll have Keser in custody.'

İkmen really wasn't ready to tell Sophia that he was the father of her boyfriend Aslan. He said he just wanted to help. She was pregnant and alone and he was concerned about her.

But Sophia wasn't convinced. 'What is it you want?' she said when he offered to find her a clean and safe place to stay. 'You want fuck me? What is about you Turkish men and pregnant women?'

He tried to convince her that he was not in any way after her body, but she wouldn't believe him. And so eventually he told her the truth.

'My wife doesn't even know about this yet,' he said to the girl as she sat stunned before him in his office. 'But Sophia, when she does she will want to help as much as I do.'

'You want my baby! Cannot have,' Sophia growled darkly. Years on the streets had made any notion of trust absolutely alien to her.

İkmen sat on the edge of his desk next to her and sighed. 'No,' he said, 'I don't want your baby. But I do want to help. I don't know of course precisely where you live, Sophia, but I know it is in Edirnekapi. I went to Hüseyin Altun's place up there, just the once, some years ago and so I think I know how you might be living.'

She turned her head away.

'Sergeant Farsakoğlu tells me you have a doctor, but I know many doctors who will really care for you.' Junkies and those associated with them did frequently have access to doctors, some of whom were the types of practitioners only just on the right side of the law. 'I know some very good doctors,' he said. 'My family will pay your costs and I can find you somewhere decent to live, at least for the moment. This isn't charity, Sophia, this is making up in part for what my son has done to you.'

He told her to think about it while he went off to join İzzet Melik in one of the interview rooms with the hospital administrator. The man now had one of the Cerrahpaşa's own lawyers with him, a nondescript man in a grey suit. İkmen sat down and looked at the piece of paper İzzet Melik passed to him. For several seconds he just read it in silence. Then he put the paper down and looked up into the small grey eyes of the administrator, Mr Aktar. He had a rather bruised split lip.

'This is a letter of resignation for your employers, not me,' İkmen said, tipping his head towards the paper on the table.

'Now that your officer has . . . discovered my addiction, I feel that, given that my job is to do with health care, I cannot continue,' Mr Aktar said.

His lawyer nodded his agreement.

'So what will you do then, Mr Aktar?' İkmen said. 'What's the career plan now? You're not ready for retirement yet, I imagine. I believe you have dependents.'

'Yes.'

'Inspector İkmen, Mr Aktar is as you can see willing to own up to his addiction,' the lawyer said. 'He has not done anything criminal with regard to care of patients at the Cerrahpaşa. In addition, he is alleging that a level of police brutality was used upon him by your officer here, Sergeant Melik.'

İkmen looked briefly at Melik, knowing with certainty that what the lawyer was saying was absolutely correct. İzzet had ideas about this case and was out to prove them whatever. Back in his home city of İzmir there had been some complaints about İzzet Melik. But any discussions about that would have to come later. İkmen said, 'The constable who was with Sergeant Melik when he was interviewing Mr Aktar at the Cerrahpaşa assures me that nothing beyond the tearing of his own shirtsleeve by your client in what I imagine must have been a fit of remorse occurred.' He hadn't actually spoken to the constable in question but he knew that in all probability

267

that was what Melik had told him to say. 'Mr Aktar, this is not about you just handing in your resignation at work and all this goes away,' he said. He looked over at the lawyer. 'As administrator of your hospital Mr Aktar is ultimately responsible for what happens in it. So far a prisoner has escaped from your institution, probably with the help of Cerrahpaşa nurses. The only surviving witness to that event died, in suspicious circumstances, whilst under the care of one of your doctors. We have that doctor in our custody right now.' He leaned forward into Mr Aktar's now lightly sweating face. 'You know, he looks as afraid, if not more so, as you. What or who are you afraid of? Is it the escaped prisoner, Yusuf Kaya? Did he threaten to kill you if you didn't agree to help him? Or is it much more selfish than that? Did Yusuf buy you with heroin?'

'No! No, I—'

'Stole it from your employers?' İkmen said. 'A hospital is a wonderful place for a junkie to work, isn't it? My own drug of choice is tobacco. It would be like me working in a cigarette factory.'

'I didn't steal from my employers!' Mr Aktar said. 'Never!'

'So where did you get your heroin from?' İzzet Melik asked.

'I can't tell you that! You know I can't tell you that!'

'We can search your house,' İkmen said with a shrug. 'I know we'll find some there, we're bound to. As for where it came from, if you don't tell us, we will ask around. We know a lot of people who know people . . .'

'Ask around!' Mr Aktar said defiantly. 'It'll do you no good!'

He was afraid. İkmen could see it very clearly in his face.

'Mr Aktar,' he said, 'you should know that if my officers find heroin at your home, I will have the right to detain you here for further questioning.'

Aktar looked over at his lawyer who simply said, 'He can do that.'

Mr Aktar looked back at İkmen but said nothing.

After a pause, İkmen said, 'It's my belief that you are probably even more afraid than I can imagine, Mr Aktar. All I can say is that I know that drug dealers, Yusuf Kaya included, are violent and dangerous people who will slaughter entire families to get what they want. But you know we can provide protection . . .' He saw Aktar's face briefly break into a small, thin smile. 'But whatever you may think of that, the fact remains that unless you decide to cooperate with us, you could be here for some considerable amount of time. Note, Mr Aktar, that we don't allow drug-taking on our premises, and think for just a moment about how long you can normally manage between fixes before you start wanting to climb up the wall.'

The administrator didn't appear to respond at all except that when he spoke his voice was obviously strained. 'What about my allegation of police brutality?' he said.

'What about it?' İkmen replied. Then he leaned forward again and said, 'Now, Mr Aktar, are my officers going to search your house or not?'

'İbrahim Keser was neither in or around the house in Dara,' Edibe Taner said with a sigh as she put her phone back in her bag. 'The American woman told our officers she hadn't seen him since the Easter service. They're hiding him somewhere.' She sat down on the low wall in front of the hospital, where Süleyman joined her. He, at least, had only been in the hospital for just over half an hour but the sky was already dark. Such a long and tiring Easter Day! In all the madness he had even forgotten to wish his wife a happy Easter. Not that Zelfa was a religious woman and cared about such things, but she was nominally a Catholic and so he should have phoned to send his good wishes anyway. But at that moment there was something else, something rather more immediate, troubling him.

'Inspector,' he said, 'if the people of Mardin believe so passionately in Gabriel's miracle, why was his father so afraid that the word of just one person could discredit his son?'

'Inspector Süleyman,' she replied, 'you are a sophisticated man from İstanbul. Even the languages you speak are sophisticated. French and English! Allah, those people don't even have a notion of clan or the power of one's neighbours or . . .'

'I think they do,' Süleyman said, 'but maybe in a way that is perhaps unfamiliar to people in a place like this. In İstanbul there are certainly clans.'

'Inspector, here, what a man's neighbours believe about him, about his sons and about the honour of his daughters, can affect his whole life! Sometimes men can even kill because of the opinions of others.'

'You mean so-called "honour" killings?'

'Where a girl is murdered by her relatives because some meddlesome or envious neighbour impugns her good name? Of course!' Taner said. 'Some vicious, bitter old hag takes it into her head that some teenage child is no longer a virgin and the poor girl is strangled by her own brother or father. There was no truth in the allegation. The old hag didn't even really know the kid, only by sight. But that is enough, that is plenty.'

'So Brother Gabriel . . .'

'İbrahim Keser is a liar. But he was undoubtedly behind Gabriel when he returned from the desert all those years ago. Everyone saw him. Minimal contact but again, enough. This is a small place, Inspector, a small poor place where people have very little of value. Their beliefs and their honour are very precious to them. But our lifestyle here is brittle because it is so old. Our beliefs and customs are threatened and made thin by a present that very few, including myself, can really understand. And so if someone might have deceived them, or they only perceive that as being the case, it can be serious. People can and do die over what you may consider such non-problems.'

The mobile telephone in her handbag began to ring and she took it out and answered it. The call could, Süleyman knew, be either business or personal and so, because he didn't want to intrude were it the latter, he drifted back into his own thoughts. On the face of it Mardin seemed very different from İstanbul. For a start, with the exception of a couple of the restaurants and hotels, there was no discernible night life in the city. Few places served alcohol, and as soon as night fell the city was, as far as he could tell, pretty much shut for business. There were certain quarters of İstanbul, the religious district of Fatin for instance, that were like that. But the centre of the city was a twenty-four-hour riot of activity and life. All of that, however, was at a very surface level. Deeper within the life of İstanbul there were, he knew, uncomfortable similarities. Honour killing was not unknown and, on a far more mundane level, people cared about the opinions of others, sometimes to a ridiculous degree. His mother, for instance, still told her friends, even her lifelong bridge partner, that her son Mehmet's wife was exactly the same age as he, even though Zelfa was twelve years his senior. His mother's friend was not a stupid woman and had eyes in her head that had to inform her that what her friend Mrs Süleyman was telling her was a lie. But the old woman had never, Mehmet Süleyman knew in his soul, even hinted that she thought her friend might be mistaken. It wasn't done.

'Inspector?'

He turned to where Edibe Taner was sitting with her mobile phone cradled in her lap. Her conversation had obviously come to an end.

'Do you remember the Jandarma captain we met in Birecik, Captain Erdur?' she asked. Her face looked suddenly small and crushed. Süleyman frowned.

'Yes? Has something happened to him?'

'No.' She breathed in deeply and then spoke on a rush of breath as if she wanted or needed her words to be over with as soon as possible. 'The body he and his men pulled out of the Euphrates when we were there wasn't an American soldier, it was Yusuf Kaya.'

'What? What!' He could hardly take it in. 'No. It was in a uniform and—'

'Inspector,' she said, 'the Americans tested the body. It was not one of their men. The DNA sample taken apparently by a doctor in Urfa matched exactly the sample taken from Kaya by yourselves in İstanbul. The dead body in the Euphrates belongs to Yusuf Kaya.'

Literally speechless now, Mehmet Süleyman simply sat.

'Someone must have put him in an American uniform,' Taner continued. 'Obviously the face was taken off to disguise his identity. According to the captain, the Americans are very worried by the fact that someone clearly from or based in this country could take the clothes and identity discs of one of their servicemen in Iraq. We all know, or those of us who are realistic know, that there is movement across the border, but this particular incident is unprecedented.'

'I've been chasing a dead man,' Süleyman said. 'For the last I don't know how long, I've been chasing a dead man!'

'The doctor in Urfa reckoned that Kaya probably died only

shortly before his body was dumped in the Euphrates,' Taner said. 'He also told the captain that in his opinion Kaya's body hadn't been in the river for more than five or six hours before it was found. You started off chasing a live man, Inspector.'

He looked at her very hard for a moment and then he said, 'You are sure, aren't you?'

'I have the captain's word. Why would he lie?' Taner said. 'This isn't his area. He didn't know Yusuf Kaya. The DNA from the body in the river matches exactly that which is held in İstanbul.'

There was another short pause before Süleyman took his telephone out of his jacket pocket and said, 'I must tell my colleagues in İstanbul.'

What woke Zeynep Kaya was no more than a click. If it had not been followed by a long sigh from the sleeping child next to her, it probably wouldn't have woken her. But exhausted by grief though she was, when it came to one of her children being disturbed, she instantly went on to the alert.

'Tayyar?' she whispered to the child beside her. 'Are you all right?'

He didn't make a sound. Poor baby, to learn that his daddy had been killed at such a tender age! The police had been with them for hours, that unnatural cousin of hers telling them all that Yusuf wouldn't ever be coming back.

'Tayyar?'

She put a hand up to his mouth and felt absolutely nothing. Zeynep's heart jumped to her throat just as she felt something move in the early morning shadows on the other side of her bed. Caught between a child who was not breathing and something or someone in the shadows who could mean her harm, she said, 'Who's there? What do you want?'

Surprisingly the voice that replied was familiar and, she had thought, friendly.

'Tayyar is dead,' it said. 'Just like you.'

And then there was another click and Zeynep felt a raging pain in her chest. As she lay dying she saw through the open bedroom door one of her daughters fall over the balcony and into the courtyard below as a bullet, from somewhere, took her life away.

Chapter 19

That morning was a lot warmer in İstanbul than the weather forecaster on the television said it was in Mardin. The southeast, apparently, was even under slight risk of snow. Çetin İkmen, who had been awake for much of the previous night, was, however, as cold as he imagined he would have been in Mardin. Yusuf Kaya was dead! He still couldn't really believe it. But Arto Sarkissian had quickly confirmed Süleyman's story and so it was certainly true. Who had killed Kaya and why were still mysteries, cloaked as they were in the gruesome details that surrounded the disposal of his body. Clearly it had not been sent down the river from Iraq to its final resting place in Birecik. The American owner of the ID tags had apparently been killed just outside Baghdad. Somehow his tags and maybe even his uniform had ended up on Kaya's body in Turkey where, it was reckoned, the drug dealer had been killed.

So the hunt for Yusuf Kaya was off. The hunt for whoever had helped him to escape and had killed to do so was still however very much on – as was the search for Kaya's own murderer. Monstrous though Yusuf Kaya had been, whoever had killed him had done so for a reason which, if İkmen was correct, was almost certainly drug-related. Someone as yet unknown was making a bid for Yusuf's property. In the meantime the Cerrahpaşa administrator, Mr Aktar, was still in the cells at police headquarters. A considerable quantity of narcotics had been found in the garage of his rather nice house in Kumkapı and, as İkmen looked down at his watch now, he wondered how Aktar was feeling after a whole night without access to heroin. It was only five a.m., but he imagined the administrator was still up. İkmen's wife Fatma certainly was. As she came into the living room he thought about pretending to be asleep but decided that it was probably best not to try to deceive her. She had been deceived quite enough by Bekir, whose potential child he had only told her about less than an hour ago. It hadn't been easy.

'So this girl, this Sophia,' she began.

'When I came back from the interview room she had gone,' İkmen said, referring to the fact that Sophia the pregnant Bulgarian girl had walked out of his office and disappeared the previous afternoon. 'I offered help, she appeared to be thinking about it, but then she disappeared. Fatma, we can only help her if she wants to be helped.'

Fatma looked outraged. 'She is carrying our grandchild! Don't you care about that?'

'Well, of course I—'

'You are a policeman! Look for her!'

'Fatma!'

'Çetin, this is our grandchild!' Fatma said with tears in her eyes. 'I know that you don't care about Bekir, but you have to care about his child! The child is innocent!'

İkmen lit up a cigarette and then leaned forward in his chair. 'Fatma,' he said, 'our son Bekir is a wanted man. When caught he will go to prison. This Sophia, his girlfriend, is an illegal immigrant who has sold her body on the streets. She is also, she says, an ex-heroin user. She may still be taking the stuff; junkies do lie, as we know. Of course I want to find her and try to protect that baby of hers. But it isn't easy.'

'Yes, but—'

'Fatma, I will try, it's all I can do!'

She knew it was pointless to keep on at him about it and so she asked him whether he'd like a glass of tea. When he said he would, she left for the kitchen. Love her as he did, İkmen was glad when Fatma went out because then, to a certain extent, he could relax. Alone, at least he could think his own thoughts, and they were most certainly focused on Mr Aktar. What was he going to be like after over twelve hours without heroin? And, maybe even more interesting, how was he going to respond to the news about the death of Yusuf Kaya?

Süleyman looked down at the photograph of Bekir İkmen that Çetin had faxed over to the Mardin station the night before. He'd never actually met or even seen Bekir, but he could tell from the image before him that he was most certainly a member of the İkmen clan. He definitely had some of his father's features and, by the sound of him, he had Çetin's sharp intelligence too – albeit in a rather more toxic form.

'This is your wanted man?' Edibe Taner said as she looked over his shoulder at the image in his hands.

'Bekir İkmen, my colleague's son,' Süleyman replied. 'Although we don't know, we think he may have had some connection to Yusuf Kaya.'

'I've never seen him before.'

'I doubt he's ever been here,' Süleyman said. 'Back home he was a "soldier" for a local beggar king and small time dealer called Hüseyin Altun. If he was connected to Kaya he may come here, if he thinks Yusuf's still alive. Or he may just come because we're near the border and he is, after all, on the run now.'

Edibe Taner sighed. 'It's horrible to be betrayed by a member of your family. Inspector İkmen has my sympathy.' Then she picked her handbag up off her desk and said, 'Are you ready?'

'Yes.'

He wasn't really. In the wake of the call from Birecik, both he and Taner had spent much of the night informing Kaya's family about his death. Their grief, especially that of his mother and his wife Zeynep, had been terrible. The women particularly kept on and on about his body and how they wanted it immediately for burial. The twenty-four-hour deadline, of course, had already passed, and getting the body to the family from the hospital in Urfa was still going to take some time. This only added to their distress which was in sharp contrast to the cold, dry grief they saw at the house in Dara later. Elizabeth Smith did not react with anything more than a hard swallow when Edibe Taner told her what had been found in Birecik. She'd stood in the middle of her wormwood-scented hall and hadn't spoken a word. When Taner had told her that they would have to return in the morning to take a statement from her, she had only just managed to nod her head in agreement. Now, together with two constables who were going to scout round the area for the still missing İbrahim Keser, they were going out to see Elizabeth Smith once again.

'We will go briefly to Mardin Prison on the way back,' Taner said as they set off, 'to see Musa Saatçi. Maybe we can get him out. But I can at least explain to him what has happened.'

'He's dead?'

'Yes,' İkmen replied for the third time in quick succession. 'Yusuf Kaya is most definitely dead.'

'Mm.' Mr Aktar was sweating but his pallor was deathly

grey and he was shivering. The Americans called this state 'cold turkey'. İkmen thought how very appropriate that term was in this situation. 'You're sure it's him? You're sure he's—'

'Dead?' İkmen sighed. 'Yes.' Of course, telling suspects lies in order to get them to offer up their guilt and that of others was not unknown and he could understand why Mr Aktar was so suspicious. But the administrator was also in the grip of such a wild need for heroin that he was now totally and utterly paranoid. Not that officially any connection between Kaya and Mr Aktar actually existed. He was where he was because of drug offences related to his personal use. But the mention of Yusuf Kaya's name now, given the state that Aktar was in, had added significantly to his agitation.

'You know what I want, what I need now, and so you have me at a disadvantage,' Aktar said as he rubbed his cold dry hands together to generate warmth.

'Mr Aktar, this is a police station. I cannot give you heroin,' İkmen said.

'I need to get out of here!' He got up, paced the room once and then pointed down at İkmen. 'Your officer assaulted me! He split my lip! I want my lawyer! Now!'

'Sir, if you want your lawyer, you can have your lawyer,' İkmen said. 'You are entitled to pursue an action regarding alleged police brutality . . .'

Bloody İzzet Melik! So keen to get a result he'd gone tearing back to methods many had given up long ago and İkmen personally had always abhorred. He'd bawled him out once and, he imagined, Süleyman would have his own thoughts on the matter when he returned from Mardin. Of course İzzet had been backed up by the constable who had been with him at the Cerrahpaşa, but that didn't make what he had done any more acceptable. Conversely it didn't exactly save Mr Aktar either. And as he sat down in front of İkmen again, this time with tears in his eyes, it was obvious that he knew it.

'Inspector İkmen, I am a weak man, I know that,' he said. 'I am not a fool, however, and I know, as you do, that I would sell my soul to Satan for some of my dear, vile drug now.'

İkmen lit a cigarette and then said, 'I know.'

Mr Aktar sighed. 'But I do love my wife and my two sons and although I know that I have put them at risk both now and in the past, I cannot subject them to real, actual harm.' He looked up into İkmen's eyes and said, 'Do you know what I mean?'

He was trying to say something possibly about his involvement with Kaya, but he was a junkie. Could what he was saying be trusted?

İkmen frowned. 'No, Mr Aktar, I do not,' he said. 'But why don't you tell me?'

'Do you swear before Allah that Yusuf Kaya is dead?' Aktar said as he leaned, sweating and panting, across the interview room table. 'Do you swear it?'

He was clearly coming apart after his night without heroin. But was what he was about to tell İkmen, if anything, the truth? There was only one way to find out. İkmen raised his right hand. 'I swear.'

Aktar licked his lips once, looked over his shoulder at the absence of anything except a wall behind him and said, 'Can I get out of here afterwards?'

'Mr Aktar, that will depend upon what you are going to tell me,' İkmen said.

Several moments passed before Aktar breathed in deeply just the once and then said, 'It's called the Wormwood Route. It is, or was, going to make us all very rich. Myself and Mr

Oner were going to be set up for life. Yusuf Kaya and Mr Oner were friends from way back. When Mr Oner died the plan was already in place. I knew nothing about it or who, apart from ourselves and Kaya, were involved until it happened. Kaya planned it that way. He also told me that, apart from owning up to knowing him or giving his location away, I was to give you whatever information you asked me for. I was to protect no one but Kaya. He called me to tell me specifically. He also wanted to assure me that I could have, come the day, all the junk I could ever want. Only if I betrayed him would bad things happen. If I betrayed him, he said, my wife and children would be raped and murdered in front of my eyes. He'd said the same thing to Mr Oner, his old friend. That was why he killed himself. He couldn't back out and he knew he couldn't go through with it either. He didn't want his family to die. He was half mad with desperation. You are sure, aren't you, Inspector İkmen, that Yusuf Kaya is dead?'

The front door of the house was open, but there was no one at home. Süleyman and Taner went right through the building but found not one living soul anywhere. There were signs, however, in what had to be or have been the American woman's bedroom, that Elizabeth Smith was probably on the move. Clothes from an open wardrobe were scattered across an unmade bed, while someone had spilled a number of aspirin tablets across the floor. Neither of the officers spoke. Occasionally one or other of them would look out of a window at the constables searching in and around the garden. But everything out there was quiet too.

After a while, and mainly because he just couldn't stand the silence any longer, Süleyman said, 'She's gone.'

Edibe Taner stood still for just a moment, looked at him,

and then continued to go through a stack of papers on a table. Elizabeth Smith had definitely said she would see the police in the morning. But she wasn't anywhere to be seen and neither were her guards, keepers or whatever the men who lived with her were called. Süleyman at least had a creeping sense of something happening over which he was failing to exercise control. It was not something pleasant.

They continued looking, playing the answerphone machine, reading letters and notes in a kind of frozen fugue until eventually, and almost mercifully from Süleyman's point of view, Taner's mobile phone began to ring. She answered it and, although he couldn't make out a word of what the person at the other end was saying, he could hear that he or she was shouting. When Taner finally came off the phone her face was white.

'We must get back to the city,' she said as she pushed the mobile back into her bag and got her car keys out of her pocket. 'Something terrible has happened.'

Constable Selahattin had never seen anything like it. He, like all Turkish men, had served in the army and had seen action and violence. Since he had been stationed in Mardin he had been witness to the aftermath of gang and clan violence. But this was off the scale.

'They're all dead,' he said as he stood in the middle of the Kaya family's courtyard. 'Five adults, including Kaya's wife and mother, and eight kids. One was a baby.'

Tayyar, the two-year-old child had been called, Edibe Taner remembered. Conceived she imagined on some visit home when Yusuf Kaya was still free. She looked down at the splashes of blood that had settled in the dust of the courtyard and fought to hold back her tears. Zeynep had been a silly, weak and easily manipulated woman but she had once been a Taner and Edibe was sorry that she and all her poor children were dead. Even Yusuf Kaya's indulgent mother hadn't deserved to die.

'No one saw anything, of course,' Constable Selahattin added bitterly. 'Thirteen people are shot and no one sees or hears a thing.'

Ignoring the ire in his voice, Edibe Taner said, 'If they were all shot as they slept then I expect the assailants used silencers.'

'There are several sets of footprints in the house,' Selahattin said as he pulled himself and his emotions back to business once again.

'It would be difficult for one person to shoot thirteen even with a silenced weapon,' Taner said. 'I'd like to know exactly how many sets of footprints we have, please, Constable.'

'Madam.' He nodded his head.

Edibe Taner looked up at Süleyman. 'The scene will have to be forensically examined. Whoever did this cannot have arrived too long after we left last night. I can't see that the entrance has been forced.'

'No.' He waited until Selahattin had gone to join his fellows in the family's bedrooms before he took Taner to one side. 'Inspector,' he said, 'we must follow up the American and her men.'

She frowned. 'You think they did this? Why?'

'How should I know?' He wanted to add that he didn't come from the back of nowhere where people believed at least five impossible things before breakfast as she did. But he just about managed to restrain himself. What had happened wasn't her fault, but this mass slaughter was so shocking and sickening that he had to get at least some of his anger out of his system. 'All I know, Inspector, is that these people are dead and Elizabeth Smith and her men are missing.'

'You don't think it could be some sort of power struggle, do you?' she said. But before he could answer she saw something that made her jerk up her head and run over to the entrance to the mansion. Süleyman took the opportunity afforded by her temporary absence to think. With someone as powerful and pervasive as Yusuf Kaya dead all kinds of fault lines could open up in his family. Even Yusuf in prison had probably had a kind of control, but Yusuf dead was just a void, an emptiness which would either remain empty or be filled. He was wondering whether any Kaya family members still remained alive and if so who when Taner returned with her father, the Master of Sharmeran.

'My father would like to speak to you,' Inspector Taner said to Süleyman in what amounted to an almost sulky tone. And then she left to walk towards the stairs leading up to the family rooms on the first floor of the building.

Seçkin Taner took Süleyman by the arm over to a far corner of the courtyard. Once there he spoke in surprisingly good English. 'I am speaking this language because not a great many people here can say more than a few words in it,' he said. 'Inspector Süleyman, because of who and what I am, people do not tell me so much of their lives, if you know what I mean. I will not lie, and no one would dare try to silence me so I know very little. But there are exceptions to this.'

'Mr Taner—'

'I tell you because I know you will use what I say with wisdom. You are not involved,' Seçkin Taner said. 'Inspector Süleyman, a person known to me has told me that figures were seen coming out of this house just before dawn. One of those figures was definitely İbrahim Keser. Apparently he had been staying with Bilqis Hanım and her family since last night.'

'But we were here last night, Mr Taner,' Süleyman said. 'Telling the family of Yusuf Kaya's death.'

'Then he was probably being hidden,' Seçkin Taner said. 'He was one of Yusuf's men. They would have trusted him.'

'Which would have allowed him to be here and possibly let others in to kill them,' Süleyman said. 'But why? Why would he do that?'

The Master of Sharmeran shrugged. 'That I don't know,' he said.

Chapter 20

'If it had been just a large amount of heroin then the idea that everyone not absolutely key to the operation was expendable would not have been worth the risks involved,' Mr Aktar said. 'The Wormwood Route is—'

'About getting heroin into the city amongst packets of wormwood leaves,' İkmen said. His face was dark, bitter at the thought of what he had found in Bekir's rucksack. And the terrible boy hadn't even cared! Holed up with his very convenient police officer father! Had Bekir helped Yusuf Kaya to escape from the Cerrahpaşa, or from the prison? Had he killed his old boss Hüseyin Altun for that, that . . .

'No, it's more than that,' Mr Aktar said as he gulped greedily from the bottle of oral morphine İkmen had requested for him from the police station doctor. Already he'd drunk enough to knock over a camel, but Mr Aktar was a junkie and so it just had the effect of making him calmer, more 'normal'. 'The Wormwood Route is what it purports to be: a route, a way in which, basically, heroin can get out of Afghanistan, through Iraq and into this country.'

'So it's a mapped-out route, a safe route through friendly towns and villages?'

'In part,' Mr Aktar said. 'I don't know the details. I was only interested in the product, you understand. I was promised money but I wanted my fix. That's it, that's . . .' He sighed.

'The Wormwood Route is more than a map. It's also contacts, names, faces, drop-off points, bribable border guards . . . Apparently it took some years to organise and only Yusuf Kaya, it was said, knew every detail of it. My predecessor Mr Oner knew Yusuf Kaya as a child; they went to school together. He told me before he died how ruthless Kaya was. He told me that he killed the Russian Mafia boss, the one he was sent to prison for, because the Russian had been competing for parts of the Wormwood Route. I should have got out then. Gone. Where? I—'

'Mr Aktar,' İkmen said, 'are you sure that Kaya was the only person to know the precise details of this route?'

'That is what Mr Oner said.'

İkmen sat back in his chair and briefly looked up at the ceiling. Kaya was dead and so, possibly, if what Aktar had said was true, was the Wormwood Route. But that was assuming that whoever killed Kaya hadn't managed to get the information from him first. 'Mr Aktar – the nurses, Lole, Mardin and Öz,' İkmen began.

'Öz, or whatever his real name was, was some relative of Yusuf Kaya. Mr Oner knew him too,' Aktar said. 'Anyway, Mr Oner gave him a job. Lole was a friend of Öz, but I knew nothing about him. Apparently his name is Armenian and that was some sort of joke to Mr Oner, although I never understood it myself.'

Lole, İkmen recalled, had been the name of Mardin's greatest architect. Clearly a 'joke' only for those in the know.

'Whether Lole and Öz were recruited to help in Kaya's escape, if they actually did, I don't know,' Mr Aktar said. 'But I have always been suspicious about İsak Mardin, the third nurse. Mr Oner took him on not long before he . . . before he died. They spoke a lot, Mr Oner and Mardin. Maybe he was brought in for . . . You have to understand my role was to know nothing. Nothing!'

'And so Dr Eldem . . .'

'Did Dr Eldem kill the prison guard? I don't know,' Mr Aktar said. 'If he did then it was via an arrangement with Kaya that I know nothing about. You have to understand, Inspector, that things like the Wormwood Route are only secure so long as as few people as possible know exactly what is going on. This route is worth billions of dollars! People die for this thing!'

'We will provide you with protection.'

'What?' Mr Aktar laughed. 'You'll what? Inspector İkmen, with all due respect, even with Kaya dead, your men can't protect me. Half if not more of the people involved in this will know of my existence at least. They will know when someone talks. They'll have contacts in the police. I could be shot dead leaving this station now. Not that it matters.' He leaned forward across the table and frowned. 'Look after my family. With Kaya gone they might stand a chance. But forget me. If they want me dead for talking to you, that is what they will have. Save my wife and children. They are innocent.'

İkmen looked into the drug-hazed eyes of the administrator and then gravely nodded his head. 'All right,' he said. 'If you want to be ruthlessly honest . . .'

'I do.'

'Then tell me absolutely everything you know.'

'And you'll get my wife and children out of the city?'

'I will put your wife and children where no one will find them.'

Mr Aktar thought about it for a few seconds and then he said, 'All right. All right. I know something about Dr Eldem . . .'

'Just let me make a call first,' İkmen said as he took his mobile phone out of his pocket and activated the keypad. 'I must update my colleagues in Mardin first.'

No one spoke until they were inside the car. The old man, Musa Saatçi, was tired, anxious and very grateful to be getting away from Mardin Prison. He was also keen to see his son.

'Can we go to see Gabriel at the hospital now, Edibe dear?' he said as soon as Inspector Taner had started up the engine.

'Of course,' she said. She was just about to ask the old man something when Süleyman's mobile phone rang. She waited a few moments for him to finish the call, but when it became clear that he was going to be some time she spoke to Musa Saatçi again. 'Uncle,' she said, 'do you have any idea why İbrahim Keser wanted you to hide those armaments for him?'

The old man hung his head. 'To my shame, I do not,' he said. 'He threatened my boy's honour. That was enough for me. Was I wrong to be so worried about Gabriel's reputation, do you think?'

'Uncle Musa, everyone who matters to you believes in Gabriel's miracle.'

'Then I *was* wrong.'

'No.' She took her eyes briefly off the road ahead and looked at him. 'You are a good father. You know there are vicious tongues in this city, people bent on the destruction of others not in their clan, their political or religious group. Gabriel is a bright light in this darkness. Gabriel brings all right-minded souls together whether Christian, Muslim, Kurd or Jew. Uncle Musa, if Gabriel were a fake it would diminish us all.'

'But Gabriel isn't a fake!'

'I know that,' she said. 'It's just that . . .' And then she told him about the death of Yusuf Kaya and the slaughter of his family. As she spoke Musa Saatçi's eyes filled with tears. He had not, by his own admission, liked the Kaya family but he had had an affection for Yusuf's mother Bilqis Hanım. She, like he, had been a Syrian. In the back of the car, Süleyman, still on the phone, was frowning and concentrating hard.

'İbrahim Keser had become one of Yusuf Kaya's people,' Musa Saatçi said as soon as he felt able to speak again. 'He was often at Bilqis Hanım's house. When he was not, he was either at his home next to my own or out about his business, whatever that was.'

'Guarding an American woman, a second wife Yusuf had taken down near Dara,' Inspector Taner said.

'An American?'

'Some sort of adventuress, I think, Uncle Musa,' Taner said. 'You know, one of those western women who are in love with "the east" and take on its culture and its customs.' In fact she felt that Elizabeth Smith's love for the Tur Abdin went much deeper than that but she didn't, even after talking to the woman, really understand how or why.

'Ah.' Musa Saatçi shrugged. 'I've heard of such women. There is, it is said, a French woman married to a man from Bingöl who has not just become a Muslim but has willingly covered herself completely. It is really quite odd. Most strange,' he said. 'Most strange.'

'Or maybe not,' a male voice from the back of the car put in.

'Inspector Süleyman?'

'That was a colleague from İstanbul,' Süleyman said.

Taner looked at him in her rear-view mirror. 'Saying?'

'Saying that they have discovered that Yusuf Kaya was a far more important player in the drugs world than even we imagined.' He put his head round the side of the front passenger

291

seat and said, 'Mr Saatçi, have you ever heard about something called the Wormwood Route?'

'The Wormwood Route?' The old man thought for a few seconds before shaking his head. 'No. I know of wormwood the plant, of course.'

'Which grows behind the American woman's house in Dara,' Taner said. 'What is this Wormwood Route, Inspector, and how does it relate to Kaya?'

'The Wormwood Route is a method whereby heroin from Afghanistan may enter this country without being discovered,' Süleyman said. 'Yusuf Kaya was, according to my colleagues in İstanbul, at the centre of it. Maybe our American woman was not just besotted with Yusuf and his very quaint land and its people after all.'

'You think she could have been part of this?'

'The Wormwood Route is reputed to be worth billions of dollars,' Süleyman said. 'What if Elizabeth Smith were part of it? Zeynep Kaya said that her husband had the American because she was good at business. What if he really did have her only for that? What if she were part and parcel of this route? It would be worth living in the middle of nowhere for a few years for that sort of money, wouldn't it?'

For billions of dollars it would be worth living almost anywhere. Also, İbrahim Keser, one of Elizabeth Smith's men, had been seen at the Kaya family home just prior to the massacre. Not that Süleyman could talk to Taner about that in detail now, not with Musa Saatçi with them in the car. Later, he and she would have to have another conversation, possibly whilst on the line back to İkmen in İstanbul.

'I have no idea what relevance this has to anything!' Dr Eldem said indignantly.

'Have you or have you not been conducting a homosexual relationship with the nurse İsak Mardin?' Çetin İkmen reiterated.

The doctor paused for a moment and then said, 'Homosexual relationship? Ludicrous! Who told you such a thing?'

'What makes you think that anyone told us anything?' İkmen asked. 'Maybe you were observed. Maybe it is a fact of record, or—'

Dr Eldem laughed. 'I am not homosexual,' he said. 'Who's saying these things? Is it Aktar?'

He knew that they had Mr Aktar in custody. But even so, why he should think that the information came from him İkmen didn't know. It had, of course, but in theory at least, anyone at the hospital could be to blame.

'Why would you think that Mr Aktar would say such a thing?' he said.

'Well, you have him here, and—'

'So? So we have him here. What makes you think that he has been talking about you?' He smiled. 'Dr Eldem, we have been talking about something quite different with Mr Aktar. With you I wish to discuss first İsak Mardin and second the Wormwood Route.'

There was a frozen, deadly silence. He'd asked Eldem about wormwood before and the good doctor had wittered on about its properties and the manufacture of absinthe. But now that İkmen knew how to talk about that plant in a significant way, things appeared to be different. Dr Eldem's eyes fixed on a spot somewhere on the wall above İkmen's head.

'Because you know, Dr Eldem,' he continued, 'we know what that is now. We also know that Yusuf Kaya, the only person apparently to know all the ins and outs of this innovative drug route into this country, is dead.' He watched the doctor very carefully but detected only a very slight shift in his demeanour. 'What this means,' he continued, 'I don't really know. But at a guess I would say that the route, unless someone has managed to get that information from Kaya, is now not as valuable as it once was. A lot of people have died for it. And of course if someone did manage to get Kaya to part with his secrets before he died, quite a few more people will still die before this thing is over. Anyone, I should imagine, connected to Kaya. Dr Eldem, you tried to make a call from your mobile to a phone registered in the name of a Syrian national an hour before the guard Ramazan Eren died.'

'You looked at my phone records!'

'Of course,' İkmen said. 'Answer the question.'

'But I didn't get through. It was . . . it was not picked up.'

'Who didn't pick it up?'

'Well, the, the er, the—'

'Were you telephoning Yusuf Kaya or was it your lover İsak Mardin?'

'But you said it was a Syrian national. You—'

'Dr Eldem, you made the call. You know!' İkmen said. 'I think that the name the telephone is registered in is a fake anyway.' He paused. 'Dr Eldem, you telephoned someone I think may well have been Yusuf Kaya or someone connected to him and very soon afterwards Ramazan Eren died. Now we know that the cause of his death was not, as you would have it, natural. He was despatched with diamorphine.'

'I—'

İkmen held up a hand to silence him. 'Doctor, you were there. Alone. The cameras outside that side room at that time indicate the presence of no other person. You plainly lied about the cause of Mr Eren's death and we know that you have been conducting an affair with the nurse İsak Mardin. You even, we have been told, on occasion repeat rather irritating little eastern sayings you have learned from him. I think that you know something about the Wormwood Route and I have a feeling you know where İsak Mardin might be.' He leaned across the table and looked intently into the doctor's eyes. 'Faruk Öz is dead; the nurse calling himself Lole deliberately gave us the slip. We need to find İsak Mardin and so if you know where he is I suggest that you tell me.'

The doctor licked his lips and then was motionless for some time before he spoke again. When he did his voice was cracked and strained with emotion. 'When Mr Eren began to come round from his coma he was in some considerable discomfort. I, er, I gave him diamorphine . . .'

'You poisoned him with diamorphine,' İkmen corrected. 'Dr Eldem, the only way that a judge will look upon what you have done with even mild sympathy is if you come clean about everything else right now. Now, who did you make that call to and where is İsak Mardin?'

Chapter 21

Edibe Taner visited the families of every man she even remotely recalled as having recognised from Elizabeth Smith's bodyguard. In some cases the wives and children of these men were in, in others they were nowhere to be found. 'Gone away' was all that the neighbours of the disappeared would say. Where families remained behind there was clearly some confusion. They knew of no house in Dara, no American woman with or without Yusuf Kaya. Ominously, the wife of one of these men said that her husband had gone out the previous afternoon and had not yet returned. Had this man been maybe with İbrahim Keser at the Kaya house too? İbrahim Keser was a sore point for Edibe Taner.

'Why would my father tell you that Keser was seen at Yusuf Kaya's house last night and not me?' she demanded of Süleyman once the two of them were alone. As soon as they had dropped Musa Saatçi off at the hospital, Süleyman had told his Mardin colleague everything – hence the widespread search for Elizabeth Smith's guards.

'Your father fears reprisals,' Süleyman said. 'If I as an outsider own such information, if it is seen to come somehow from me, no one is at risk. Everyone in your department knows it came from me. That will filter out. It is I who suggested we trace Elizabeth Smith's guards, Inspector.'

What had been done had been done at his suggestion, it

was true. Also, she knew full well why her father had done what he had. She, much more than Süleyman, knew all about clans and how they worked.

'Madam!' Selahattin ran up to her as she leaned against the wall of the mansion where two of Elizabeth Smith's guards had, apparently, lived.

'Yes?'

'Madam, no one fitting the description of the American has passed legally into Syria,' Selahattin said. 'None of the other names you've given me have come up either.'

'What about the airport?'

'Nothing,' he replied. 'Of course, madam, there is always the possibility that they crossed into Syria illegally. Or into Iraq.'

'Where they might just as well have disappeared,' Taner said. PKK fighters were known to come and go across that particular border all the time. And although neither Elizabeth Smith nor her men were Kurdish, deals between organisations of all sorts and clans were known to happen often.

'Maybe if Elizabeth Smith has somehow found out the details of the Wormwood Route she and her men are using that,' Süleyman said.

Taner was silent for a few seconds before, frowning, she lit a cigarette. 'But how, if Yusuf Kaya was the only person to know all the details of the route, would she come into possession of that knowledge?' she said. 'Kaya was killed in or around Birecik where someone dressed his body in American paraphernalia from Iraq.'

'How do we know that person wasn't Elizabeth Smith?' Süleyman said. 'Not even you knew that she existed until a few days ago. She or some of her men could easily have gone to Birecik. Maybe Kaya's aunt was lying? Maybe Elizabeth met up with her husband at his aunt Bulbul's house?' And then he frowned. 'But then . . .'

'But then what?' Taner shrugged.

'But then Brother Seraphim told me that rumour has it that Yusuf Kaya's father put out the eyes of Bulbul's husband Gazi Kaplan.'

'That old story.'

'You've heard it?'

'Years ago,' Taner said dismissively. 'I know that the Kayas are ruthless and tough, but . . .' She shrugged again. 'It can't be true. Apart from anything else the Kaplan family would have retaliated.'

'Yes, but . . .'

'Mrs Kaplan told us her husband was blind,' Taner said. 'She also, if you recall, said that her husband had had surgery on his eyes. Why would he have eye surgery if he has no eyes? And how would Bulbul Kaplan know Elizabeth Smith? Yusuf kept her very quiet. Why would he tell a very distant aunt about her?' Edibe Taner began leading her small squad of officers back to the police station.

'My informant knew about the American woman,' Süleyman said as he took his cigarettes out of his pocket and lit up.

Taner turned to look at him. 'And your informant was?'

Lütfü Güneş the Kurd, had sworn Süleyman to secrecy. Now maybe he would have to break that confidence. In light of the existence of a drug route apparently worth billions could Süleyman allow anyone anonymity? Could he allow anyone trust? He looked up at the high yellow stone walls around him, walls behind which were many, many eyes and ears, and then he said, 'I'll tell you back at the station.'

They finished the journey in silence. It was only broken, at the end, by Süleyman's mobile phone which rang just after he had entered the station and was about to ascend the stairs. He turned away from his Mardin colleagues in order to answer it.

'Süleyman.'

'Mehmet, it's Çetin!'

İkmen. He was very breathless by the sound of it.

'Çetin. Are you all right?'

'Mehmet, listen,' İkmen said. 'You and Taner have got to go to the place where Kaya's body was found.'

'Birecik?'

'A Captain Erdur of the Jandarma, you've met him I believe—'

'Çetin, what is this?' İkmen was, he knew, perceptive but he hadn't realised that the man was now reading people's thoughts at long distance. 'I've just been talking about Birecik.'

'My son Bekir is in Birecik,' İkmen said. 'Dr Eldem of the Cerrahpaşa told us that the nurse İsak Mardin left İstanbul with Aslan, in other words my son. They are headed for or have already reached the town now.'

'But why? Why is your son in Birecik, Çetin?'

'Because the Wormwood Route, this thing these people all fight and kill to find out about, is something that he has a keen interest in,' İkmen said sadly. 'Mehmet, I fear my son may have killed for this. Like the hospital administrator, he is addicted to heroin. He will do anything to secure his supply.'

'The administrator has told you about Birecik?'

'No, I told you, one of his doctors. I'll tell you about it later. But both the administrator and this doctor are implicated. In exchange for protection for his family, the administrator told me some interesting facts. Mehmet, this drug route is huge. Those involved in it have a very long reach. I don't know who or what you will find at Birecik, but Yusuf Kaya died there and Captain Erdur of the Jandarma is going to see the aunt who lives there now.'

'Bulbul Kaplan?'

'If that is the woman's name, yes,' İkmen said. 'He said he'd call you, but you must get out there now, Mehmet. You must . . .' He faltered just a little and then he said, 'Mehmet, my son is a bad man, and he must pay for whatever he has done, but . . . Look, just try, if you can, to . . . try not to let them kill him, will you?'

'Çetin . . .'

'It would break his mother's heart, you understand. Break his mother's heart.'

Süleyman took a deep breath and then said, 'Of course I will try to do what I can, Çetin.'

'Thank you.'

And then he cut the connection. Süleyman looked across at Taner who was standing at the bottom of the stairs staring at him, frowning.

The Kaplans' smart villa was quiet save for the sound of a television broadcasting some sort of sporting fixture inside. That Mrs Kaplan was reluctant to let members of the Jandarma into her house wasn't unusual. Her husband was upstairs asleep and she didn't want to wake him. However, when she learned that the captain and his men were looking for out-of-towners, bad people from İstanbul apparently, she let them in to have a quick look round. One could not, the old woman said, be too careful in such circumstances.

As soon as the jandarmes had satisfied Mrs Kaplan and themselves that her house was quite safe, they left. Captain Erdur even telephoned Inspector Süleyman from İstanbul to tell him that everything was quiet. But he didn't really believe in his soul that that was the case. Süleyman was trying, he said, to persuade Inspector Taner, that rather formidable female from Mardin, to join him on the journey, apparently, across to Birecik. She was not, however, entirely convinced of the need to leave her home city at this point. Many people had died there in the last twenty-four hours.

Erdur had spent some time talking to Inspector Çetin İkmen from İstanbul before he'd been to the Kaplans' house. One of the people the inspector was seeking in connection with drug offences was his own son. Not that Bekir İkmen had turned up yet, to Captain Erdur's knowledge. In fact everything at Bulbul Kaplan's house had been just perfect. The lady herself had been modestly dressed, busy and cheerful. The house was clean and quiet and even old Mr Kaplan, always a problem apparently with his somewhat erratic sleep patterns, had not so much as stirred when they had looked round the house. But then that was the issue really, that was the reason, in part at least, why Captain Erdur could not feel content. Gazi Kaplan, though rarely seen by anyone in recent years, was a mad old man who shouted, appealed to Allah for help and sometimes screamed as well. The story was that he'd contracted an eye disease many years before and had ever since endured a lot of pain and had needed some surgery. He was, famously, very easily agitated. Not, however, it would seem, by a troop of heavy-footed young jandarmes.

And so Captain Erdur drove back to the Kaplan house later on that afternoon. He told Private Yüksel exactly where he was going and why. Nevertheless, it wasn't until very much later, when inspectors Süleyman and Taner, a couple of constables and some bizarre-looking civilian arrived from Mardin that anyone thought to try to contact the captain. Inspector

302

Taner called his mobile phone but it was, apparently, switched off.

'Why, Edibe, do you think that a person like my father fears and despises the Kaya family so very much?' Gabriel Saatçi said as he walked out of the Jandarmerie towards Inspector Taner's car.

They had gone to the hospital so that Taner could bid the monk goodbye before they set off for Birecik. But then he had insisted upon accompanying them. When he'd first seen them together, Süleyman had been convinced that Edibe Taner was in love with Gabriel Saatçi, but he had not been entirely sure that her feelings had been reciprocated. Now it seemed, from the looks that he gave her and the words that he spoke, that the monk loved the police officer in return. He also had information, it transpired.

'Your father has never liked the Kayas,' Edibe Taner replied as she unlocked her car door and then got in. 'No decent people do. My father was horrified when my uncle let Zeynep marry Yusuf Kaya. But then my uncle isn't a very nice man.'

Süleyman, who was going to travel with Taner and Brother Gabriel, signalled to the small group of jandarmes who were going to follow them to the Kaplan house that they were about to move off. As he stood by the car, the monk repeated what he'd said back in the Jandarmerie.

'Yusuf Kaya's father could not bring himself to tell another Muslim the fearful violence he had done to Gazi Kaplan. He told only someone who was a very young monk at the time: Brother Seraphim.' Then he looked at Süleyman. 'Inspector, you must think badly of us. That Brother Seraphim only shared his certain knowledge with his brothers for such a long time must seem strange to you.'

'It would seem to me, Brother Gabriel,' Süleyman said as he got into the car, 'that a lot of people had their suspicions anyway.'

The monk climbed into the front passenger seat and said, 'Indeed. But no proof. Had there been proof that the story was true the truce between the Kayas and the Kaplans would have been worthless. More blood would have been spilled.' He turned round in his seat to look Süleyman in the face. 'That was the deal, you see, the one that no one at St Sobo's could speak about.'

'What deal?'

'That the Kaplans pay for the dishonouring of Bulbul Kaya with Gazi's eyes.'

Edibe Taner fired up the engine while Süleyman sat and struggled with feelings of shock and revulsion. The Kayas and the Kaplans had actually traded a young girl's body for a young man's sight! It was so monstrous that he began to feel his head pound with rage. Allah, but what could that young man and that young woman have felt about their vile relatives? What could Bulbul Kaplan have felt about Yusuf Kaya?

'Inspector, we'll go off with Private Yüksel and the others now,' Constable Selahattin said, bending down to talk to Taner through the window.

'All right,' Taner said. 'You're looking for strangers, remember? Any strangers, but particularly any young men resembling the man Bekir İkmen, also known as Aslan. He may or may not be travelling with another young man called İsak Mardin. We don't have a photograph of him but just be aware that this İkmen or Aslan may not be alone.'

'Yes, Inspector.'

He left to join his other colleague and a group of jandarmes around a jeep which then sped off towards the centre of Birecik. Edibe Taner waved to the other jeep behind her car to let privates Güzer and Bilge know that they were heading along the banks of the Euphrates river towards the house of Bulbul and Gazi Kaplan.

Just before she put her foot down on the accelerator, she turned to Gabriel Saatçi and said, 'When we get there, you stay in the car, understand?'

The monk did not so much as turn in her direction. He just looked up into the now rapidly darkening sky and frowned.

'Fatma?'

She was standing at the window, looking across towards Sultanahmet Square and the darkening bulk of the famous Blue Mosque. It was dusk but she hadn't as yet put any of the apartment lights on. No one apart from his wife was, seemingly, at home. It was preternaturally quiet and it made Çetin İkmen shudder.

'Fatma, are you all right?' he asked as he walked over to her and put a hand on her heavily cardiganed shoulder. He felt her flinch beneath his touch and he shook his head and sighed. 'I had no choice,' he said. 'Even you must see that.'

'They will kill our son, your *colleagues*!' she responded bitterly.

'Bekir is involved in a drug supply operation that is probably the biggest this country has ever seen,' İkmen said. He sat down on the arm of the chair that stood beside his wife and lit a cigarette. 'People have been murdered because of it.'

'Our son hasn't—'

'Fatma, I don't know whether Bekir has killed anybody or not.' The words almost choked him but they were nothing but

305

the truth. Bekir might very well have killed someone on his road into or within the Wormwood Route plot. The prospect of billions of dollars did that to people. 'Mehmet Süleyman is out there and he has gone to the town the corrupt doctor told me Bekir was heading for,' he continued. 'Fatma, Mehmet will protect him if he can. That's all we can do.'

'You ordered his arrest.' She said it in a frighteningly quiet voice. 'You.'

İkmen puffed on his cigarette, his back to his wife, the Blue Mosque, the ancient Byzantine Hippodrome. 'I had no choice,' he said.

'Because of your job?'

'Because what our son has done is wrong,' he said. 'As well as being whatever he is in this plot he also gave Kemal cocaine, he got that girl pregnant and then just left her . . .'

'He is our son.'

'He was stealing from his brothers and sisters when he was a teenager!' İkmen turned to look at his wife with anger in his eyes. 'For years we put up with his drug-taking, his lying, the violence he perpetrated wherever he went! He was a nightmare and I will be honest with you, Fatma, I was glad when that boy left this family all those years ago! I was glad!'

They looked at each other, her eyes wide with the fury his words and even the look on his face was making her feel. Then she drew one hand back slowly and deliberately and smacked him full on across the mouth. For several seconds neither of them so much as breathed. İkmen, his face sore from the great slap she had dealt him, simply sat as his eyes watered with the pain. It wasn't the first time she'd hit him. It had happened when Bekir had originally left the family home. Then, as now, she was completely unrepentant.

'Bekir needed you and you let him down.' Fatma turned to

look back at the Blue Mosque once again. 'Always at work. Always spending what time you did have with the children who pleased you. Sınan and Orhan with their medical studies, Çiçek learning languages to travel the world.'

'You are as proud of our children as I am!' İkmen growled, now for the first time touching a hand gently to his aching mouth.

'Of course I am,' she said. 'But Bekir was different. He needed . . . he needed . . .'

'He needed what, Fatma?' İkmen looked up at her face in profile. She was still very beautiful to him. 'Needed what?' He sighed. 'Go on and say it, woman, because it's what is in your head.'

His words made her angry again, but then that had been the intention. Making Fatma angry got to the root of her worries, made her say the things he did and did not want to hear. 'He needed moral guidance!' she said.

'Religion.'

'Absolutely religion!' she shouted. 'Islam would have saved that boy! I begged you, Çetin İkmen, to give our children the choice about religion, to at least take the lead with them, guide them! But you wouldn't have it!'

'You wanted me to take them to the mosque and I said no,' he said, struggling to control himself now. This if anything was the fault line in their long, long marriage. It had always been, and remained, the only real point of disagreement between them. 'You took them from time to time. I was not averse to your brothers' taking the boys . . .'

'But whenever we came back you ridiculed us!' Fatma said, beginning to weep with the sorrow of it all. 'You looked at the girls with their heads covered and it angered you!'

'Yes,' he said, 'yes, it did.' He stood up, calm again now

307

for some reason he couldn't even begin to fathom, and began to move back to the living-room door.

'Religion is a wonderful thing, Çetin. Faith is—'

'Faith would have done nothing for Bekir.' İkmen cut her off cruelly and then said, 'I have asked Mehmet Süleyman to do what he can for our boy, I can do no more. You pray if it makes you feel better. I don't believe it. You knew that when you married me.'

He made to leave the room and, suddenly panicked by his unusually cold demeanour, she said, 'Where are you going?'

'Back to work,' he said with a small, tired shrug. 'Back to work.'

And then he left. Fatma İkmen, alone again, tried to pray with all her heart, but found that she could only cry.

Chapter 22

'What do Gazi and Bulbul Kaplan do for a living?' Süleyman asked the Jandarma officer Private Bilge. They were looking round what was turning out to be a very empty and silent house.

'I don't know,' the young man replied. He took a piece of paper off the kitchen table, looked at it and then put it back again. 'The actual Kaplan family are rich,' he said. 'They all live off each other, and . . .'

Edibe Taner came into the kitchen and both men looked towards her.

'There's no one here,' she said, running her hands agitatedly through her hair. 'Where can they have gone? The old man is blind, and—'

'I'd just like to find the captain,' Private Bilge cut in darkly. 'It's not like him to be out of contact. Can't see his jeep anywhere.'

'Maybe, Private, he's gone on somewhere else.'

The house did not, to Süleyman's way of thinking, have any sort of ominous atmosphere. Maybe it was because it was so modern. But there was a smell. It wasn't, he knew, the vaguely sweet and metallic smell of blood, but it was faintly disturbing. He didn't know why.

'Where's Private Güzer?' Taner asked.

'Outside,' his colleague replied.

'Let's go and join him,' Taner said. 'There's no point being in here; there's nothing.'

They went outside to where Brother Gabriel stood beside Taner's car looking up at the stars. He wasn't supposed to have left the vehicle and Edibe Taner was very quick to hustle him back inside. Süleyman meanwhile took his small pencil torch out of his pocket and switched it on. The earth was poor, dusty and rutted, and as he made his way towards the back of the property he was very aware of the fact that his shoes were really quite unsuitable for the countryside.

Private Güzer, a figure also shining a torch down towards the ground, was over by an outbuilding of some sort, a garage or a barn.

'Anything?' Süleyman asked as he walked over to where the young man was standing.

'Not in that shed, sir, no,' the jandarme replied. Then he frowned. 'But if you look on the ground there are some fragments.' Cloth by the look of them, torn pieces that looked as if they had been dragged into or embedded in the dust. Some of them were quite bright, like fabric women might favour.

'Have you looked behind the shed yet, Private?' Süleyman asked.

'No, sir. Not yet. I've only just got here.'

'Let's do that now, shall we?'

They walked together round the side of the shed, past what Süleyman imagined was a very old piece of agricultural machinery – a large rusted metal thing. The smell he'd noticed earlier was getting stronger.

'Nothing inside, sir?' the young private asked as they rounded a corner of the shed.

'No,' Süleyman replied. 'No one in. Do you have any idea about where Mr and Mrs Kaplan may have gone, Private?'

'No, sir,' Güzer said. 'People out here in the country generally don't go far. Especially not the old folk. Not at night.'

Süleyman scanned what he could see of the flat area around the house and its outbuildings. His small torch was useless here and so he just squinted unaided into the darkness. The banks of the Euphrates were less than half a kilometre away and he began to wonder whether indeed this was where Yusuf Kaya had met his death. At the hands of his aunt? Could that possibly be the case? Could the old lady have done it on her own, or—

'Sir, the earth's been turned.'

'What?' He'd seen something, just very faintly against the almost black horizon, something sticking up above the olive trees in the field behind the house.

'Sir, the earth has been turned here,' Private Güzer said.

Because he couldn't make out what the object in the field might be, Süleyman looked down to where the jandarme was shining his torch. At his feet was a large area of churned and scuffed-up earth.

'Do you want me to get a shovel?'

But Süleyman just pushed at it with his foot. The smell he'd noticed earlier became much stronger. It didn't need any more force than a foot because in less than thirty seconds a very dead and dusty human hand had come to light. It was attached to an equally dead and dusty arm.

Mrs Bulbul Kaplan wasn't alone in what was in fact a very hastily dug and shallow grave. Captain Erdur lay beside her, his throat cut, his still open eyes filled with surprise. Private Güzer put a hand up to his head and then breathed deeply through his mouth. The captain had been his superior, and he had respected him.

Süleyman took his mobile phone out of his pocket and said, 'We'll need the services of the police in Şanlıurfa. This is a crime scene; we need forensic support. I hadn't been expecting this. I don't think any of us had.'

He had just started to work through the directory of numbers in his mobile and had heard what he thought was Güzer shuffling his feet next to him when the phone was suddenly and violently wrenched out of his hand.

'Güzer!'

But Private Güzer hadn't touched Süleyman. In fact Private Güzer was unlikely to touch anything again. Before he could even look to see where his phone had gone, Süleyman gazed on horrified as Private Güzer slumped slowly to the ground. Blood poured out of his mouth and also out of the great gaping stab wound in his back. The person standing behind him holding what had certainly killed the jandarme was a man he had never seen before. Probably in his early thirties, he held, as well as the knife, a small pistol which was pointed at Süleyman's head. He said nothing. Even when Süleyman wheeled round to try to locate his other colleagues the man just stayed where he was, smiling.

'What?'

And then lights! The thing he had vaguely seen on the horizon in the darkened field behind the house lit up. Its engine roaring into life as its lights came on, a truck of some considerable size lumbered through the trees and over towards what was a very rickety back fence. The person who had knocked Süleyman's phone out of his hands, the person standing behind him now, rammed the barrel of a gun hard into his temple and then ripped his own gun out of its holster underneath his jacket.

'Who . . .'

'Get them all over here; we'll finish the lot of them together!' a male voice behind his head called. Süleyman tried to speak but as he watched the truck heading towards the fence he found that he was completely dumb. What were these people going to do, run them all over? And where were the others anyway? Where were Inspector Taner and her beloved monk? Where was Private Bilge? The person behind him pushed Süleyman in the direction of the smirking man who had killed Private Güzer. Stumbling over the bodies of Bulbul Kaplan and Captain Erdur, he almost fell on to the outstretched knife, but he recovered himself in time. However, as he stumbled, he did look behind again and saw that Taner, Private Bilge and Brother Gabriel were being herded by the man who had grabbed him plus someone else too. It was a woman.

'You can't get any more in that pit, for God's sake!' Elizabeth Smith said to her two men. 'In fact let's just finish them and leave them where they fall. We're leaving. What does it matter?'

The truck had stopped moving now and someone had got out. As the figure moved towards the rickety garden fence, Süleyman saw that it was İbrahim Keser.

Her face a splash of white horror in the darkness, Edibe Taner looked down at the body of Bulbul Kaplan and said, 'Did you kill her? What—'

'She'd done her bit,' Elizabeth Smith said simply. Then, leaning in to place her gun against Taner's head, she said, 'That's how this operation works, Inspector. Haven't you worked that out yet?' She smiled. 'Yusuf did his bit when he set the whole thing up. All sorts of people did their bit when he got out of prison and then escaped from the hospital. Now . . .'

'The Wormwood Route. You or your people have just killed

for it as you've gone along, haven't you, Miss Smith?' Süleyman said. 'That's what it's been about all the time – money.'

'Yes and no,' she responded. 'Very good detective work.' Then she turned to the man at her elbow and said, 'Bekir, this is Inspector Süleyman.'

The young man was far from the image of his father but he was enough like Çetin İkmen for the experience of seeing him to take on an air of the surreal. Süleyman stared. To be killed by someone who looked like his friend, was indeed part of his friend, was a monstrous concept. Bekir looked at him with barely contained glee. It was almost as if he were looking forward to it.

'You need money to survive in the cradle of civilisation,' the American said. 'Money buys you immunity from all sorts of clan violence and terrorist activity. Like the Persians and Byzantines, Inspector Süleyman, I want my little empire and I want it to be here. Yusuf would have squandered the money on women and shitty apartment blocks in new Mardin. Now get over to the pit.'

Pushing and shoving, the American's men lined them up behind the pit where Bulbul Kaplan and Captain Erdur lay. Like a firing squad. Every part of Süleyman's body was cold and although he wanted to turn to Edibe Taner and tell her he was sorry for not having at least attempted to protect her, no part of him could actually move. As the three men now in front of them prepared their weapons to fire, Süleyman inwardly railed at the fact that İkmen's child was part of this. And all for what? For a method whereby death-giving drugs were about to swamp every city, town and village not just in Turkey but in many other countries as well. All because Elizabeth Smith wanted to live in some sort of eastern fantasy.

'Put your weapons down.'

For just a moment he thought that they were saved, that maybe the other Mardin constables and the jandarmes they were with had come to rescue them. But the voice that urged Miss Smith and her men to give up their violence was neither demanding nor in any way alarming.

'Put your weapons down and just go,' Gabriel said. 'You were leaving anyway, so leave. We will not follow. You've taken the officers' weapons and telephones. What can we do if you go?'

He was, Süleyman noticed, moving very slowly towards the American and her cohorts.

'Go!'

'Brother Gabriel!' Süleyman said.

The monk turned, and by the light of the truck's headlights Süleyman saw him smile.

'It's all right,' he said calmly. 'It's fine.'

And then he began to run towards them. Edibe Taner screamed. 'Gabriel!'

All three men shot at him and all three men had terrified expressions on their faces as they did so.

'Allah, what was that!' Bekir İkmen said as he turned to the man on his left. 'What happened there?'

Edibe Taner, screaming, threw herself across Gabriel Saatçi's body and shook him by his lifeless shoulders.

'That was a saint,' İbrahim Keser said with both arrogance and fear in his voice. 'You killed a fucking saint! I killed a fucking saint!'

'Bekir,' Süleyman began, 'you—'

It was like a curse at first. There was nothing to hear and yet suddenly there was blood. Pouring out of Bekir İkmen, out of İbrahim Keser and out of the mouth of the other man who stood beside them. They'd killed a saint and now they were paying. And to think that he, Süleyman, hadn't believed in any of this! To think that Edibe Taner, an officer hidden away and obscured in the country, had known what he had not. There was something, there was a—

'Don't move, Miss Smith! If you move I'll kill you too!'

Whose voice was that? He couldn't make any sense of it until he heard Taner screaming once again.

'Selahattin! Selahattin, help me!'

And then the men came forward out of the darkness. Two Mardin policemen and three jandarmes. They all held pistols with silencers attached. Two of them grabbed the American by her arms and then forced her down on the ground so that they could search her.

'Madam!'

Constable Selahattin ran to Taner and helped her to cradle the monk's head against her shoulder. Her clothes were drenched in his blood, her mouth full of it where she had kissed and kissed and kissed his face.

Once he could speak again, Süleyman said to Private Yüksel, 'How did you . . . how did you get here?'

Private Yüksel put a hand on his shoulder and said, 'It was the river again, sir.'

'The river?'

'When we got into town some kids reported seeing a vehicle down this way in the river. They said they thought it might be a jeep.'

'And?'

'And, sir, we don't know yet,' Yüksel said as he looked down at the dead body of his former boss, 'but I imagine it was probably . . . his.' He grimaced. 'Sir, the river gives and takes – bodies, vehicles, everything.'

'I must go to Inspector Taner,' Süleyman said. And he stepped over corpses and mindlessly went to her.

'Edibe . . .'

Her eyes were blasted. A for ever sleepless, tortured and brutalised animal. She folded herself over the dead body of her love and then she began to ululate her grief. A trilling mourning overpowering and snuffing out the sounds of the American being led away, and the death agonies of the three men on the ground in front of her.

Chapter 23

Bekir İkmen didn't actually die until he had been in the ambulance on the way to hospital in Şanlıurfa for nearly half an hour. Süleyman, who chose to ride alongside his old friend's son, saw all the efforts that were made to save his life, but he knew inside that none of them would work. The young man's internal organs were shattered by bullets. There was no way back.

When the vehicle arrived at the hospital he was given the option of having the doctor who pronounced life extinct call Çetin İkmen. But Süleyman said he would do that himself. He owed it to İkmen to let him know that he had failed. Bekir İkmen had proved impossible to save.

'You didn't kill him,' İkmen said when Süleyman's story finally came to its bloody and horrific end. 'And even those who did, did so for a good reason.'

His voice was not only tired, it was dead too. Like a ghastly horror movie one can only just stand. In the background the sound of Fatma İkmen screaming a hellish soundtrack.

'Çetin, I am so sorry.'

He didn't reply. The screaming continued and then he just said, 'I will get the first flight that I can.'

Süleyman heard his friend light a cigarette and then he heard his wife berate him for it. İkmen did not react at all. İkmen was just doing what he always did, getting everything done. There was almost no option, for Süleyman at least, but to take the same stance himself.

'I have to go back to Mardin,' he said. 'Inspector Taner needs me. She can't interview the American woman without some support. And . . .'

'And you want to know how this all came about,' İkmen said. 'Of course you do. Of course you do.'

'Çetin, I will tell you everything. I—'

'My dear Mehmet,' İkmen said, 'we already have part of the picture. If this American is to be the key to more knowledge about the Wormwood Route . . .'

'I think she knows it,' Süleyman said. 'I mean all of it. I hope that is the case.'

'So . . .'

'It's my belief that Elizabeth Smith orchestrated almost everything.'

There was a pause and then İkmen said, 'Well, you get her then, Mehmet. You get her so that she never sees the outside of a prison again.'

And then he ended the call. Alone until Constable Selahattin arrived to take him back to Mardin, Mehmet Süleyman stared into the night with still, exhausted eyes.

The small community of monks at St Sobo's monastery were not accustomed to keeping irregular hours. Times for sleeping, eating, praying and working were strictly prescribed by rules going back millennia. But death is no respecter of tradition and when Edibe Taner knocked on the great gates of the monastery at four o'clock that morning she knew that she was about to turn their world upside down. Not that she cared. Leaning on her father's shoulder for support, she looked down at the litter the two young constables had carried to the gates in front of her and wept all over again. By now, not just her colleagues and her father but almost all of Mardin knew that their saint was dead.

'He died to save the rest of us,' she said to Brother Seraphim once the other monks had taken the body away to be washed. 'None of us knew that help was on its way and Gabriel just . . . he . . .'

'God was working through Brother Gabriel,' Brother Seraphim said as he took the shattered woman and her father into the monastery refectory. He sat them down and then poured mirra for them both to drink. The three of them sat in silence for a long time. Seçkin Taner, though stunned by his daughter's news, was nevertheless trying to maintain at least an aura of composure for her sake. Seraphim didn't really know anything beyond the fact that Brother Gabriel was dead. He had died protecting others, which was something that Seraphim could easily imagine happening. But how had he died? How had he got into a situation where others had wanted him dead?

Shivering as she spoke, Edibe Taner said, 'I killed him. I put him in the way of danger. It was my fault.'

Seçkin Taner grimaced in pain. 'Edibe . . .'

'My dear, I'm sure you didn't cause Brother Gabriel's death,' Brother Seraphim said. 'You loved him. And he loved you. You were the very best of friends, I know that. Edibe, if Gabriel died protecting you then I know that he died a happy man.'

But his words just seemed to inflame her. 'Tell me this, Brother,' she said bitterly. 'Why did Gabriel survive the bites of the snakes but die with just three bullets? If Allah was looking after him, if he was an immortal saint, then . . .' She broke down and wept, howling her pain on to her father's chest as he stroked her hair and cooed into her ear.

321

Brother Seraphim, clearly upset by her words, said, 'I don't know the answer to that question, Edibe. I wish I did. Maybe Gabriel needed his Sharmeran by his side for God to protect him. Maybe our brother was just too good for this wicked world. Who knows?' And then he too put his head in his hands and wept.

They put the American woman into the smallest cell they had. If they had been able to find one that was actually window-less they would have pushed her into that. Nothing was too bad. Not because she was American, not even because she had killed or ordered the deaths of people that they knew and sometimes loved. The young constables put her where they did, said the bitter things they did to and about her, because she had killed their saint. Muslims to a man, the Mardin consta-bles had all grown up with Gabriel, all knew him to be a special person, and they had all, without exception, liked and respected him. If this woman didn't go away for ever they would want to know why. The police were not alone, either. As dawn broke over the Tur Abdin people began to come into the city and position themselves in the streets, tea gardens and cafés around the police station. Lütfü Güneş stood at the head of a small group of his people outside the Sehidiye Medrese. As Süleyman passed him on his way to the station, the Kurd smiled enigmatically in his direction. The İstanbul man wondered, as he had done before, just how and why this man had known about Elizabeth Smith, but he didn't dwell upon the question long on account of the restive nature of the crowd around him. Whether they all knew who he was he couldn't tell because none of them, so it seemed, was choosing or able to speak Turkish. In fact, amongst the many languages that he could hear around him there was only one word that he could recognise and that was 'Gabriel'. Their saint, who was dead and whom it was obvious they wanted some sort of justice for. That was his job, or rather it was partly his job. When he reached the front entrance to the station the crowds behind him parted and he turned to see Edibe Taner walking towards him. Dressed in black, her face as white as paper, she wore an expression of such hatred that it took Mehmet Süleyman's breath away.

Chapter 24

'It is my intention to conduct this interview in English,' Süleyman said as he sat down in front of the American woman. He looked briefly over at Taner, who just shrugged before folding herself stiffly into the seat beside him. 'This is because,' he continued, 'I want to have no mistakes, Miss Smith. I want you to understand exactly what I am saying and I want your answers to be free from any ambiguity that may arise if you have to translate what you say into Turkish. Do you understand?'

She shrugged. The fact that she didn't actually answer him was annoying. But the irritation he felt was nothing compared to the anger that had flooded him as soon as he was once again in her presence. Not because of Brother Gabriel, whom he had hardly known, but because she had albeit indirectly been responsible for the death of İkmen's son and she it was who had turned Edibe Taner into a silent, shadowy, almost ghost-like figure.

'Miss Smith,' he said before he could think too hard or too deeply about his own feelings, 'I understand that you do not wish to have a lawyer.'

'No.'

'That is your choice,' he said. He looked down at his notes and then briefly at Taner again, but her face was as blank as the wall behind Elizabeth Smith's head. 'Miss Smith, let us be rational, shall we?'

She frowned.

'Miss Smith, you ordered my death and the deaths of my colleagues,' Süleyman said. 'I was there. I heard you. You witnessed the death of Gabriel Saatçi. Jandarma Private Güzer was killed by a man clearly associated with you and you were apparently aware of the place where Mrs Bulbul Kaplan and Captain Erdur of the Birecik Jandarma were buried. Captain Erdur we know was unlawfully killed, Mrs Kaplan we have yet to receive forensic evidence about. So, Miss Smith, make no mistake, you are going to prison. It is highly unlikely that you will ever get out. So when I say you must be rational what I mean is that you must look to your future, in prison, and you must consider how you might make that as easy or comfortable or however you wish to express it for yourself.'

'You want me to spill?'

'I want you to die,' he heard Edibe Taner say in Turkish under her breath. He put a hand on her arm and held up a warning finger. The last thing he needed, because he was exhausted and furious himself, was a loose cannon at his side.

Whether Elizabeth Smith had heard what Taner had said he didn't know. She didn't respond until he said, 'I want you to tell me everything. Miss Smith, we do not have capital punishment in the Turkish Republic and so the most a judge can sentence a criminal to is life in prison. I think we both know that that is already very possible for you.'

'You want I should finger other people?'

'I want you to start at the beginning and talk until your story is finished,' Süleyman said. 'I want you to tell me what happened when your husband Yusuf killed the Russian gangster, Tommi Kerensky.'

*　　*　　*

Çetin İkmen went to Atatürk Airport accompanied by his son Bülent. Because the young man worked for Turkish Airlines he had managed to talk to those who could get his father quickly on to a flight out to Şanlıurfa.

'Dad, you mustn't worry about Mum. She will be all right again, in time,' Bülent said as he placed a hand on his father's sloping shoulder. They both stood in front of the large departure board in the middle of the domestic terminal, İkmen openly smoking underneath a new No Smoking sign.

'Your mother blames me,' he said. 'And maybe she is right.'

'Dad, you couldn't have prevented Bekir's death. You told me he'd just killed a man. How could the officers who shot him have done anything else?'

'No. No, I know I couldn't have . . .' He sighed. 'Bülent, I did very little to find Bekir when he left home all those years ago.'

'Çiçek told me he was a nightmare,' Bülent said. 'He stole from everyone. Mum was always in tears.'

'But he was fifteen!' İkmen said. 'He walked out of our apartment and he was on the streets at fifteen!' His eyes filled with tears. 'Oh, I looked for him in all the obvious places at the time. But I didn't really get stuck in. I didn't go to the terrible, awful places.'

'You probably couldn't imagine him in that sort of context,' Bülent said. He was having some trouble feeling anything about this brother who had appeared so late on in his life, disgraced himself and then run away and died. 'Dad, you and Mum brought us up well. In some ways it's a curse.'

'What do you mean?' His emotions sharpened by grief and tiredness, İkmen puffed on furiously.

'I mean I couldn't possibly have gone on the streets like Bekir did,' Bülent said. 'I think I speak for all of us, Dad, when

I say that we as a family are all too pampered to be capable of such a thing. You've looked after us all much too well.'

'Except Bekir.'

'That was his choice,' Bülent said. 'He wanted to take drugs and beg and get involved in criminal activity. We didn't and so he left.'

It was all so simple to Bülent. But then he'd been just a child when Bekir left; he'd never had any sort of relationship with his brother really. And although he was as shocked and sad as the rest of the family he did not feel any pain. İkmen looked up at the departure board and saw that his flight was boarding.

'I have to go,' he said.

Bülent put his arms round his father and kissed him. 'We will start to make funeral arrangements,' he said.

'I'll do my best to bring my son home tomorrow if I can,' İkmen said. 'But as I told your mother, it may be that Bekir's body has to remain in Urfa until . . .' He swallowed hard. 'Your mother cannot understand why the body may have to be treated as evidence. She just hates me.'

'Dad, go and get your flight,' Bekir said.

İkmen kissed his son on both cheeks and then headed towards the passageway leading to the departure gates. Bülent, shaking his head with agitation, made his way back towards the front entrance to the terminal. Outside in the car park one of his brothers was waiting to take him back to their parents' apartment and the agony of his grieving mother.

'Tommi Kerensky knew something about the Wormwood Route,' Elizabeth Smith said as she looked Mehmet Süleyman clearly in the eyes. 'The Syrian whore Yusuf used to bang when he was in İstanbul—'

'Hana Karim?'

'Yeah. She spilled it. She was doing Tommi too, which was why the both of them had to go. Yusuf for all his vision was a poor judge of character.'

'He was a psychopathic killer.'

'Yes, but he was a psychopathic killer who had nevertheless built a drug route into this country that was second to none.'

'Why second to none?'

'Because every part of the chain was discrete,' she said. 'People even half the way along the line had no idea who was at the end or the beginning of the process. Each took his cut in goods and no one knew more than was necessary to do his job.'

'Except for Yusuf.'

Elizabeth Smith leaned across the table and said, 'He wasn't scared of going to prison. Tommi Kerensky had put it about that Yusuf had something big on his hands before he was killed. Yusuf had already made millions of dollars and everyone wanted in. No one in that prison gave Yusuf any hassle and that included some of his gaolers.'

'How did he get out?' Süleyman asked.

She smiled. 'I bought a lot of people,' she said. 'Some of them at Yusuf's request and some off my own bat. Some of the nurses at the hospital were known to him. Mardin people, as I'm sure you already know, are kind of close.'

Süleyman looked down at the file on the table in front of him and said, 'İsak Mardin, Murat Lole and Faruk Öz. Some of these are pseudonyms, as I am sure you know, but . . .'

'The then administrator of the Cerrahpaşa, Oner, was a friend,' the American said. 'Unfortunately he couldn't really handle what Yusuf had in mind and started to get a bit wobbly.'

'Wobbly?'

'He wanted out,' she said harshly. 'Yusuf sent a message that that wasn't really an option and so he topped himself. You don't split on your nearest and dearest out here – not unless you're prepared to take the consequences. It could have all been over at that point if Oner's replacement hadn't been a user. Aktar, who fortunately got the job, has a big habit. Not that he knew too much until Yusuf was sprung.'

'So who apart from the nurses—'

'İsak Mardin had this doctor who liked to fuck him. Eldem. Not averse to getting rich either. He did as İsak said. We placed Mardin in the Cerrahpaşa to get Yusuf away. That was his purpose. He was waiting outside the hospital and got Yusuf and the others away from there.' She leaned across the table and said, 'The prison guards who went out with Yusuf to the hospital did as they were told, too.'

Edibe Taner looked at Süleyman. 'But they died, didn't they?' she said.

'Yes.'

Elizabeth Smith shrugged. 'That was the plan.'

'I'm sure neither they nor the police officers who accompanied Kaya to the hospital knew that,' Süleyman said.

'Of course not!' She laughed. To the inspectors in front of her this was a very disturbing phenomenon. 'The coppers were entirely ignorant anyway. They had nothing to do with it. But that was, in part, Yusuf's idea. If those who knew his movements were dead they couldn't tell anyone what they'd seen.'

'No. But you say in part. What do you mean by that?'

She sat back in her chair then and looked down at her hands, suddenly subdued. 'Some of those who died were not on Yusuf's mental list,' she said. Then she looked up with sharp, cold eyes. 'But they were on mine.'

'Because you wanted to take this Wormwood Route from

Yusuf Kaya so you could use the money to forge some sort of "empire" or fiefdom here,' Süleyman said, recalling what she had said to him back at Bulbul Kaplan's farm in Birecik. But she didn't react to the obvious jibe.

'Murat Lole, İsak Mardin and Faruk Öz sprang Yusuf,' she said. 'But then afterwards Lole got greedy and killed Öz. İsak Mardin was with Yusuf by that time; that was the plan. Lole I believe either offed Öz at Mardin's place or took the body there afterwards. Whatever, Mardin's apartment was never going to be used by him again. The cleaners were taken care of by Yusuf, although one of them did prove useful, as you saw last night.'

'One of the cleaners?'

'The copper's son, your friend's son, the guy who worked for that beggarman, that Fagin character back in your city. You know the—'

'Do you mean Hüseyin Altun?' Süleyman asked. 'From Edirnekapı? He and Bekir İkmen posed as hospital cleaners?'

'Bekir İkmen and there was some kid as well,' Elizabeth said, 'but he was offed too, as I said. The İkmen guy killed Hüseyin Altun at Yusuf's request. Altun had put Yusuf and İsak Mardin up for the night after his escape, which was risky. He had a big mouth. Yusuf was always going to use İkmen to kill Altun and to front his İstanbul operation because he was so smart. It was apparent, so Yusuf said, from their first meeting. But, well . . .' She shrugged again. 'I used him myself. I used anyone and everyone not in bed with the Kaya family.'

'What did İsak Mardin do then?' Süleyman asked.

'Lay low just outside İstanbul until I called him and Bekir to join us in Birecik last night,' she said. 'Yusuf, remember, had me plan his escape with him. What he didn't know was

331

that I was planning to double-cross him with guys I'd done deals of my own with.'

'So let me see this correctly,' Süleyman said. 'To go back in time again now, you helped to arrange your husband's escape from Kartal Prison. You got him out to Birecik where you extracted information from him and then you killed him, or someone else killed him.'

'His aunty Bulbul did the actual killing,' the American said. 'She wanted to.'

'Bulbul Kaplan?'

'Yeah. You know that Yusuf's dad pushed out her old man's eyes?' Elizabeth Smith shook her head in apparent disbelief. 'Yusuf told me it was an agreed thing between the Kayas and the Kaplans. Gazi's eyes go and there's no more feud. Honour on both sides is apparently served. The Kaplans get to keep Bulbul, while the Kayas get to blind Gazi. All square. Good deal, huh? Except that old Gazi could never get a hard-on from that moment onwards and so Bulbul never had any kids. Resentful? I think so, don't you? And not just of Gazi but of her family too. So there she is, she's given up her whole life for a man who never touches her again.'

'But why did she agree to see Yusuf Kaya?' Taner asked.

'Originally? I don't know,' the American said. 'He fetched up there, she was nice to him and that was that. Maybe she saw him as some sort of child substitute. I don't know. I never cared. Anyway, Yusuf himself hadn't actually hurt her husband, had he? But then later I realised that she maybe had other plans for Yusuf all along. He took me to meet her a few months before he was arrested. We were business partners – he only married me because he wanted to feel he had some sort of control over me. He wanted me to know where his safe houses were. But when he was in prison I contacted her myself, just to be nice, you understand. She it was who started on about how she really wished that her nephew could get the old death penalty. I started thinking, because I knew I wanted the Wormwood Route for myself by this time, that maybe she had sussed me out and maybe also I could use her justifiable rage. She was a very ruthless woman, you know. Very ruthless.'

'What do you mean?'

'I mean that when her husband Gazi got wind of her plans to kill Yusuf he ordered her not to do it. He'd given his eyes to stop such things happening; the whole reason behind his sacrifice was to stop any further feuding. You can appreciate the man's point of view.'

'Gazi Kaplan was blind. He couldn't do very much to stop his wife, surely.'

'He could do even less once she'd stabbed him in the chest,' Elizabeth Smith said.

Both Süleyman and Taner were truly shocked. Gazi Kaplan had not been found at the house in Birecik, it was true, but no one until now had thought about the possibility that he might actually be dead. Gazi Kaplan, until this moment, had simply been missing.

'She killed him weeks ago,' the American continued. 'I don't know where she buried him.'

'And now Mrs Kaplan is dead I cannot ask her, can I?' Süleyman said.

'There's no one left to ask,' Elizabeth Smith replied. 'She was dead by the time you got to the house. By the way, most of my boys were long gone by that time too.'

'Your guards? To where?'

'To where I'd arranged to meet them,' she said. 'That left only İbrahim Keser and the two boys we met in Birecik.'

'Bekir İkmen.'

'And Yusuf Mardin, yes.' She smiled. 'We'd agreed in advance to tidy Mrs Kaplan away. She did what she did for money. That was the bait, as well as Yusuf's death, that I used to tempt her. She wanted to get away and have a bit of a life somewhere. But her price was high and I couldn't have that. The captain of the Jandarma, however . . .' she shrugged, 'that was unfortunate. We didn't know he was coming back. I got in the old woman's bed and pretended to be sleeping Gazi. The captain didn't disturb me and I thought he had to have bought my act. When he came back, Bekir and myself had just offed the old woman and so the captain . . . well, he had to go too, didn't he?' She smiled. 'You guys did well, really. Although whether the Mardin posse would have done it without you, Inspector Süleyman, is probably doubtful.'

Süleyman looked at Taner and then said, 'Oh, I don't know.'

'Sure you do.' The American smiled. 'Take the compliment, Inspector. I mean nothing by it. I'm doomed. What on earth can I get out of you now?'

Süleyman ignored her. 'Miss Smith,' he said, 'you have told us that you had arranged to meet the rest of your men somewhere. Where is that? Where are the rest of your men now?'

Elizabeth Smith took a deep breath and then leaned back into her chair. 'Ah, well then, that would be telling, wouldn't it?' she said.

Süleyman thought about all the Mardin families who had either disappeared or no longer had a patriarch. He thought about the proximity of Syria and Iraq and about how someone had dressed Yusuf Kaya's corpse in an American uniform from Baghdad. Borders, even Turkish borders, were easy – if you knew the right people.

334

'How did you get hold of an American serviceman's uniform from Baghdad?' he asked.

She smiled, but did not speak.

Süleyman felt himself shudder. He tried a different tack. 'Tell me about Murat Lole,' he said. 'We know that Faruk Öz's real name was Hasan Karabulut and that he was one of your husband's cousins. Where did Murat Lole come into this?'

'Van,' she said.

'Van?'

'Where Faruk Öz trained as a nurse,' the American said. 'Where in fact Hasan Karabulut became Faruk Öz.'

'How and why did he change his identity?' Edibe Taner asked.

'I believe he paid some criminal in Van to get him a new ID,' the American said. 'As to why . . . To get away from here, from Yusuf and from his connection to the clan. He was really a gentle boy. But Yusuf found out.'

'And did what?'

'And was very angry,' she said. 'Yusuf never liked to lose anyone. Faruk/Hasan was intimidated into telling Yusuf that he and his friend Murat had plans to work in İstanbul. He said that if Yusuf ever needed him while he was there he would be on hand to help him. He was buying himself some freedom. The poor kid was so desperate to get away he would have done anything. I think he planned eventually to just disappear. Mind you, if Murat hadn't been in the picture . . .'

'Murat Lole?'

'Murat whatever he was calling himself that wasn't Armenian, yes,' she said.

'So the name Lole . . .'

'Is his real name, so he says, yes,' the American said. 'Claims he is a Lole whose family came originally from Mardin, just like the architect.' She leaned forward in her chair then. 'But as we all know only too well, some Armenians have changed their surnames over the years. I don't know what Murat's had been, but I do know that my husband fixed it for him to get all his papers changed into the name of Lole when the boys went to İstanbul. Murat had this belief that away from the east he could be who he wanted to be and use whatever name he felt like using. Yusuf believed that in a tight spot an Armenian would keep his head. Some people have this view of Armenians, you know.'

'But Lole, surely, works for you?'

'No, no,' she said. 'He killed Faruk/Hasan on Yusuf's orders.'

'You said before,' Süleyman said, 'that Lole killed Faruk/Hasan because he got greedy.'

'So he did,' she said. 'Yusuf offered him money to kill Faruk. The boy had tried to leave the Kaya clan! When he was of no further use he was killed.'

'But surely,' Edibe Taner said, 'Lole and Hasan Karabulut were friends?'

The American woman crooked an eyebrow. 'Honey, he was or is a man with a dream and big empty pockets wanting money. Bleak, I know, but the whole point about the Route and everyone around it is that no one can be trusted. Everyone double- and triple-crosses for billions of dollars. It's Darwinism in action.'

'And of course Lole is still out there somewhere,' Süleyman said. 'Do you have any idea where this man might be, Miss Smith?'

'No, why should I?' she said. 'He's Armenian, or at least that's what he claimed. You Turks always say they're so clever. He could be anywhere.'

* * *

336

The man wept. Not a nice man, Dr Eldem had in all probability murdered the prison guard Ramazan Eren without so much as a flicker, but now that he knew his lover had died it was another matter. İzzet Melik looked across at Ayşe Farsakoğlu who just very slightly raised her eyebrows.

'Dr Eldem, was the plan that you go and meet İsak Mardin somewhere after his rendezvous with the American woman?' İzzet asked.

It took the doctor a moment to gather himself. 'Well . . .' He gulped. 'Well, of course. We—'

'Where? Where were you going to meet up with İsak Mardin?'

'I . . .' The doctor wiped his eyes with a handkerchief and then gulped down a sob once again. 'He was going to call me.'

'Except that he wasn't,' Ayşe Farsakoğlu said. 'Why would he? You'd done what he needed you to do. He was off to Miss Smith.'

'I didn't know anything about that. I—'

'No, you didn't,' İzzet Melik said. 'You killed on the orders of İsak Mardin.'

'No!'

'Yes. Dr Eldem, you are a doctor. You are not going to kill on the orders of a thug or a madman or even a superior. You will, however, kill for love,' İzzet said. He looked briefly across at Ayşe Farsakoğlu before continuing. 'Many of us would. Now listen. Tell us who you phoned the night Ramazan Eren died. Who did you not manage to get through to?'

'I don't know.'

Ayşe Farsakoğlu pounded one fist down on the table in front of her. 'Sir, that cannot be! You must know who you were supposed to telephone and why. Why did you call this person, this apparent Syrian national?'

There was a pause. Dr Eldem moved his head from side to side in agitation. Once he opened his mouth to speak and then changed his mind and retreated into silence again.

'Dr Eldem, we will find the truth. İsak Mardin is dead. He died attempting to escape the Jandarma in Birecik along with a man called Bekir. You are protecting no one.'

'Oh, no?' He looked up sharply, his eyes full of tears. 'How do I know he's dead? How do I know you're not just lying to me so that I will implicate İsak in something?'

İzzet Melik sighed. 'Doctor, if you want a photograph of the body, I can arrange it,' he said. 'But consider this: our conversation is being recorded. Our superior, Inspector İkmen, will not tolerate dishonesty or cruelty. If we lie to you, sir, we will be the ones to get into trouble. İsak Mardin is dead and so whatever you say about him now cannot possibly do him any harm. Now, how did you know to give Ramazan Eren an overdose of morphine and why?'

His eyes welled with tears again but this time he held them back. 'If Eren started to wake, İsak said, I was to call the number that I called,' he said. 'I didn't know that the phone was registered to a foreigner – I thought it would be İsak who would answer. He would tell me what to do. I knew only that İsak said we would make big money.' He put his head down. 'I was greedy. I am . . . İsak had told me that if Eren began to wake he would have to be killed. He said I should confirm it by phone but that wasn't possible. No one answered.'

'So you acted on the say-so of your lover,' Ayşe said.

'Yes.' He shook his head slowly. 'Eren wasn't supposed to survive Yusuf Kaya's escape. İsak and the other nurses and cleaners were meant to get away with him and leave all the guards and the police officers dead.'

'But Ramazan Eren survived.'

He looked up. 'He would have talked.'

'Because he had been double-crossed,' İzzet Melik said.

'Yes. Apparently he was part of it.'

'Just like İsak Mardin's fellow nurse Faruk Öz,' İzzet said. 'Found dead at Mardin's old house in Zeyrek. Was he double-crossed too, Dr Eldem?'

The doctor was beginning to shake now, and with good cause. 'Suddenly İsak was working not for Kaya but for some American woman,' he said. 'But Faruk Öz was related to Kaya and indebted in some way to him. He was from back there, back in their home out east. Murat Lole killed Faruk Öz apparently with Yusuf Kaya's blessing. Lole was greedy. It all became confusing then. Then I didn't know who was working for whom or . . . or if İsak really loved me.'

Chapter 25

'It was in effect a violent putsch,' Süleyman said to Edibe Taner. 'Everyone who was in the way, knew too much or was a threat had to go.'

The interrogation of Elizabeth Smith was going on well into the night and they were taking a short break before going back in to speak to the woman again.

'Elizabeth Smith identified two types of people she could target,' he continued, 'those local people who secretly disliked or actively hated the Kayas and those outsiders who didn't know or care about Yusuf Kaya. It was all motivated by greed, of course. Makes you wonder how Miss Smith ever managed to get even a thug like Kaya to marry her. After all, it was the place, here, that she was in love with, not Yusuf. But then she says, and Zeynep Kaya told us too, that their marriage was a business arrangement on Yusuf's part also. She wanted an "empire"! Allah!'

'She had all the Kayas killed,' Edibe Taner said as she hugged her tea glass to her chest. She was cold with weariness and grief, and what they had just been told by Elizabeth Smith had made her feel no better.

'And that was always the intention,' Süleyman replied. 'At least some of the arms that İbrahim Keser blackmailed Musa Saatçi into hiding for him were to be used against the Kayas. The rest I imagine were to further her own power and influence in the Tur Abdin. To terrorise. But then this thing, this route, is worth billions and so of course you're going to use guns and grenades and even rocket launchers to protect it. She wanted the Wormwood Route to herself and so wanted no pretenders to rise up in the future to challenge her authority. Not even Kaya's children. And as an outsider that made perfect sense. Her men could have defected to Zeynep or any other Kaya family member had they thought there was some advantage to be had there. Elizabeth, by killing the whole family, prevented a war. Very sensible.'

'But she killed Gabriel too,' Taner said as yet again she descended into her grief. If he were honest, Süleyman had to admit that his colleague was of little use in the current interrogation. From the searing misery at the death of the monk she had now slipped into a quiet, horrified hopelessness. In the interrogation she hardly spoke. She regarded their prisoner simply with a cold, implacable hatred. But then she wasn't alone in that. Even at nearly midnight those who had loved Gabriel Saatçi still ringed the station, waiting to catch a glimpse of or maybe even mount an attack on the woman responsible for the death of their saint as well as, in some cases, their own relatives too. Süleyman knew that the situation was volatile. He also knew that he had to remain calm. Others around him may very well lose their heads, but that was not an option for him. He had to remain in control.

'Inspector,' he said, 'I have two priorities here.'

Edibe Taner looked up from her drink and said, 'Oh?'

Süleyman offered her a cigarette, which she took, and then lit one up for himself. 'To trace exactly how Yusuf Kaya escaped from prison – who helped him, who died, et cetera – plus the exact circumstances of his death. And secondly we must try to get this Wormwood Route out of her. We know that heroin and other drugs passed through here and that part of the operation involved packaging the drugs with bundles – or whatever one calls such things – of wormwood flowers.'

'Do you think that Elizabeth Smith knows all the details of the Wormwood Route?'

'I don't know,' he said. 'That was clearly her intention and she must have got something out of Yusuf before he died. But then we don't know the exact circumstances of that yet, do we?'

'No.' She sighed. 'Inspector, who was it who told you about Elizabeth Smith and her men out at Dara?'

Although he had intended to tell her for some time, he now realised that he still hadn't. 'Lütfü Güneş, a Kurd,' he said.

She frowned.

'What?'

'Oh, his family are poor. They, like a lot of people, have by turns been given employment and hospitality and then bullied by the Kayas,' she said. 'There is no love lost there. Yet Lütfü has – or had – quite a surprising best friend.'

'Oh?'

'Yes,' she said. 'He and Elizabeth Smith's right-hand man, İbrahim Keser, were friends since their school days. Like brothers, they were.'

Çetin İkmen knew that he would never be able to sleep. Even without the noisy ladies' henna party in one of the rooms at the bottom of the hotel.

'A lady, she getting married,' the hotel owner had explained to İkmen in his fractured, slightly guttural Turkish. Şanlıurfa was far too 'east' for İkmen. Most people communicated amongst themselves in a variety of languages and dialects, none of which he could speak. Not that that was what was

343

exercising his mind as he lay on his bed now, awake and motionless save for the lifting of his hand up to his mouth as he smoked cigarette after endless cigarette.

He had not spent long at the hospital. Just enough time to formally identify his dead son. Bekir had looked as if he were sleeping. He'd been shot in the back, basically in the lungs which, as İkmen knew only too well, made a hell of a mess. Blood poured out of the mouths of such people. But the hospital, to their credit, had cleaned him up and apparently Mehmet Süleyman had done his best to make sure that the body was not further damaged when it was taken to the mortuary. But it was still dead and it had still been his son. Whatever Bekir might have done he would always be that. First thing in the morning he would fly back to İstanbul with the body and then they would put him in the ground. There were no questions about how or why he had died. The jandarmes and the Mardin policemen who had shot Bekir, İsak Mardin and some man called İbrahim Keser had had legitimate cause. The three men had just executed a defenceless monk. Just the thought of it made İkmen want to cry, even though he knew that he wouldn't be able to. It was as if his tear ducts had run out of moisture.

Fatma had of course been relieved that the boy would be buried soon. Not that any of that meant much to İkmen. But it was important for his wife, whose voice when he had spoken to her on the phone earlier had been as cold as winter. She didn't so much blame him for what had happened as feel nothing for him. Whether this was temporary or not he couldn't know. But he had an unpleasant feeling that nothing would ever be quite the same again. The happy and united İkmen family had somehow produced a killer from its midst and the reverberations were going to take years, if not decades, to subside. Because even if the drugs and the drink were put to one side, Bekir İkmen had not been like other people. Even as a child he had not wanted to conform to the norms that governed what was a very liberal household. There'd always been a kind of itch inside that boy, a something that agitated and threw off balance even his sometimes sincere attempts to fit in and make himself agreeable. All the children had had moments of adolescent angst and awkwardness but with Bekir it was as if something extra had entered his soul somewhere along the line, something that had ultimately killed it.

'It was Hüseyin Altun, the beggar king or whatever you call him, who got Yusuf a car,' the American woman said. It was well past midnight now and she was looking shadowed, pale and exhausted. But that was not Süleyman's problem.

'He stole it?'

She shrugged. 'Yusuf dropped İsak Mardin off somewhere outside the city to hole up and then drove to Birecik. Hours and hours and bloody hours.'

'While Hüseyin Altun was being murdered by Bekir İkmen?'

'Yes.' She shrugged again. 'I guess. I don't know when he killed him exactly.'

'Who was involved in the plot within Kártal Prison?' Süleyman asked. He already had a list of names but he wanted it to be absolutely comprehensive.

'The two guards.' She shook her head as if to try to get it to work properly now she was so tired. 'He bribed some prisoner to pick a fight with him.'

The simple Ara Berköz.

'The governor?'

'No, but there were other guards too.'

'Names?'

'I don't know.' She looked up and yet again shook her head. 'Honestly. Look, I'm bushed. Can we rest?'

'No.' He leaned across the table and said, 'Tell me what happened when Yusuf got to Birecik. Did he get any more help along the way?'

She looked as if she might be close to tears. But she didn't cry. 'Not that I know of. I think he may have stopped briefly in Gaziantep . . .' she said. 'I was waiting for him at Bulbul Kaplan's house.'

'Why did you agree to meet there?'

'It was all part of Yusuf's plan,' she said. 'To hole up at Bulbul's. No one knew, or rather the police couldn't make any connection between him and her. She was just this woman, you know? Not related to him. It was very finely calculated.'

'And he knew that you were going to be there?'

'I'd called him, yes,' she said. 'He was happy about it.'

'Yusuf Kaya had a phone?'

'Hüseyin Altun gave it to him. It was registered in the name of a foreigner, a Syrian. Once Yusuf was at the Kaplan house we, Bulbul and I, got rid of it.'

'So', Süleyman said, 'you had Yusuf Kaya at his aunt's house with the intention of getting information from him that he had killed, put his own life at risk and spent a lot of money to protect. Did you think he was just going to tell you because you were his wife? Did you think you might seduce—'

'Oh, I had sex with him shortly after he arrived,' she said coldly. 'He expected that.'

'And?'

'And I knew that wouldn't work. I'm not a fool. I just did it to relax him, get him off his guard.'

'And so?'

She sighed. 'Inspector, what can I say? You're a man, you know how men are when they've just had sex.'

He did not respond and for a few seconds no one spoke. Then the American said, 'We tortured him.'

'You and . . .'

'Bulbul. She threatened to put out his eyes. We . . .' She looked up and blurted it out seemingly as quickly as she could. She was clearly not one of those people who took pleasure in such things. It had been a purely fiscal expedient. 'We tied him to the bed and then it was stuff like burning him with cigarettes, cutting. I held a gun to his head at one point. I tried to pull a tooth, but . . .'

'But he didn't talk?'

'No. It was only when Bulbul Kaplan had a knife at his eye that . . . He told me something, Inspector. It was detailed and it all made sense.'

'How did he die?' Edibe Taner asked.

Only then did Elizabeth Smith give vent to what was, what had to be, a terrifying ruthlessness. 'We cut his face off,' she said calmly.

Süleyman felt his heart jump inside his chest.

'It had all been planned,' the American said. 'Several of my guys went in and out of Iraq at that time. We got a US army uniform. We put him in it. Threw him in the river.'

'Thinking no doubt that both ourselves and the US authorities would be fooled into thinking that the body was that of an American serviceman,' Süleyman said. 'Miss Smith . . .'

'We were supposed to be long gone when you came to the house that day,' she said, referring to the first visit Süleyman and Taner had made to the house in Dara.

'Long gone where?'

'I had people ready to run the operation from this end when we'd gone,' Elizabeth Smith said. 'We'd slip over the border into Syria and stay there until it was safe to return. In Turkey or not we'd still be making money. The Kayas were going to die that night.'

'Get rid of any possible competition.'

'They knew. Even though she didn't know much herself, Zeynep knew about the existence of the Route. I couldn't have my guys changing sides. I, or rather İbrahim, had persuaded them to change once and so I feared they would do it again. No one can be trusted, can they?' Then suddenly she looked up and said, 'So who told you where we were?'

'How did you, or İbrahim Keser, get your husband's men to change sides, as you put it? And why?'

'İbrahim hated Yusuf,' she said. 'He always had. İbrahim told me about the Wormwood Route quite independently of Yusuf. Of course I knew already, but İbrahim didn't know that.'

'Why did he do that?' Süleyman asked.

'Because I slept with him,' she said. 'I fancied him and I slept with him and he told me everything. He was much better in bed than Yusuf. We decided to double-cross him together. İbrahim had the confidence of the other guys and, of course, money talks, as I am sure you know, Inspector.'

Süleyman sighed. 'Because you desired İbrahim Keser . . .' He shook his head. 'Miss Smith, the only way in which any judge will even consider leniency is if you tell me everything you know about the Wormwood Route.'

In that cold room in the middle of the night the murderess and torturer laughed. 'And what kind of leniency might that be?' she said. 'My very own mattress complete with bedbugs just for me? Inspector, no judge is going to hand down anything less than life. Who told you about me?'

'Miss Smith,' Süleyman said, 'your lover Mr Keser had other friends.'

'What do you mean?' she said. 'You mean that İbrahim told someone else, someone outside, about the Route?'

'I don't know. Miss Smith, did Yusuf Kaya, to your knowledge, tell you the truth about the Wormwood Route?'

She didn't answer.

'Miss Smith . . .'

'Tell us or you'll be sorry.' It had been said very quietly but that was what made Edibe Taner's words all the more threatening.

'There's nothing *you* can do to me . . .'

'You killed a saint. A saint!' Edibe Taner said. 'You don't think you're going to get away with that, do you?'

Süleyman reached across and put his hand on his colleague's arm. She was shivering with rage.

'Inspector Taner . . .'

'I get the feeling you two aren't working from the same script any more,' the American said. 'You want the Wormwood Route but all she wants is revenge. That won't work.' She leaned back in her chair and crossed her arms over her chest.

'I don't care what you think!' Taner said. 'I don't care!'

Her grief was getting in the way. Süleyman had to get her out of there, and quickly. But he had to find out what he was up against first, because the Wormwood Route was important. The Wormwood Route, if all the hype about it was true, was very important indeed.

'Miss Smith,' he said, 'are you going to provide us with details about the Wormwood Route?'

Her answer was immediate. 'No.'

Edibe Taner was nearly shaking herself on to the floor by

this time. Süleyman took hold of her arm and pulled her to her feet.

'Why is that, Miss Smith?' he said. 'What use can that information be to you in prison?'

'Same use as it was to Yusuf,' she replied with a smile. 'People knew that he and only he knew it and they left him alone. Also, a lot of people were willing to help him get out.'

'Miss Smith, if İbrahim Keser told his friend . . .'

'Friend? What friend?' She was frantic now. 'Tell me his name and I'll . . .'

'You'll what?' Süleyman said. 'Give me the Wormwood Route?'

There was a moment of silence and then she said, 'I'll get out.'

Aware that Taner was about to explode or collapse, Süleyman knocked on the door to attract the attention of the constable on guard outside. As soon as the man opened up, he pushed the shaking Taner through the door, and then he turned back to Elizabeth Smith.

'If you plan to escape . . .'

'Oh, I will escape,' she said. 'You won't be able to even think about holding on to me. Solitary, putting me in some godforsaken hole in the middle of nowhere . . .' She laughed.

'But if those who decide these things put you in a prison with Suriani inmates you will find that your escape plans will fail,' Süleyman said. 'You killed their saint.'

'You mean they'll try to kill me?'

'What do you think, Miss Smith? Between the Surianis and any influence that friend of your lover might have in prison, you'll be at risk. There are a lot of Kurdish people everywhere.'

Her face froze. Had she suddenly made the connection

350

between her lover and one of his friends who was a Kurd? Had she even known of the existence of Lütfü Güneş?

He gathered the papers and files on the table together and made for the door once again. He rapped once on the metal grille and then turned back towards the woman. 'I would urge you most strongly to rethink your position. You can be in danger or you can be out of danger.'

'Or I can be out,' she said, and then she pushed her features into a broad smile. 'Because you and I both know, Inspector Süleyman, that where billions of dollars are involved there is no such thing as an honest person. I love this land purely and truly. But when billions of dollars came into view, to ensure that I would never have to leave it, that I could in fact control it and that all I had to do to get that was to kill . . .' She sighed. 'Saints, sinners, foreigners, whatever, it all don't mean diddly squat.'

Chapter 26

There were quite a few absences from Gabriel Saatçi's funeral. Men once resident at the house in Dara and, in some cases, their families too had just disappeared. Of course there were rumours. Because these men were known to have gone in and out of Iraq and Syria on their various errands and missions, those countries seemed to be likely destinations. There were also places not on easy terms with Turkey where one could easily fall off the radar. Elizabeth Smith wouldn't say one way or the other. That she had been leaving the country in some way when she was captured, however, was certain. But then, after the killing of the Kaya family, how could she have stayed? Now the house in Dara, the centre of the Wormwood operation, was silent and empty. But for how long, Süleyman wondered as he looked at the long line of mourners standing in the streets waiting for Gabriel Saatçi's funeral cortège to make its way back from Mar Behnam church to St Sobo's monastery. It was nearly two weeks now since the monk had been killed and in the meantime Süleyman had been back to İstanbul to attend Bekir İkmen's funeral. Apart from the fact that he still had work to finish up in Mardin, he had promised Edibe Taner that he would attend Brother Gabriel's funeral. Dressed in a black suit and tie, he bowed his head as the coffin passed in front of him and the woman at his side began to weep. He knew her and so, in the absence of any kind of visible handkerchief, he offered her his. Lucine Rezian, Edibe Taner's Armenian aunt from Gaziantep, thanked him.

'My son Rafik usually takes care of me when we leave our home,' she said. 'But he couldn't come today and my brother-in-law Seçkin is too busy with his daughter to be bothered with me. Not that I am complaining. Edibe is a soul in torment.'

He had seen his Mardin colleague earlier. Veiled and dressed in black, she could barely walk, even with the support of her father on one side and Constable Selahattin on the other. Everyone looked at her and spoke behind their hands about her. Everyone, after all, did know.

'She has lost the love of her life,' Lucine continued. 'The light has gone out in her world. Her soul is in exile and there is no way back. I know.'

When he had first met this woman he had found her talk about times past fascinating. He had in fact been rather aggravated by Edibe Taner's apparent desire to lend her words no credence and to keep him away from her. She'd described the old woman as 'mad' which hadn't seemed fair then and didn't now. But there was a hopelessness about her, a sorrow, that was disturbing.

'Exile of the soul?'

The old woman nodded. 'When one is detached from something so loved, just the thought of it can bring the urge to kill oneself,' she said. And then, reading the graveness on his face, she continued, 'It can be a person, a place, even a time in one's life. Sometimes, as in your case, it is a time you do not even remember.'

'I beg your pardon?'

'You are an Ottoman,' she said. 'Edibe told me. She heard it from someone she works with who had been in İstanbul. She's very thorough. Remember when I told you about the Cobweb

354

World? The Cobweb World is where exiles go. It is where I am. Where else would an Armenian be? Modern Armenia has nothing to do with me. It's an awful place. I don't belong there. As an Ottoman you don't belong in modern İstanbul. You don't even want to be there, not deep down in your soul.'

He watched the end of the cortège pass before him and then offered his arm to Lucine Rezian as they joined the rest of the mourners following on behind the coffin.

'So where do I want to be?' he asked.

'In your palace, riding out with the Sultan, doing things that Ottomans do.'

Edibe Taner had been right after all. This woman was clearly foolish. He didn't want to do any of those things. Did he?

'Now you are poor like the rest of us and you have accepted that like a good Muslim,' she said. 'But in the dark of the night you think about what might have been had history been different. You don't even know that you're doing it.'

'Yes, but . . .'

'Why do you think that people refer to you as an Ottoman?' she asked. 'Because they do. I know that because just the look of you tells me that is what happens.'

She was right. A lot of people did refer to him as an Ottoman. Some people resented him because of it.

'But you cannot go back to the past any more than I can. So you do what you can. You keep your standards, you talk to the old members of your family, you live with ennui, you live *in* the Cobweb World.'

Süleyman thought about someone else possibly in the Cobweb World too. An Armenian without a name who had chosen, according to Elizabeth Smith, to take money to fulfil what he saw as his destiny. Murat Lole was still at large some- where.

'Madam, do you know anything about the Lole family?' he asked.

'The family of the architect Serkis Lole?' She smiled. 'All gone. Years ago.'

'Gone? Gone where?'

She looked away from him. 'Who knows?' she said. 'Out of the country, I think.'

'So there couldn't be any family members here or say in Van or anywhere like that?'

She regarded him levelly for a moment and then she said a very firm and final, 'No.'

In spite of his reluctance to engage in any more stories of Armenians and why so many of them had emigrated from eastern Turkey, he was wary of her last answer and said, 'Madam . . .' But at that moment they were passed by Constable Selahattin, Edibe, and Seçkin Taner making their way to the top of the procession to walk alongside the priest of Mar Behnam, Musa Saatçi and Brother Seraphim. The dead man's father was grey with grief, crying bitterly with every step. As she passed, Edibe Taner looked through her thin black veil into Süleyman's eyes. The self-inflicted rents and scratches on her face aside, her eyes were so full of pain that the look of her was almost too much to bear. Behind him the many Christian women in the crowd began to ululate.

'Arabs!' Lucine said with a shrug. 'They are Christians and yet they are Arabs too. They live in the Cobweb World. Islam came and it moved the Arabs to a different place. These Syrians got left behind. My niece will go there too.'

Whether she meant to the Cobweb World or into Christianity he didn't know. But Lucine explained. 'To the Cobweb World,' she said, nodding gravely as she did so. 'There is nothing for her, not now that Gabriel Saatçi is dead.'

'But she would never have married Brother Gabriel. She is a Muslim, he was a Christian and he was a monk.'

'Of course not. Edibe worshipped from afar. But that was enough,' the old woman said. 'Now he has gone, however, now he is no longer in the world, her life has no meaning. She will enter the Cobweb World with the rest of us. Her life will be one of compromise, regret and sorrow.'

But wouldn't Edibe Taner one day recover? People did, after all, weather the storms of bereavement and somehow come through them. He had visited the İkmen family when he had returned briefly to İstanbul. Grief there was in degrees, from not much more than an awareness of it amongst Çetin's younger children, those who had known Bekir only briefly, right up to the black despair of Fatma İkmen. His friend, as usual, was getting on as he always did. But then Çetin, for all his deeply unfashionable traits like agnosticism and smoking, was a modern man. The fact that his mother had been a witch notwithstanding, Çetin lived in the now because with so many children to support and think about he just had to. The Cobweb World, as far as Süleyman could perceive it, was where the lonely and disjointed and only they could afford to go. And he saw himself with them. As he walked in procession towards St Sobo's monastery and the last resting place of Gabriel Saatçi the saint, it became clear. He sprang from a past that could hardly be imagined any longer. Old people blithely called his father a prince and gave him respect because of that, but the reality was that he was an elderly man with little money who was a prince of nowhere. Like Süleyman himself. Had Mehmet Süleyman lived the life of his ancestors he would have had a harem and had lots of sons who would probably now be adults. In his head he was an honourable man of some standing but he wasn't royal and other men were coming up in the police force behind him now, younger, fitter, more in tune with a city that wanted to be *modern* – something he just was not. He was a dinosaur. And yes, just as Lucine Rezian had told him, he did think about what might have been in the dark, dark watches of the night. He was there with the rest of them: the Armenian woman, the dead saint, the Master of Sharmeran and the hordes of ululating women behind him. In the Cobweb World.

Because Ayşe Farsakoğlu knew the girl anyway there was no problem about Sophia's gaining access to the police station.

'She's with me,' she said to the officer on the front desk, who had been just about to shoo the dirty girl and her filthy bundle away when Ayşe came into the building.

'I want to see Inspector İkmen,' Sophia said as Ayşe ushered her through the reception area and into the station. The filthy bundle in her arms was making small snuffling and squawking noises. Given Sophia's radically different shape, Ayşe assumed it had to be her new baby.

'Where have you been, Sophia?' she asked as she led the girl up the stairs towards her superior's office. 'Inspector İkmen and I have been worried about you.'

The girl looked down at the bundle and said, 'I have baby.'

Ayşe both did and did not want to see the dead man's baby, the child of a murderer. Her boss Çetin İkmen had been so marked by what had happened. He was going through the motions of his daily life because that was İkmen, that was what he was. But the death of a child, even a troublesome, even an 'evil' child, leaves whoever suffers it irreversibly changed. İkmen had aged and he was, Ayşe had noticed, just occasionally drinking brandy again.

'Did you have a doctor?' Ayşe asked as she led the girl

down one of the long green-and-white-painted corridors on the top floor of the building.

'I go to hospital,' Sophia said simply. Probably one of the social security hospitals, where one didn't pay but one did wait, sometimes until it was far and away too late.

When Ayşe reached İkmen's office door, she knocked on the glass before calling out, 'Sir, someone to see you.'

A very smoke-dried voice from within said, 'Who?'

'Sophia, sir.'

She waited for him to come and answer the door, which he did with alacrity. Stinking of cigarettes and with eyes red from weeping and lack of sleep, Çetin İkmen was not a pretty sight. As soon as he saw the girl he looked down at the bundle in her arms and said, 'Is that . . .'

'I call him Aslan,' the girl said. 'For his father.'

İkmen looked across at Ayşe and said, 'Does she . . .'

'I know your son is dead, Inspector İkmen,' Sophia said. Her eyes were quite dry and she showed no emotion. 'I come to show baby.'

He ushered her into his office and Ayşe Farsakoğlu, even without a sign from her boss, left. She had no place in whatever conversation was to pass between them. She went back to Süleyman's office where she and İzzet Melik were following up on possible sightings of the nurse Murat Lole.

'I will see the rest of the year out and then I will retire,' Edibe Taner said to Mehmet Süleyman.

The man from İstanbul took a sip from the glass full of sweet red wine Brother Seraphim had given him and said, 'Why? Inspector, I know that Brother Gabriel's death has upset you, but I would urge you not to act too hastily. You're a really good officer. It's been . . .'

She put a hand on his arm and smiled. 'I have been honoured to work with you, Inspector Süleyman,' she said. 'I would not have survived the interrogation of Elizabeth Smith had you not been there. I might have killed her. But . . . Gabriel's death is only part of the story.'

'Part of the story?'

They were standing outside the huge main entrance to the monastery, smoking. In front of them the vineyards and olive groves belonging to St Sobo's disappeared into the misty distance that was the border with Syria.

'Did you notice Lütfü Güneş, the Kurd, back there in the monastery garden?' Taner said.

'I noticed he was there,' Süleyman replied.

'Talking to clans once powerless in the face of the Kayas,' she said. 'He gave us, or rather you, Elizabeth Smith.'

'Yes.'

'His friend İbrahim Keser was sleeping with the American and he passed the information to you so that he could destroy her plans.'

'You really believe Keser told Güneş about the Wormwood Route?'

'I believe it's possible,' she said. 'Lütfü is an ambitious man. He has a big family. Lütfü Güneş was not one of those who would have profited from the Wormwood Route had the Kayas or even the American controlled it.'

'You think that he spoke to us behind İbrahim Keser's back?' Süleyman said. 'That he really did in effect use us?'

'Possibly. I think that Güneş would eventually have killed Keser, as I believe Elizabeth Smith would have done in the end.'

Süleyman, though horrified, knew it could easily be true.

'All the surviving men who worked for Elizabeth Smith would seem to be abroad,' he said.

'With little or no money, not to mention direction,' Taner said. 'New masters will, I believe, piece together the elements of the Wormwood Route. Lütfü Güneş the Kurd talks to the clan leaders at Gabriel Saatçi's funeral and maybe he even talks to men he once knew who now reside abroad, on his mobile telephone.'

'You really do think he told us about Miss Smith so he could ultimately displace her?'

'Why not?' she said. 'Here in Mardin we are on the route westwards from Afghanistan, a country bulging with heroin that is now almost completely out of control. Miss Smith was right: billions of dollars are at stake here. Not, thankfully, that we will have to endure her "empire" here in the city. Someone else will control and organise our lives now. The new owner of the Route.'

'Mardin will need someone to fight that,' Süleyman said.

'Yes, it will.' She sighed. 'Just not me.'

'Why not?'

She looked up at him and smiled. 'Because I'm tired,' she said. 'Because my heart is broken and because my poor father must teach someone to beat copper and speak to the Sharmeran before he dies.'

He didn't know how to respond to that and so he just stayed quiet. The reality or otherwise of the snake goddess was not something he felt able to discuss with her or any other Mardin native.

'I used to have a brother,' Taner said as she squinted into the distant vistas of the great Mesopotamian Ocean. 'Like poor Captain Erdur he was in the Jandarma. He died. Now there is only me, and so although our Sharmeran requires a master by tradition she must now settle for a mistress.' She looked again at Süleyman and said, 'I want to be who I am.

I will not run away and hide under a false name like Hasan Karabulut. I will not kill to be who I am like Murat Lole. I belong to the Sharmeran and I want to be with her. It is my destiny.'

It was also lonely, old and ephemeral. The Cobweb World.

'Elizabeth Smith thinks that she will be able to use her knowledge of the Wormwood Route to buy her way out of prison,' Süleyman said.

'If she does even know it, Lütfü Güneş or someone else will have taken it over by then. The Wormwood Route is just the first, I think, of such "super routes",' Edibe Taner said. 'I think ultimately they will proliferate. Making those around them rich, of course. In the end they will be like leaking buckets: as soon as one hole in one route is discovered, so another one will arise to take its place. That is my prediction.'

'But the Wormwood Route was foolproof.'

'Nothing in the end can be perfect,' she said. 'Only Allah. The Wormwood Route is mythical and exciting because it is new and because Yusuf Kaya was totally intoxicated by what he had made. But nothing is for ever. It will have its day and people other than ourselves will profit from it.'

He frowned.

'Even saints die,' she said. 'Even if our love for them does not.'

She made to go back into the garden where the wake was taking place, but Süleyman took hold of her wrists and held her back.

'Edibe,' he said, 'you must not give up on the notion of finding love somewhere else some day. You are a very impressive person.'

This was only the second time he'd ever used her first name

and he had blurted what he had said because he was neither comfortable nor competent with strong emotion. She appreciated that, even if her reply was not what he had wanted to hear – just because it was so unutterably sad.

'That's very kind of you, Mehmet,' she said, 'but my heart died along with Gabriel and I will not be seeking to try to revive it. I am already in the Cobweb World. Let the drug men peddle their poison. My life belongs to my Sharmeran now.'

He let her hands go then and she began to walk back through the monastery gates.

'I will look out for Lütfü Güneş and his associates in the future,' Süleyman said just before she disappeared. 'I will not forget. I may belong to the Cobweb World, as your aunt Lucine has told me, but I've realised that I do not live there, Edibe, not yet. I will keep you as safe as I can from the poison, Inspector. I promise.'

'You're a good man,' he heard her say from inside the gates. 'The Sharmeran loves you. I know she does.'

The baby was clearly undersized for his age. He was also bundled up in a really disgusting succession of rags. But he was healthy and when İkmen picked him up he smiled up into his face with such joy that the tired policeman felt himself begin to laugh.

'I really, really appreciate you bringing him to see me,' İkmen said as he sat down behind his desk and held young Aslan on his lap. Sophia had just told him that it was her intention to return, with the baby, to Bulgaria.

'I have mother there,' she said. 'Now I no do drugs, I can go to her.'

Like a lot of young eastern European girls, Sophia's flight

from her own country had not resulted in her becoming either wealthy or famous. Since her arrival in İstanbul she'd become a junkie, a prostitute, a thief and the girlfriend of a murderer. At least she had little Aslan, however, a child she seemed genuinely fond of.

'Do you have money?' İkmen began.

'I have train ticket,' Sophia said. 'Some lire for food also.'

İkmen sighed. He didn't know what kind of environment Sophia was going back to. In all likelihood it was far and away inferior to the kind of life little Aslan would have with the İkmen family in İstanbul. Bulgaria was still a very impoverished country with huge social problems and very low levels of health care. But Aslan was half Bulgarian at least, his only surviving parent was Bulgarian and she loved him. He was her baby.

'Sophia, I don't know whether I will see you again, but . . .'

'Oh, I come back sometime,' she said. 'For sure.'

'I'd like to give you some money,' İkmen said, 'for the baby. I . . . Just let me know where you are and . . . Look, you can always ask me for money, you know?'

She looked at him levelly, suspicious he could tell, but then she said, 'I know.'

'There's something else too.'

'Something?'

He handed the baby back to her and then put his hand in his pocket and took out his wallet. He had taken out Fatma's housekeeping money earlier that day, and now he handed it over. The girl's eyes grew large at the sight of it.

'My wife,' İkmen said. 'I don't know whether you know where I live or not, Sophia, but I must urge you to keep who you are and what you are doing to yourself until you leave İstanbul. I don't want my wife to know about you until after you have gone.'

The girl looked confused. 'You . . .'

'Sophia, if my wife found out that you were leaving the country with the baby she would try to take him away from you,' İkmen said. 'Our son . . .'

'Aslan died.'

'Yes, indeed.' İkmen wiped a nascent tear from his eye with the back of his hand. 'Your baby is our grandson, the only connection left with our son,' he said. 'But he is your child, Sophia, and if you want to take him back to your country you must be free to do that.'

'I contact with you all the time!' Sophia said as she stuffed what was to her a huge amount of money into her pockets.

'That would be nice,' İkmen said. 'That would be very nice.'

Later, when the girl had gone and he had had a chance to think about what had happened, he wondered whether she had just come to him for cash. He wondered if he would ever see her or his grandson again. The thought that maybe he wouldn't made him feel sick. But then how much worse would it be if he told Fatma and then had to deal with her worry and grief over the baby? Things had changed so much already and she was barely talking to him now. For selfish reasons as well as Fatma's sanity, he couldn't put her or himself through any more traumatic scenarios.

His son and many other people's sons and daughters had died since Yusuf Kaya escaped from Kartal Prison. A lucrative drug route into the country had been uncovered if not, as yet, plugged. Had that been worth what had happened in İstanbul, Birecik and Mardin? He really didn't know, and as he took his latest bottle of brandy out of his desk drawer and gulped long and hard from its neck, he had no idea what, if anything, was the point of any human act at all.

In fact he would have drunk the whole bottle had it not been for the phone call that came then. He was, he knew, and had been since Bekir's death, descending into the alcoholism that had characterised his forties. So he answered the phone slowly and without enthusiasm.

'İkmen.'

'Çetin!' said the clearly excited voice of Mehmet Süleyman.

'Yes.'

'Çetin, one of Elizabeth Smith's guards has come across the Iraqi border and given himself up. He was terrified out there. Couldn't wait to get home even though he knew he'd be punished.'

'I'm not surprised. Iraq . . .'

'Yes – and Çetin, listen to this,' Süleyman said. 'This man is going to tell us what he knows about the Wormwood Route. We have another piece of the puzzle. And with İzzet Melik and Ayşe Farsakoğlu looking into possible sightings of Murat Lole . . .'

İkmen put his brandy bottle down on his desk and said, 'There might just be some hope, do you think?'

'I think that's more than a possibility,' Süleyman said triumphantly. 'Çetin, what was done was not done in vain. It wasn't.'

'No.'

Çetin İkmen looked at his brandy bottle, picked it up and put it into his desk drawer, which he shut. Then, as Süleyman began to tell him more details about the man from Iraq, just very slowly, he began to smile.

Acknowledgements

This book would not have been possible without the help I received from my fellow travellers, both known and unknown, back in March 2007. This is a novel that relies upon myths and folklore and for these I have to thank the people of the east themselves: shopkeepers and officials, priests and singers, artists and those who tell the stories of the past. *Teşekkürederim.*

Turkish Alphabet

The Turkish Alphabet is very similar to its English counterpart with the following exceptions:

- The letters q, w and x do not appear.
- Some letters behave differently in Turkish compared with English:

  C, c   Not the c in cat and tractor, but the j in jam
            and Taj or the g in gentle and courageous.

  G, g   Always the hard g in great or slug, never the
            soft g of general and outrage.

  J, j   As the French pronounce the j in bonjour
            and the g in gendarme.

- The following additional letters appear:

  Ç ç   The ch in chunk or choke.

  Ğ, ğ   'Yumuşak ge' is used to lengthen the vowel
            that it follows. It is not usually voiced (except
            as a vague y sound). For instance, it is used
            in the name Ayşe Farsakoğlu, which is
            pronounced *Far-sak-erlu*, and in öğle (noon,
            midday), pronounced öy-*lay* (see below for
            how to pronounce ö).

  Ş, ş   The sh in ship and shovel.

I, ı	Without a dot, the sound of the a in probable.
İ, i	With a dot, the i in thin or tinny.
ö, ö	Like the ur sound in further.
Ü, ü	Like the u in the French tu.

Full pronunciation guide

A, a	Usually short, the a in hah! or the u in but, never the medium or long a in nasty and hateful.
B, b	As in English.
C, c	Not the c in cat and tractor, but the j in jam and Taj or the g in gentle and courageous.
Ç, ç	The ch in chunk or choke.
D, d	As in English.
E, e	Always short, the e in venerable, never the e in Bede (and never silent).
F, f	As in English.
G, g	Always the hard g in great or slug, never the soft g of general and outrage.
Ğ, ğ	'Yumuşak ge' is used to lengthen the vowel that it follows. It is not usually voiced (except as a vague y sound). For instance, it is used in the name Ayşe Farsakoğlu, which is pronounced *Far-sak-erlu*, and in öğle (noon, midday), pronounced *öy-lay* (see below for how to pronounce ö).
H, h	As in English (and never silent).
I, ı	Without a dot, the sound of the a in probable.
İ, i	With a dot, the i in thin or tinny.

J, j	As the French pronounce the j in bonjour and the g in gendarme.
K, k	As in English (and never silent).
L, l	As in English.
M, m	As in English.
N, n	As in English.
O, o	Always short, the o in hot and bothered.
ö, ö	Like the ur sound in further.
P, p	As in English.
R, r	As in English.
S, s	As in English.
Ş, ş	The sh in ship and shovel.
T, t	As in English.
U, u	Always medium-length, the u in push and pull, never the u in but.
Ü, ü	Like the u in the French tu.
V, v	Usually as in English, but sometimes almost a w sound in words such as tavuk (hen).
Y, y	As in English. Follows vowels to make diphthongs: ay is the y sound in fly; ey is the ay sound in day; oy is the oy sound in toy; uy is almost the same as the French oui.
Z, z	As in English.

Pretty Dead Things

Barbara Nadel

When flamboyant beauty Emine Aksu suddenly goes missing, Inspector Çetin İkmen's investigation leads him deep into Istanbul's strange and mysterious past.

Emine was a hippie in the sixties who enjoyed the liberated free-love lifestyle that swept across the city when the western Europeans flooded into Istanbul. Her husband suspects she was visiting an old friend at the time of her disappearance.

Meanwhile, Inspector Mehmet Süleyman discovers the hideous remains of a woman in the old banking district of Karakoy. Could these two bizarre incidents be linked?

While the atmosphere in Istanbul reaches fever pitch as it hosts football's European Champions League final, both policemen are about to uncover the darker legacies of the old city's past: anger, resentment and deadly obsessions . . .

Praise for Barbara Nadel's novels:

'Nadel's evocation of the shady underbelly of modern Turkey is one of the perennial joys of crime fiction. İkmen is a magnificent character and I can't think of a better summertime read' *Mail on Sunday*

'A searing emotional authenticity' *The Sunday Times*

'A wonderful setting . . . a dizzying ride' *Guardian*

978 0 7553 3563 3

headline

A Passion for Killing

Barbara Nadel

A serial killer is stalking the streets of Istanbul, seemingly targeting gay men. A man is found dead in a hotel room, a single stab wound in his heart. Could he be a victim of the 'Peeper'?

Inspector Mehmet Süleyman is assigned to the case, and is shocked to discover that the victim's body has been delivered to forensics entirely 'clean'. Has someone tampered with vital evidence?

Meanwhile a young carpet dealer, on the brink of a huge sale, is discovered on the mangled remains of his Jeep, a bullet between his shoulder blades. The deal would have made him – the carpet he wanted to sell used to belong to Lawrence of Arabia. Did the young salesman know too much?

Inspector Çetin İkmen and Süleyman uncover an incredible story and quickly realise that behind even the most seemingly innocent and respectable façade lurk passion and jealousy, savagery and madness . . .

Praise for Barbara Nadel's novels:

'Intelligent and captivating . . . her storyline has a searing emotional intensity' *The Sunday Times*

'Inspector Çetin İkmen is a detective up there with Morse, Rebus and Wexford. Gripping and highly recommended' *Time Out*

978 0 7553 2134 6

headline

Now you can buy any of these other bestselling
Headline books from your bookshop
or *direct from the publisher*.

FREE P&P AND UK DELIVERY
(Overseas and Ireland £3.50 per book)

The Murder Stone	Louise Penny	£6.99
Unspoken	Sam Hayes	£6.99
The King of Thieves	Michael Jecks	£7.99
The Drop-Off	Patrick Quinlan	£6.99
The Spies of Sobeck	Paul Doherty	£7.99
Afraid	Jack Kilborn	£6.99
Monster	Jonathan Kellerman	£7.99
Soul Murder	Andrew Nugent	£7.99
Buckingham Palace Gardens	Anne Perry	£6.99

TO ORDER SIMPLY CALL THIS NUMBER

01235 400 414

or visit our website: www.headline.co.uk

Prices and availability subject to change without notice.